SHADOWS ACROSS AMERICA

SHADOWS ACROSS AMERICA

A THRILLER

GUILLERMO VALCÁRCEL

Translated by Kit Maude

Text copyright © 2017 by Guillermo Valcárcel
By agreement with Pontas Literary & Film Agency
Translation copyright © 2019 by Kit Maude
All rights reserved.

Previously published as *Sombras que cruzan América* by Harper Collins in Spain in 2017. Translated from Spanish by Kit Maude. First published in English by AmazonCrossing in 2019.

Published by AmazonCrossing, Seattle
www.apub.com

Amazon, the Amazon logo, and AmazonCrossing are trademarks of Amazon.com, Inc., or its affiliates.

ISBN-13: 9781503958821
ISBN-10: 1503958825

Cover design by David Drummond

Printed in the United States of America

SHADOWS ACROSS AMERICA

1

Synchronicities

By way of an example I shall share an event I observed myself. A young woman I was treating had, at a critical moment, a dream in which she was given a golden beetle. As she told me about the dream, I sat with my back to the closed window. Suddenly, I heard a noise behind me, a slight tapping sound. I turned around and saw an insect knocking against the glass from the outside. I opened the window and caught the animal as it flew inside. It was the closest thing one might find to a golden beetle in these latitudes: a scarab beetle, the common cetonia aurata. In a departure from its ordinary behavior, it had clearly felt a need to enter a dark room at that precise moment. I must admit that nothing like that has ever happened to me before or since and that the patient's dream remains unique in my experience.

—C. G. Jung, *Synchronicity: An Acausal Connecting Principle*, 1952

Suddenly he was dreaming about her again. She was no longer the small, charming girl he'd known but a skinny, precocious preteen from Central America. She was about eleven or twelve, just as she would be in real life. With the omniscience of dreams, Ethan was certain it was her even though he had no way of knowing what her face actually looked like. It came like a mysterious premonition. Although in real life he wouldn't have recognized her if they passed on the street, this was definitely the girl. Later he would realize that he might not have seen her face in the dream; maybe she hadn't even had one.

A weak, frightened, disembodied voice arrived like an echo: "I'm still alive." The words flowed around him in a mist. A chill ran down his back, but he was unable to turn around. There was something unsettling about where she was. Something inexplicable and threatening was approaching, an abstract presence that defied comprehension. It set his teeth on edge. Then the girl's ghostly whisper faded, and he sensed her crumble away. He couldn't see her anymore, but he knew that she was still there. He felt that she wanted to run away but that such a move would entail unimaginable danger. His muscles grew tense, and a nauseating smell filled the space. Afterward he would wonder whether it had actually happened, whether you could dream smells or if it had just been simple suggestion, but at the time it had felt viscerally real, a detail that had borne the ring of a terrifying truth.

She spoke again without moving the lips of a face that may not even have been there: "I'm still alive," and her timid, childish voice merged into the horror of what was to come, the horror from which he wanted to save her. It swelled around them like a swarm of insects, enveloping her, swallowing her up until she was completely obscured from view. Everything around him had turned pitch black; he couldn't move and was barely able to breathe. He could feel his constricted chest, his empty lungs, his heart struggling to keep beating. It felt . . .

Ethan woke up, his eyes bulging.

He patted the bed, utterly disoriented, trying to reconnect with something solid and real. He was sad to leave her. It felt like he was abandoning her, as though the simple act of waking up was actually a betrayal. His eyes still bleary, he stared up at the ceiling and said her name several times: "Michelle. Michi," trying to summon his memories of the child and keep them separate from the sinister fog. But for the rest of the day, he couldn't shake off the unsettling dream.

He didn't know how long he lay there, trying to think of when he'd last had a nightmare, the last time he'd clutched at the sheets, afraid that he was about to be dragged off. When he was twelve or thirteen? Finally, her image came to him: Michi, a dark, small child. The way she'd waddled like a doll, chasing him around with clumsy, duck-like steps when she was four years old, her dress flapping in the wind like in a cartoon, laughing like crazy, her black hair flopping over her cheeks. She had coffee-colored eyes and Latin features that already hinted that she would inherit her mother's looks. His fear faded into melancholy.

2

He hadn't dreamed of her before, but he often remembered her whenever he saw a child do something endearing. He couldn't understand why his subconscious would place her in such a horrible situation, and it unnerved him still more that the dream had updated her to her current age. And yet she had been bodiless, like a spirit trapped by some primeval fear. Michelle. Wherever she was.

Coming back to reality, he looked at the clock: nine. He couldn't believe that he'd slept through the rising sun or that Ari had left without saying anything. But she had. Her side of the bed was empty and cold. Ari must have left an hour ago, and for some reason she'd let him sleep in. He wandered through the house, unable to focus. The dream had gotten under his skin. He was even more surprised when he saw that everything was clean and tidy. She must have made her breakfast and washed the dishes herself; it was the kind of thing she did when she was mad. He thought back to the night before but couldn't remember anything out of the ordinary. They'd stayed in to do the quarterly accounts and watched a couple of episodes of a TV series, and Ari had gone to bed exhausted. When he'd come up, she had already been asleep, and he hadn't woken her. There had been no suggestion of sex. He had no idea what might have happened to upset her. Now thrust unceremoniously back into the trials and tribulations of his everyday life, he set off for the office, still puzzled and worried.

It wasn't a long commute. The hard part was usually getting out of the residential district, but at that hour the roads were practically deserted. After crossing Madison Avenue and its long lines of office blocks, Franklin Boulevard led to the single-story strip mall where his office was located, an unremarkable horseshoe-shaped lot designed for small businesses, although half the units were vacant. His office window was barely distinguishable from the pet shop next door. It was only just big enough for the sign: **GONZÁLEZ BAIL BONDS FIANZAS 24/7**. His surname and the bilingual message had been useful in the early years, but now all the bail bondsmen knew they had to speak some Spanish, including Ari, who spoke it well. These days the company survived more on inertia than any real momentum, and they were beginning to get concerned. He parked the SUV next to her pickup. He could see her through the window, with her back to him. The office was narrow but long. It had been divided into two equal spaces: the office Ari used as a reception and, separated by a screen, his office, which he rarely occupied given that he spent most of his time transporting prisoners and suspects from one place to another. When he went inside, Ari was on the phone.

"What crime has your son been accused of? Yes, I understand. The important thing now is to stay calm. We're here to help . . ."

Ethan slipped around her desk, his eyebrows raised.

"Do you know how bail bonds work? I understand. OK, fine. We've paid your son's bail before? What's his name? Yes, I remember—the kid with the Batman tattoo. What? Oh, this is your other son, the younger one. I'm sorry, madam. Well, listen: if you know us already, we can save some time. Clients can download the form from the website . . . yes, that's right. Yes, the guarantee plus ten percent. Exactly. Yes, all right. We'll be here waiting. You too. Good luck. Yes, yes, goodbye."

He didn't know what to do. He'd been thinking hard, but he couldn't find a single reason for Ari to be pissed. But he certainly wasn't imagining it. She was so unpredictable; it was usually best just to stay clear. Also, if she wasn't angry about something and he asked, that was a sure way of aggravating her. He was trapped in a blind alley: the only way out was past her desk. He heard her hang up but still couldn't decide what to do. Before he could react, she came over to stand in the doorway.

"You haven't said good morning."

Ethan shivered a little. "Hi, honey. You were busy."

"Yes, I was, but now I'm not."

Maybe she wasn't angry with him after all.

"Did Bear call you?" Ari asked.

"No. I haven't spoken to him in a few days."

"That's strange. He called me to ask for some help tracking down someone. He asked me to tell you to pick him up at home."

Ethan gave her a questioning look that she returned twofold. "Why didn't he call me?"

"That's what I want to know."

"He must be worried about something."

"I think so. If not, he would have called you. He's always afraid that you'll find something out before he gets a chance to see you. He still hasn't worked out how slow you are," she said, her voice taking on a slightly acid tone.

So Ari was annoyed about something, but Ethan had no intention of finding out what it might be. Now he had a perfect excuse to let the comment pass and spend the day out of the office. If he was lucky, she'd have forgotten all about it by the evening.

"What did he say?"

"A kid missed his court date. I didn't get whether it was for possession or for not paying child support. He was nervous—he just blurted it out."

"He must have been in jail for one of the two. What was the bond?"

"Five hundred dollars. Do you think he needs money?"

Ethan laughed incredulously. "Bear? He's loaded."

"What are you laughing at?"

"I'm not laughing at you. Why would he need money from us?" Now Ethan knew she was mad about something. "Come on—I know that look."

"Don't start that again. I didn't give you any look."

Ari was restraining herself, and Ethan respected that. She was always struggling with her anger, and Ethan wasn't exactly a calming influence.

"You seem a little on edge today."

"It's nothing," Ari mumbled.

Her tone didn't sound angry, just tired.

"Why don't we take off into the mountains for a couple of days? Just forget about everything? Back to that cabin. The guy would let us have it cheap."

"And what about the business?"

Ethan shrugged. That was how he was: he came up with ideas and then shrugged. He was a good tactician; he could plan for the future and had brilliant ideas. But he was lazy about putting them into practice. He needed help, someone to execute things while he got distracted by new projects. Ari knew that very well; she'd known it since the day she'd met him, before Michelle had left him, when he'd barely noticed she was alive and she had been nothing but a troubled teenager.

Ethan went over and gave her a hug, a little wary of how she might react. He didn't dare try to kiss her. By now, nothing about their relationship could be fixed with a kiss, but his hunches were usually right. Ari allowed herself to be hugged, sharing her heat and the reassurance he needed. He could feel how stiff her neck was, the tension in her shoulders, and her frayed nerves. They'd been going through a difficult period, and to cap it all off, she'd been up all night listening to him whispering the name of his ex-girlfriend. Her muscles relaxed as he held the hug, and although she tried to keep up her guard, he could feel her defenses dropping; she was softening slowly, reluctantly. But when he pulled away, she was just as cool as before.

"So I'll go see Bear. I guess we'll be having lunch together."

"Goodbye." She sat down and stared into space, struggling with everything she hated about herself, at a loss to explain her inability to communicate.

Ethan drove away regretting what he'd said, as usual. Ari might not have known it, but she had that power over him. When he was with her, he could be eloquent and convincing; he could calm her down or drive her crazy. But when he was alone, Ari's silences and arguments, which were often simplistic and poorly expressed, kept on coming back to him, making him feel deeply guilty. Why did he prey on her low self-esteem? Why did he have to hurt her?

As Ethan liked to describe it, he'd stumbled into this life "as a moronic twenty-year-old looking for adventure and a broken nose." He'd certainly managed the latter and, just occasionally, the former. His diplomat father had taken Ethan to live in several different countries when he was a boy, and Ethan had run away several times. He'd regularly flirted with hard drugs and spent some time living on the street, a wholly bitter, unpleasant experience. Until his sixteenth birthday his life had been cushy, his future all planned out. His older sister had agreed to follow that path without complaint, but he had resisted, too thirsty for excitement and intensity. The thrills you chased, he now realized, when you'd never had to worry about money. He'd always been well off, so it had never seemed important. Ethan had spent the early years of adolescence railing against the world he knew, rejecting its benefits and obligations, and his later ones struggling to find the place he imagined awaited him on the streets, the only place where he believed genuine experiences, the truth, could be found. He spent several years passing from one gang to another, long enough to be betrayed, to get his face smashed in repeatedly, to betray others, to grow disillusioned, and to learn that lies and misery were not exclusive to the gilded cage in which he had been raised. And yet he had eventually come to the conclusion that the street was where he belonged.

When he was twenty years old, he'd found himself presented with the opportunity to turn in a dealer for whom he'd been working for the past few months. Said dealer had slept with his girlfriend right under his nose and then taunted him about it before withholding a payment he'd promised. Ethan hadn't thought twice. Jealousy and pride had driven him to become an informant for a bounty hunter, but it had been the same rebellious nature that had made things impossible for him at home that had spurred him to ask the bounty hunter for a job. After he'd become familiar with the gutters of drug trafficking, the willfulness of youth had sent him right over to the other extreme. He'd been a poacher turned gamekeeper. He hadn't had any trouble passing the exams for the necessary qualifications, had gotten the requisite licenses, and had stridden into yet another exciting new world that had turned out to be the worst yet. Far from tracking down dangerous kingpins, he'd found himself seeking out pathetic fugitives who usually reacted like strays being taken to the pound. And just like strays, these wretched people treated anyone they had power over, usually children, in just the same way. That was how he had met Ari and the abusive man who'd supported her and her sister, Sasha, when the girl had still been in diapers and tried to follow her older sister everywhere on her wobbly legs.

Now, if anyone were to ask, he'd say that he helped to keep people out of jail, not to put them in there. Most of the time, when he had to track down someone who had skipped out on bail, it was because they'd forgotten or misunderstood the instructions they'd been given or were afraid. The majority of people who didn't turn up for trial were fools incapable of getting their lives in order; more trouble was the last thing they were looking for. They simply couldn't handle the responsibility of important decisions. Their biggest crime was that they couldn't help making mistakes. When he came by, they answered the door in a civilized manner and were usually more scared than angry when he took them away. Some of them burned with shame, while others broke into tears. His world was not one of criminals and gangsters but rather fools and losers struggling for survival, caught in a bind that got more difficult with every passing day. Over the years, Ethan hadn't developed the killer instinct of a hunter but rather a painful empathy for victims of the system. To him that meant that the problem must be with the system itself.

Under his supervision, Ari had gone back to school in order to start studying law. She'd dedicated herself to this goal. He was amazed at how much she had matured in the time that he'd known her. Although they didn't have a fixed plan, they wanted to make a change, and her academic success was a hopeful sign. Meanwhile, the business kept limping along, often getting to the end of the month thanks to a little extra income from jobs like this one for Bear. Logically speaking, it should have been Ethan hiring Bear to find fugitives, but that rarely happened, so in the end he'd become Bear's occasional assistant.

His car pulled up in front of a quintessential image of the American dream: front lawn, pastel shades, a peaked attic with a round porthole. He honked the horn three times. The front door opened, and out came Candy, ruining the picture. She was dressed in a vest and leather pants, tattoos covered her rippling arms, and her jet-black hair was pulled up into a ponytail. She waved to indicate that she didn't have time to stop. The threshold remained empty for a few more seconds before it was occupied by Bear's huge form, which did full justice to his name. His outfit, however, did nothing of the kind: a cream linen suit, dress shoes rather than his usual leather boots, his shoulder-length hair gelled back. Bear, at just under six foot six and 280 pounds, had always been insecure about his body. He was endlessly searching for an aesthetic to call his own, and the results could be somewhat variable. Now, nearing the age of fifty, he'd plumped for a look that he imagined gave him a respectable, executive air but was really that of an oversized Bible salesman in a bulletproof vest. He got into the car with some difficulty and greeted Ethan with a curt hello. Bear spoke in short, direct phrases with a slightly mechanical tone that intimidated fugitives, thus facilitating their successful capture and delivery. Before they pulled out, Bear gave the day's docket to Ethan.

"Look, this is the guy. Twenty-one. A two-year-old daughter."

"Fuck, I'm sick of these people. Why do they even have kids if they're going to treat them like shit? They leave them to grow up on the street, like Ari's mother: three kids by three different fathers, and she didn't raise any of them. They're the worst. And I say that with all due respect, may she rest in peace. Where do you want to start, with the mother or the girlfriend?"

Eighty percent of the time, the search boiled down to finding one of the two. Most of the punks lived with their parents well into their thirties. They didn't have anywhere else to go and in any case had no idea what to do with themselves on the outside. Their plans for the future rarely stretched beyond the upcoming weekend. Meanwhile, they loaded up on video games and sports clothes and spaced out, living a day-to-day existence.

"The mother. After that we'll go see the girlfriend, but the baby's there. Let's avoid that if we can."

They rolled out. When they got to the neighborhood, Ethan parked two blocks away from the house on a hill so they could assess the lay of the land. Bringing in someone who had jumped bail wasn't about high-speed chases but spending hours in your car on stakeouts, surveillance, listening to police reports about the suspect's whereabouts, and, when they were unlucky, absurd fights.

"Look, that's his car. He has a Toyota."

"He parks it around the back? The guy's really looking out for himself."

Bear neatly folded up his jacket and put it in the back seat. They went down the hill in their high-visibility vests, their weapons in full view. They walked down the alley without coming across anyone. The silence grew more oppressive the closer they got. By the time they got to the porch, it was almost tangible. They could feel unseen eyes trained on them from either side of the street. The front porch was full of children's toys, a couple of beach chairs, and a deflated wading pool, while the paint on the house's facade had long begun to flake. The kitchen window was dark. Ethan found the bell and rang. Nothing happened. He pulled back the screen door and rapped on the front door with his knuckles before shouting, "Hello? Knock, knock! Hello?"

"They're in there," Bear said confidently.

After waiting for a few seconds, Ethan slammed his fist against the door hard enough that the frail carpentry shuddered. A weak voice mumbled something unintelligible from inside. Ethan answered quickly.

"Good morning! Tyrone?"

The voice of an elderly woman came over to the door. "Huh?"

"Good morning, ma'am. How are things?"

"Huh?"

"We need you to open the door."

"Who is it? Who's there?"

"We need you to open the door, please."

"Who is it? This is my house."

"We're officers of the peace. We have our IDs right here—if you open the door, you can take a look."

"This is my house."

"Of course it is, ma'am. But we need—"

"I'm right here."

While Ethan spoke to the old woman through the door, Bear stepped back and looked up at the upper floor.

"We know that Tyrone is with you. We need to pick him up so he won't get into any more trouble."

"I'm here!"

"It'll go much better for him if he cooperates, ma'am."

"He's not here."

"We know that he's with you."

"No, he isn't."

"Do you know where he is?"

"Oh, my poor boy, my boy. He hasn't done anything wrong—who knows him better than his mother?"

"We believe that he's innocent, but if he doesn't come to court, things are only going to get worse for him."

"He hasn't done anything!"

"That's not what we're discussing right now, ma'am. Could you please open the door?"

"My boy hasn't done anything. The judge hates him. He wants to lock him up."

With one ear on the conversation, Bear stepped back onto the road to get a better overall view.

"I know that he has to go see the judge, and I'd tell him if he was here, but he ain't."

"I see. What about his girlfriend? Is he still seeing his girlfriend?"

"Oh, no, my poor son. He has no time for a girlfriend. He's being persecuted! And then there's the baby."

"So you have no idea where he might be."

"Yes, yes I do. He left for Alaska. He was always complaining about the heat down here."

Ethan couldn't help but laugh. "And of course you don't have an address or a telephone number."

"I sure don't! My poor boy . . . he's in Alaska!"

"Listen, ma'am, this is a criminal investigation. If you say that your son isn't hiding in your house and the neighbors say otherwise, that's obstruction of justice. Do you understand? I need you to listen to me because I know that you think you're doing him a favor, because you love him. But I need to explain what's going to happen if you keep—"

A brief whistle from Bear cut him off. He turned and saw Bear waving from the sidewalk opposite. The kid must have jumped out the back. Ethan gave up his speech, and they ran back to the car.

"Do you think she would have opened up?"

"Never."

"So why did you keep talking?"

"How else were we going to flush him out?"

When they pulled away, Ethan accelerated to the corner, but the fugitive was nowhere to be seen. He thought he saw something to his right, a glint off the asphalt and an almost imperceptible gray streak in the air.

"OK, I've got a hunch. It's all or nothing—what do you think?"

Without waiting for an answer, Ethan followed his instinct. A couple of streets farther on, they caught sight of the target's beat-up Corolla. They stopped at a traffic light a block away to give him some space, then followed for just over a mile, apparently undetected, before he parked outside a bar and disappeared inside. The building was just one story, but it took up the whole block.

"Let's split up. I'll go in through the kitchen," Bear said.

"He doesn't know that we're following him. There's no need."

"Amateurs . . ."

They pushed open the bar's door. Behind it was a black curtain. Beyond that the place was large with Irish decor and had a long bar to the right that came to an end just before the bathrooms. There was a crowd of tables, each with its own lamp, all of which were empty. At the back was a door marked **Private** and smoked-glass windows that almost completely blocked out the sun. The waiter turned to look at them, while in one corner a pair of shadows appeared to be enjoying a late breakfast. Ethan and Bear took note of all three and brandished their Remington 870s, which were loaded with nonlethal bullets.

"Good morning, we're looking for Tyrone, the kid who just came in here."

The barman pointed toward the bathroom. They smiled.

"Well, well, well, he didn't get time to take a piss."

As they approached, one of the customers stood up.

"Well, who would have thought it—Bear and Ethan!"

They recognized him immediately.

"Tony!"

"I don't believe it, Tony!"

"How long has it been?"

Tony gave Bear a hug. Everyone knew Bear, and in spite of Bear's intimidating appearance, Ethan didn't know anyone who had a bad word to say about him. They talked happily for a little while until they heard the sound of the hand dryer, and the kid came out, eager to find out what all the commotion was about. Suddenly he saw the two vests and went pale, as though his girlfriend had told him that she was expecting another baby. He stared at the scene, completely confused. Then he looked at Tony, who just stared back while his pursuers calmly lowered their guns and grabbed him.

"Hello, Tyrone. We've been looking for you. You need to come with us."

"Hands behind your back, please."

Bear took out the cuffs. The prisoner allowed himself to be turned around but then kicked out and ran off through the tables. Ethan sighed, threw his gun to Bear—who hadn't even felt the kick—and set off after him.

Tyrone ran as fast as he could, turning over chairs as he went, until he got to the heavy curtain, which he furiously pulled out of his way. He shoulder-charged the door, and the momentum tipped him over onto the sidewalk, but he got his hands down in time to stay upright. Instead of going for the Corolla, he decided to cross the street.

Confronted with a forest of overturned chairs, Ethan jumped onto a table, hopping from one to another. The first two were sturdy enough, but the third folded up, spilling him onto the floor. He got up feeling pain but rushed to the door in time to see the curtain fall heavily back in place. Untangling himself, he was able to jump through the still-swinging door. He saw the kid push himself back up on his feet, but the delay gave Ethan enough time to dive for Tyrone's shins just as he was about to cross the street. Tyrone kicked out instinctively and immediately fell forward. This time his hands weren't fast enough to break the fall, and his face smashed against the asphalt, scalding in the midday sun. Ethan straddled and cuffed him, meeting no more resistance. The kid ran his tongue around his mouth, checking for broken teeth, completely disoriented. Bear caught up with them, and they shoved Tyrone into the SUV.

"They run because it's what they see on TV. Fucking reality shows are the bane of our lives."

They went on talking as though they were alone.

"After we hand him in, I'll buy you lunch. I was thinking about this before," Bear said. "Have you ever known a mother to hand over her son?"

"No, never . . . no, that's not true. One did tell me where he was hiding once, but she wasn't trying to be helpful. It was to keep him away from his girlfriend. She blamed her for everything and figured that if the kid spent some time behind bars, the girl would lose interest. That was what she wanted most of all."

"You're kidding."

"Nope. She was willing to lock up her son just to get rid of a girl she didn't like. People are fucked up."

"What happened?"

"How the hell should I know? Do you think I go visit them when they get out?"

"Why not? I do with some of them. A bunch of good kids—they've formed a group to help reintegrate former offenders into society."

"Bear, you're one of a kind."

After they'd dropped off Tyrone, Ethan felt free to talk about Tony.

"Bear, I wasn't going to say anything in front of the package, but . . . that was Tony."

"Yeah, it was a surprise to see him."

"I've never noticed that bar before."

"Me neither. Tony's hiding."

"You think he was worried to see us?"

"I'm sure he was. He knows that we're not looking for him, but he doesn't know if we're going to tell anyone."

They went into a faux-Mexican chain restaurant.

"I thought he'd left town," Ethan said after they'd ordered.

"So did I. It's not smart to be here, given the situation he's in."

"But his business is here. If that Tyrone worked for him, he might have a problem."

"You think he'll squeal?"

Guillermo Valcárcel

"I doubt they know anything about it, but if they find out and offer him a deal, Tony's fucked. What's his reward up to now?"

"I don't know. Listen, Ethan, I wanted . . . I wanted to tell you something . . ."

Hearing Bear trip over his words, Ethan knew that they were finally going to get down to whatever had been bothering him all morning.

"M . . . Michelle wrote to me."

The name came like a slap to the face. Michelle. This was the last thing he had expected. Michelle. Even the sound of it hurt like a gut punch. His discomfort was palpable. Bear anticipated what he was going to say.

"I know. I . . . couldn't believe it either. Sh-she sent me an email. She must have kept my address. Maybe she has yours too."

"Who cares? I'm sure she does."

Michelle. He had no idea it would be such a shock. But then he hadn't thought he'd ever hear of her again. It had been six years since they'd last been in touch, maybe a little less. She'd sent him a few emails and some letters, but he'd never answered any of them. Eventually she'd gotten the point and stopped trying to contact him. She'd walked out of his life the same way she'd come into it, without asking for permission, steamrollering everything in her path. Michelle was hell. That was how he remembered her and their relationship: the roller coaster of emotions, the fights, the mood swings, the ridiculous jealousy. Four years during which she was all he'd been able to think about, when there was nothing else in his life. Michelle was extreme in every sense of the word: an ebullient Latin beauty with a wild, explosive character. A woman who existed to be adored and demanded every last second of your time, who put all her energy into fully occupying the role of lover—and she had a lot of energy. Ethan remembered it more like an addiction than love, not something that you enjoyed but a state where you felt as though you'd die if you didn't get your daily dose. And that was how he'd felt when she'd left: as though he'd died.

One afternoon she'd just up and vanished, taking the girl with her. Later on, she'd written to say that they'd gone back to Central America, that she still loved him but not like before, so she'd left to make things easier on the both of them. She hadn't mentioned that she'd run off with a handsome con man who'd persuaded her to pay for his plane ticket and then abandoned them at the airport. The bum, who'd promised to treat her like a queen, hadn't expected her to buy her own ticket, and especially not another for her six-year-old daughter.

14

Ethan would find out about that through mutual acquaintances a long time later, and it had brought all the pain and torment back again. Michelle had lied to him, as she so often had. But even after everything he'd gone through, Ethan couldn't hate her. The main victim of Michelle's conniving and deceit was usually Michelle.

"Why did she write to you? Did she ask you to talk to me?"

"Ye-yes. I haven't answered."

"What did she say?"

Bear rubbed his face, not sure how to say what had to come next. He made a couple of false starts before finally getting it all out.

"The . . . the girl has been kidnapped. Michi. She was taken coming back from school three days ago, and they can't find her. The kidnappers haven't been in contact. The police have looked into it, but they aren't very hopeful. She doesn't know what to do. She's desperate."

In a flash, Ethan's dream came back to him. It exploded vividly in his mind while the unnerving feeling he'd had when he'd woken up returned. Suddenly it seemed as though he was missing something. He hadn't heard from either of them for six years, and then he dreamed of the girl just hours before receiving this news. His face must have crumpled up in dismay because Bear was looking at him worriedly.

"You OK, man? I'm sorry. It . . . shocked me too. I know she was like a daughter to you. I don't know—whatever you want to do, I'll support you. Anything, no matter what."

"No, it's not that. It's . . ." He saw the image in his mind's eye; his head was spinning. Michi speaking in an almost teenage voice from a face he didn't recognize. *I'm still alive.* The sound had just seemed to float in space. It hadn't come from her mouth. He relived it over and over again and then started to gasp for air.

"No, it's not . . . ," he said mechanically. "Did she say anything else? Did she give you any more details?"

"Just that. She wrote everything in one long string of words, no punctuation, like it was a vision. She just told me and asked me to tell you. 'Please tell Ethan because I can't.'"

"She didn't ask you for help or money?"

"No. She didn't ask for anything. Just to tell you. I think she was trying to come to terms with it. She hasn't been given any hope of finding her. They know what it means when a girl disappears in that city. And so do you." Bear's lower lip began to tremble.

"She's not dead. Michi is alive," Ethan replied with a confidence he didn't recognize, as though the information were being transmitted to him from outside, although hearing himself say it, he realized how illogical he was being, that the only likely outcome was that she'd been murdered. They hadn't even demanded a ransom. What kind of ransom could they ask for anyway? The family was poor. Any professional, himself included, would have advised beginning the search at the morgue, and yet somehow the idea never even crossed his mind.

"Michi is alive," Ethan said again. "I don't know where she is, but she's still alive."

Bear's eyes opened wide in a mixture of incredulity and amazement.

"Let me see the email."

"Of course, buddy," Bear said, pulling out his phone.

The long, rambling, repetitive plea read as though it had been written in one go and sent. It wasn't Michelle's usual style, but some of her distinctive expressions remained in the hurried, confused account. Three days ago a friend of Michi's who'd been walking her back from school had called Michelle in tears. A car had stopped in their path, and the occupants had said they were friends of her mother; they knew things about her and offered to take her daughter to the hospital because she'd been in an accident. Michi had reacted with surprising maturity and had refused to get in, but the kidnappers hadn't given her a choice. They'd shoved her into the car without too much difficulty and immediately disappeared. Her shocked friend hadn't even been able to say what color the car was. The email didn't say anything else about the assault or what Michelle had done in the first decisive hours. Instead Michelle mentioned a detective she described as a saint and a genius who was helping her, although she didn't say whether she'd hired him, whether he was investigating the case, or whether he'd just given her advice. She finished off the email saying again and again that no one could hate her that much, and even if they did, they couldn't possibly want to hurt Michi to get to her. She brought up God several times, both in gratitude and begging for help, and that surprised Ethan too. Although he knew that she was Catholic, he'd never heard her express her faith so vehemently.

He reflected that in such a desperate situation, reverting to one's core beliefs was part of the process. After one of the few periods in the email, she begged Bear to tell him because she couldn't. Ethan, who knew her well, tried to read between the lines, but there wasn't any resentment, accusation, or hidden message. It was a harrowing cry for help from a distraught mother, an outpouring of the anguish she'd been through in the past three days. Maybe all she wanted was for someone to lie to her, anything to lift her spirits in a hopeless search.

On the one hand it was frustrating that she hadn't sent it to him, not just because of their relationship but also his connection with Michi. But on the other, it was understandable: he hadn't answered her for years. He read it three more times and each time felt more chilled.

"Have you told Candy?"

"No, I thought I should tell you first."

Neither of them spoke for a while. What should he do? Michi's father had left before she was born, and her mother had given her the same name to reinforce the fact that she was the only thing that truly belonged to Michelle. She'd grown too used to constant movement and instability, plagued by lotharios, passing encounters, con men, and generally unreliable, occasionally dangerous adventurers. All that instability had had its effect: Michelle had grown tough but also extremely practical, sometimes frighteningly so. It was her only defense against the world. Michi, the invisible daughter, had quietly moved into Ethan's life, and he'd begun to think of her as family. Then, just when they'd started with the adoption papers—the prospect of marriage was another regular cause of arguments—they'd disappeared.

Losing Michi had been just as painful as losing Michelle, if not more so. In many ways, it was the real cause of Ethan's depression. There was one aspect of the breakup that he hadn't revealed to anyone. It still tormented him. It hadn't just been Michelle who'd written: Michi had started to send him letters a few weeks after they'd left, but he hadn't been capable of answering them. When the first one had arrived in his mailbox, he'd thought it was from her mother until he'd seen the childish handwriting. The shock had been so great that he hadn't been able to open it. He'd spent months living in fear of another one arriving, and eventually three more had. He'd suffered from a nonsensical emotional paralysis. He'd needed her so badly that those envelopes should have been his salvation, but they'd done nothing but stir up despair that incapacitated him for days. He hadn't opened or torn up any of the letters but kept them in a box along with other old documents. In the end he'd moved, just so he wouldn't know whether she was still writing to him.

"I don't know what to think or what to do." His stomach was churning. "They're all wrong."

"Let's go home, have a cup of coffee with Candy, and decide what to do," Bear said, clearly concerned by Ethan's disorientation. "When we've worked it out, you can talk to Ari, or we can do it together if you like."

"No, sorry, I was a million miles away. I'm starting to think a little more clearly now. Will you help me?"

"Of course."

"I need . . ." Ethan was sweating. "I need to see my accountant. Will you come with me?"

"What are you thinking?"

"You know very well."

"You want to go down there? And what are you going to do, Ethan?"

"It's just an idea. The first thing I need to do is find out if I can afford it."

"We can lend you the money."

"Are you kidding? Do you know how much it'll cost? It could be weeks or months. You couldn't even if you wanted to. You're going to tell Candy that you're giving me money to go find Michi? You've got plenty to deal with as it is."

"Maybe. But you don't need to go see your accountant. You know what he's going to say."

"Let's get out of here. I'm suffocating."

Ethan left the restaurant, but instead of heading back to the car, he walked down the street to the corner and then back again. Bear was waiting for him at the door. Ethan walked up and down again. Bear could hear his breathing growing faster with each pass. By the fourth, Ethan's face was bright red, as though he'd been running for half an hour. He bent over, gasping for air. Bear didn't move.

"Are you OK?"

"Huh, huh, huh. Yeah. You know what I think?"

"I think you need to sleep on it. Or at least talk it over with Ari."

Ethan felt the tension rising, the adrenaline bubbling up inside of him like a soda, his fear increasing. "When will we get another chance? Tony won't be there tomorrow."

"What if he's already gone?"

"Then I'll have to come up with another plan."

"Ethan, you're being crazy."

"How much is it, Bear?"

"I don't know."

"It's enough to pay for the trip. Can you help Ari at the office for a few weeks?"

"Ethan, I'll do whatever you ask, but this is crazy. Also: it's Tony, man. We can't do this to Tony. Can you imagine how people will look at us afterward?"

"I can't just let him go—it's like he's been served to me on a plate. And you know what? I doubt this is a coincidence. Strange things are going on. If we don't do this now, and I can't . . . I'm not saying that I'm going to look for Michi." He was finding it difficult to speak; his hands were trembling. "I don't mean that I'm definitely going. I mean that I need to be able to. If I decide to go tomorrow, and we don't find him . . . if I want to go, and I can't afford it . . . Christ, if I don't do anything for her, how long will I regret it?"

Ethan parked the SUV in the lot next to Tyrone's Corolla. Both men got out, and they started toward the bar.

"Watch the barman. He'll be behind us—armed, probably."

"If we're lucky, it'll be a bat."

"If we're lucky. And we won't know if there are any customers or someone in the back."

"That could work in our favor."

"We need to cover the doors," Ethan said, his expression hardening. "Do we both go in the front or come from both sides?"

"We don't even know if he's still there. We'll go in together."

They slowly pulled back the curtain so their eyes could adjust to the dark. This wasn't the kind of place where people lingered over their lunch. The bar was still empty. First, they located the barman and then confirmed that Tony was still there. His companion from earlier had left, and Tony was slumped in front of a tablet, idly tapping away. At another table, two young guys were drinking beer. Ethan and Bear assumed that they were Tony's guys, waiting for orders, though it was clear they were like Tyrone, posers more likely to run than fight. The bounty hunters were more worried about the barman, who looked like a professional. Tony looked up. His expression changed. His smile grew more bitter, but he tried to keep his composure.

"I wasn't expecting you to come back."

"Tony, you need to come with us," Ethan said. "This is my move. Bear has nothing to do with it."

Bear pointed his gun at the barman, while Ethan covered the kids at the table, who didn't react at all.

"Then he should have stayed at home," Tony said, standing up to show that he wasn't armed. "Bear, if you're not a part of this, then you can leave. I'll go quietly with Ethan."

Bear remained focused on the barman, who didn't look like he was in the mood to back down.

Ethan went over to Tony, keeping his gun trained on the two underlings. They stared at him with bulging eyes, their engines revving. They'd forgotten their drinks but didn't know what to do with their shaking hands. The longer the situation went on, the more unstable it became. If Bear's man wasn't cooperative and he had to go in to get him, he'd be turning his back on them, and that worried Ethan. The four adults knew what they had to do, but these kids didn't seem to know their roles. They might behave and wait for Tony's orders, or they might try to be heroes. Or, even worse, they might just get scared, and then they'd be even more unpredictable. And that was exactly what was happening. Ethan could see it coming.

"You two, stay there. Keep your hands raised, right up. Keep them where I can see them."

They looked for Tony's approval, but he offered no instructions. They were lost, and he was encouraging their confusion. Their eyes met, and Ethan took advantage to increase the pressure.

"Your fucking hands! Didn't you hear me?"

Bear, trying to keep facing them, backed along the bar to immobilize the barman, but the employee stepped back, just out of reach. Bear sighed in annoyance and swept the glasses from the bar with a crash. The barman understood the threat and froze. The underlings jumped back like a pair of frightened cats, and one tripped against the table, knocking it down. The clatter of the beers and plates echoed around the large room. Tony instinctively stepped back, and Ethan pointed his gun at him.

"Stay there."

Bear looked at them, grunted, and leaped with surprising agility onto the bar to grab the barman by the collar. The first kid, pushed back by the table, tripped on his chair and fell backward, shoving his companion, who, wild with fright, took cover behind the table. Squinting, he took a revolver he'd clearly never used before out of his pants and aimed it blindly at the strangers. The first shot rang out sharply, unleashing a brief bout of chaos. Tony went for the booth to take cover, but Ethan blocked his path. The second kid curled up behind a chair and started to scream, covering his head. The barman got away from Bear while the shooter continued to fire blindly with his eyes closed. Bear turned his Remington to where the firing was coming from but immediately switched back to the barman, who was reaching for something under the bar. The barrel of a Mossberg appeared in his hands. Ethan grabbed Tony by the hair, lifting him up. The third shot smashed a bottle a few feet away from Bear, but he ignored it. Deafened by the kid's panicked screams, he aimed at the barman and raised his voice threateningly.

"Drop it, or I'll blow you away!"

The random shooter somehow aimed his gun at the source of the sound and instinctively let off his last three bullets. Bear was watching his man, who'd dropped the sawn-off shotgun. The first bullet hit Bear's vest, but the two others went right into his side under the protective straps. He let out a gasping scream and collapsed among the stools, increasing the confusion. Tony shouted something amid the commotion, and Ethan saw his best friend fall, tangled up in a footrest and a stool, his gun three feet away. With that image in his mind, he pointed his gun at the table and fired. The table exploded into shrapnel, and smoke filled the room. The shooter dropped his gun. He had no idea what he'd done. Ethan turned around in time to see the barman stand up, taking advantage of this turn of events. Ethan anticipated him with a shot aimed a foot away from his head. The barman reared back from the explosion next to him while glass and wood flew everywhere, cutting into his cheek. Ethan, who was just as disoriented, used the only fraction of a second he had to get ahold of himself. He refrained from firing again, steadying his trembling legs and wavering voice.

"Drop it! Drop it! Hands up!"

Keeping the gun trained on the barman, he pulled Tony's hair. The barman dropped the Mossberg without firing and patiently put his hands behind his head.

"Out! Get out of here! You: on the ground, for fuck's sake! On the ground, hands behind your back!"

Tony obeyed him, but they were both on autopilot, moving without thinking. They went through the established routine while their attention was fixed elsewhere, entirely occupied by their friend's inert bulk. Bear had fallen, and they could see his body amid the rising clouds of dust floating through the air like ash after a fireworks display.

2

The Beast

The Beast looked at himself in the rearview mirror. He liked to call himself the Beast; it made him feel powerful and prepared him for the aggression to come. He had a gaunt face and a fixed, piercing stare. He liked the word *piercing* too. It was something a woman had once said to him before she'd discovered his true nature. It excited him—not that he fully understood what it meant. He told himself that he was an invincible conqueror, the omnipotent master of all he surveyed. Herds of women belonged to him; they were his possessions. His gaze tamed them, because it was so piercing, before revealing to them his terrible power. He was a cruel destroyer, a beast without conscience or pity. He would teach them lessons until they fully understood the grandeur of his evil. The Beast was a powerful, fearsome harbinger of doom; his piercing eyes promised death and unimaginable pain. He seethed with resentment, although he preferred to think of it as just another facet of his greatness, not his primary impulse. He felt no hatred toward his victims; he didn't even scorn them. Deep down in his rotten soul, they were nothing more than a consequence of the satisfaction demanded by his ego. He was their lord and master, and he could mistreat them as he wished, the way one might break a toy. Bewitched by his own gaze, convinced that the word *piercing* had obscene, disturbing connotations, he pulled up his shirt to examine his scars. Then he stroked them indulgently. He pulled his shirt back down. Now he felt ready, hungry for action.

He turned the key in the ignition, and the great animal rumbled to life with a threatening roar, inhaling the aroma of the thousand oil wells on which it fed. The truck growled as it headed uphill, and he revved the engine like a hell hammer announcing his presence to the world. Reveling in his own brutality, he drove up to the shack just off the road. Night had fallen, and the wooden shacks with corrugated iron roofs, most of which were connected to the public grid, glowed from the inside, revealing the gaps between the boards, while the sounds of multiple televisions leaked into the tense, quiet night. Outside, however, there was no one to be seen. At night in the slums of Latin America, the outdoors belonged to beasts like him.

The shack opened up, and a wiry girl appeared, a thick mane of black hair wrapped around her neck like a feather boa. She was wearing red high heels that were utterly impractical on the dirt road. She gave the truck a challenging, flirtatious look and stretched out her right leg, showing off her tiny, frayed cutoffs. She waved her leg like an invitation.

"So, honey, what'll it be?" she said in a rough coastal accent. "You in the mood tonight, old man?"

The Beast licked his lips. Two nights of generous payment to soften her up and earn her trust. Young whores could be very trusting.

"Get in, babe. Tonight, I'm gonna show you my palace."

The girl laughed in a mannish way. "No, honey! My mom won't let me go off with strangers. We do it here."

The Beast jumped out of his truck, pleased to be able to show off his gleaming cowboy boots, which were soon covered in a layer of dust, and his open white shirt. She wasn't used to these kinds of clothes; it made her suspicious. He noticed.

"What do you think, babe? I look good, don't I? Here, touch them if you like. They cost over five hundred dollars. Snakeskin, handmade just for me."

The girl looked at them more curiously when she heard the price, although she still thought they were ridiculous. It occurred to her that this bastard might have something worth stealing in his old trailer. Confusing her curiosity with admiration, he took her gently by the chin.

"I want to do it at home tonight, honey. It really turns me on. And I'm not a stranger anymore, am I?"

The girl shook him off in annoyance while she weighed up the potential risks and benefits. As they talked, another figure appeared in the doorway. The Beast smiled at the silhouette, whose expression was impossible to read in the dark.

"Come on, madam, tell your daughter that she's safe with me."

He took out a wad of bills, more than triple what he'd paid on the previous visits, and put it in her hand. Both women were stunned. The madam tried not to show her excitement, but she couldn't help licking her lips as she counted the money. The Beast puffed out his chest and fixed his eyes on the girl in an absurd attempt to impress her. She met them with the tough glare of a girl who'd grown up on the streets.

Feeling irresistible, he murmured, "How do you like my piercing eyes?"

She had to stifle a laugh. Then she turned to her mother, who nodded imperceptibly, and took his hand.

"They're great. You're a hottie."

But the Beast caught the hint of mockery. The insult wounded his pride, stoking his resentment still further. *I'll show you who's in charge, you whore. You're about to learn the meaning of fear.*

After they got into the truck, the girl brazenly opened the glove compartment and looked inside.

"Do you have any gum? There's a field over there where it's great to do it . . ."

He didn't answer. After waiting until they'd driven over a mile, he grabbed her hair with an anger that took her completely by surprise. He turned to face her, taking his eyes off the road.

"Look at me, bitch. Look me in the eyes! They're piercing! I'll show you!" He smacked her head against the dashboard as hard as he could while the truck swerved wildly from one side of the road to the other. Then he let her go and regained control of the truck. The girl, spitting blood, her nose broken, tried to reach for the door, but it was locked. The Beast let out an ominous laugh and felt himself grow, filling the interior with his presence while she shrank down to the size of a puppy. A puppy that he, the great demon, would crush without remorse. Grabbing her hair again, he shouted with the full force of his lungs: "I am the Beast! *I am the Beast!*"

The cafeteria smelled of disinfectant, and the light was cold and weak, creating a sickly, bloodless atmosphere. The white walls with their faded double lines only enhanced the feeling. The cavernous space echoed with the murmur of different conversations. Couples and groups with devastated expressions were scattered around, talking in ghostly voices. Ethan thought that this was absolutely appropriate, given the circumstances. The people sitting around him were either waiting or hurting: when you received good news, you didn't come down to the hospital cafeteria to celebrate. It occurred to him that the bewildered feeling it gave you was intentional, demonstrating a kind of empathy with the distraught visitors. The only relief came from the window that looked out onto the garden. It might once have promised sunny mornings on the patio, but instead the sun had scorched the building's facade and withered the garden into a lifeless shell. He had the impression that this was the kind of place one only saw at night, in dim light when the cold had sunk into your bones. Candy came back in; her bitter expression seemed burdened with the weight of the world.

"The nurse says that he's going to be sedated until tomorrow, so we should go. There's nothing we can do here."

"I want to stay with you."

"You can go. Actually, I'd rather you did. The way Ari left, I think maybe you have some stuff you need to talk over."

"This isn't about us."

"Yes, it is. Or you, anyway. This whole mess, this shitty situation, wouldn't have happened if you hadn't suddenly decided to become the masked avenger. Seriously, Ethan, what the hell were you two thinking? Don't think that fat bastard in there has got away with it—he'll get his when he wakes up. You've told me the story three times, and I still don't get it. I remember little Michi very well—you know I loved her—but do you really know what you're saying?"

Ethan didn't answer. He hadn't told them about the dream. That would only give them more reason to think he'd gone crazy. And he understood completely. In their place, he'd have reacted the same way. Instead of trying to explain himself, he just kept silent. It didn't matter now. What they'd just been through had forced him to give up on his plan anyway. Waiting for the ambulance for Bear had been some of the worst minutes of his life. He had had to help them lift him onto the gurney. After the legal complications, the questioning, Candy's reaction, and the fear, panic, and fury, now there was the waiting. The tense, exhausting waiting. They'd gotten lucky: the bullets hadn't done any major damage to Bear, but his vest had stopped them from exiting, and that had aggravated the wounds. Then Ari had stormed off, screaming that she couldn't understand how he could have let things go so far. And now he felt triply guilty about Michi, Ari, and Bear.

"It's over now. I'm not going anywhere. Ari won't run the business if I go, and she couldn't do it on her own anyway."

Candy took out another cigarette and tapped it against the pack. "So it's over? Just like that?"

"You know I don't have a choice. It's not up to me."

"I don't know. Fuck, you're with Ari, not Michelle, right?"

"You never liked Michelle."

"That's not what we're talking about. What we're talking about is your girlfriend's reaction to you going off to visit your ex in another country."

"You never liked Michelle."

"No, I didn't. I thought she was a bitch then, and I still do, but I guess that's on me. Maybe I'm being unfair."

"You're entitled to your opinion."

"Ethan, you're a great guy. I love you lots, but sometimes you're a fucking douchebag. Listen, I'm not going to sit here arguing with you, because you always manage to twist things around to your point of view. But even if we were to say you were right and that you're the only one who can help Michi, you could have asked Ari to go with you, and we could have run the business. You know she'd have said yes. I don't want to break your balls here, but you'd better think hard about what's on the line. Ari isn't the little girl who used to stare up at you wide eyed, repeating whatever you said to everyone, or the girl you used to get back on your feet when Michelle left you. She's changed, and it seems you're the only who hasn't noticed."

"I never used Ari."

"Sure, but you always found her in your bed when you needed it, and she never asked you for anything in return. Maybe it's better this way. Maybe she's grown out of you."

Ari was brushing her teeth and wondering whether she'd overreacted at the hospital, if it had been selfish to have made that scene over Michelle instead of trying to stay calm. But she'd gone crazy. She'd been distraught about Bear when she'd arrived, on the brink of tears. Then suddenly, the moment he was out of immediate danger, Ethan and Candy were talking about that bounty, the trip, a kidnapped girl. And who had been right there in the middle of it all? Bam! Michelle, admiring the chaos she'd created. Ari could understand the impulse to go look for the girl, but to her it was so obvious that it was all a big lie. There were all these strange details: the email to Bear instead of Ethan, the random encounter with Tony on the same day they got the news during a seemingly routine capture . . . she'd seen through it all while Ethan had just gone on and on with that silver tongue he always used to trick her. He could fool anyone. But not this time.

He'd spent the night before murmuring "Michelle, Michelle." He'd seemed so upset that she'd tried to wake him. When she'd been unsuccessful, she'd gotten out of bed in a rage. At the hospital, she'd listened to his little tale and watched her friend, listening and accepting it with surprising credulity. She'd wondered how to expose him without screaming what she thought of him. But then he'd finished his story and told her that this wasn't the time to talk about it. It was the way he'd dismissed her so lightly that she couldn't stand. She'd stared at Ethan, and for a moment he'd seemed unrecognizable. They'd had a lot of fights, but he'd never treated her so coldly before. It was so cynical. He was like a compulsive liar convinced he'd never be caught out. It made her wonder whether she really knew him at all or if the mask had finally slipped after all these years. She realized that if he'd told one lie like this, he might have told dozens, hundreds. And this wasn't an innocent white lie—it involved Michelle. Why make up something like this? How long had they been in touch behind her back? Why was he really going on this trip?

Instead of smashing everything within reach and telling him to go to hell, turning back into the violent teenager she'd once been, she'd restrained herself. She'd learned from the best, and she couldn't be more grateful to him for that. She'd repressed her confusion, her uncertainty, and her anger, and she'd left. On her way back she'd racked her brain for possible excuses: confusion, forgetfulness, maybe some kind of well-meaning intention she couldn't understand. But every time she thought it over, it came back to the same thing: deceit, betrayal, lies, cheating, ingratitude, sleaze, and, ultimately, loneliness.

Voices were eating away at her from the inside. She couldn't go to Candy; she was still at the hospital, going through something even worse. Unable to share such a deep wound, she'd locked herself in the bathroom, hoping it would be a long time before he came back. Then she'd cried as she hadn't cried in years.

An hour later, she had calmed down and decided to keep going until she'd exposed him for the dirty liar he was. She'd had a quick dinner and gone to brush her teeth, sure that he wouldn't be back until the next day. But then she heard his keys in the lock. He called out a greeting. She froze, feeling nervous, as though they hadn't seen each other in months. Her instinctive reaction was to lock the door.

Ethan stomped heavily into the bedroom and sat on the bed. He looked at the closed door and for a moment wished he were on the other side, hugging her. He tried to think of what to say, feeling ridiculous, annoyed, and guilty all at the same time. For one thing, he didn't understand anything that had happened over the past twenty-four hours. He'd been caught up in a sequence of events completely beyond his control. It annoyed him that he had to explain his actions as though he'd done something wrong, and he was especially irritated by Ari's childish behavior. With Bear out of danger, he'd taken full responsibility for the botched arrest, and he'd felt as though he were a hostile witness being interrogated, having to justify himself for wanting to help with something that he felt was important: a girl's life was at stake. But he also felt terrible about what Candy had said to him: he'd made sure to keep Ari out of it right from the start, and he was ashamed. And he was frightened by what Candy had said, by the idea that Ari had outgrown him.

Ari had lived a difficult life. She had been forced to grow up fast, confronted with problems no girl of her age should have had to deal with, and she'd gotten through them with incredible strength. That was who she had been when Ethan had met her, and he'd accepted her immediately. But who was she now? What could be scarier than not knowing who your girlfriend was? Wasn't it that very fear he'd seen in other aging couples? His parents, for instance. Ethan was afraid to poke his head over the ramparts Ari had put up. What if there wasn't any room for him in there? After her childish outburst at the hospital, once the initial indignation had faded away, he'd only felt tenderness for her. He'd been given a glimpse of the insecure, aggressive little girl he'd once known, and he'd been grateful to finally see a little vulnerability. It was a reminder of how much he loved her. Now he wanted to make it up to her. But his good intentions began to wilt in the glare of real communication. The gap between them was getting wider and wider. He cleared his throat but didn't know what to say.

"Hello!"

He could hear Ari gurgling.

"Candy's going to stay the night. Did you have dinner?"

"Yes, there's lasagna in the oven."

"Thank you. But . . . about before. I'm not going. There won't be any trip. I don't know what I was thinking. I know it was crazy, but . . . I need you to understand. The news . . ."

Ari came out and stood there expectantly, but Ethan couldn't find the words. She raised her eyebrows and looked at him with a feeling she couldn't identify. Still, it was comfortable. She shrugged. "I'm sorry too. I acted like an idiot. I'm glad. I'm very sorry about Michi, but I'm glad that you're staying."

She went over, and he wrapped his arms around her without getting up, feeling her stomach against his cheek. The hug was short lived. She stepped back, and he let her go and went off to the kitchen. She wanted to ask him to stay, but she didn't. She asked herself why she had pushed him away. She asked herself whether she believed him. Who was the real Ethan? How could they get things back on the right track? That was what she wanted. He'd comforted her with just a few words. It was like a bad dream that had lasted a whole day. She wanted to take his hand and lead him somewhere to talk and work things out. She wasn't going to give up. Their relationship meant something. It had to.

She got into bed, knowing that he wouldn't join her. He'd have dinner in front of the TV and fall asleep on the sofa. It was a flashback to their early days. She had been very temperamental, and in certain situations, not just when she was angry but when she felt anxious or in crisis, she'd asked him for space. She needed to breathe, and he'd crash on the couch. One summer night he'd slept in the hammock. Respecting her wishes was the act of a Hispanic gentleman. Now it had become a habit: during tense periods like this one, it was a preventative move. But she could go to him and ask him to keep her company. She wouldn't even have to say anything; she just had to go and kiss him on the cheek or stroke his hand. But she didn't. She didn't know why. She just didn't.

An hour or two later, she felt his warm body slip in next to hers. She turned over and saw his shape under the sheets.

Ethan whispered, "Go to sleep."

And she turned around, pleased that their tacit agreement had been consigned to the past.

Ethan felt the darkness closing in around him. He sensed danger. He didn't know who he was with, only that they were familiar to him. Confused, he tried to focus on the people, but for some reason he couldn't see them, though he sensed their presence. He walked on, realizing that he had no idea when he'd started moving or from where he'd started. He soon found himself far away, alone, with nobody close by. The hallway (since when had he been in a hallway?) got narrower and darker as the echoing voices grew quieter. He focused on the sound and realized that it was coming from a party. That was right—he'd just left a party and was sliding down this poorly lit hallway. A vague fear welled up inside of him, and he realized that it was a dream. *I need to wake up*, he told himself, trying to sit up in the hopes that he could shove his body out of this oppressive limbo. But nothing happened; he wasn't in bed. He was standing in the hallway. *This is a dream, a dream I can wake up from.* His fear grew as he went deeper into the darkness and approached a closed door. He recognized the sensation of danger and knew that he had to wake up. *I need to wake up.* He knew that he was lying in bed next to Ari, but he was unable to move or get out of his self-imposed prison. The door opened, and he walked down some stairs, his terror growing with each step. *This is a dream—it's not real.* He started to hear whispers. The noise from the party (what party?) had disappeared completely, and now the space was filled with the ghostly sound of a pair of women's voices. Their invisible voices came closer, and Ethan worried they'd give him away to whatever was stalking him. He knew that they'd expose him and tried to quiet them without making any noise. *It's a dream*, he told himself. *I can change this. I'm in charge of my dreams. The only thing that's stopping me is my fear. I just have to decide to change it and wake up.* But one of the whispers echoed clearly in his head, as though it were right at his ear, even though he was still alone. It was Michi's voice. He'd known it was her right from the start. Another feminine voice was trying to reach him. Someone was talking to her, telling her to say something. He couldn't tell whether it was trying to help her or catch him. The voice became clear; there was nothing he could do to avoid it.

"Don't go any farther, or they'll catch you."

"Your voice, Michelle. They'll hear you."

"They can't right now. They're blind right now—they're worried about the fire."

"I can't stop. I can't help it."

"Yes, you can. This is a part of your dream. If you don't stop, they'll find you."

These words made Ethan shiver. His hair was standing on end. A nameless fear trickled like ice water down the back of his neck. Then he stopped. Everything stopped. He could see a glow in the distance.

"See? You stopped. But if you move, they'll find you. And then you'll never come back."

"Back where, Michi? Where are you?"

"I don't know—in another country. To the south."

"Why can't I see you?"

"Because you're not here. She is. And you'll get here. Now you have to get ready."

"Where are you talking to me from? What do you want me to do?"

"There are two of them. They're coming down the passage, but I can see them for you. Don't be afraid. They don't know that I'm talking to you."

"Are these the men that kidnapped you? Are they the men you're afraid of?"

"I'm afraid of the other one. Very scared."

"Who's the other one, Michi?"

"He's one of them. He says he's a man, but I know he isn't. He's one of them, and if he finds me, he'll take me away."

Now Michi was clearly crying; she was terrified.

"Don't worry, Michi. No one is going to take you anywhere. I'm going to come find you."

She wasn't speaking anymore, just struggling to keep her crying silent. She took a deep breath. "Are you coming to find me?"

"Of course, but I need your help. I need to know where you are. Something."

Michi's voice grew taut, like it had crystalized, as though the soundwaves had turned into glass scratching at his ears.

"He's coming now. You have to go. He'll take you away along with me."

Ethan felt the girl's fear increasing. It spread to him and became a part of him. He tried to reassure her.

"Michi, listen: nothing's going to happen. You're dreaming."

But the voice didn't belong to her anymore. A monstrous groan swelled and replaced it with a demonic roar.

"Get out!"

He jolted awake in terror. It took him a long time to calm down. The bedroom was dark, and the house was silent. In the distance, a dog barked at something. Next to him, Ari was breathing slowly. It was a normal early morning. He gulped and got up to go to the bathroom. He decided to go to the guest one so as not to wake Ari. His legs were trembling, and he was afraid to leave the room. Ethan was amazed to find himself scared in his own house, as though he were seven years old again, but he couldn't control it. He turned on the lights in the hallway and the bathroom and looked at his reflection in the mirror, expecting to see something unfamiliar. But everything looked normal. He scolded himself incredulously. How could he be having a panic attack? But the fear wouldn't go away. As he took a piss, his head cleared a little, and his vision came back into focus. He washed his face in the sink, and when he looked up, he saw a silhouette in the mirror. A few feet behind him, a figure in the shadows. His dream was merging with reality. He jumped.

Ari stepped back, nervously saying, "Are you OK?"

Ari had woken up and followed the lights. Now she was looking at him with a sleepy but alarmed expression. "Ethan? What's wrong?"

As though coming out of a trance, Ethan wanted to explain himself and reassure her at the same time, but the words seemed to have a mind of their own.

"I . . . it was a dream, just a dream. She . . . she's alive. And I'm going to find her. I—I . . . I know it's not right, but I'm going to find her. I have to . . . I'm going, Ari. Forgive me, please, or come with me. I'm going to find Michi."

3

The Lost Children

Like an automaton, Ari ran the faucet; wet the toothpaste on the bristles, even though Ethan had told her a thousand times that it wasn't necessary; and brushed industriously for a few minutes. As she stared into the mirror, she got lost in the ritual, and her mind wandered. Memories came to her like in a daydream as she was lulled by the sound of the running water. She recalled all the times Ethan had come up behind her and turned off the faucet. Ari knew she should save water. She knew all about recycling and being environmentally conscious, and she did everything she was supposed to, except for when she brushed her damn teeth. But Ethan was always there to remind her. It had become a running mini-argument, like a constant drip, drip, drip falling in the same place in a relationship, eroding it away. Ari just wanted Ethan to leave her alone, to let her have her fucking bad habit. To leave her be while she let her mind wander for three goddamn minutes.

Now she stared at the stupid faucet and calculated how much water she was wasting. Even though Ethan had gone, she couldn't even enjoy this little indulgence. His absence filled every corner.

The definitive breakup had occurred on the same day Ethan had woken up so strangely in the middle of the night. Ethan had tried to explain, making her promise that she wouldn't tell anyone and then telling her about his nightmares. He'd told her about his irrational hunch, a kind of conviction that the girl was alive and communicating with him. He was determined to go look for her. He hadn't asked her to believe him, but he had wanted her to come with him.

She'd made an effort with the first part, but it was impossible. She hadn't even considered the second. Someone had to maintain some degree of sanity. She had tried to reason with him, suggesting that he see a therapist. Maybe the help he needed was with getting over the trauma of the news, not doing something in real life. But Ethan had reacted in a way she'd never seen before: he'd turned her doubts back on her, reminding her of every time she'd lost control. Suddenly he'd been judging her. He'd never rubbed old flaws in her face before. It had been then she'd seen just how lost he was. Ari had known that if only she kept her composure, she'd be able to win the argument, but she hadn't cared about winning. But Ethan hadn't let up, insisting she was difficult, impossible to live with.

"Of course I'm difficult!" she had yelled, finally taking the bait. "So what? You knew that before you decided to move in with me. Don't start complaining now. I'm the addict; I'm the irresponsible one. But I've never fucked with you. I go to the meetings, and you just sit there watching TV and ask me how they went. I haven't gone off to meet a lover. Let the past stay in the past!"

"I've helped you with everything you've ever needed. Do you want me to start coming to the meetings again?"

"I want you to shut the fuck up!"

Ari wanted to forget their argument. He was the last person she wanted to act like that with. And again she felt the fear that came with passing a point of no return.

"I think it would be better for the both of us . . ."

"Stop it. I've never been jealous—don't make me out to be something I'm not. You're going to leave, and I'm not going to stop you. You can explain it however you like. Michelle calls you asking for help, and you run back to her like a good little doggy."

"That's just your point of view."

"Yes, it is, and you're right, as always. I'm going for a coffee. I don't need this. Do whatever you want, but you'll be doing it on your own."

She'd gone to a diner to clear her head, and Ethan had started looking up flights. Later that morning they'd sat down again, and she, after thinking it over in a calm, measured way, had explained the situation the way she saw it. From her point of view. She'd gotten used to reacting to him. For better or worse she was always responding to him, whether as a companion or an antagonist. Now that role was over, and she had to plan for her future, which bore no relation to what he wanted to do.

Ari had told Ethan that she'd look after the business while he was gone. If Bear couldn't help her, she'd do it herself and hand it back to him when he got back. She'd use the time to find a new place to live. Then she'd change careers. She didn't mind being a waitress if it meant that she could continue her studies. She liked the idea of moving close to Sasha so she could see her sister every day, especially now that she was about to become a teenager. She wanted to be there for her at such a crucial time; it was something she'd been thinking about for a while now, although she'd never brought it up. Most of all, she had concluded, Ethan had to understand that this wasn't an ultimatum. It had nothing to do with what he decided, even if it was to stay. In fact, she wanted him to go on his trip. It would give her the time she needed to deal with things quietly and make sure everything was done properly.

That was when Ethan had understood how things really were. He had remained quiet and hadn't even dared to touch her. He hadn't touched her again until the day he'd left. They'd taken turns sleeping on the couch, and he hadn't had any more dreams. He'd bought a ridiculously expensive ticket to fly in a couple of days, and she'd approved of that too. There was no point prolonging things just to save some money when a girl's life was supposedly at stake.

But when Bear had regained consciousness, they'd talked, and he'd repeated Ethan's story so exactly that it had only made Ari more confused. She hadn't known what to believe. The idea of Ethan's departure had felt like a relief but had begun to hurt more and more as it had neared. Organizing the trip in such a short period of time, Ethan had spent the last few days in a state of nervous panic. He had had no time to get an international gun license and especially not a permit to carry his own. He'd been afraid of getting stranded. By the end, Ari had preferred to stay at the office rather than go home. She'd felt as though she'd already left it behind. She'd become the serene counterweight he needed, staying friendly and active, but on the last night, when the departure had been inevitable, she'd felt as though her life had been falling apart from the inside.

Candy had offered to take him to the airport, and Ari had happily agreed. When they'd last seen each other, she'd offered him her cheek and given him a quick hug, wishing him luck. As she'd watched them drive off, she'd felt a sudden emptiness and collapsed into tears. Utterly distraught, she'd wandered through the rooms, looking for something she'd never find until she'd eventually decided to do what came naturally to her.

To outside observers, Ari seemed to exist to solve problems and improvise solutions. They assumed that it was an innate talent, but that wasn't true. It was a virtue she'd acquired in order to survive with her little sister. Optimizing non-existent resources, making sure they had enough to eat or somewhere to sleep. In any given situation, she could now envision a way out or at least a suitable reaction. So she employed these skills to help deal with the breakup while also keeping the business going while he traveled the world chasing shadows.

That morning after he left, without thinking, without really knowing why, she'd sat down in front of the computer and started to do research. She hadn't thought about this at all while Ethan had been there, but she wasn't going to wallow in self-pity just because he'd left. She'd begun with search terms like *kidnapping, Central America* and *disappearances, Central America*. The first results had contained descriptions of crimes they were already familiar with, carried out by gangs, especially the Mara.

Since the nineties, the so-called Northern Triangle of Central America, which was made up of El Salvador, Guatemala, and Honduras, had been dominated by Mafia-like gangs known as the Mara; their violence reached levels unheard of in other criminal groups. Their members, which numbered in the hundreds of thousands, recruited destitute teenagers and street children. Rites of initiation could be performed by children as young as ten, sometimes even younger. Their life expectancy was similarly short: few of them lived past the age of thirty. Their lives were summed up in a common tattoo: three points of a triangle representing "my crazy life," the fate that awaited every member of the Mara: prison, death, or the hospital. The very term was associated with the *marabunta*, huge swarms of predatory ants that invaded and devoured everything in their path.

Their power rivaled that of entire provincial governments, making them, like Mexico in narco territory, failed states. Their income was based on extorting businesses, families, and transport networks, supplemented either by drug trafficking or through taxes levied on drug dealers operating in their territory. Struggles over different neighborhoods led to constant battles in which the security forces were reduced to the role of referee. Central America had become the most violent region in the world without a war ever being officially declared.

Ari had also learned that kidnappings—another source of income—when not organized by the local gang, were at the least authorized by them.

Now, several days later, she was going out every day but wasn't opening up to anyone. She had plenty of company, especially male company, but it wasn't loneliness she was feeling. It was absence, grief. She knew both emotions well. Loneliness wasn't unique; it was generic and related to fear. An abstract pressure that got stuck in your throat and crippled your self-esteem. Absence was a deep wound in your chest caused by something specific and unique, something you knew well, and the pain that came with it was harsh and cutting. You were forever fooled into thinking that the person had come back, like phantom limb syndrome. Ari, who had watched her mother die of an overdose when she was fourteen, had suffered from them both but was upset to find that she was still so susceptible.

The mountain chains between the tropics and the equator formed undulating, leafy profiles, like gods sleeping under a blanket of vegetation. On top of these mythical creatures, which were known to shed whole hillsides during torrential rain as though they were sloughing their skin, the presence of humans seemed like an anachronism. The local inhabitants, inconsequential creatures, had struggled through centuries of injustice. The poorest people living on the richest land.

After cresting one of these peaks, the Beast drove to a village he'd kept under surveillance for weeks on a client's orders. He drove down the narrow track around the volcano; there was barely enough space for the truck to get through. He parked in the extra space set aside for braking around a curve, a semicircle of dust and gravel added next to the road overlooking a deep canyon. Under his wheels, hundreds of feet below, was an even mat of jungle interrupted by the occasional zinc roof and small plantations belonging to subsistence farmers. From his precarious vantage point, he leaned on his seat, smoking as he surveyed the land, keeping an eye on the huts spread out along the asphalt and barely walkable tracks. Wood-and-corrugated-iron or at best adobe shacks with one or two rooms separated by a chipboard screen, with holes in the walls for windows, hinged sheets of metal for shutters, wood ovens outside, and altars with crucifixes at certain strategically prominent points. *Jesus, protect this home.* Domestic animals moved around freely; hens scattered from the road every time a car came by. The locals walked to the store or farther down to the school, frustrated by the lack of opportunity but well adapted to their lives. A motorbike drove up the hill carrying a fat man and three kids, one in front and the two others behind, casually clinging on in their distinctive way. The Beast looked at all this and chuckled to himself. He despised them, but he found their poverty amusing.

A little farther down the slope, one of the makeshift shutters opened, and his gaze was met by the tough, wizened face of a local whose expression was part question, part challenge. He cursed his carelessness and sat up, throwing away his cigarette. He was upset with himself: he'd been sloppy and had allowed himself to be seen. It was an unacceptable risk. He had to make a quick getaway and avoid the area for the next few months. It wouldn't be difficult. Once his job was over, he would be glad to be rid of this filthy land and its starving people. As soon as he picked up the package, he'd have to change his license plates, paint the truck a different color, and maybe get a new trailer. It wouldn't be any trouble; he knew exactly who he needed to talk to before he got to the border. While he settled in to start the engine, their eyes met again: the man was thin and scrawny with no obvious muscles but also not an ounce of fat on him. He was pure nerves and fiber, a patriarch with a tough, unwavering hand, or so his greenish tattoos suggested. He leaned on the window frame, asserting his status. Here was someone who'd been raised in a school of hard knocks with the taste of his own blood in his mouth. The local alpha male, here to mark his territory in front of this outside presence. The Beast had been singled out.

The Beast wasn't stupid. He sized up his chances realistically. He thought that he probably had nothing to fear from the jungle-hardened man. In theory, he kept telling himself, he should be able to handle him easily enough, but still, the man was probably younger than he looked. His appearance reflected what he had been through over the years, not the years themselves. The Beast understood that well enough. He knew that someone with so few possessions and probably a small family also had nothing to lose trying to defend them. He pulled away, making sure to seem like a casual onlooker, nothing to write home about, and drove down the hill. He could feel the keen gaze still on him and knew that it would remain there until he'd disappeared into the undergrowth. Annoyed and frustrated, he hid in a lot near the school that would give him access to his target without him being seen. He allowed his anger to build, telling himself that it was because he'd been forced into an unforeseen change of plans, not because he'd been humiliated. He reached into the back seat for his latest trophy, a pair of red shoes spattered with dark-pomegranate stains of dried blood. Just the feel of them turned him on. His body swelled with pleasure, and he felt his indignation fade away.

When Ethan closed his eyes, exhausted by the stress of the past few days, he saw what he'd left behind at home, the traumatic ending of something that shouldn't have ended. When he opened them, jolted awake by the announcement they'd be landing soon, he found himself back in the present, heading for a country that in many ways was a whole new world, one he wasn't sure he belonged in. It was a strange, unsettling place where he'd have to speak in his second language, which he associated with some of his worst memories. Nothing of what he'd been through over the past few hours existed in this new place, but he still wouldn't be able to get away from Ari. He couldn't get her out of his system, though he feared that she could get him out of hers. And now the pain, the emptiness in his guts, mingled with the tension he felt at the prospect of seeing his ex-lover. For a few moments, he thought he might throw up before they landed. But he held on. The immigration official stamped his passport uninterestedly and wished him a pleasant stay, while in customs he put his suitcase through an x-ray machine being run by a pair of policemen so engrossed in their conversation that they almost forgot to take his declaration form.

When he walked into arrivals, amid dozens of travelers, she stood out like a film star, standing behind the velvet rope with a childish fixed but exuberant expression. She looked like a potential model completely unaware of her good looks, exuding a grace and style that didn't go unnoticed by any of the men around her or fail to attract the enmity of their wives. Michelle's patterned dress flattered her curves. She was pretty as a pagan virgin in sandals finished with ribbons wrapped halfway up her shin; her toes poked out like cute little trophies while the platforms underneath camouflaged her short stature. She was radiant, oozing sensuality with a raised hip to one side and her head slightly tilted to the other in an innocent, flirtatious pose. Her long dark hair fell down over her shoulders, framing thick, pouting lips; thin, impeccably shaped eyebrows; and dark almond eyes staring into space. When Michelle saw Ethan in the crowd, there was no perceptible change in her expression other than tiny tics that only he knew how to interpret: her pupils came alive with a spark while her lips formed a smile of cryptic sweetness. Everything about her suggested hope, anxiety, and a sincere welcome. Ethan suddenly felt a rush of adrenaline, a shiver down his back that turned into a weakness at the knees. *Like a little kid,* he thought. Michelle took a step forward; she wasn't about to run to him or make a scene. She maintained the dignity he'd always remembered as one of her distinctive traits. Still attracting the full attention of the arrivals hall, she latched on to Ethan with seductive confidence and pulled him to a stop. Then he heard the full, deep voice for the first time in six years.

"Ethan, this means so much to me. Welcome."

Somewhat hesitantly, he moved closer to her, and her unmistakable aroma filled the space around him, blocking out the airport with a torrent of feelings. A pair of cool, slightly moist lips brushed his cheek before she wrapped him in a warm, tropical hug. The embrace was emotional and lasted several seconds. Her hands rubbed his back, and her head nestled into his neck as she breathed into his chest.

"Hello, Michelle."

"It's amazing to see you again."

"And you."

"You're . . . you're so different, so . . . handsome," Michelle said, blushing.

"You look the same as ever."

They hugged again, a little disoriented by the moment.

Standing next to Michelle was a character to whom Ethan took an immediate dislike: a tall, gawky kid with narrow shoulders and thin arms in a string vest, chains, and pants pulled down below his ass to reveal designer underwear. His skin was covered in common, rather unimaginative tattoos, while he was further adorned by thick reflective sunglasses and multiple rings. The hair under his baseball cap had been cut into shapes. He didn't look dangerous, but it wasn't for want of trying. Ethan had brought in the type thousands of times over—he knew how to deal with them, but it worried him that one had appeared before he'd even left the airport. "Ethan, this is my little brother, Beto. I told you about him, remember?"

"Uh . . ." Ethan looked the kid over again. Not a promising sight. "Yes, of course. But he was much younger then. He was a little kid."

Michelle responded with a forced laugh. "Of course! But he grew up! He's much bigger now. Look how big he got!"

Beto nodded disinterestedly while Michelle went on.

"Beto loaned me his car to come pick you up. He asked to come because he was excited to meet you. I've told him all about you. Tell him, Beto."

Beto's answer, a kind of snort as he examined his iPhone, belied her words.

"But you can drive," Ethan said. "You don't drive anymore?"

"Of course I do. It's Beto who can't drive—I have to take him everywhere—but he asked to meet you."

"You're not very talkative, kid."

This was answered with another obnoxious grunt that might have meant anything. Ethan saw that Beto was going over his Snapchat history.

Michelle cuffed him like a small child. "He's shy, but he's a good kid. You'll see."

Unsurprisingly, the vehicle matched its owner. Ethan raised his eyebrows at the cheap Korean model covered in stickers set off with blue LEDs under the chassis, giving it an electric, ghostly gleam.

"Wow, very nice. I see that you've tuned it up."

"Customized, bro."

Beto called shotgun, making Ethan sit in the back. During the drive, he got bored of his phone and started to chatter away just as casually as he'd previously stayed quiet.

"How ya doing?"

"Fine, thanks. You?"

"Is it true you're a *body hunter*?"

"Well, something like that."

"How many men have you killed?"

"I've shot at a few and wounded even fewer. But I've never killed anyone. How about you, Beto?"

Beto heard the sarcasm in his voice and laughed through his nose, grunting unpleasantly.

Michelle chided him with a look that shocked Ethan as much as it did her brother. "That's not something you talk about like that, as though it doesn't matter."

Beto laughed again to assert his independence.

"That's enough, Beto. Stop it," Michelle said in her very measured tone.

For a while an uncomfortable silence hung in the car. Ethan didn't recognize this prim Michelle. She'd been to the hospital with him twice, once for a bullet wound, and had handled his job without blinking. Michelle had listened to his tales of arrests happily, laughing when he laughed, supporting him no matter what. Maybe this wasn't the same Michelle. Maybe, he thought, she wasn't as lighthearted as she seemed. Then, in the blink of an eye, she was herself again, smiling into the rearview mirror.

"Let's talk about nice things. You should see the meal my mom made to welcome you. I hope you're hungry."

"Sounds great."

"Everyone's coming."

"Everyone?"

"The family and some friends who remember you. You'll see. Everyone loves you around here! My brother Andrés will be there."

"Andrés is coming? How many people are we talking about?"

"Well, about twenty, maybe?"

"Are you serious?" Ethan's mood soured, although he tried to hide it.

"You don't like the idea?" Unexpectedly, Michelle began to overreact. "Shall I cancel it? You're right! Beto, tell Mom we have to cancel. I don't know what I was thinking; I was so happy you were coming. I wanted to—"

"No, Michelle, don't worry. Relax. It's fine. I'm very happy to be seeing Andrés, but I thought . . . considering why I'm here . . . I don't know. Maybe we should be a little discreet. You never know . . ."

"You're right. I . . . the barbecue was Beto's idea. He was so excited you were coming, even though it doesn't seem like it. And I thought it was so sweet. He's even invited his girlfriend and her family to meet you."

"Good vibes, man," Beto said, very proud of his achievement.

"Fine. Forget I said anything. I'm sure it'll be great. Did you find me a hotel nearby?"

"You're staying with us. It's not up for discussion—the room is ready. There's even a closet for you."

As the conversation went on, Ethan felt trapped in a spider's web he was afraid he might get lost in, surrounded by a city of wide avenues and skyscrapers, its hillsides swarming with shacks and half-naked children staring listlessly at the traffic. They turned off the freeway and cruised along narrow roads with high-walled drains for storm water, heading for a more remote neighborhood. Working-class housing appeared: a mixture of adobe and brick with prefab and cement houses, accentuating the improvised, provisional feel of the city. In the background the mountain peaks stood out against the cobalt sky with dark storm clouds skidding across from one sea to another, periodically blocking out a harsh, merciless sun. Central America: a strip of land caught between the two largest oceans on earth. The bodies of water stared back at the land's inhabitants with insolence, emphasizing the fragility of its resigned but tough, sensuous but repressed, innocent but criminal offspring. There was only one way to understand Central America, and that was to immerse yourself in it. You needed to delve into the soil of its fertile jungle, the cruelty of its aggressive beauty, the desolation of its desert of men, and especially the danger of its volcanoes and violence of its earthquakes, the twin powers that both decimated the land and kept it afloat.

Michelle's mother's house was located in one of the city's poorest settlements. Doña Maria shared it with Michelle and Beto. The settlements were like twisted reflections of American towns. The suburbs in the north, neat but repetitive, were laid out in impersonal patterns that down south turned into rutted streets festooned with worn-out but attractive and colorful facades surrounded by fences and barbed wire that served as reminders of the fear in which the residents lived: the stark contrast of pain and vitality that one only found in the tropics.

Doña Maria's house was Caribbean green, flanked by a sky-blue one to the right and a purple one to the left. Wide and shallow, a short drive ran between what might one day be hedges and an earth patio to the rear separated by a ditch from three other identical patios. There was an outhouse nobody used, a modest living room, four bedrooms with just one bathroom, a kitchen, and a utility room annex.

When they parked, Doña Maria came out, making a huge fuss over the greeting, certain that the neighbors, who spent most of their time in the shade of their doorways, would be watching. She was elegantly built but overweight, wearing plenty of well-applied makeup, though her skin was tough and weathered. She kissed Ethan and wished a thousand blessings upon him as she pressed a card with the image of a saint into his hand.

"You have no idea the good it does us to see you, *m'hijo*. God has brought you here, and God will see the girl brought back safe and sound. God wants everything to be well. God protects me."

She shared her daughter's flirtatiousness, but her conversation was sprinkled with the chaste outbursts of prayer and blessings so common to the elderly. Nonetheless, she lacked the goodness that Ethan still sensed in Michelle, in spite of her actions. Now Michelle surprised him again by ignoring her family's celebrations and slipping indoors with a humility very unusual for her. In his room, once free of the family's welcome, Ethan saw that she had unpacked his suitcase and set aside items that needed to be ironed. He found her tending to things in the kitchen, and Ethan was made uncomfortable by this servitude, but the others didn't seem to find it out of the ordinary.

"Michelle, what are you doing?"

Doña Maria stepped in. "Sit down, *m'hijo*. Let her look after you; it makes her happy."

No, it doesn't, he thought.

"Michelle," Ethan said. "We need to talk about Michi. I need photos, information—"

"She doesn't have any of that. You can get it from Andrés. He's taken charge of everything."

"It's true. Andrés is back with us," Michelle said, offering Ethan a glass of guava juice. "He's been the most help."

"Wouldn't you rather have a beer instead of the guava juice?" Doña Maria said. "Michelle made the juice, but I bet you'd rather have a beer after that horrible journey. I don't know what it's like to fly on a plane, but you must be tired. Oh, I'm so scared of them! Why don't you lie down before the others arrive?"

"I'd like a beer, Mommy," Beto said, trying to twist the situation to his own advantage.

"Not you, Beto. What will Don Ethan think of us?"

Ethan picked up the glass. "Juice would be just fine."

Doña Maria offered him a plate of fried plantain and yucca. "The meat will be wonderful. My son-in-law, Jonathan, is coming to make it. He's a grill master."

"Your son-in-law?"

45

"Leidy's brother. She's Beto's girlfriend. A lovely girl—they live a few blocks away, in Colonia Trece, on the other side."

Michelle, who hadn't even sat down, made to leave. "Well, I'm going to get ice and everything else we need before they arrive. I'll let Mom explain everything: what we've done so far and what we know."

Doña Maria fixed Ethan with an inquiring gaze. "We hired a detective, you know. The best in the city, God bless him."

Ethan looked at Michelle, but she avoided his gaze and walked out to Beto's ridiculous car.

"Wait, Michelle, I'll go with you. I've barely even said hello."

Beto sighed in exasperation and got up reluctantly. "Fine, let's go."

"No, Beto, I'd rather go alone, if you don't mind. That way you can get ready for the party." Ethan's expression brooked no argument.

Michelle's mother sent them on their way with feigned enthusiasm. "Of course, Don Ethan! Michelle, you know what we need; make sure you get everything."

At first Michelle didn't say anything. She was deep in thought or immersed in the strange melancholy that seemed to have haunted her since she'd come under her family's sway. After giving her some time, Ethan started to ask questions.

"Whose idea was it to hold a big party, Michelle?"

"Beto's. I'm sorry. I know it's a bad idea, but Mom got excited. He's the youngest, her baby. And I thought you might like to see some old friends."

"It's OK; don't beat yourself up. I'd rather have gone incognito, but it'll be nice to see them. And I suppose that Beto and your mother were going to tell everyone about me anyway, so it's not like any harm's been done. I am surprised that Andrés is coming."

"You know him. We hadn't seen him for years, but as soon as he heard about the kidnapping, he came right away and told us that he'd take care of everything. Anything we needed . . ." Michelle choked up as she spoke. "He asked me why I hadn't called you. That was when I wrote Bear, after what Andrés said. You know how good he is. He still isn't talking to my mom or Beto, but he's doing everything. He's the only one I trust to help me no matter what. I . . . you can't do anything without a man to help, can you?"

This woman was nothing like the liberated, independent Michelle that Ethan knew or thought he knew. He worried that he'd never really known her.

The fear had always been there, but now that he was faced with this new side of Michelle, a completely different Michelle, it grew exponentially.

"I've never heard you say anything like that before."

Michelle shrugged. "That's how the world is."

"I remember when you didn't want to be tied down, when you didn't know if you could live with anyone after Michi's father. You didn't know if you wanted to get married, to lose your freedom . . ."

"I haven't changed. You feel different things at different times. And look who's talking—you couldn't live on your own. The moment I met that kid Ari, I knew she'd be a problem. I acted badly, but we would have broken up just the same."

"Broken up? You left without saying a word!"

"I knew that girl would get in the way. I just went a little early."

"A little early?"

They rode in silence until they got to the supermarket. When they'd gotten out of the car, they looked at one another, trying to make up for lost time.

"I'm sorry. I did it all wrong," Michelle said. "I was a coward. I messed up everything. I've gone over it so many times—I was so horrible . . . I've never forgiven myself."

"You would have done things differently if you could?"

"Yes, of course."

Ethan was caught by surprise. After her confession, Michelle moved toward him, her face a picture of anguish, and wrapped her arms around him. She was being so gentle, but he couldn't help notice her breasts pressing against him. He felt trapped and disoriented.

Michelle whispered, "If I could change things, my darling, if I could go back in time . . . I'd stay with you. But it wouldn't have changed anything."

"Why is that?"

"The girl would still have come between us."

He stepped back. "That's what you're telling yourself now to justify what you did."

"But I told you, didn't I?"

"Yes, but . . ."

"Women know these things."

"That's not true, and you know it."

"You don't like me saying that women aren't born to live alone, but you went off to live with that girl. I don't have any men in my life. I've learned to live without them. The men here are no good. They're macho—you know that. They don't care about us; they forget you like the father of my little girl did. They don't even care about their children. They leave you. You say you've never heard me talk like this, but I never looked for anyone else, and you did. Now you think that I've changed?"

"I don't know, Michelle. I never know with you."

"You don't know if I'm the same person, but listen: Andrés stopped talking to me because of Randall. He was the biggest mistake of my life, but we talked it over and made up. And now it's settled."

Randall. Just the name made him choke on his own bile. The lounge singer, the starving ladies' man with musical pretensions who turned up with nothing but debts and his guitar and had ended up dragging Michelle back to her home country only to abandon her with the breezy declaration that "he was born to be free." The no-good con man. A bum whose only goal in life was conquest and deceit. He was addicted to feeding his ego. Randall was a home-wrecker: he got what he wanted out of women and then disappeared, leaving behind a trail of hatred that meant he could never go back. If Ethan ever saw him again, he couldn't be held responsible for his actions.

"I know I hurt you. I was acting crazy, but that's all behind me. Like I said, if I could, I'd change everything. I'd be there right now with you and Mi . . . safe and sound."

Her voice broke. Ethan thought that this was the first sincere emotion she'd revealed since he'd landed, but she immediately got ahold of herself.

"What I said about men. Not all men are the same. Here they're all misogynists, but I know that some men really do share their lives with you and make you happy. I had a life like that, and I ruined it. I know that you don't get a second chance with things like that. That's why I choose to be alone."

Here comes the sugar. Ethan recognized the telltale signs: the demure eyes, the sighs, the way she somehow made you feel guilty . . . she was still a master of manipulation.

"Michelle, forget about the past. That's not why I'm here."

"But still, you're here, and everything's OK. I'm calm now. I know that everything's going to be all right. You're going to make everything all right."

"I can't work miracles."

"I know that, you idiot. I'm not getting my hopes up, but you came to help. Things can only get better from here."

When they'd finished their shopping, Michelle's wide smile returned. She even tickled the back of his neck as they put the groceries in the trunk. Ethan took advantage of the relaxed moment to get back to the subject she seemed to be continuously avoiding.

"Who's the detective your mother mentioned?"

"I don't know. You can talk about that with Andrés. I know he's made an appointment to go see him tomorrow."

"And you'll be coming with us."

"No, I have to go to work. Andrés is dealing with it."

"I don't understand. Why are you trying to avoid this?"

"I'm not avoiding anything, but Andrés came to help me, and I—I . . . it's good for me. Everything's fine now. Now that both of you—"

"Tell me exactly what happened. Tell me this afternoon: how it happened, what you did. I don't understand why you're not telling me anything."

"Talk to Andrés. He knows everything—he has—"

Michelle was in a hurry to get back home, but Ethan stopped her. She struggled weakly to get free of his grip, avoiding his gaze.

"Oh, let me go! The guests are coming, and we still have to—"

"Look at me. Talk to me, Michelle."

"I want to—"

"Talk to me about your daughter. I've come to find her. Where's Michi? Why can't you even say her name? What happened before the kidnapping? What can you tell me that might help us? Why don't you want anything to do with this? Talk to me!"

"I . . . I . . . my . . . my . . . girl . . ."

Michelle exploded in pain. Her face contorted into a devastating grimace. She doubled over and collapsed like a rag doll, as though she'd lost control of her body. Ethan caught her before she hit the ground, saving her from hitting her head. If she weren't still sobbing inconsolably, he'd have thought she'd fainted. He slowly lowered her down to the ground, where she curled up, still sobbing, repeating, "My girl, my little girl . . ." over and over again.

It was the most devastating sound Ethan had ever heard. The only thing he could think to compare it with was an image from his childhood, a dog whose puppies had been taken away from her. They'd been shoved in a bag to be drowned in a river. He'd never forgotten how she'd looked, chained to a post, pulling against her collar so hard that it had drawn blood, chewing on the links until her teeth broke. Eventually, she'd worn herself out. Afterward she'd just lain on the grass like a dead body, her eyes glassy, staring at the never-ending flow of the river. Now Michelle reminded him of that zombie animal, curled up like a little kid in a nondescript parking lot, oblivious to the passersby and to him, sucked into an apparently bottomless pit. She cried ceaselessly, sniveling and hiccuping, having lost any trace of dignity or shame. She began to bite her own lips, pushing little pearls of blood to the surface.

More than ten minutes passed before she was able to move, but as soon as she'd caught her breath, she leaped back up, covering her face. Without saying a word, she locked herself in the car, where she checked herself in the mirror and neatly took a pack of baby wipes from her bag, tidying her makeup and applying eye drops. Ethan, who was completely dumbfounded, waited at the door until she lowered the window and told him to get in.

"Forgive me. We're very late. We need to run."

He got in the car full of doubt.

"So you'll talk to Andrés? He knows everything."

"Of course."

"Great. I know that you're the only ones who are really with me. Now things are looking up."

They headed back to a party that was a perfect metaphor for the absurd situation in which Ethan found himself. The barbecue dragged on as the sun gradually dropped in the sky, and the suffocating heat began to let up. Several locals came over and bombarded him with questions, so much so that he began to grow suspicious. Doña Maria proudly strutted among her guests, introducing them to the gringo detective who was going to find her granddaughter. Whenever he stepped away, Ethan also heard her crowing about how he'd asked Michelle to marry him, but she'd rejected his advances. But the worst part was when Beto's girlfriend, Leidy, and her family arrived. They were a veritable catalog of the worst society had to offer. Jonathan, the older brother, took charge of the barbecue. He was clearly a role model for Beto, acting like a cut-price king surveying his domain under the fawning gaze of his sister's boyfriend. He was spoiled by Doña Maria, who did everything she could to satisfy his whims and lauded his work at the grill as though it were a banquet laid on by God himself. His sister Leidy, Beto's girlfriend, wandered around like a high-maintenance housewife, and something about the way Beto treated her aroused Ethan's worst suspicions. Their mother sat in a corner playing with a two-year-old they called Patito whose true parentage seemed something of a mystery: either he belonged to an absent sister, Jonathan, or the mother herself. Something about the family seemed deeply unhealthy, but Ethan had the odd feeling that he was the only one who could see it. The only saving grace came when most of the guests were getting ready to leave and Doña Maria proudly announced that her eldest son had arrived.

As Andrés approached Ethan, they both smiled nostalgically. In some ways, Andrés was responsible for this whole situation. He'd gone to the United States as an immigrant when he'd been little more than a boy. He had been stopped at the border, illegally detained, and deported. But he'd come back. You couldn't fight desperation with walls and watchtowers. Ethan had no idea what had happened on those trips. Andrés had never told him, but the deep pain in his eyes said it all. Many years later, now a legal resident, he'd gotten back in contact with his mother and siblings, who were much younger than him, making his relationship with them more paternal than anything. He'd helped do the paperwork for Michelle to follow him to the United States, and Ethan had met her through him. After she'd left Ethan, Andrés had stopped talking to her but still kept tabs on his niece. He had blind faith in both her intelligence and essential goodness. Eventually, now that the economy in his home country had improved and he'd felt ready, he'd moved back and made a life for himself. Now he owned several stores and paid for his two children to study in the United States. Ethan knew that he was the only one who could have taken charge of the search and paid for a private detective.

Andrés was short and squat. Everything about him was stumpy: his fingers, neck, and all his limbs appeared to have been stunted by some invisible force, giving him a rough, compact air. He always wore a suit, and his straight, short sleeves and pants legs looked like tubes sticking out of his torso. His bald head gleamed; his thick moustache was going bright white on either side. The gray hair and bags under his eyes were the only features that indicated his true age. It touched Ethan's heart to see this evidence of the passing of time. They hugged with hefty slaps on the back, and the new arrival served himself a drink, ignoring the rest of those present, who pretended not to notice the snub.

Ethan held up his beer. "No beer?"

"I stopped drinking. It's forbidden by the congregation."

"Congregation?"

"When I got back, I learned a lot. I turned my back on the beliefs of a family that did so little to help me, and now I go to an evangelical church. My life has changed completely. They taught me that alcohol is not permitted by the love of Lord Christ. Blessed be his name."

"I see a lot has changed over the years."

"I'm a good believer, closer to God than I ever was. Now that I think of it, you never had much time for that kind of thing."

"Well, we discussed it often."

"I remember. And I also remember that in addition to my having the good fortune to call you my friend, you're also a good man. My wife never forgets to pray for you."

Ethan was deeply honored by the compliment because the man he was talking to was one of the few people in his life whom he truly respected. After twelve years, Andrés still addressed Ethan in formal Spanish, and even though they hadn't seen each other in six, the first thing Andrés had brought up was their friendship. They shared a bond that Ethan had probably never experienced with anyone outside his family.

"I came to welcome you, but now I'm leaving. I don't belong here. We'll have time to talk tomorrow. I'll come pick you up at twenty to nine." He handed Ethan a basic cell phone.

"Thanks, but I have my phone."

"This one has a prepaid SIM card so we can keep in touch. I've put some money on it. If your phone is unlocked and you prefer to use it, then you can just put the card in that one without any trouble. But keep it—it'll be your number while you're here."

"Thank you."

"It's a pleasure to have you with us. I'll give you as much help as I can, not that I know anything about the business anymore. These days I sell secondhand clothes."

When Andrés had left, the party came to an end, and the family was left alone with Leidy. She and Beto locked themselves in his bedroom. Michelle finished tidying up and slumped with her mother in front of local TV, which was showing a lurid news program whose only purpose seemed to be terrifying viewers. Ethan went off for a shower and to get ready for bed.

As soon as he got some alone time, the events of the day hit him like a landslide. He was deeply confused. The biggest questions revolved around Michelle's evasive behavior. There was almost a physical change whenever she was with her family. The constant sensation that she was switching between the person he knew and a stranger was disorienting. He remembered her in the parking lot: he'd never seen her looking so vulnerable and distraught. Never in their time together had she revealed such an intimate side of herself. Never had she been so genuine. Then he thought about Ari and the way she exuded raw truth in everything she did.

When he got out of the bathroom, he tried to write to Ari on WhatsApp but gave up when he saw that his messages weren't getting through. He was able to get through to Candy, and he asked how Bear was doing; after a brief conversation she told him that Ari had gone out with some friends. He felt bad about his immediate reaction: asking Ari who she was out with. This time his message went through. He kept an eye on the phone until he saw it indicate that the message had been read. But that was it.

A tap on the metal roof made him jump. He put down the phone and got up to take a look. The tap was followed by several others. They were footsteps. He looked up and guessed there were two or three people on top of the house. He went into the living room to find Michelle and her mother curled up on the sofa with the TV volume turned down, waving at him not to make a sound. Ethan waited and listened. The only sound was the quiet murmur from the television. The light behind Beto's door was off; he and the girlfriend must have been sleeping or at least sitting quietly in the dark. The steps went from one end of the house to the other, accompanied by high-pitched teenage laughter. Ethan tried to reassure the two women, but he could see the fear in their eyes. He looked around for a weapon, and Michelle, reading his mind, led him silently to the kitchen and gave him a knife with a trembling hand. She pressed herself against his body, shivering with fear and nuzzling him on the neck like a puppy looking for safety. Ethan stroked her hair but pushed her away gently so he'd be free to move and follow the path of the footsteps.

Suddenly a rock crashed through a window. Beto's door swung open, and he came out in his underwear, brandishing a metal baseball bat with a wild, paranoid look in his eye. Ethan thought that he must be stoned. He gestured to Beto to show that there was nothing to worry about, and Beto lowered his guard. Doña Maria started to squeak while an equally stoned Leidy appeared in a sheet, mute with fright. Ethan waited. They all did, frozen in place, but nothing happened. It all melted into the night: the footsteps, the laughter, the tension. If it weren't for the broken glass on the ground, they might have dismissed it as a mass delusion. Ethan cautiously went to the entrance, but Michelle's mother begged him not to open it with a sob in her voice.

"No, *m'hijo*, don't. Better not to."

After waiting anxiously for a quarter of an hour to make sure that the danger had passed, Michelle got a broom to sweep up the glass, and Doña Maria stuck a sheet over the hole. Ethan helped her while Beto and Leidy locked themselves back in the bedroom. This was followed by ten more minutes of silence, which Michelle eventually broke.

"It's n-not the first time this has happened, Ethan. There's nothing to worry about."

"No, *m'hija*, that's not true."

"I was going to explain, Mom. There is something to worry about. These neighborhoods, the ones where the rent isn't hundreds or thousands of dollars . . . are slowly falling to the Mara. They come in, take control, and make it Mara territory."

"This isn't Mara territory."

"No, it isn't. This neighborhood is safe enough, but Colonia Trece, where Leidy lives, already belongs to them. When they get to a new neighborhood, they move into an empty house and try to scare people away. They're called destroyer houses. They stay and live there like a commune, but a very poor one. They don't even have enough money for food, and to keep themselves and their children alive, they search through garbage, beg, or steal. Extortion rackets and bus robberies are run by the bosses. There's a destroyer house over there. It's only a matter of time before they get here."

"Don't say that, honey; it'll bring misfortune down upon us."

"That's what's going to happen, Mom. They walk over the rooftops, climbing around, talking on their phones, and sometimes even sleeping up there in case the police come. They're always up there, talking away while the hawks, the youngest kids, keep an eye out. Do you think they don't know you're here? They know everything. People here still go out and live their lives, but in Trece they stay in their houses in case there's a shoot-out or worse."

"So they do this a lot?" Ethan said.

"Walking around on the roof, sure, lots. Jonathan says they do it at his house every night, but they've never broken a window before . . ."

"They were laughing."

"Yes, they were."

"It's because of me, isn't it? Even if you don't want to say it, I know. They're letting us know that they know I'm here."

"Who knows . . . ?"

"If it's because of me, maybe they won't bother us again tonight."

The three of them went to bed, still worried. As soon as Ethan stepped back into his bedroom, he instinctively checked his phone. Ari still hadn't answered.

The sun came up a little after five, and Ethan's exhausted body insisted that he get up. He reluctantly obeyed. Doña Maria made him a traditional breakfast of eggs, rice, and beans. Michelle left for work before he'd finished. When Andrés came by to pick him up, Beto and Leidy still hadn't come out of the bedroom.

They drove along narrow streets where elderly women made tortillas and set them aside in piles. They joined the traffic and turned off into a modern business district, which boasted rows of intelligent buildings watched by helpful porters and guards armed with shotguns.

"So who is this detective?" Ethan asked. "How did you make contact with him?"

"He's famous for being good at what he does. Plenty of rich people have hired him to deal with kidnappings, and he never fails."

"Does he get involved?"

"No, but they say he has a lot of contacts with the police and the gangs, so he can negotiate where others can't. They say that his methods aren't always very nice. I'm sorry to say that he has in the past paid off the Mara so he can enter their territory and kill the perpetrators, God forgive him. But mostly he makes sure that the payments are made and the hostage gets back unharmed. He doesn't get into bed with anyone. That's what he's famous for. He gives it to you straight:

if he thinks there's a chance, he'll tell you, and if not, he'll tell you that too. The problem for us is the talk, which doesn't lead anywhere. His services are very expensive, and for what we've paid him, he's only promised to keep an eye out."

"I understand."

The office was high up in a building that also housed a shopping mall on the stories below. First you had to show your ID at one of the reception desks on either corner attended by friendly receptionists and at least three armed guards; then you got into an elevator. Once you got to the right floor, you walked down a marble-lined corridor into a minimalist office. The reception led into a midsized room with four work desks and behind them a large wooden door that opened into the boss's office. The lavish decor, carpentry, and shiny floors contrasted with the shoddy plasterboard walls and visible screwheads, giving the place a provisional feel. The secretary asked them to follow her in. The detective was over fifty, smug, and quick off the draw; he wore a comb-over, a bespoke suit, an amused demeanor, and an intelligent gaze. He got up from his leather office chair and greeted them warmly.

"You must be Evan."

"Ethan."

"Ethan, forgive me. I have to say I was curious to meet you. I've already had the pleasure with your companion. Good to see you, Don Andrés."

"Good morning."

"Here, Don Ethan: my card. Adrian Calvo at your service. Would you like something to drink? A coffee?"

"Yes, please."

"You'll take it black, won't you? We're in the land of coffee. Sugar or sweetener? My secretary will bring it along in a moment. So how has my country treated you so far?"

"Fine, I guess. I've only just arrived."

"Oh yes, those flights. Fortunately, there's not a big time difference. Don Andrés told me that you're a detective, a personal friend of the family, and that you'll follow your own line of inquiry. I'm to provide as much help as I can. Is that right?"

"Well, I'm not sure. You know the country. It makes more sense to me for you to take the lead in the investigation and for me to assist you. But I suppose there's the matter of your fees."

The secretary came in with the drinks. Adrian Calvo waited until she left to reply, but his face had lit up with an answer. As soon as the door closed, he continued the conversation with a different degree of friendliness. "Forgive me . . . would you mind my asking where you learned your Spanish? You hardly seem gri . . . American."

"You can say *gringo*; it doesn't bother me. My father was Spanish. We traveled a lot when I was a child. I spent some time in Spain."

"Good, good, that's good to know. Hence your accent and style. I won't lie to you, Don Ethan—I'm surprised by your answer, but pleasantly so. You don't have an Avatar complex: that explains a lot."

"I'm glad to hear it, although I'm not sure that I understand."

"I've worked with gringos before and always come up against the same problem. Maybe it's Hollywood—do you watch a lot of films? I love them; I watch everything. But when they go to another country . . . have you seen *Avatar*?"

"Who hasn't?"

"I blame the movies. If they want to make a film about indigenous people, in the end it's a gringo who has to lead them because they're apparently too stupid to do it themselves. If the gringo goes to another country, let's say, he ends up saving it single-handed. If he goes to another planet, it's the same thing. Such fantasies don't do them any good—believe me. Three years ago a gringo detective jetted in looking for a surfer chick who'd disappeared on her vacation, without a trace. He had an Avatar complex."

"He couldn't find her?"

"Oh, she turned up on her own when the stoner she'd fallen in love with got tired of fucking her. He left her for a menopausal German woman who promised to take him home with her, and the girl called her daddy in tears."

"Well, a happy ending."

"Not for the detective. No one was going to pay a ransom for him. He was a tall white guy, very sure of himself, and he'd definitely seen a lot of movies. I won't bore you with the whole story, but we offered to help. He, however, thought he was better off on his own. He went straight for the narcos like he was Bruce Willis. We never heard from him again. It's a good life here if you avoid the dangerous areas—wonderful beaches, virgin jungle, friendly country folk always willing to help—but in the war zones . . . gringos disappear there too. When you're in a foreign country, you're never the smartest guy in the room."

"Thanks for the warning."

"I don't think you needed it." Calvo sipped his coffee before continuing. "Now that we understand each other, let me ask again before we get into the details of the case. Is there anything I can do to help you during your stay here? Between professionals."

As Ethan drank his coffee, he decided to trust this man, who brandished his sincerity like a weapon. "I need a gun."

"Are you sure?"

"Yes, we got a warning yesterday. I think I'm living in Mara territory. I'm not planning on getting into any fights, but from what I've seen, it's sensible to have protection."

"You're staying with the grandmother?"

"Yes, Doña Maria."

"The Matapatria. I don't know if that area belongs to them yet, but they're close. The cantons are theirs. Have you seen much graffiti saying 'MP' or 'MP12' around? That's their symbol. Mara Matapatria Zone 12. What happened?"

Ethan gave them a brief account of his experience the night before.

"What a mess. I'll get you a clean gun without a serial number. But be careful—an illegal *ferro* is an illegal *ferro* here and everywhere else. But that doesn't mean that they've necessarily come for you. The Mara are always walking over roofs around there. And the window was meant to scare you because they know a stranger has moved in, but I don't think it's about the girl. I don't think the Doce does that kind of thing."

"I don't understand. We shouldn't start with the Mara?"

"Well . . . they could have riddled you full of bullets instead of breaking a window. Take it as a good sign. It would be best for us if the Mara weren't involved. The fact they haven't killed you means we're off to a good start."

"That's a relief. But if it isn't the Mara, where do we start the search?"

"I'll tell you what I think. Firstly, and I'm asking in confidence because the mother isn't here, and she might get upset by the question: Are we sure that it is a kidnapping?"

Ethan hesitated. He looked at Andrés, who stared gravely at the ground. "I don't know. I really have no idea."

"Look, lots of kids run off with a coyote for the north, for the States. Some mothers even encourage them, set them up with the smugglers, pay them to go away . . ."

"No, that's not what happened here."

"From what I understand, the girl lived in a poor neighborhood, the mother works in a call center, and her uncle is a little . . . I understand you've met him."

Now Calvo looked for help from Andrés, but he remained stubbornly silent. It was the reverential silence of a peasant in the presence of a landowner. Ethan remained true to his convictions without feeling the need to explain himself.

"Yes, I've met him, but I don't think that's what happened. She was taken off the street, shoved into a car."

"Yes, I know the story. But it came from the other girl, you understand? A girl the same age. There's no note, no remains; she just disappeared. I'm forced to consider other possibilities."

"That seems reasonable, but for now let's concentrate on the kidnapping hypothesis."

"However you wish," Calvo said. "Look, to cut a long story short, the Mara don't do kidnappings, but you can't do anything on their territory without their permission, which means that if someone kidnapped the girl, they paid for the right to do it. As Don Andrés must have told you, I've had some dealings with them in the past, but that's not necessarily going to help us. Contacts are one thing, and power is another. It would be very risky to show an interest in the girl without knowing more. They'd probably ask for a lot of money, and we wouldn't know whether they really have her or whether we'd be picking her up in a box without our ever finding out what happened. Do you see my point? We can't go to the Mara because in my opinion it would be counterproductive, and at best they'd be intermediaries. That's what has worried me since the beginning. In all this time, why haven't we received a ransom demand?"

"This might be a stupid question, but aren't there any other reasons someone might want to kidnap her?"

"This is a business. No one organizes an operation like this if there isn't profit to be had. They spy on families they think might be able to pay, but there's no guarantee. Their informants come from the same neighborhood. Kidnappings have happened based on errors, mistakes, and envy. They tend to end badly. When they find out that there's no money to be had, they have no reason to keep the victim alive and especially not to risk being caught. Those hostages don't come back. With a little luck they're found in a river some time later. But this girl didn't live in a private condo; she didn't travel around in a chauffeur-driven car. No one would want her for her money."

Andrés grew even more pensive. Ethan got up, stretched his legs, and maintained a tense silence until he finally said what they were all thinking.

"The problem is finding out the motive."

The detective coughed before replying. "In this country, sadly, girls disappear all the time. It's not safe for them to be walking the streets alone. I imagine you're familiar with the situation—it's like an epidemic. It's awful."

"I've read something about it."

"If you ask me, the main motive for a disappearance like this would be rape, not a kidnapping. If a group of Mara decided to have some fun with her . . ."

"*Fun* seems a rather casual way to describe rape."

"Well, you'll get used to it. If they attacked her and the girl fought back, or even if she didn't fight and one of them got rough, a crackhead maybe, she's probably lying in a ditch somewhere. Other motives might be private vengeance, abuse by a relative . . . but they all end the same way."

"She's dead, and we won't find her."

"That's right."

"But none of that fits with what her friend said."

"That's true. Hence my suspicion: when one detail doesn't seem to fit with everything else we know, it's the first thing I begin to doubt."

"But it's not a detail. It's the only eyewitness account. We have no other evidence. Did you speak to her?"

"As soon as I was hired."

"And what did she say?"

"Here's the recording, but you know already. A car, some men who called her by name . . . it's a professional kidnapping, the kind where they've been watching the target and planned everything. And also the kind that you see on TV. It's an easy story for the girl to make up. If they'd asked for a ransom, I might believe it, but they haven't. And that's the first thing they'd do—they'd call right away."

"I'm sticking with the kidnapping theory. What options does that leave us with?"

"The obvious move is to wait for the call and negotiate. It's the safest way to get her back. Now that the call hasn't come, we can try to find the group that *might* have done it, but they know how to hide. They're hard to track down. It might be just three or four guys, and all they need is a cellar to lock her in. It's like looking for a needle in a haystack, and on top of that it's often cops, and if they've paid off the Mara, they're under their protection. That doesn't mean that we can't take action against them—the Mara can be bought off like anyone else. But their demands might be too high. If you can tell me why someone would invest all that time and money in the girl, I can move things forward."

"I thought you were going to give me answers, not ask me questions."

"Avatar. You're asking me to believe in a crazy story, and then you complain that I can't explain it."

"Try to see things from my point of view. I've come all this way because I need to believe that she's alive."

The detective's smile returned. "You win. That's the best argument I've ever heard. I can counter anything but that. Fine, you win: I'll play along. Look, I've considered every possible option. If you want my opinion, I'd say that it was a relative or someone close to her, but again, that would be the end of her, and I know that you won't accept that. If I accept that she's still alive, after all this time, she *must* have changed hands. In similar cases, they don't hold on to them for longer than twenty-four hours. If we concentrate on the client, we'll avoid upsetting the Mara and confronting a band of kidnappers."

"So who could pay for something like that?"

"If we discard the people close to her, we're left with human traffickers. I'm thinking of pedophiles or illegal adoptions, but she's too old for that. Then there's organ theft or prostitution, and that kind of thing's easier in rural areas."

"Fine. So where should we begin the investigation?"

"My boys have been on it for a week. If it is a smuggling network, she'll be valuable to them, and we may be able to get her back. But then they'd take her across the border, and she'd be gone. It's been too long. That's not what happened. You can't do that without the help of corrupt officials who charge their cut, and my contacts with the immigration authorities are solid. I've paid what's necessary to ask my questions, and there's been no movement."

"Isn't there a chance they could have moved her without them knowing?"

"Why? This isn't just one trip we're talking about here; it's a business. They have too much at stake. The other way is safer and cheaper."

"What about an individual?"

Calvo thought about it for a few moments and ended up nodding. "Yeah, an individual in a car, with the girl hidden in the trunk . . . yes, that could be. Then I'd have to refund your money, and we'd all have to go home, because if that's the case, she's just as likely to be dead. We'll never see her again. It's beyond my reach."

"You're right. Let's assume that she hasn't been taken out of the country."

"I've been thinking it over for the past few days. About who might be willing to pay from inside the country. To our shame, and yours, gringos and Europeans hide out here to find children. Usually they don't need to use force; wherever they look, there are people short on cash and morals willing to do what they say. I won't go into details, but if one of them had their eye on her and had enough money . . . I've come across cases like that."

"And is there any way to get access to that world?"

"There's a gringo who's been coming in and out of Central American countries for five years now. He's almost been caught twice, but he escaped. He's been around so long that he's become a key player in pedophile circles. So you make contact with him, he makes his own inquiries, he talks, and you pay well. That's how he makes his living. I've found him before, but he disappears for months. As soon as this case came to me, the first thing we did was try to track him down, and my boys finally found him yesterday. If you give me another day to confirm my sources and his routine, we can catch him at home."

"That sounds great."

"So I'll call you tomorrow with a plan. It's not the best lead, but it's the only one I can offer. Finally, I want to reiterate: I know how much it costs to pay for this service, and I consider myself an honest man, so I don't want to mislead you. We might not be able to find her. If you give me permission to investigate the family and friends, I'm sure that I'll come up with something, and then I'd only have to find out why the other girl lied, whether she was afraid or wanted to cover up something. It's almost always an adult who was close to the child, and if it was the Mara, I'd know that too. At least then you can bury her. It might not be consolation, but at least it brings an end to the uncertainty."

After the visit, Andrés asked Ethan if he wanted to come along with him as he made a tour of his stores. Ethan was grateful for the offer; it was much better than going back to spend the day with Doña Maria and the lovebirds while Michelle was at work. On the way, he got an answer from Ari: she said hello, told him about the progress she'd made in her research, and asked how he was settling in. The message made him happy but also gave him a pain in the pit of his stomach. Although it was just a couple of phrases, he reread it several times as though he were inspecting it for a hidden message.

"What did you think of the detective?" Andrés said after a while.

"He knows his business better than we do. There's no doubt about that."

"How much do you trust him?"

"Until his fees become too high. Why do you ask? Didn't you hire him?"

"I'm not paying for everything. It was Michelle's idea."

"But she can't pay for everything herself."

"Forgive me. You know I don't like to stick my nose where it's not wanted, but do you trust my sister?"

"Do you think she's hiding something?"

"I don't think so. But it's not just the case; she's always lived one lie or another. How has she been acting since you arrived?"

"I don't know yet. I don't understand what's wrong with her. Well, I can imagine, but even so. She seems too calm. We've barely spoken."

"You don't know what's going on inside. No one does. You didn't see her during the first week—she was wandering around like a zombie. She forgot things, got confused. She didn't eat for three days. I kept an eye on her. She lived on coffee. I wanted to take her to the hospital, but she was afraid that they'd drug her and she'd forget about Michi. She agreed to eat in return for not going. When you said you were coming, she was a new person. You became her savior."

"I tried to tell her how things really are. She seemed to understand."

"She's idealized you. Now that hope is the only thing that's keeping her going. It's as though she thinks because you're here, everything's going to work out. Listen, I think contacting you was the right thing to do, but I'm worried about what might happen if this all ends how we know it might, God forbid."

Andrés hesitated before going on. "Tell me if I'm out of line, but do you really love her so much? Forgive me; it's so strange . . . to have you with me, investigating . . ."

"Don't worry. I'm glad you asked. I haven't come for Michelle—I'm looking for Michi. It's my duty. There's no other reason. And I won't stop until I find her."

Andrés indulged in a rare show of emotion for such a reserved man. "I'm so grateful to have you here. I . . . I'm moved by your charity. There's nothing that obliges you to be here. The girl, you haven't seen her for years. She has a gift. She's different from the rest of the family, better than any of us. She has a talent for helping people. She's special, like my grandmother."

"Michelle told me about her. Your family was from . . . Hungary, wasn't it?"

"Yes. My grandmother was an angel, but my mother . . . it doesn't matter. The Lord has blessed the girl, and I'm not going to forget my responsibilities as an uncle. They think she's dead—they'd prefer her to be so as not to shake things up. They live in fear. I'm not afraid. Nothing's more important to me than getting her back, to be at peace with the Lord and myself. If they have to kill me, then I'll die happy in the knowledge that I wasn't a coward."

The journey ended at a café with flaking walls and a scarlet-and-cream checkerboard floor: early twentieth-century architecture that had all but disappeared, not unlike the customers—all male and older than Andrés, who was willing to break his church's rigid rules by entering the premises even though he didn't drink alcohol. Ethan felt forced to join him although he was beginning to feel the accumulated exhaustion of the past twenty-four hours. The visit stretched on for hours amid conversations about soccer and chess, to which a couple of the old men seemed particularly addicted, and the notable absence of any mention of women or sex, topics that were not to their taste. Andrés's traditional, austere, and somewhat solemn worldview appeared to be shared by his fellow regulars, but Ethan found them a little dull. Game after game of chess was played, and time appeared to be defined by what was happening on the board. When the last game was over, they gathered up the pieces, and Ethan, the only one who was drinking beer, yawned in relief.

The noise from the school had died down. He could still hear children's voices in the distance, but the area appeared to be safe from unwelcome intruders. Finally, after a string of bad luck, fortune was smiling on him. He forced himself to be patient and kept watch, staying still and out of sight. He was very good at his job. He was precise and never made mistakes. That was why they had hired him. He'd never been visited by the police, no one had ever linked him to the disappearances, and he continued to cross Latin America without a criminal record, but that was because of the precautions he took. Recently, he'd grown a little lax. To make sure that he rested easier in the future, he decided to reintroduce his security protocols. The hours of waiting bore fruit, and the girl appeared with the groceries, but, as though fate were trying to test him, she was accompanied by a friend she must have met at the store. He considered waiting until the following night but decided to go ahead so as not to risk any further exposure in the village. It wasn't the first time he'd had to deal with a situation like this. In fact, he didn't mind the idea of a second package for his own personal enjoyment.

Because of the changed circumstances, his pursuit was more convoluted than usual, and he almost lost them before they got to the first curve, where they were out of sight of the village. Just as they were about to cross the limit he'd set himself, he quickened his pace and caught up with them. He took out his bar and brought it down quickly against the back of the head of the companion, who fell, just as expected. Before his prey could react, he covered her mouth and nose with a handkerchief and injected the tranquilizer into her neck. The girl kicked out, and he struggled to catch the cans of food before they hit the ground. Staying calm, he lifted her up and threw her over his shoulder, carrying the bag in the other hand so as not to run any more risks. The job took priority; he couldn't do anything to compromise it. He got to the empty shack and crossed through it to the truck hidden in the undergrowth. The girl's struggles grew weaker as the drug took effect, and he was able to shove her inside fairly easily. He put her in the back, and they wrestled for a few moments more before he tied her up and gagged her with the necessary care. Finally, once he'd made sure of the primary objective, he decided to go back for the other one. Then he'd make his getaway before the alarm could be raised. He slipped back through the undergrowth and, after making sure that the road was still clear, stepped out again. To his horror, he saw that the body had disappeared. He froze for a few moments before making a decision. She couldn't possibly have regained consciousness so quickly. He checked his watch again; the whole thing hadn't taken any longer than five minutes. He'd held back with the bar to make sure he didn't kill her. He was skilled: he knew exactly how hard he'd needed to hit her. That girl shouldn't have woken up until they were a long way away and he was ready for her. Maybe she'd stepped aside at the last moment, and the blow hadn't hit her full on . . . no, he'd made sure, and he didn't make mistakes. Suddenly his mind cleared, and he ran as fast as he could to the truck so he could get away from the accursed mountain. Someone had picked her up; that much was obvious. How had he not seen it coming? Some fucking scrawny, flea-bitten peasant had come down the mountain for a drink—that was what all these *indios* did. They must have found her lying there and taken her away. That was what had happened. Who knows what they'd thought was wrong with her. They must have taken her to a doctor or the local witch doctor or whatever these backward *indios* had. He tried to laugh at the idea, but there was nothing funny about it. He sat up in his seat, checked that the package was unconscious, and started the engine, desperate to get away from the stinking village before some local cop heard that two girls had been attacked and decided to play the hero.

If they followed him, he'd have to kill them, he said to himself, like he should have killed that turd of an *indio* who'd stared at him from his window. Once he'd reached the safety of the road that ran downhill to the freeway, he started to shout.

"*Indio, indio*! They're all *indios*! I should have killed her!" He smacked the roof of the cabin, trying to wake up the hostage even though he knew she was knocked out. "You hear me, you whore?" If her friend said something about the disappearance, he needed to get back to the city where they'd never find him. "Fucking whore!" He took all his frustration out on the steering wheel. "*Indios*! Savage sons of bitches, filthy pigs!" he went on, insulting people who looked pretty much exactly like him. "You're lucky you're a special order; if not, you'd soon learn to fear me." He was blinded by his hatred of the hillside where everything had gone wrong. "That other bitch doesn't know how lucky she is. Whore!" He hoped she was dead or disabled; he hoped with all his might that he'd given her irreparable brain damage. "Whatever happens to her, the whore's still lucky she's not here." He lost sight of the damp forest. Around him, smoke snaked up from chimneys, dirtying the air, making it as black and thick as his dark monologue.

On the way back, Ethan felt beat. Andrés said goodbye, and on the short stretch back from the gate, Ethan found it hard to stay upright. Michelle met him happily, ready to see to his needs, but it felt as though she were speaking to him through a long funnel. After a brief conversation he could barely understand, he excused himself so he could go to bed. She suggested it might be better for him to get some air, and he reluctantly agreed. They stepped out into the neighborhood, where it was getting dark but still, he thought to himself sardonically, safe to walk in. As they went along, Michelle turned out to be right; the breeze revived him a little. Their conversation wound around like a creeper, covering all kinds of topics, which ran into and jumped from one to another as though they didn't have enough time to cover everything that had brought them together. The walk energized him, and Michelle laughingly invited him to dinner, offering to take him in Beto's car if he could stand it, on the condition that she paid. In fact, she'd already chosen the restaurant. Ethan was tempted, but although he was feeling better, he knew that his exhaustion would catch up with him by dessert. He asked if they could do it the next day. Then he excused himself for a second time, leaving her looking resigned and a little lonely. He went into the unfamiliar bedroom, feeling almost weightless, unreal, as though he hadn't slept since the airport. He managed to get himself undressed in jerky movements and lay down on the mattress without switching off the light, trying to think clearly about the day. He lost consciousness before his head hit the pillow.

Like the night before, Michelle found that she couldn't get to sleep. She'd barely slept for two weeks since her little girl had disappeared, and she was grateful that it didn't show in her appearance. But for the past two nights, it had been for a different reason. For the first time since this nightmare had begun, she felt better. It was because of Ethan. Michelle closed her eyes and felt his arms around her. She thought she could smell his chest, his bittersweet, manly scent, and felt something stir inside of her. She was sorry they couldn't spend more time together, but she also feared the moment when questions would have to be asked and answered. It would come sooner or later. Ethan would want to know everything; he wouldn't give her space to breathe. She stopped herself: that was the Ethan of the past. He had been a different man then, and times had been different. Then he had had enormous potential but hadn't known how to tap it. His weaknesses had always won out. The man sleeping a few yards away from her was different. This Ethan had restored order to her life just by being there. She was slightly disoriented by the emotions rising up within her but excited by the idea of sitting down with him in the dark so they could express themselves freely. They'd listen to one another and give each other companionship. She'd rest her head on his firm chest and feel the noose loosening; her flesh would relax and bloom. Maybe she should go see him, pay him back a little of the time she owed. She would go, they could talk, and then she'd come back to her room to sleep having released the tension that so tormented her. Yes, Ethan would release the tension; he'd been doing that since he'd arrived.

She closed her eyes and pictured him. In her memories he was like the day they met. Then her memory started slipping into the present—no man had ever treated her with such tenderness and understanding—but even knowing that, Michelle had rejected him. This Ethan was different. Now he was big and powerful. Her recollection got caught in the neurotic loop of the past: If he was the perfect man, why didn't he turn her on? Well, he did, and they had sex, but why didn't he drive her crazy? Why wouldn't she have followed him to the ends of the earth the way she had Randall? With Ethan she'd never felt that she was being led by her man, someone who took charge of the situation. She knew that if she'd gone back to him, all the doñas, her mother first and foremost, would have been green with envy. They'd love to be claimed by a man like him: *Yes, Mom, we're going to get married, and I'm going to live with him. We're going to give little Michi an education in English so she won't have to grow up in this horrible city.* But her words had drifted away on the wind, and when Randall had come along, she'd felt she'd found a knight who could truly tame her, who told her where she could and couldn't go. Actually, he hadn't had to say anything: she'd guessed. Randall went wherever he wanted, free as the wind, and she'd had to follow him, always seeking a moment of his time, making sure that he never forgot her. That was Randall, such an artist, so committed, and she'd had to be there to show him her love so he would deign to share his greatness with her. But he sometimes got lost; she knew that it wasn't his fault. He was easily distracted. He'd been surrounded by whores who wanted to sleep with him, and sooner or later he'd given in. He couldn't help it. She remembered being in bed with Ethan. No man had ever performed oral sex on her like he had, not many had at all and none with his touch, his ability to give her multiple orgasms. But it had never seemed a very masculine thing to do. In spite of the waves of pleasure running through her, she'd never felt comfortable. Her kneeling in front of her man—that was different.

It was a question of vibrations. She'd always known that, but now she saw it clearly. She and Randall vibrated at complementary frequencies, like it had happened with the father of her son. It was a shame that all the men she'd known who were on her wavelength were no-good bums who never loved her and ditched her whenever it suited them. But she'd always had plenty of suitors, then and now. Michelle knew that her wavelength was a sensual purple. It was deeply feminine, and it excited men. Her mother had taught her that it wasn't their fault; she had to forgive them. It wasn't her stepfather's fault that she'd given off those vibrations when she was practically a young woman. The good man couldn't control himself: he himself vibrated red with passion, and that was why he'd gone to her when she'd first had her period. His kisses, his drool all over her, his hands everywhere. Fortunately, in the end he'd never done anything too bad. She should be grateful for his restraint. That was when Michelle had learned what attraction did to men and began to experience fear as she walked the streets. She was always on the receiving end of catcalls and innuendo from strangers or worse: aggressive groping. She couldn't even come back from a party alone for fear of being assaulted, but her mother had taught her to take it all with good grace, telling her that they didn't mean it badly. It was their nature; it was the woman's fault for stimulating their virility. However, she also told her that it was a form of power she could use to manipulate them.

Michelle's thoughts turned back to Ethan and how she had studied his vibrations when they were together. Ethan's wavelength had been orange, like a peach, soft and tender like coming home but lacking the authority she needed to control her. Ethan's wavelength was a space where she could rest and recover, but her feminine purple needed a more energetic accompaniment, like the navy blue of the two lovers she'd chased but who had rejected her. So selfish but so masculine.

But since he'd come back, Michelle had noticed a change in his wavelength. She knew that it changed as one matured, that the pink tones in her purple were fading along with her youth and that since she'd become a mother, she'd grown a more saturated violet. But with Ethan she could have sworn that his wavelength had changed completely, not just its shade but its very color. She'd have to check and read the stones, but she could have sworn it. Ethan gave off a different color. Could a man change that much? Could he become the companion she needed? If she'd never met him before, she'd have been sure that his wavelength was blue.

The need to sit with him and inhale his aroma grew inside of her like a blooming bud; it was almost painful. She remembered what she used to tell herself: *He'd be a good father. It's not about my needs but Michi's.* What did these new circumstances mean—how would they change things? What would she say to him, or . . . ? She pushed these tangled thoughts aside and replaced them with images of him playing with the girl, the strange feelings that came when she saw them together. Why had they played so much? Why had she always been with him? She regretted having reminded him so often that he wasn't her real father. She regretted her jealousy and tried to forget those painful truths. Something was keeping her awake, something more than her fear and nerves, something more than the fact that they were together again in completely different circumstances. The connection was going to be made that night, and she knew it. She trusted her intuition; she trusted in the vibrating cores of her stones and decided that she had to share them with him, let them resound with their energy as she watched it flow. She felt as though she was being pushed to go to him, and although she told herself that it wasn't sexual, that that had nothing to do with it, she could feel the call of the energy. Positive energy flowed between them both, and it could easily become a column of white light rising up into infinity, bringing them together. But when she left her room, she realized that in her excitement she'd never considered that his lights were off and that he might be asleep. She hesitated over waking him up but reassured herself that her intuition was foolproof. Mother Pachamama was sending her the energy to go do what he was waiting for; surely he was lying awake, like her, without knowing why. They were going to experience the communion of their energy once more. They were two lights—hers was white, and his was blue—but there would be no sex; sex had nothing to do with it . . . and in that moment she realized that her intuition had been correct, as always, and that was why it had sent her to him. She wasn't supposed to merge their energies. She was there because he needed her. Ethan was in some kind of danger.

The door to his bedroom was open, and the ceiling lamp was on, swinging from side to side as though someone had hit it. The bed was empty, the sheets messed up; his suitcase was open, and a trail of blood led out onto the patio. Michelle was shocked by the blood, but her curiosity overrode her fear, and she followed the trail, which led to the outdoor bathroom by the back fence. Its light was also on, and the door was half-open. She could see a shape inside, the unmistakable profile of Ethan under the light bulb, standing still in front of the small mirror.

Michelle went on, getting more and more frightened: something in the stance, in the way Ethan was moving, bringing his hands to his face and then back down again as though he were hypnotized, wasn't like him. Ethan was standing right there in front of her, and yet something about him was unfamiliar. The hair on the back of her neck stood on end as she approached, but she didn't stop. She forgot all about energy and belief and confronted him on her own in the orange glow of a light bulb swinging in the dark night. The face of her ex-boyfriend had three red streaks cut across it. The blood from the gashes dripped onto the ground. She stared in horror as Ethan looked straight into the mirror with blank eyes, as though he were trying to see something beyond it, something invisible on the other side of the wall. He raised his hand mechanically and continued to mutilate his face with a razor without flinching. Michelle didn't dare scream; she was overwhelmed by anguish and fear. Fighting back her rising panic, she walked toward him and gently stopped his hand, which put up no resistance. Ethan stood there like a toy whose pull string had run out, his pupils inert and expression frozen. His only movement was the rise and fall of his chest. He didn't blink for an unnatural period of time.

Eventually she managed to choke out a barely audible whisper: "E-Ethan? Are you there? Are you OK?"

Ethan answered with a grunt. The words from his dream emerged from his chest. "She's alive."

Michelle held back her sobs, trying to stay quiet. She covered her mouth with both hands, and the tears ran down them and onto her neck. "Michi?"

"Yes, she's alive. But she's suffering. The room is very strange. I don't understand what it is. It's like a classroom in an old school." He closed his eyes and went quiet again, as though he were hesitating.

Michelle cried for her daughter, for him, for her pain, and for the pain she was witnessing.

"Yes, I think it's a classroom in a school. The windows are narrow and very high. They're wooden, but there's no light. Michi is very scared; so is the other girl."

"She's with another girl? Are they both OK?"

"No, she hasn't gotten there yet. The other girl is very afraid, and her voice sometimes reaches her, but she's still far away. The men are pleased—this is what they were hoping for."

"Who are the men, the kidnappers?"

As he spoke, his voice grew deeper. It was very different from his normal voice, as though something from another world were speaking through him. Part of him was gone. The sensation that she was listening to someone else made her even more afraid.

"I don't know. They're there. Their souls are black, sinister, but one is worse. I don't think he's from the real world. The others can't see him. They don't know he's with them."

"Does Michi know?"

Before Ethan could answer, something behind Michelle made her jump.

"Michelle! What's going on here?" Her mother had come out in a robe. She stared at Ethan in horror. "Blessed Virgin! What happened to the poor man? Christ Almighty, he's bleeding! Why aren't you helping him? Why can't you do anything right? Wake up, *m'hijo*. Don't worry—you were dreaming. It's just a nightmare. You need to wake up, my dear."

She reached out to draw a cross on his face, like a child, but Ethan stared at her with the whites of his eyes.

"No, it isn't. She's alive, right now, trapped in that prison."

Michelle's mother jumped back in shock as though the angel of death himself were standing before her. Even so, as she crossed herself, she managed to ask a question, more to confirm that he was still in there than because she wanted to hear the answer.

"How do you know, dear?"

"I'm there right now. With them."

4

Caribbean

At the breakfast table, silence reigned. Doña Maria steamed the tamales she'd made for their guest but said nothing. Leidy and Beto, who'd decided to join the others this morning, were still staring, transfixed by the light coming from under the bathroom door, where Michelle had led Ethan to treat the cuts, which had reopened when he'd tried to drink coffee. A trace of blood could still be seen on the tablecloth while three drops rested intact on the floor leading into the bathroom. When the door opened, the couple had already finished half their plates, and Doña Maria, who hadn't touched her food, got up to serve them more.

Ethan smiled and sat down, but nothing about the silence changed. It was as though bad news hung in the air. Doña Maria said something about the chili sauce and invited him to try it. He tried to thank her for the special dish, which was usually reserved for Christmas, but everything he said sounded so forced that it just made things worse. Finally, the young couple got up and found an excuse to go back into Beto's room. Doña Maria pouted.

"Does . . . does it hurt?"

Ethan had bandages wrapped around his head to cover three deep gashes and another over a shallower one, which had opened up a few times already.

"No, with the painkiller I can barely feel it."

"And . . . how does it look?"

"The nurse told me that there'll be some scarring, but it'll just make me look more handsome. Do you remember, Michelle?" Ethan laughed a little, stretching the wounds on his cheeks.

"Yes. She was so shameless, Mom. She was coming on to him so obviously."

"Fortunately, I have health insurance, and there wasn't any trouble. Also, the new thing they used means no stitches."

"Cutaneous glue."

"That's it. It'll just fall off on its own."

But Doña Maria was having none of their casual attitude. She cleared her throat, and her voice began to crack. "My boy, I know that you've come to help us—and God protect you and bless you in all you do—but what happened last night had nothing to do with God. I don't know if it's because of my daughter, because of something she's done to offend the Almighty—"

"Mom, I—"

"Don't answer back. We'll discuss this later, Michelle. I don't know what happened last night, but it wasn't Catholic, and—Don Ethan, forgive me, but you weren't talking to a little girl. I don't know what it was, but the fright almost killed me. Beto is here and his girlfriend. They're both innocent; I can't let them witness such things. Not in my house."

"Don't worry, *señora*. We thought you might feel that way. While I was at the hospital, we called Andrés, and he's coming to pick me up in a little while. He's found me somewhere to stay, and I'll continue the work there. I'll come to see you every day to tell you how things are going. I think we should have done it this way from the start."

"I'm so sorry, *m'hijo*. I wish things didn't have to be like this but . . ."

"Don't worry. This is best for everyone."

Michelle had swapped shifts so she could take care of Ethan and now stood next to him as he packed his bag, stroking his cheek to alleviate the pain. Ethan, who was still under the effects of the painkiller, let her do what she liked. She made small talk, and neither of them brought up the big issues hovering over them like a dark cloud.

By lunchtime, Andrés was able to get away from work for long enough to come pick up Ethan. Michelle had to go to work.

"I'll get back late tonight, honey, but I'd love to see you tomorrow so we can talk properly. I owe you dinner, remember." She finished with a gentle kiss on what little free space remained on Ethan's cheek.

Once they were underway in the car, Andrés told Ethan that he'd found an apartment that could be rented by the week in one of the city's newly built areas, far away from Mara territory. Ethan was pleased to hear it. To his surprise, however, they stopped in front of a luxury hotel in the middle of the city. Andrés asked him to be patient and without saying another word led him into the lobby, where they picked up a key for a room that had already been booked. Ethan was confused.

"What's going on?"

"This is what I always thought we should have done, but they insisted that you stay with them."

"What are we doing in a hotel? I thought you were taking me to an apartment?"

"I've arranged that, too, but I paid for four days here. Then there's this," Andrés said, handing over a set of car keys. "It's downstairs in the parking lot. The boy knows which it is."

"Have you gone crazy? I can't accept any of this. I won't let you pay for everything. I'm not your guest."

"It's less than you think, and I'm not paying for everything."

"I don't care."

"You know how much I respect you, Ethan, so if you just listen, I'll explain. Then you can decide for yourself."

Ethan nodded, and the two men started walking to the room.

"I know a man. He knows more than us—he's very smart and well educated. He was a police inspector before he retired, and we've been friends since childhood. I trust him completely. He's fully informed, and I've told him all about it, and he can help us, thanks be to God. But no one can know, he says. Not even Michelle."

"You still don't trust her."

"It's not her. It's the people around her. The Lord gives us the freedom to choose, and people make bad choices, either out of evil or ignorance. But that doesn't matter; my friend has agreed to help us."

"And you don't trust the detective either?"

"I do, but there's more than one way to do this. I know—I've seen my friend in action. Calvo will do his own investigation. Everyone knows him, and everyone knows he's on the case, but my friend will go his own way. I'm grateful that he's with us, and you will be too. I'm sure of it. But only you must know about it, not even me."

They arrived at the room, and Andrés unlocked the door. Once inside he held up another basic new phone and put it and the room key on the bed.

"If you agree, you can use this one to talk to him. It has a number saved on it that he uses, just as he instructed. He says not to talk to anyone else on it, not even me. When you go back to my mother's house, you mustn't take it out of your pocket or show it to anyone. Keep it with you at all times, even if you think it's safe, and don't leave it alone if Michelle visits you here."

"She wouldn't go through my things."

Andrés raised his eyebrows skeptically. "He told me to bring you to this hotel and give you the car. You'll spend the first few days here, and then you can move into the apartment. After that the two of you can decide how best to move ahead."

"Why?"

"He knows what he's doing."

"So you're not going to be a part of this?"

"That's how he wants it, and I trust him."

"Who am I to argue?"

They said goodbye, and Ethan spent some time unpacking and thinking. He didn't understand Andrés's friendship with this enigmatic character. He was mulling over his doubts when he heard the muffled ring of the new phone. It was vibrating on the mattress. The name on the screen just said *cell phone*. It continued to bounce around the duvet cover for a while before Ethan decided to answer.

"Hello?"

"Good afternoon, Don Ethan."

"Who is this?"

"You can call me Suarez."

"So what are we doing? I don't like all this mystery."

"Number one is never to call this number or any other from this phone. I'll call you. Anything you want to tell me: send me a message. I'll read them all, but don't call me. That will be our code. If you call, I'll know you've been compromised and someone is forcing you to make the call. Neither should you answer any calls from a different number."

"What if you're compromised? How will I know?"

Suarez ignored the question. "If you want to meet, you should leave in twenty minutes. Pick up the car that was left for you, and I'll call in fifteen minutes."

"Why all the secrecy? We're looking for a girl, not—"

"I think you're being tailed. Will you let me find out?"

The news hit Ethan like a bucket of cold water. He didn't like the man's condescension, but he had to listen to him.

"Fine, I'll wait."

In the garage, he found a pearl-gray RAV4, a large but discreet 4x4, and sat in it waiting for the phone call.

"Ready to go?"

"The engine's running."

"Good. Put it on speakerphone, and I'll give you directions. It's important that they think you're on your own and not talking to anyone. When you get to where I tell you, make sure that you leave the back doors open but without them seeing. That's the most important thing."

"So they can steal it?"

"You should have left by now."

Ethan put the phone between his legs, drove up the ramp, and went down a crowded avenue until he got to a large, busy traffic circle. As he hesitated, he was overtaken by a pair of taxis and assaulted by a barrage of horn blowing. He finally got around it and made a left onto a smaller street with even more traffic where the different vehicles' conversations with each other amounted to a kind of symphony: people honked their horns to attract attention (briefly if they wanted to be polite), to ask to be allowed in or to say thank you for having been let in, to salute women pedestrians in lieu of an obscene comment, or, in the case of the angrier drivers, to express their displeasure at anything they deemed to have gotten in their way, including pedestrians. The mood was constantly shifting between a lively tableau and sheer brutality.

"What the hell is going on? Why is everyone honking like that?"

"Many of my compatriots appear to be compensating for inadequacies elsewhere," said Suarez through the phone.

Ethan drove around an enormous mall with little stores running along its facade like remoras feeding on scraps. Large speakers were turned outdoors, blaring strident music or advertising *Wonderful Offers!* while a sea of people coming and going only added to the chaos. As he followed Suarez's instructions, he realized that he was going around the entire building again.

"Once again for luck?"

"This makes things easier."

"Fine, I get it. How many times do you want me to do the circle?"

"I'll let you know when I need you to do something."

Ethan thought for sure he'd hit another vehicle or a pedestrian as he circled. Finally, Suarez told him to enter a parking garage and which floor to park on.

"Now head for a very large mobile phone accessories store on the opposite corner, and buy a charger for your phone. Then come back, and I'll give you more instructions. Don't forget to leave the car unlocked."

"You don't need to remind me."

Ethan crossed the mall, which was filled with advertisements louder than the street outside. Hordes of students and schoolchildren saw it as their home away from home, especially the food court. Eventually, he completed his stupid mission. When he got back to the car, he saw that it had been locked from the inside and quickly checked the back seat, where he saw a crouching shape. He sat down and pulled out without saying a word.

"You can go back to the hotel now," said the voice in the back seat.

"I hope that our little trip was worth the effort."

"You had a tail. Not a very good one."

When they'd parked in a place far from prying eyes, Suarez sat up and introduced himself. Ethan was surprised to see that he recognized him: an elderly man with a good head of gray hair and what had clearly once been an athletic body. He was fairly pale for these parts and had a kindly gaze that was a long way from the hard-bitten stare Ethan had been expecting. He was one of the chess players from the night before. He looked far more like a retired professor or wizened elder than a detective. He'd beaten his friends in game after game with a certain measure of condescension, barely saying a word as he concentrated on his next move. But of course he had been using this as a front so he could study Ethan.

"A pleasure to see you again, Don Ethan."

"Oh . . . the pleasure is mine. I wasn't expecting it to be you."

"That's good. What happened to your face?"

"It's a long story."

"It shouldn't concern us?"

"No, it shouldn't. So?"

"So."

They both eyed each other warily.

"I was expecting you to start," Ethan said. "I wanted to hear your thoughts."

"I don't have much to tell you, and you should be going up to your room. I'm familiar with the case and have all the details. Andrés has explained everything. He asked me for help."

"He told me. Also that you used to be a cop, but to be honest you don't look like one."

"That's true, and no bad thing."

"OK. Why are you doing this? Is he paying you?"

"No. And he's not paying you either. Why are you doing this?"

"For personal reasons."

"Likewise."

"You don't have a relationship with the girl."

"Neither do you. We're both helping Andrés, her relative. If you're interested in my help, I'll continue. If not, this is where we part ways. You're looking for a girl, and I came to observe you. Sometimes you learn more from watching someone doing something than from doing the thing yourself. That's how children learn."

In spite of the man's measured tone and immaculate appearance, or maybe precisely because of them, Ethan felt uncomfortable. "Fine, go on."

"You've hired that detective. He's good; I know him. But he'll always be looking ahead of you. He has to show you the way. I, in contrast, can follow behind, watching out for what you leave in your wake. I thought that given all the fuss over your arrival, if you're right and the girl is still alive, it was quite likely that someone was keeping an eye on you. Hence the hotel and the car."

"You've made me the bait in my own investigation."

Suarez shrugged. "I did what your expensive detective couldn't do. Watching you rather than the rest of the city. It's cheaper and produces better results. I thought you do this for a living."

"I'm more used to being the one doing the following."

"Well, be careful. The rules are different here."

His advice wasn't so different from what Calvo had told him, but it was much more infuriating. "And what have you found out? Who's tailing me?"

"I don't know yet. I don't have our detective's resources, but I've seen a car and a license plate. I need you to be visible over the next few days, to move around. That will help."

"You want to keep using me as bait."

"You continue with your investigation, and I'll go on with mine. We'll each come to our own conclusions."

"So I can go on without waiting to hear from you."

"I'll report to you and Andrés if I find something. If not, it's not as though you have anything to lose."

"Andrés said that he wasn't going to be involved."

"That's right. If I need help, I'll call you, not him. But I still have to report to him. He's my friend and the girl's uncle."

"You can count on me. So long as you don't mind that I have a tail, that is," Ethan said sardonically.

"I'll take care of that."

"Fine. Will you be dealing with the Mara too?"

"If the Mara are involved, Calvo's the only one who can help you. He's the only one who can negotiate with them. But I don't think so. What makes you think they're involved? They wouldn't be having you followed like this." Suarez held out his hand. "That's all for now."

Ethan shook Suarez's hand but was still dubious. "I'm not sure . . ."

"About what?"

"About anything you've told me."

"Of course. As I said, if you don't want me, we'll say goodbye, and you'll never see me again."

"But that doesn't mean that you won't be working for Andrés."

For the first time, Suarez allowed himself a little smile. "And if I do?"

"Then I'd rather keep you close by. To know what you know."

"Shall I take that as a yes?"

"It's a necessary evil."

"I've never known an agreement that wasn't."

Ethan could see the man assessing him, analyzing his weaknesses as though he were preparing for a potential confrontation. They went their separate ways. The painkillers had him dozing until dinnertime, when he forced himself to leave the hotel, allowing himself to be seen—and followed, if he were to believe

Suarez. He felt ridiculous. During dinner, Calvo confirmed their appointment for the next day and offered to pick him up. Ethan accepted politely. Then he got an unexpected message that almost gave him a heart attack: it was from Ari. At that precise moment, thousands of miles away, she was writing to him. He envisaged an almost magical connection between them: she was looking at her screen, wondering how he was. Ethan was filled with innocent, almost childish happiness and answered immediately. She told him that she was going out but wouldn't be long. Then she suggested they talk in about three hours, if that was OK. She felt like talking. Suddenly the day lit up, and everything that had happened, beginning with his conversation with Suarez, seemed important news.

That night, he managed to keep his drooping eyes open until Ari wrote. She started out telling him about her research. Ethan saw this as an intimate connection, like a wonderful declaration. He knew it was a fantasy, but it made him happy all the same. Halfway through their chat, he received a loving message from Michelle wishing him good night and lamenting the fact that he wasn't with her at that moment so he could put his hand on her heart and feel how it beat for him. It made him shudder. For the next few minutes, he switched between the two conversations, his feelings growing ever more confused. Ari wasn't tender or intimate; it wasn't her style, but her involvement made him feel a sense of deep communion. Michelle didn't stray from romantic clichés, but she knew how to use them. She topped off their conversation with a photo of herself blowing him a kiss from bed. The photo revealed nothing but invited his imagination to run wild. After Michelle signed off, his messages became more and more flirtatious until Ari put an abrupt stop to it: Really? You're trying to get it on with me now? Ethan didn't answer, and she signed off. After that it took him a long time to get to sleep.

Outside the hotel the next morning, the sight of Adrian Calvo in a suit tucked over a Kevlar vest was both amusing and ominous. He was accompanied by three men wearing the same protective gear over sweatshirts, black pants, and military boots. They were carrying two AK-47s and an MP7, making them indistinguishable from a team of drug traffickers or special ops. Their aggressive paramilitary appearance didn't overly impress Ethan. When Calvo saw him, he jumped back.

"What happened to you? Did you get into a fight with a cat?"

"A domestic accident."

"You're not doing a very good job of going incognito."

"You might call it a lot of effort with little reward."

"Let's hope that doesn't apply to all your ventures. Do you want one of these?"

He held out a vest, which Ethan took reluctantly. "Do you really think it's necessary?"

"Not at all, but it looks intimidating. Don't wear it if you don't want to—you know how much they make you sweat."

The party got into a pair of black Range Rovers that only enhanced their military aesthetic. Ethan noticed that the license plates were factory issue.

"They're not registered?"

Calvo smiled. "We won't have any trouble with that here. Better this way, don't you think?"

They drove out of the capital and up into the northern hills, which were sprinkled with high-end residential areas linked together by malls. Soon afterward they came to more dispersed, villagelike settlements and turned down a street blocked by a barrier with a guard post manned by a bored security guard. Ethan saw the signs posted on every corner: **This community is protected by private surveillance.** The guard came out to question the driver of the first vehicle, and they had a brief conversation finished off with a friendly smile and the handing over of several bills. The employee lifted the barrier, and the small convoy got through the checkpoint. They parked close to a small country house surrounded by enormous hedges. It looked idyllic. The commandos got out and pulled on balaclavas, exuding violence from every pore. Ethan came last, just behind Calvo, who was mopping the sweat from his brow with a handkerchief, gasping in the heat.

"Oh, the heat, it's so draining . . ."

"Are we just going to knock on the door? I thought we were going to break it down."

Calvo smiled under his hood. "It's all just for show."

A small explosion blew the lock open. The three assistants set out running, pointing their guns and shouting as they searched each room. Ethan heard the detective's stifled laugh.

"We like to use the plastic explosives with foreigners. It scares them shitless."

They followed their companions inside while Calvo expounded on all the different ways in which one could intimidate a suspect. Ethan looked around the house. It was cool and colorful, with plenty of plants, tasteful blinds, and ethnic decor: an intimate, inviting space. As he walked through a bedroom, he noticed a camera tripod and shivered. In the living room, a large window looked out onto the jungle. The three hooded men were holding down a man in his thirties. One of them pressed his head against the floor with his knee. His boss gestured to let him go. Next to him was a pair of hard drives he had been trying to hide when he was caught. Calvo gestured again, and one of his men opened a backpack and took out a laptop, which he then connected to one of the drives.

As Ethan watched, he realized that no one was in any hurry. They didn't appear to be expecting the police or for anyone around to report them. He suddenly understood the culture of impunity in which he found himself: right now it was working in his favor, but that situation could change at any moment.

The target didn't look like a stereotypical pedophile: he wasn't morbidly obese, covered in acne, or lacking in personal hygiene. In fact, in his designer glasses he looked like an attractive surfer. His naked torso was shaved and toned, his beard was carefully trimmed, and his mat of red hair gave him a dreamy look. He wouldn't have had any trouble attracting the company of either sex. Instead, he was sweating, begging them not to access the secrets on the hard drives. The second hooded man came back from another room with another laptop belonging to the detainee.

"The password, you bastard."

He tried to play dumb.

"The password, you son of a bitch!"

Sobbing, the man spelled it out, and Ethan noticed that they weren't doing him any harm. Even the way they held him down was gentle enough not to leave any marks. They were professionals and knew exactly the purpose of their mission. They were limiting themselves to verbal violence, and it seemed that was more than enough.

The two specialists searched through the computers while the third stayed on the ground; Calvo searched the house, more out of curiosity than because he was looking for something in particular. They opened hundreds of folders and focused on the ones dated around the time that Michi had gone missing. Each of them contained thousands of pictures of girls posing clothed and naked in many different positions, most of them obscene. For a few minutes, the owner denied that they belonged to him. Then they started to delete them, and he screamed at them to stop. His whine attracted Calvo's attention from his iPhone. The detective looked up at Ethan and felt that he needed to explain himself.

"I wasn't chatting—I don't do that kind of thing. I don't know how to work these devices."

Their prisoner was still whimpering. Calvo addressed him, still struggling with his phone. "So they are yours after all? We're deleting every single one."

"No, please. They're my angels. I don't hurt them. I *give them things*; I *help them*. I just take photos dishabille. They know; their mothers know; they're so pretty . . . they're completely safe . . ."

His voice was trembling. His captors responded to his pathetic display with disgust. Calvo finally found what he was looking for.

"Here it is!" He turned to Ethan. "I was about to ask you if you had any photos of the girl. I couldn't find them."

This made Ethan realize that, oddly, he hadn't asked for a picture of Michi, as though the image were somehow already fixed in his brain. Somewhat apprehensive, he went over to Calvo, who showed him the screen.

"This should be good enough for him to recognize her, shouldn't it?"

Ethan nodded, knowing that he shouldn't let his accent give him away but mostly because his fears had been confirmed. He hadn't seen her in six years, but five minutes ago he could have described her in detail and would have been spot on. Disoriented by a disturbing sense of déjà vu, he realized that he knew exactly what her voice sounded like as well: he'd spoken to her only a couple of nights ago.

Oblivious to his discomfort, Calvo started his interrogation in Spanish, clearly trying to upset the subject, who had difficulty understanding.

"Where is she? Where have you stashed her, cocksucker? Tell me, or I'll rip your balls out through your mouth!"

The abuser cried out, swearing that he'd never seen her before. He had no idea what they were talking about. Unfortunately, he was quite convincing.

"We know you sell them, you motherfucking son of a bitch. To other perverts like you, you sack of shit. Tell us who you sold her to, or we'll give you something to remember us by."

Sitting on the ground, the abuser tried to speak as best he could. "No . . . I've never seen her before. I promise. They . . . no one, no one here paid for that girl. I promise—"

"We want the names of your customers! They'll tell us the truth once we're done with you!"

"They're all here on my phone, in my pocket. And on my computer. But I promise you none of them did anything to that girl. You can check."

"Why are you so sure?"

"She's . . . too old."

Calvo stepped back in disgust and went outside. Ethan followed him after making sure that the computer searches didn't turn up anything. Calvo took off his mask to smoke a cigarette.

"We'll take the material to search further, but you saw his face. I told you."

"Yeah, this isn't the guy. Aren't there any other leads? Is there anyone else?"

"There always are, but this was our best bet."

"The police aren't coming."

The detective smiled his mischievous smile. "They gave us an hour, and we still have half an hour left. Let's go back inside and make him squeal like the little shit he is."

"And after that?"

"After that we go home. It's lunchtime. I'll let you know what we do from here."

"No, I mean him. Aren't you going to hand him over to the police?"

"To who? The captain we paid before coming here? The same guy that bastard pays every month to cover up his disgusting ways? Who makes sure that no one ever sees the photos or that a judge never gets wind of it? Then he really would be fucked. If you ask people around here, they'd have nothing bad to say about him. He's generous to the girls and their families; no one has complained. You're telling me this doesn't go on in other places? Hypocrisy isn't exclusive to the first or third worlds. But that's not what prevents me from killing him here and now. You can do it if you like."

Calvo unfastened his vest, stuck his hand underneath, and took out a medium-caliber handgun. "Here's the gun you asked for. It's clean, filed, untraceable. We'll leave and let them know that he's free and unharmed. He'll call the guards that keep him safe, and they'll come by to console him—'Why didn't you call before, man?' 'We'll protect you, my liege'—and they'll take money from everyone, him and us. If I don't hand him over or something happens to him, tomorrow I'll turn up in a sewer somewhere wrapped in plastic. But no one knows about you. We can leave you in an unmarked car; then you wait until we leave and do it. No one knows you. No one will come looking for you. You go in, shoot, leave. It'd be as simple as that."

Ethan didn't answer.

The detective threw away his cigarette and stepped on it before going on. "There's another reason to keep him alive. It might sound terrible, but he's useful. It's not the first time we've had to find a child. He's at the center of all the networks of foreign pedophiles. At least we know where we can find him and that he's weak. It's awful, isn't it? The world isn't how we'd like it to be, I know. It's tough."

The drill bored into his head, filling it with light. It was about to pierce his brain. Ethan realized he was asleep, or at least he had been. The sun was flooding through the curtains. The shrill motor continued to pound at his skull until he finally realized it was the vibration of his phone from the drawer in the nightstand. What a way to be woken up. He opened it and realized that it was the phone Suarez had given him dancing from one corner of the drawer to the other. The voice on the other end of the line was just as grating as the drill.

"We have a problem."

Ethan yawned as he answered. "Have you been exposed already?"

"Don't be stupid. I have some information about your tail. You know her."

"Uh-huh?" Ethan said. The only thing on his mind was that he needed to take a piss.

"Her name is Leidy Durán Zamora, girlfriend of a kid named Beto, whom I assume you know because he's the missing girl's youngest uncle. The girl was following you and then met up with her brother, a boy named Jonathan. He runs with rather unsavory characters. What does that suggest to you?"

Ethan sat up, now fully, almost painfully awake. "What's the problem? What do they know?"

"Nothing so far. Yesterday, I paid a girl to hook up with Jonathan at a bar, slipped a little something in his drink too. She came back out with everything, including his phone. The kid's still probably passed out somewhere with no idea what happened to him or that he's missing anything. That could work in our favor."

"I'm getting tired of this. Tell me what's going on."

"Once I'd got confirmation, I talked to Don Andrés and told him. I asked him to be patient and wait for us to decide what to do."

"Why didn't you call me before? Why don't the three of us meet up? Of course we have to wait; we need to follow them and turn the tables."

"Don Andrés agreed, but it doesn't sit well with him. He went to talk to his pastor, and he told him that he had to deal with the situation through dialogue and by letting the truth come to light. Only the serpent deals in lies and works in the shadows. He called me a few minutes ago to tell me. Now I'm calling you."

"Andrés can't talk to them!"

"No, he can't. I told him so."

"You should have stopped him."

"That's why I'm talking to you. I'm working as fast as I can, but you didn't answer your phone."

"You should have called me first!"

"I've done my duty in accordance with my instructions. Nobody changed them."

"You fucked up!" Ethan shouted in a rage. "You know it. Admit it!"

"Nobody here has made a mistake, not even Andrés. Each of us has made a decision, and we must accept that. These are what are known as consequences. Now, do you want to go on arguing or resolve the situation?"

Ethan hung up before he said something he'd regret. He looked for the other phone to try to stop Andrés. It took him a few minutes, which felt like a lifetime. He remembered Andrés's moral scruples well, and it seemed he'd only grown worse having found religion. Finally, he got through, and after a couple of rings, Andrés answered. He was driving.

"Good morning, Don Ethan."

"Andrés! Andrés, listen, stop for a moment. Where are you?" He tried to get dressed as he spoke, hopping from one side of the room to the other.

"Suarez called you. I know. I know that you don't agree with what I'm doing, but you must forgive me. The Lord knows what's right, and he's never wrong."

"OK, OK, you're right. It's not like that. I think it's the right thing to do, too, but give me half an hour, and we'll sit down and talk about it. Let's meet, without Suarez. We don't need to involve him in this."

"I understand: you're detectives, and this is how you work, but there's another world, one more important than your investigations—"

"Andrés, this could be very bad for Michi, do you understand? Think of her and what we're trying to do. We have a very good lead—"

"My brother. My own brother, her uncle. Forgive me, Don Ethan, but that little kid . . . oh, praise be the Lord, he wanted this to happen because it's best for us. We shall never understand his plan, but . . ."

Ethan thought he heard a repressed sob.

"I knew . . . I always knew, but I couldn't set him right. I need to talk to that unfortunate young man. He—he always . . . he isn't to blame. He grew up without a father, and our mother couldn't . . . but . . . forgive me, Don Ethan. I need to deal with this myself."

"Do me a favor: wait for me. I'm going over there right now. Just give me a chance; we'll all sit down together and say what we need to say. Please, just wait for me."

"I'm almost there, Don Ethan. I'll talk to my mother first, but with or without you I'll talk to him just the same. It's God's will."

Ethan couldn't stand his evangelical sanctimony. He couldn't help thinking that it was suffering that pushed people into believing in promises of a better life. He picked up his local telephone and weighed the pistol in his hand for a few moments. He didn't want to bring it to Michelle's home, but he knew that talking to Leidy and her brother would lead to a confrontation, and he had no idea what the consequences might be. He looked at it and put it back down, reassuring himself with the thought that he wouldn't need to pacify Beto and Jonathan at the same time.

When he arrived at Michelle's house, he saw Beto's ride and Andrés's car, leading Ethan to believe that they'd all be together for some time. He went to knock on the door but saw that it was half-open already and pushed it. He heard a muffled conversation coming through the closed kitchen door. The remaining rooms were empty. He knocked, asking permission to come in, and found Andrés and Doña Maria inside. They jumped when they saw him.

"Did Beto let you in?"

"No, the door was open. I didn't see anyone."

"Betito, are you there?" Michelle's mother called from her seat.

The sound echoed without response. Andrés, surprised, called out too.

"Beto! He was here a moment ago; where is he?"

Ethan got straight to the point. "Andrés, have you spoken to him?"

"No, I was waiting for you, like I said. I was telling Mom—"

"Listen, I don't like accusations—"

"Let's go!" Ethan said, ignoring Doña Maria. "We have to get to Leidy's house!"

Andrés jumped up, and both men ran outside.

"Here, we'll take the car."

"Where's the house?"

"Over there, it's the one on that corner—"

Ethan was off and running. Andrés tried to keep up, but he didn't have the stamina and soon fell behind. The brief run was enough to attract the attention of the entire neighborhood. It was used to such scenes, but they generally featured half-naked Mara, not a pair of well-dressed men.

When Ethan was about 150 feet away, he saw a guy leaning haughtily in the front entrance, wearing a string vest, sweatpants, and designer sneakers, his eyes glaring. It was Jonathan. Ethan stopped. A neighborhood audience watched expectantly. Trusty Andrés came trotting along, sweating and surrounded by gawkers. Some of them started to ask what was going on.

"Hi, Jonathan," Ethan said. "Is Beto with you?"

Jonathan stepped away from the wall to block his path. "No one's here, gringo," Jonathan said. "Go back where you came from—you look hot. Why don't you get Michelle to make you a lemonade?"

"Jonathan, I don't want any trouble, but we need to talk."

"I don't know you. I don't know you, gringo. I saw you the other day at the barbecue, but I don't know you, and I don't trust you. Go back if you don't want to start eating shit."

Ethan saw that several of the locals had crept forward; they were almost at the porch. He wasn't sure of their intentions, but for the moment their body language didn't seem threatening. He raised his hands in a sign of peace and kept walking forward. "I just want to talk, Jonathan. I know Beto is with you. I only want to ask some questions, and then I'll go."

Jonathan took a territorial stance. "No. Go away. Now."

The locals waited a few feet away without revealing their allegiances. Then Jonathan's mother poked her head from the doorway, distracting him.

"Go back inside, Ma."

Ethan tried to guess the mood of the crowd, but it was impossible to read. There was something electric in the air that made him anxious, a kind of anger and thirst for violence that grew with every new arrival. He considered stopping and going back; the potential danger seemed too great, and he didn't want to imperil Andrés. He knew that he could handle a couple of bums but not a crowd. He was relieved that he hadn't brought the gun. If the locals decided to defend their guy, he and Andrés might not get out of there alive. But he also knew that if he turned back now, they'd be missing out on their only chance. He plunged on into the unknown.

Just then, a group of Andrés's friends began shouting.

"He says that they're part of a gang!"

More joined in.

"Jonathan sells names to kidnappers!"

"Our people!"

The crowd began to murmur. Jonathan and Ethan looked for the source of the shouts, each just as surprised as the other. Now the man closest to them stepped up to question the accused.

"Is that true, man?"

Jonathan waved him away dismissively. "Get out of my way, scum." He turned back to Ethan, trying to turn the attention back on him. "Come here, gringo. I'm gonna smash your face in."

But his accusers weren't going to fall for it. Another voice chimed in. "Hey, kid! We're talking to you. What are these strangers saying?"

Jonathan turned to face the newcomer. "If you don't want something bad to happen to you, you'd better get on back home."

The man recoiled from the threat. But his companion stepped forward. "Young man, we're only asking a question. There's no need to get upset."

Jonathan turned to this new man and strode toward him aggressively. His opponent stood his ground, and soon they were within punching distance.

"Oh, yes? You want some too? Come here!"

Jonathan's mother watched from the doorway, trembling. The commotion had now spread to the entire block; every door and window was open. Children hung out in groups while the elderly slowly approached. Andrés had stopped a few feet away without intervening. Ethan was keeping an eye on the house, where he saw a shadow scurrying around. The wives of the men confronting Jonathan shouted encouragement. A truck stopped, and the driver shamelessly sat watching with a passive expression. Ethan ignored the distraction and focused on the movement inside. He realized that now Jonathan's protection was faltering, Leidy might try to slip out the back. Jonathan's opponent wasn't backing down.

"Hey, my friend here is asking if you're one of the pieces of shit who provides information to fucking kidnappers."

Jonathan's face reddened in anger. "Calm down, man! You're the piece of shit, just like that other fucker! Get out of here, or I'll—"

His companion stepped forward again, speaking firmly but calmly. "I need to know."

Andrés took advantage of a slight drop in tension to separate them, seeking the help of the third man.

"Listen, we can all talk about this in a civilized way . . ."

But his prospective ally wasn't as helpful as he'd hoped. "Yes, because if not, I'll call the police, and we'll see if they can get to the bottom of this."

Ethan, passing unnoticed amid the confusion, headed for the house, but Jonathan's mother stood in his way.

"You're not coming in here, you bastard!"

Ethan heard a door slam and gently pushed the mother out of the way before rushing inside. His actions distracted the others, and Jonathan seized his moment. He head butted the man closest to him in the nose, and he fell back in a daze, bleeding profusely. Before the other two could react, Jonathan ripped off his belt with his right hand and skillfully started to whip it at the others. While they protected their faces, he swatted the belt around so he could hit them with the buckle. Meanwhile, Ethan was chasing Leidy. He was followed in turn by her mother, who was screaming hysterically.

"Run, girl! He's coming for you!"

The old lady jumped on Ethan with surprising agility given her frame and grabbed his arm, but he pushed her back down. After he'd shaken her free, he came face-to-face with the toddler he'd seen at the party. The sight of the baby in bare feet and just a T-shirt worried him, given the unstable situation.

"Quickly, run to the kitchen and stay there."

Patito obeyed silently, marching off like a half-naked soldier.

Jonathan was flailing around with his belt, hitting Andrés and the neighbor, who protected themselves with their arms, trying to deflect the blows. The buckle caught the other man in the cheek, ripping out a chunk of flesh. The attacker let out a grunt not dissimilar to laughter. The crowd filled the street and spilled onto the property, asking questions and shouting accusations, both horrified by and savoring the spectacle. When blood started to flow, the mood grew more heated.

"They're old men! Why don't you mess with someone your own age?"

"Killer! Bastard!"

But Jonathan went on exultantly until Andrés managed to get ahold of the belt. There were shouts of encouragement and even some applause. The truck driver had left his vehicle parked in the road and was striding purposefully toward the altercation. A man of intimidating size with a muscular frame, it looked as though he might prove a different prospect entirely. And he was coming right for Jonathan. Seeing Jonathan look away, Andrés pulled the belt away from him. Jonathan, now aware of the danger, let it go and headed back inside to fetch a gun.

Ethan got to the door to Leidy's bedroom and kicked it. He knew it would open easily given the flimsiness of the house, but he hadn't expected just how flimsy it would be: his leg went straight through the cardboard-and-balsa-wood door. He fell forward, wondering how he could be so stupid, and he tried to extricate his leg. Then he saw Jonathan run into the hall. Seeing that he'd caught Ethan in a vulnerable position, Jonathan changed course. What he didn't know was that as fast as he might be, Ethan was trained, and he wasn't. The kid took three strides forward and got ready to turn the fourth into a kick to Ethan's face. But even with his leg stuck, Ethan was able to avoid the kick and punch Jonathan in the balls. Jonathan gasped for air and collapsed, too hurt even to scream in pain.

Ethan finally shook himself free and assessed the scene before his next move: the mother, convinced until very recently that her son was about to smash Ethan's head in, sat still, stunned by what she had just witnessed. Patito was hiding under the kitchen table just as he'd been instructed; Jonathan was curled in the fetal position, unable to get up. A quick glance through the hole he'd made confirmed Ethan's suspicion that Leidy had already escaped. However, he noticed that the noise outside contrasted sharply with the silence indoors. Leaving the house, he saw a huge man striding forward, flanked by a pair of opportunists. The trio entered the house and headed straight for Jonathan, who was still lying on the floor. Surprised to find him in that position, the giant truck driver gave Ethan a complicit wink that Ethan didn't return. He effortlessly lifted Jonathan up, and the two other men spat at him before the giant set about rearranging the boy's face with his fist. The mother reacted by hauling herself up and screaming desperately.

"My little boy! What are you doing to little Jonny? Bastards! Motherfuckers!"

Ethan's apprehension about what might happen next grew. It wasn't the coming beating: the activity around the house had increased, and he knew from experience to pay more attention to that than what was about to happen indoors. He couldn't hear much rage, but the initial tension had reached a critical point. He sensed a thirst for blood that would demand more than Jonathan being beaten to a pulp. The mother's screams were echoed by the conversations out on the street. The tone grew darker, changing from initial indignation to suspicion, accusation, and condemnation. Soon, the latter was all that would matter. Having got his wind back and left his companion in the hands of some good Samaritans, Andrés came into the house. His arms were covered in scratches and bruises. Curious onlookers followed closely behind, eagerly filling up the space. Ethan saw what was going on and decided to move quickly. He met Andrés's eyes and nodded to him to get out, but the anguished Christian forgot his own injuries and rushed to halt the pummeling of his erstwhile attacker.

"Brothers! Brothers! Stop before you do something you regret!"

By way of an answer, a brick came through the window, getting tangled up in a curtain. This new development made everyone freeze for a moment, all except for Ethan, who saw himself in the middle of a potential riot. The atmosphere was about to explode; it only needed a spark. He could hear what they were saying through the broken window.

"Murderers! Kidnappers! You've killed our children!"

Mixed in with the general agitation were the laments of mourners, relatives of people who had been murdered, and angrier exclamations from hotheads demanding justice. Then a cry of genuine pain rang out, quieting all the others. It was a deep, gravelly male voice that cracked halfway through.

"They took my Sheila! Those motherfucking sons of bitches sold my Sheila. They asked for money, and we gave them everything we had! Then they left her in a field with no clothes or underwear—they threw her away like she was a thing."

The account broke down into a howl that sounded strange coming from such a dignified man. A shudder ran through the crowd. Soon the chorus was echoing his words.

"They killed her! They abused her! The bastards! They killed Sheila!"

Ethan took hold of Andrés's wrists to pull him away from the beating. "Let's go! We need to get out of here. Leidy escaped, and this is getting out of control."

"But they're beating him! We can't leave him like this."

"This is the best thing that can happen. If they take him outside for people to see, things might cal—"

The situation changed in a flash. Jonathan's mother went into the kitchen, where Patito was still sitting under the table, and came back with a large knife in her hand. "Get back, you motherfuckers! I'll cut you, you pigs!"

One of the men said, "*Señora, señora*, calm down—stop for a second!"

But the woman was out of her mind. She threw herself upon him, plunging the whole blade into his side. He screamed out in pain while, blind with rage, she stabbed again and again, pushing it right to the hilt each time. Those in the crowd waiting outside who saw this swarmed into the house. Ethan grabbed Andrés by the arm and pulled him against the flow. The living room exploded into a maelstrom of shouts and screams, crashes, broken glass, smashing furniture. Ethan dragged his friend away. Andrés, stunned by what was going on, didn't resist. As they were slipping through gaps in the mob fighting to get inside, they heard the kitchen window shatter. Ethan desperately tried to shout over the commotion.

"The kitchen!"

But Andrés didn't understand. He was just trying to avoid getting crushed in the press of bodies. An obese older woman came between them, and Ethan let go of Andrés and pushed back to the kitchen, where there were fewer people. Slipping through a gap, he saw eight intruders calmly stealing whatever they could find. One of them had found Patito and was trying to corral him with a broom. The boy was crawling around under the table, hiding from the broom and rushing feet while the rest of the looters ignored him. Ethan smashed a frying pan over the head of one of them and hit another in the ear as hard as he could. The man stumbled to the side in a daze and was trying to recover his balance when he got a frying pan to the face. The other looters, who had stopped to watch the show, went back to what they were doing. Andrés had managed to make his way through the sea of bodies and immediately understood as he saw his partner lift the howling child. Ethan had seen something like this before; it was a vivid, horrifying memory. The kind of thing few ever experienced in their lives. Then, he had rescued a fifteen-year-old girl who had been determined to defend a baby from a mob even though she could have been knocked out easily and possibly killed. Acting with preternatural calm and calculation, Ethan was determined to prevent it from happening again. Andrés caught up with him and was chilled to see that his friend didn't appear to be fully aware of what he was doing. He was relying on survival instinct and body memory alone.

"You're very good."

Ethan didn't hear him. His mind was elsewhere, his gaze blank. "The patio."

They went out into a small, barren space barely six feet square, separated from other similar patios by wire fences. Andrés climbed over and asked for the boy, who was still clinging to Ethan's neck like a screaming monkey. Just when he managed to shake the boy free and hand him over, someone came out from the kitchen.

"Hey! What are you doing? Are you family members? You're not going to—"

Ethan interrupted the man with a few punches before jumping over the fence. He took back Patito, and they ran through another tiny patio, pulled away another weak fence, and ducked into a shed. As they went inside, Andrés sniffed the air.

"Do you smell something burning?"

Ethan went back out onto the patio. Black smoke was rising up through the gaps in the corrugated iron roof.

"Come on—let's go."

Their ears ringing with the sound of the chaos behind them, they crossed through the shed and came out into an alley. As they left, they bumped into a young man in a vest and baseball cap, a sartorial style like that of Jonathan. They stopped uncertainly. Fortunately, he held up his hands in a conciliatory gesture.

"Are you trying to save the baby?"

Ethan sized him up, trying to guess his intentions, but then Andrés recognized him. "You were in the kitchen. You're one of the looters!"

The man stepped back in fright. "Yes, I was there with my guys. But I saw you take the kid and came out to see where you were going. I was ashamed that I didn't do anything to help."

"And now you're going to help us?" Ethan asked suspiciously.

"If I don't, my grandma will be pissed. I'm Lorena's grandson."

The name meant nothing to Ethan, but Andrés stepped forward to reassure him. "I've heard of her."

The young man smiled. "Are you coming?"

"Where?"

"To see my grandmother, of course."

The three of them crossed the road to get away from the flames, which were beginning to threaten the neighboring walls as they rose higher and higher. They could hear sirens in the distance. They didn't see anyone else for the rest of their journey. Still, they felt eyes on them from all corners. They didn't care; they were just happy to have Patito with them. The boy had passed out from the stress, but he was safe. They stopped in front of another precariously built house that looked no different from any of the others. Their guide asked them to give him five minutes to explain things to his grandmother. He asked for Patito so he could show her, but Ethan refused with a smile that required no further explanation.

"Fine, I wasn't going to steal him. You'll soon see that I'm telling the truth."

He disappeared, giving them their first minute alone since all hell had broken loose.

"Was that how it happened?" Andrés said. "I mean, I'm sorry to ask, but is that how you saved Ari?"

Ethan continued to stare into the middle distance. His gaze was fixed firmly in the past. "Ari had more of a chance than this poor kid . . . it was very different. But yes, it was similar with Sasha." He paused for a long while. "I didn't think I'd ever see faces like that again. I didn't think it could happen so easily. There's something wrong with us. Whatever you believe, there's something dark in us, in how we're made . . ."

Before he could go on, the kid reappeared and invited them in. They headed through shabby rooms that had apparently been decorated in the eighties and then never touched again. At the back, sitting next to a sink with a large bowl of lentils, they found the grave-faced Lorena drying her hands.

"Why don't you give him to me?"

She held out her arms to take the child, but Ethan made no move. She accepted this with equanimity and invited them to sit down before going back to her lentils, cleaning and draining them little by little. She spoke to her grandson in an authoritative voice. "Tinin, you haven't offered them anything to drink."

"I'm sorry, Grandma. Would you like a beer or some juice? My grandma makes it."

"Juice, please. Thank you," Andrés said. "I'm parched."

"Nothing for me right now, thank you," Ethan answered.

Lorena finished washing and went on making her stew, studying them all the while. "Because you don't want to put him down?" She gave Ethan a defiant smile and turned to the child. "Patito, Patito, wake up. Patito, come to Grandma."

Hearing her voice, Patito opened his eyes and suddenly looked more relaxed and began to smile. He saw the old woman and leaped into her lap, paying no attention to Ethan. She hugged him tenderly and whispered something. He nodded. Then she repeated it so everyone could hear. "Would you like to go to bed to sleep a little? You're tired, aren't you?"

He lovingly collapsed onto her chest, and she handed him to her grandson, who was giving Andrés a drink.

"Listen, Tinin will take you to his bedroom and lie down with you. He'll give you a few cookies, and then you'll go to sleep like a good little boy. OK?"

Patito didn't answer, but he allowed himself to be passed over gently and left, clinging to Tinin. He didn't give his saviors a second glance.

"Don't worry about it; he's a baby."

"That wasn't what I was worried about," Ethan said. "After what happened at his house, he doesn't seem very upset. But I will have a beer now."

"They're in the fridge. Make yourself at home. The kid is going to have to learn to forgive and forget. His mother and brother are dead; his house has been burned down. Leidy escaped. I don't know where she went. Nobody paid her any attention."

"How do you know that?" Ethan said. "You were here the whole time."

"I know everything that goes on in these streets."

"And did you know that family sells their own people to kidnappers?"

"I know what happens in the streets but not what goes on in the privacy of their own homes. Families turn bad inside the walls. With their partners and children. I try to take care of them as best I can. That's why I'm everyone's grandmother."

"But you're not Patito's grandmother."

"Not Patito's, no. I only have one grandson left alive. The other two were killed. But I'm a grandmother to all the children. They know that they can always come here; for some of them it's the only place where they feel safe. But Patito: he didn't suffer. His family loved him. From what I could see, anyway. I have no way of knowing what they do in secret. Jonathan and Leidy were like all the other kids around here. You saw what Tinin was doing, and he's a sweetie pie. He has a big heart."

"Like Jonathan?"

"Maybe not. I imagine that Jonathan was the troublemaker. But then I don't know what happened to him in his childhood or with his father. What I mean is that you can't judge people without knowing what it's like around here, in this country."

"I've lived in my country, and I've seen enough," Ethan said. "It's the same story in every city, wherever you are. It might be more violent here, but the principle is the same."

"That's true. Jonathan was the way he was. But we couldn't know . . ." She turned to Andrés. "Neither could you—how could you have imagined that your brother's girlfriend would sell out your niece?"

"How do you know that?" Ethan said.

Lorena laughed as though she were dealing with a naughty schoolboy.

"Oh, my boy. Who do you think I am? I've heard all about it. They were shouting it in the street. I knew a little already: you came to find Michelle, Leidy's boyfriend was her uncle, and they threw a party so they could check you out. Now they're saying that Beto called her to warn her. Did he know something already, or was it just to protect his girlfriend? I don't know that either. If you didn't know, how could I know? I'm just an old woman."

Ethan accepted this explanation and started to stride from one end of the room to the other, chastising himself. "It was right under my nose. How could I not see it?"

"Let me ask you another question. How did you see it?"

"What do you mean?"

"How did you work it out? Suddenly you arrived and knew everything. You knew more than any of us."

Ethan avoided Andrés's gaze so as not to give him away and grew cautious once more. "I'm sure you understand that I can't reveal that to either of you."

"You're right," Lorena said with a shrug. "And it's not as though I care. I may be nosy, but I'm an old woman, aren't I?" She smiled at him sweetly. "Let me tell you why I let you into my home."

"Because we brought you Patito."

"Of course not! Where else were you going to take him? The police? Do you think that no one saw you leave? They let you go because you were with my grandson. I don't care about that. Patito would have come to me one way or another. I just thank God that the police didn't find you. If they took him away, then his life really would be hard. There's no place for orphans in this country, other than the street."

"So what will you do with him now? Do you think that I'm going to leave him here just like that, because you say so? You think I don't care?"

"I can tell from your eyes that you're sincere. That's why you're in my home and I let you have him for as long as I did. Now you're going to go and leave him here. I don't know what we'll do exactly, but he's just another orphan now, and if we don't take care of him, he'll be a Mara before he turns eight. If Jonathan was already part of the gang, only God knows whether he might have met an even worse fate. The kid will grow up with us, and you, young man, will never see him again. He saw you get his mother and brother killed. Have you thought it through? Don't ever forget that, gringo, because he won't, and I don't know how much forgiveness I can teach him."

Ethan didn't reply. He walked up and down a couple more times, thinking. "What about the sister?"

"We don't know where she went. But I know her: she'll assume that they killed him, too, and even if she doesn't, she won't come back. Patito's on his own."

"I'm sure you're right. But that doesn't mean that this is the best place for him. Andrés, you must know someone who can take him in? Someone from your church, maybe. I don't know . . ."

Andrés raised his eyebrows doubtfully. Now Lorena was annoyed. She addressed Ethan in the same authoritative tone as she'd used with her grandson. "Look, young man, don't make me mad. You don't seem to understand. If you call the police, you're the one who's going to be in trouble. They'll take you away. And what do you think's going to happen to you in jail? Who do you think they'll lock you in with? The Mara won't forgive you for what you've done. This is their territory, and they don't like it when things like this happen. I know you're not stupid; you knew that, and that's why you escaped. I may be an old woman, and I may not know everything, but don't treat me like a fool."

"I didn't mean to offend you. I know you're right. What should we do now?"

"You'll leave Patito here. I'll help you to get out. You need to hide, I think, until the police have shut everything down. It won't be hard; the people around here will tell them the whole story, that the family sold kids to kidnappers and they confronted them. Then the house caught on fire, and they were trapped inside, but no one killed anyone. And no one will mention the gringo who got there first. They don't tell the cops things like that, but the Mara must know already. Now, my boy, you have an easy choice to make." She turned to Andrés. "Leave now, and don't come back for a few days. The car you came in is still parked in the same place—you can get it later. They won't ask you any questions. They don't know you. But the *gringuito* who came around asking questions about the girl . . . he can't stay here."

"And why are you going to help me?"

"Because I'm everyone's grandmother. I've been watching you—you've done things that no one has done to find the girl. And today my grandson told me everything. That's why you were allowed in my house. If I don't help you after everything you've done, including saving the boy, then I don't deserve the name anymore. That's why no one is going to report you or stop you from leaving."

"Well, I suppose I have no choice but to believe you. Thank you."

"Thank you, my son. I've rarely seen anything like it in my life. You do think the girl's still alive?"

"I'm sure of it."

Lorena didn't answer, but she looked deep into Ethan's eyes. He felt as though she were looking right through him. "It's true. You really think so."

"I wouldn't be here otherwise."

"You're strange . . . interesting but strange . . . I'm glad to have met you. Listen, I can only give you some advice. Listen to me if you want, and if you don't, the two of you are free to drive off in your car."

"I'm listening."

"My advice is for you to leave the city right now. Don't stop anywhere or talk to anyone so that the people who know you won't know what to say when they're asked. I can suggest a lovely place on the beach. It's close by, and buses leave for it regularly. If you take my advice, my grandson will take you to the station. He'll hide you in his car, and no one will stop him, not even the police, because they know him. You go to the beach for a few days, three or four or for however long it takes until things calm down, and then you can call Andrés, and he'll tell you if it's safe for you to come back. Don't leave an address or anything; just take money. Make yourself impossible to find. Don't let any of your friends let it slip by mistake."

"You want me to go to the beach, out of touch with everyone? Are you sure that that's a good idea?"

"Don Ethan, forgive the interruption," Andrés said. "I think I know what she's saying . . . and I think she's right. You shouldn't be here when they start asking questions. They mustn't see you, because if they do, the best that can happen is for you to be deported. We mustn't know where you've gone. I have money to lend you. I'll make sure it's enough so you don't even have to use your card."

Lorena received this unexpected support with an inquisitive gaze. "This isn't any old beach. I'll tell him which hotel to go to. I know some people there. He'll be safe with them. Only they and I will know. I'll give you the name of the place when your friend leaves. You have a choice: do what I say, or go your own way. It's up to you, but you need to decide now. Good deeds are rare, and they should be repaid. If I let you go without helping, God will punish me. That's why I let you into my home."

Ethan was utterly caught off balance by the turn the situation was taking. Before the first problem was even over, he was having to deal with the next.

"Don't take this the wrong way, but I don't know you." He looked for support from his friend but was met with determination.

"Forgive me for contradicting you, Don Ethan, but I think she's right."

"Fine, fine." He led Andrés to one side. "Can we pass by the hotel?"

"It's the wrong way."

"All my things are there, as well as the gun Calvo got me. I need you to pick up my suitcase and keep it safe. I can't leave it in a hotel for three days, especially not with a weapon."

His lunch was *arepas a la reina pepiada*, or so the owner of the establishment had said. He wasn't going to come back. The food was heavy and oily, and he knew that later on he'd get indigestion. Eventually the old man summoned him on the phone, and he drove there with his trailer. The bastard complained again, asking why he hadn't left it in the garage—it got in the way. He explained, once again, that he couldn't let it out of his sight. The man knew that very well— they'd been over this already, so there was no point arguing about it anymore. The old man laughed, assuming that he was smuggling something, and the Beast laughed even harder inside, thinking that if this *indio* knew what he was really transporting . . . but if he told him, he'd have to kill him. No doubt about it.

So he stood by the truck while they changed his license plates, and the old man's assistants gave him the fake documentation and talked him through it. When they'd finished, he contacted the distributor to ask if he could pick up the new trailer yet. He told the mechanics to hurry up; he was worried about the merchandise. This wasn't compassion—he'd left her locked up for a long time. She might wake up, although she couldn't make much noise bound and gagged like she was, but if she suffered from dehydration, it would be very bad. He knew that if he ever lost a package or if it arrived in poor condition, he might pay for it with his life. So as the hours dragged on and he worried that she would choke on her own tongue or die of heatstroke or stress, he grew more and more irritable. He hurried them along as much as he could, desperate to get out of there. Finally they gave him the OK to leave, and the old man told him that it was a pleasure doing business with him again. The Beast was just as friendly—and false—with his goodbye.

He had grown so anxious that he decided to stop before picking up the trailer, choosing a deserted rest stop. He took the bottle of water and reached under the chassis for the lock to the lower compartment. When he opened it, he found the small body curled up in the false bottom. She was breathing quickly, but apart from the sweat and urine, she seemed unhurt. He took the sack off her head, and she nodded in confusion, still feeling the effects of the drug. He was pleased to see that she didn't understand what was going on. He removed her gag and offered her the drink, which she accepted eagerly. When she'd taken her third gulp and started to open her mouth, he pulled up the gag and covered her head again. With that much water, she'd piss herself again, but it would cool her down, he thought, laughing to himself. He calculated that it would take another half hour for the drug to fade away completely, so he had just enough time.

He headed for the large warehouse and asked for the foreman, who was waiting for him. He looked over the trailer, which was smaller than his last, and they gave him a signed and sealed delivery slip. He was assuming the identity of a truck that had gone in the other direction and would be coming back once it had been unloaded, which would allow him to cross the opposite border. Once they got to the safe house, he'd give the truck a new coat of paint: all red—he was tired of black—and he'd have it detailed with a devil and a pole dancer. It was a design he'd seen somewhere that he liked a lot. Maybe he'd even modify the hood. He felt like resting for a few days; it was something he'd been thinking about for a while. But the most urgent thing right now was to put the merchandise in the top bunk so it could sleep and rest before they went through customs and immigration. He had to make sure that she survived the journey.

Ethan was hiding under some blankets on his way to the station, wondering how things had come to this. What was he going to do when he got to the beach without a change of clothes and only the money Andrés had given him? He was going to disappear for three days. Three days without showing any sign of life, without calling Ari or answering her messages. She'd go crazy before he could explain anything. After what felt like a hot, stuffy eternity, Lorena's grandson pulled away the blankets, and Ethan followed him into a bustling crowd on an esplanade lined with repurposed American school buses known as chicken buses. The owners had decorated their vehicles with a lively mixture of colors and took obsessive care of them. They were especially keen to make sure to polish the hubcaps so that they gleamed before they headed out onto the dusty or muddy roads. The buses were treated like moving works of art, and in some ways they were. If you inspected each bus separately, you'd get an idea of the driver's personality, while if you stepped back from the whole, the effect was certainly remarkable. In the United States, these vehicles had been headed for the wrecker's yard.

Squawking at hundreds of passengers loaded down with suitcases, bags, and packages of all kinds, livestock included, the loudspeakers announced the destination of each new departure, directing the different groups like sheepdogs herding their flock. The effectiveness of the chaotic system stunned Ethan, and before he knew it, he found himself on a seat he might well have used as a child. Seats designed for two were soon taken up by three people. Before they set out, he was able to get a look at the sticker with the weather-beaten face of Christ decorating the driver's-side window, accompanied by the words THIS MORNING I WENT WITH JESUS. IF I DON'T COME HOME TONIGHT, I LEFT WITH HIM. Long-distance passenger buses had become prime targets for extortion. The drivers, who coddled their property like a pet, had to pay a "war duty" to the gangs that controlled the territory their route went through. Any who refused were killed, sometimes shot in the middle of the road, filled full of bullets right in front of their passengers to teach them a lesson. After reading the rather unsettling message, Ethan decided to try to get some sleep.

The journey was long, and its comfort level depended on the number of passengers crammed into the vehicle. The main freeway was smooth and well maintained, but the road became a double-headed snake as soon as they got into the mountains. A snake on which the buses changed lanes whenever they felt like it, forcing cars they came across to make way if they didn't want to risk being pushed over the edge. Looking through the clouds at the other peaks in the distance, Ethan saw that right-of-way was defined by size, not traffic regulations.

As they passed through the villages, the bus grew more crowded. The two-seat rows were filled by up to four people, and standing space was populated by a crowd that was made to hop with every bump. Right at the top of the mountains, just when it seemed that no one else would fit, the collector shouted at them all to move farther back, and when no one paid any attention, he opened the emergency exit and shoved in ten more passengers. They spent the rest of the journey with the door half-open, the collector clinging to it to make sure that no one fell out. At the height of the crush, Ethan could have sworn that he heard a clucking sound, although he had no idea where it was coming from.

Now the almost-empty bus had reached the final stop, a metal post with no signs that Ethan took care to remember for the return journey. Beyond the village, which spread out in six irregular strips from the main road, a narrow path to the beach ran underneath an irregular canopy of palm trees. In the distance he could see several very pale women, Americans or Europeans, riding bicycles; they were about sixty years old, clad in bikinis, wraps, Caribbean braids, and other hippie-style attire. Somewhere among the trees the dust turned into sand, and after five or six rows of palm trees, which covered the path with fallen fronds, the sand turned into a beach. The coast consisted of a series of peaceful bays, over which leaned arching palm trees like an image on a postcard. The beach was so narrow that the sea reached right up to the trunks at high tide.

In spite of the setting, the village lacked character, like all towns ruined by tourism. Its uneven streets were excessively wide, as though designed to accommodate nonexistent traffic. This gave it a bleak look compared to the lush surroundings. In the center, which was sandwiched between the road and the coast, generic stores lined up offering clothes, artisanal products, surfing equipment, and bicycle rentals. These alternated with restaurants and hotels, the latter being the only buildings that rose higher than two stories. The housing had been pushed out right to the other side and crowded around a supermarket that hid them and their residents from the tourists. In that seventy-five-foot strip the ground itself changed color, turning black, while garbage littered the facades. Chickens scurried around patios filled with mechanical and electronic detritus, motorcycle chassis, and metal bed frames.

Ethan had come on the last bus of the day, and the sun was going down behind him. Every corner of the commercial district was lit, and visitors were wandering around happily. There weren't many families to be seen, and the atmosphere was dominated by low-volume music coming out of the bars, which eagerly awaited the surfers and dark-skinned hunks trying their luck with adventurous women who had come to this remote place hoping to experience precisely that fantasy.

Like all unfamiliar places, certainly anywhere in Central America, nightfall had an unpleasant, unsettling sheen to it. Ethan saw a pair of men in municipal uniforms sitting on a dilapidated stone bench and went over to ask for directions. When he got closer, he realized that he didn't understand what they were saying; they were talking in *garifuna* or some other dialect. But with Ethan's approach they happily switched over to Spanish, albeit a heavily accented coastal Spanish.

"I'm looking for Hostel Anunga."

"Eww! No, buddy, no go there."

"Nasty, bro, that place is nasty."

They pointed to the unlit part of the village.

"Don't go there, buddy. I'll take you to a much better one."

"Take him to the Miriam."

"Not the Miriam, bro, the Caribe, bro, they have a much better breakfast. That's where you'll get the real rice and beans."

"Oh yeah, they do good rice and beans there. The cook is the best, better than at the Miriam—she's my cousin."

"The real *Caribe*, man."

They both laughed at this witticism. Ethan began to suspect that they were under the effects of a well-rolled joint. The younger one seemed to read his mind and tried to help him out.

"Are you looking for some good stuff, bro? We can hook you up."

"Very good stuff, creepy."

"Yeah, man, very good."

They laughed again, as though it were an inside joke.

"All the Americans come to try our stuff."

"Straight from the jungle, man."

"Pure jungle, man."

"It hits you hard, bro."

Seeing how high they were, Ethan started to laugh along with them. "Thank you, but I've only just arrived. The thing is I have to go to Hostel Anunga."

"No, bro, it's nasty. It's not for tourists."

"Yeah, man, don't go there."

"A friend of mine told me to go there. She said it had to be that one."

"Has your friend been there?"

"She said she had, and she phoned ahead. They're waiting for me."

"Duuuuuuude!"

They both shook their hands and clicked their fingers in triumph.

"That's different, man. That's great!"

"Good on you, brother—they're going to treat you so well."

"Your breakfast, man."

"Very good, the best rice and beans. My cousin makes it."

"Pure rice and beans with coconut sauce."

"I thought your cousin worked at the Caribe."

"She works for them both, man. But it's cheaper there because it's not for tourists."

Their goodwill was so enticing that Ethan ended up sharing several beers with them, and the day ended as the polar opposite of how it had begun, which only made everything seem more unreal. At some point they walked him to the Anunga and helped him to sign in because the tokes they'd shared with him had clouded his head. He dropped onto his mattress like a lead weight and had unsettling, claustrophobic dreams during which he relived the terrible night when he'd met Ari, only this time she was Sasha, a baby he kept trying to rescue but failed each time. He was beset by anguish and guilt, so much so that he started to cry in his sleep. At one point he had Patito in his arms, but something was taking him away, and the impotence and desperation grew until he gave up. He saw himself repeating the same word over and over again like a mantra: *impotence*. He went on saying it, unsure whether it was in English or Spanish. Eventually the sound itself took on a physical form, like honey flowing from his throat, relieving it of its emotional weight. Then, finally, he was able to rest.

He woke up hot and confused. The sunlight shone brightly in his room, giving him a chance to actually see the room. It was a ramshackle place, painted in a flaking green with a dirty bathroom. Seeing that it was before eight and he was already sweating, he wondered what the advantage was in going to the Anunga rather than a hotel on the beach. At reception he asked whether they had rooms with air-conditioning, and they moved him to the top floor, to a corner where the damp was even more evident and not much more comfortable than the room without air-conditioning. At least his new friends had been right about the breakfast. He looked for an internet café and told Ari on Facebook that he'd be offline for a while but made no further contact with the outside world. It felt as though the horrors of the day before had never happened. Finally, he was able to relax and enjoy his impromptu vacation until he got back to the Anunga and found that the air conditioner was just an embedded portable refrigerator with the back facing outside. Kneeling down, he saw the dangling wheels. He went down to the beach with the basic telephone Andrés had given him. Andrés was his only contact with the rest of the country; his was the only number he could remember. His smartphone and the private one Suarez had given him were back at the hotel. He bought a newspaper with garish, sensationalist headlines. Inside, one story stood out amid the litany of violent crimes: TWO BURNED IN THEIR OWN HOME. It didn't explain how the fire had started or make any reference to mob justice, saying only that "local residents suspected the family of involvement with a criminal gang."

Before he had a chance to call Andrés, his friend sent him a message to reassure him: all his luggage had been safely transferred to his house. They had a brief exchange of texts in which Andrés reported that he hadn't been back to the neighborhood and that his mother, who was still trying to take it all in, swore that she hadn't heard from his brother. He had apparently run off with Leidy. After apologizing, even though he still thought he'd done the right thing, he showed some indication that he was rethinking his approach. He'd asked Michelle to wait until they could decide what to do next; Suarez was apparently following his own leads. Andrés didn't get on well with Calvo and hadn't contacted him to share the new revelations.

Trying to anticipate how long it would be before he was able to return, taking into account the funeral and the time it would take for the investigation to blow over, Ethan decided to plan his next steps. They had to track down Beto before he vanished off the face of the earth. He wondered whether he should set Calvo on the case or whether it should be that arrogant bastard Suarez. Just when he might have used his skills, he'd apparently washed his hands of the whole thing. Ethan missed having Ari there to go over the different options; she'd suggest doing something direct, and he'd have to calm her down, but something good always came from their clash of styles.

On the other side of the road leading into the palm groves, whose traffic was just a few cars and bicycles, a row of hawkers' stalls set up during the day selling different wares: coconut milk, fruit juices and smoothies, local jewelry, and a pair of women offering braids and extensions. One of them, a small, elderly woman sitting in a fold-up chair next to the coconut vendor, whistled at Ethan across the traffic, the way one called a child. Surprised, he turned to either side to see if she meant someone else, but she continued to whistle, clearly pointing at him. He crossed the road and said he wasn't interested in braids. But she'd seen him come out of the Anunga.

"Why that place? They don't even have air-conditioning."

Ethan gave a sigh. "I'm backpacking. It's the only place I can afford. I know the Hotel Caribe is better, but I like the Anunga. I don't care about air-conditioning; it pollutes. Think global, act local, you know?"

"Yes, of course, young man. I was surprised because foreigners don't usually know it, just the people who live here. Did someone give you a tip?"

"I asked around. If you can recommend another place, I'll take a look."

"And where are you going to have lunch?"

"I haven't thought about that yet."

"Don't worry. I know a very good place."

"Thank you—I'll come by later."

Ethan walked away, smiling. He went to check the bus schedule and then spent the rest of the morning thinking about the terrible scenes he'd left behind in the city. The image of the horror was still very fresh. He was dozing in the shade when he felt a gentle tap on his shoulder. He opened his eyes and was faced with the coconut vendor, whom he assumed was the old woman's husband.

"You'll burn if you don't put on sunblock."

"Thank you. I put some on already."

"Rosita sent me to tell you about lunch." The man paused as though this was a grand revelation. "That's Rosita." He offered Ethan a peeled coconut with a straw.

"No, thank you."

"It's a gift. Rosita wants you to have lunch with us. She's invited you."

Ethan looked him in the eyes. They seemed kindly; he must see the invitation as a great honor. As he woke up, something occurred to him. He asked, "Does she know who recommended the hotel?"

"Lorena."

Incredible how they communicate with one another, Ethan thought, following the man.

And so he found himself with an elderly couple in a run-down shack, a small space with a table for four, a flat-screen TV, and a worn-out sofa covered in crochet. The fish-and-rice dish was exquisite and was followed by an excellent drip-filtered coffee. After lunch Rosita invited Ethan into a private back room that was in much better condition, decorated with niches full of saints and religious figures he'd never seen before. The paraments were decorated with light-blue mosaics while the altars themselves were an intense vermilion, creating a pleasant effect. His host started to light candles, solemnly murmuring some kind of litany for each while her husband watched television under a bare light bulb. Eventually, she closed the door, separating them from the outside world. She pulled a dark curtain across the only barred window, and the atmosphere soon grew thick. Then she asked Ethan to sit at a garden table and removed the crochet tablecloth. In its place she lit another candle.

"You see? There was nothing to worry about. Now it's time for your questions."

Ethan didn't understand what she was getting at. He thought it might be a local saying. "What? What questions?"

The woman's face crinkled up in offense. "Lorena didn't tell you about me?"

"We didn't get a chance to talk much. She told me where to stay, nothing more."

"I'm Rosita. Didn't Lorena explain why she sent you to me?"

"She didn't explain a thing."

Rosita didn't get up from her chair, but Ethan could feel her presence fill the room. Finally, she shed the last vestiges of her humility and began to project power and authority. "I can answer your questions."

She closed her eyes and brought her hands close to the candle, mumbling. Ethan started to ask something, but she silenced him with a raised finger. The sun was still out, and although the room was dark, the heat radiated through the metal roof and settled around them. Ethan felt a drop of sweat roll down the side of his face. After a few strange minutes, Rosita spoke again, her eyes still closed. Her eyeballs were moving under her eyelids as though she was asleep, and even so he felt them go right through him.

"The girl. Tell me about the girl."

"The . . . what?"

"Why are you looking for her?"

"Because she was kidnapped. Did Lorena tell you about her?"

"You know we haven't spoken. You have a presence. You're looking for a girl who was taken away. You came to the country to rescue her. It won't be easy; many people are against you, and you have few friends."

"What do you mean?"

"You don't know?"

Ethan shivered. She was reading him like a book.

"Who's stopping you, my friend? Who have you had to cross to come here?"

"My girlfriend," he said, stunned but trying to recover. "You know about the girl, but you don't know that?"

"I can see, but I don't know. You must tell me what I need to know, and I'll help you to see."

"I don't believe in this kind of thing . . ."

"But you believe her."

"My girlfriend?"

Rosita sensed the sarcasm and defensiveness. She leaned back in her chair, staring at him from her unseeing eyes. He could feel a wave of genuine power emanate from her. This was her territory, and everything within it belonged to her.

"The girl. She speaks to you in her dreams. Is that why you came to look for her?"

"I came because she was kidnapped, and I lived with her for a few years. She's kind of like my daughter."

Rosita was slightly mollified by this but not enough. "What does she say?"

"You can't see that?"

"I see you. In danger. Someone here is helping you, but they're not who they say they are."

"I don't understand."

"Yes, you do."

"Her mother and uncle are helping me."

"There's someone else too. A man." She rocked back and forth as though she were in a trance. "I can see him. You think he'll help you, but you shouldn't trust him."

"I don't."

"You don't understand. He knows where the girl is."

Ethan tried not to react, but the shaman sensed his horror.

"How did you find him?"

"The man?"

"He found you. I can see it. He was in . . . a hotel?"

Sweat ran down his neck.

"Tell me, how did you find him?"

"Uh . . . through Andrés."

"Yes, I see. He led you to the ones who took the girl. Didn't you ever ask how he knew?"

"He told me."

"And you believe him?"

Ethan felt a drop of sweat run down his eyebrow and wiped it away with a finger.

Rosita couldn't see him, but she smiled. Her smile was terrifying. "You don't believe him. See what I see. The man has used you to cover his own tracks. Now I need to know what you know."

He was paralyzed, hypnotized by the psychic like a rabbit in the headlights, intimidated by a gaze that wasn't even there. His body began to grow weak from his shoulders down, as though he were leaving it, and his voice began to utter the name. Suarez, the teller of tales, the man who had deceived him and sent Andrés to clean up his mess. Suarez, the traitor who pretended to be a mysterious vigilante to conceal the fact that he was the man Ethan was looking for . . .

Instinctively, without thinking, Ethan reached out to snuff out the candle burning between him and Rosita, removing the glare that had been blinding him and keeping him from seeing the old woman's face. The flame disappeared, and he felt himself released from the spell. He saw a brief twitch in Rosita's face, concealing something just before she opened her eyes.

"What have you done? You mustn't interrupt my communication with the other world! It could be very dangerous for both you and me."

Ethan answered quickly, like a nervous child trying to fool his teacher. "His name is Adrian Calvo, a detective Andrés hired. Now you know what I know. Help me."

"Fool! I can't help you just like that! You almost cut the silver cord." She was furious, raging, exposed. "You've missed your chance to find out more."

"Forgive me. I don't know why I put out the candle. I was afraid." His forehead was drenched in sweat. Now that he was being submissive, Rosita relaxed.

"I gave you the name. He's the one helping us."

Once she realized that she had the name she was looking for, she returned to the role of charitable grandmother.

"You're right, son. Forgive me; you broke my concentration, and that can be dangerous for psychics. I got scared too. Say the name again—I forgot it when you disrupted my flow with the beyond. Tonight I will try to communicate with the spirits again to see if I can find anything else. If so, I'll come to find you and let you know."

Ethan gave her Calvo's name and information again, knowing that whatever Rosita did with them, he'd be able to handle it. He felt bad about dropping him in it like that, but Calvo had demonstrated very clearly that he was a survivor and would be able to defend himself better than Suarez. Doña Rosita must be the local witch doctor, the spiritual leader of the area, maybe even of Lorena and the whole neighborhood. Ethan now knew that he'd never have escaped the trap without giving her a name. She was perceptive and uncommonly sensitive; there was no doubt about that. She must have perfected her skills of suggestion throughout her life, learning how to conjure a kind of trance, a pseudohypnotic state in which she could make her victims do what she wanted. She had never completely closed her eyes: she'd fooled him with the darkness and flames. Ethan thought that was how she controlled her followers or whoever fell into her clutches, leading them down the paths she chose for them. They said goodbye with false affection, and he was pleased to be released from the cage.

Outside, it was almost dark, and the back part of town had returned to its unsettling nighttime atmosphere. Two doors down from Rosita, Ethan's gaze met that of a large, very dark male with unnaturally blue eyes and a muscular body; he was leaning on a doorframe with his arms crossed in a territorial pose. Something about him chilled Ethan's blood. He avoided eye contact and limited himself to a brief nod. The man responded politely with a nod of his own.

Once he was safely back at the Anunga, he called Andrés before his dutiful friend went to bed and asked him to warn Calvo. The detective needed to know that someone might come looking for him in relation to the case. That way he'd be expecting it. The next day Ethan didn't hear from Rosita, and she wasn't at her post on the road. He wondered at her intentions. Why did she want to know who he was working with? Had Lorena known about this when she'd sent him here? After going over their conversation again and again, he reached the conclusion that she had gotten her information from Lorena. Everything she'd said was common knowledge. She had revealed no secrets, but with a little show-manship she'd lent it all a supernatural aura that her believers must have found very convincing. Still, she'd planted a seed of doubt that he couldn't get rid of. It seemed very plausible that Suarez was using his friendship with Andrés to cover his tracks. But there was something unnerving about accepting the woman's version of events. Leidy had disappeared with Beto at the same time as Suarez had stopped answering Andrés's calls, ostensibly to continue his investigation. What was he doing? Following the fugitives so he could kill them and complete the job? Every new piece of information Ethan got just confused him even more.

Sometimes, the ferry journey across the Central American isthmus could take a day or more, especially if you were heading north: a day of sticky heat in your seat or a night in the bunk with nothing to do but nurse your hatred and make sure that the shipment didn't spoil, especially the ones that needed to be refrigerated. Fortunately, the frontier ahead could be crossed quickly; unlike elsewhere, the officials were efficient. Even so, it could easily take three hours, and the Beast worried about the package. It had been deteriorating since the changes in the garage, and he was anxious. He thought there was a chance it would wake up and try to make its presence known by banging on the side of the trailer. Concerned by the girl's slow responses, he'd given her a much weaker dose of the tranquilizer, and now he worried that it might not have been enough. He kept going down into the hold to check, wandering close to the second water tank, listening hard so as to anticipate any unforeseen circumstances. But there was no sound. By the second hour, he was afraid that the opposite might happen: that the long, suffocating road journey had given her heatstroke. But there was no way he could poke his head in there to see. He just made sure to check the temperature of the water in the real tank and, as a precautionary measure, sprayed the other tank with water. Anyone watching would think he was either crazy or just an idiot.

During the final half hour he thought he heard something. He redoubled his rounds, growing more and more nervous. Finally, he was allowed through customs. He didn't have anything to declare, so he quickly got through to the immigration window to have his passport stamped. The officer greeted him with a familiar smile.

"You haven't brought back anything with you? That's bad business, man."

"No, boss. I'm going home to rest for a week. I've been away for a month."

"Get some rest, buddy. It's a hard life, being away from your kids like that."

"You're not wrong."

"God be with you!"

And after three nerve-racking hours, he saw the barrier open before him. *Like a whore's legs*, he thought. *Like a whore—you're all my whores.* But this relief did nothing to calm his fears over the health of the merchandise. Just a couple of miles farther on, he turned off onto the verge and crawled under the belly of the beast. There she was: dehydrated, drenched in sweat, choking on the exhaust fumes. Her face was covered in tears and mucus that dripped down from the handkerchief he'd wrapped around her face, but she was alive and well. He put her in the driver's cabin and forced her to sip from an isotonic drink and eat some cereal bars. He waited for almost half an hour, letting her enjoy the cool breeze. A few minutes later, the girl started to stir and stretch. The Beast finally felt the burden that had been weighing down on him float away. He had a powerful urge to put on his boots. Wearing them made him forget his troubles, the slights he'd suffered and the lack of respect he was shown. They restored the feeling of greatness that the world had not yet seen fit to bestow upon him of its own accord. The only therapy more relaxing was to go to a shoeshine boy in the street and sit down to get the full treatment: it was like a massage, seeing his feet being taken care of from on high. It ensured that everything made sense again. He admired himself in the mirror, raising his feet up onto the dashboard in the absolute certainty that they would impress the girl, like all the females who'd ever seen them. That was their power. He was great—he was smarter than the immigration officer, smarter than all the immigration officers—traveling across the continent with his merchandise as though it were all a grand estate that belonged to him. He stroked the embossed side, feeling its effect on his breathing. He was smarter than anyone who crossed his path, smarter than the girls he stole and their scummy families, smarter than the old man who'd changed his license plates, than the Mafia who'd provided him with his forged documents. Poor fools: they had no idea what he was transporting. He was the Beast. They didn't know what he was capable of.

Pumped up on self-satisfaction, swollen with pride, he took the trouble to open a packet of baby wipes and clean the package's face and arms to cool her skin. He even lifted her shirt, which by now had been torn to shreds, and cleaned her torso. As he did so, he flipped her over a couple of times to examine her body. In a couple of years she'd be just right for him. As he turned her over, he unselfconsciously groped her stomach and buttocks. The girl, revived a little by the cool towelettes, kept still during the deeply invasive inspection. The Beast felt her soft skin and, almost without realizing it, began to speak.

"Have you seen these, babe?" He grabbed her hand and placed it on the boot leather, but this didn't draw a reaction either. "Don't worry; you can touch them. They're very expensive, handmade from snakeskin, just for me. Your family could never afford anything like these."

The girl, still half-drugged, stayed rigid.

"Look at my eyes. Look at my piercing gaze. It's piercing." Every time he said the word, he felt more and more pleasure. But she still didn't react. "Whatever— you don't even know what the word means, babe."

As he felt his excitement grow, he stopped himself, remembering that the merchandise was off limits. He took off his boots to avoid further temptation and put her in the back of the cabin to recover for what was left of the journey.

"Come on, whore. Get in there. Stay quiet, and sit tight if you don't want to get into any trouble."

Ethan was flicking through a Roberto Bolaño book he'd found in the only thrift store in town. It stocked everything from sports gear to canned food and CDs. It was a charming place, slightly run down, managed by a half-crazy Dutchman who barely spoke any Spanish. It was now quite late, and he was surprised to hear a knock at his door. When he opened up, he found the beaming concierge.

"Good evening. I'm sorry to bother you so late. Some friends are waiting for you downstairs."

"I don't have any friends here."

"They're your friends."

"Like I said, I don't have any friends here. Tell them that, and if they don't leave, call the police."

But instead of doing what he said, the receptionist kept on smiling and persevered in a tone that he imagined to be friendly but came off as simply wheedling. "Forgive me: I didn't explain myself properly. I meant that they're friends of the hotel. They're good people. I'm sure they'll help you with your problem."

Ethan stepped over to the door to close it, looking for his phone, but the intruder got in his way.

"You only have to go with them."

"Get out."

The receptionist stepped back, keeping up his friendly front. "They're friends."

Ethan slammed the door and jumped across the bed. He peered out the window, trying to stay hidden, but the street was completely dark, and all he could see were the tops of the palm trees lit up from his own window. There was no way to know if someone was spying on him. While he was still at the window, he heard the key turn in the lock. They weren't trying to force it—the key could have come only from reception. He jumped to try to block it, but it was open by the time he got there. The receptionist reappeared, bolstered by three shadows standing behind him and his tense smile. His grimace widened with obscene pleasure, distorting his face and narrowing his eyes. He looked like a hyena, showing the few teeth he had left, several cavities, gold fillings, and all of his gums. He was the very image of a cut-price assassin.

"Forgive me. There's nothing to worry about; they're friends."

Ethan didn't really mind the ambush and the imminent danger. What really got to him was that he'd allowed himself to be trapped by a soap opera villain, someone so obvious that he seemed to revel in his own stupidity. The concierge stepped aside to reveal the dead-eyed, intimidating individual Ethan had seen near Rosita's house the night before.

"You should be grateful. They're friends of Doña Rosita. This is a great privilege."

Not knowing what to expect, Ethan was led back to Rosita's cabin through a dark, quiet town whose streets hid secrets he didn't want to know. Rosita's husband opened the door for him, and his escort stayed outside. No one said a word. Their quiet footsteps were drowned out by the rumbling of the waves and rustling in the nearby jungle. Rosita waited for Ethan in the back, the same place where she'd tried to scam him before, sitting among her candles. These were the only source of light in the house. Her husband closed the door behind him, and so once again they found themselves facing each other in candlelight. Ethan was surprised that they'd discovered his lie so quickly and wondered if he'd be able to get away again without selling out Suarez. Then, the question that had been tormenting him for a while now raised its head: Should he sell him out? Who were they working for? Rosita remained expressionless. She didn't ask him to sit down, and he remained standing, trying to make eye contact. This time, she made no pretense at keeping her eyes closed. He was surprised by what he saw in them: fear.

"Who is he?"

"I told you yesterday, a detective we hired. He has contacts—"

"I don't care about your detective or your kidnappers," Rosita raged in a booming voice. "You know what I'm talking about. What have you done to me?"

Now Ethan heard danger in her voice, the danger of a cornered animal. For the first time, he realized that this woman could do him harm.

"I haven't done anything to you. I promise."

She fixed him with a terrifying stare, but he looked past it, seeing her properly for the first time. The woman seemed to have changed since the afternoon before; she was in a nightshirt and old robe, as though she didn't care about her appearance. Her sparse hair was messed up like she'd just rolled out of bed or hadn't gone to bed at all. Her burning eyes continued to bore into him. "How did you make me dream of her?"

The veil was lifted, and now he saw her for what she was: a frightened little girl. Suddenly she had become the only person in the world who had shared his experience. Apparently it had been quite traumatizing.

"Have you dreamed of Michelle?"

The old woman nodded, looking uncertain.

"What did you see?"

"I don't know. What did you do to me?"

"I didn't do anything. I thought you were the psychic."

Rosita held back a sob. "You don't know who he is either? I've never seen anything like it. It was real. Oh, God save me, it was real, and I saw it."

The statuettes of saints and offerings remained unmoved. Rosita's gaze had lost its depth and confidence. She seemed afraid she'd never get it back. She fixed her eyes on Ethan again, angry but imploring at the same time. "How do you see him?"

"Who?"

"The man."

"What man?"

"You know who I mean; stop playing the fool."

"You mean in the dreams? I've never seen a man."

"He was there. Close your eyes. Remember him."

Ethan did so and immediately began to feel afraid. He tried to remember the dreams, but he couldn't. He regretted not having written them down.

The frightened voice of the psychic tried to nudge him along. "He was there the whole time—you must have seen him. With the girl."

Then, although he couldn't have explained how it happened, an idea formed in his mind, something like a blurry face in a negative. A looming, expanding body. A shape that wasn't seen but rather felt. A volume, occupying space. "It was the presence that Michi saw."

The woman broke into a nervous laugh, crying a little. "Did you see him? He's there all the time."

"Is he a man?"

"No, no," Rosita said, shaking her head. "I think that she creates him. I don't know what it is. He only has one eye, did you see?"

"I'm not sure. I think so."

"What did he look like to you?"

Ethan made an effort to describe him but failed. It wasn't a visual idea but a concept that was also somehow three dimensional. He knew that she was right: one of the eyes was blind, but he didn't know because he could see it. It was just how the man was. "I . . . I don't know."

"The jacket. Look at the jacket, the vest."

That nudged a memory. "A three-piece suit, I think. With a waistcoat and leather shoes. Pearl gray. It looks old fashioned, like from the thirties."

Even though he could describe him, Ethan knew that he hadn't seen him. It was as though he were describing something he'd read in a book.

Rosita giggled again, her jaw trembling. "That's how she sees him. She doesn't want you to find him; she wants to protect you. Now focus on him. Forget everything else. Forget the girl. What does he look like?"

"I don't understand."

"Think of the man outside the room where you saw her. Focus on his face, his complexion, his height. Tell me, if you saw him in the street, would you be able to recognize him?"

Ethan tried to isolate just the distinguishing features. It was obvious; it hadn't occurred to him before, but a man with one eye must be easy to pick out in a crowd. And yet he was still unable to provide a description. "Uh . . . but this can't be. I can't say anything. The suit wasn't there; I didn't see him at all. Just the eye, like you said."

"It's as though he doesn't have a body, isn't it?"

"Yes. I can't actually see what we're describing."

"Because it doesn't exist. He looks like that because that's the image he has of himself—he creates it because it's his idea of reality. The girl creates a body, like all children do, to make him more human and assuage her fear. You didn't see him. You saw the image of him she created."

"I don't understand. What about the clothes? Why would a girl dress him like that?"

"I don't know—it's the mind of a child," Rosita said. "Maybe it means something to her or she saw a movie where an evil man dressed like that."

"He's evil," Ethan answered instinctively.

Rosita laughed but soon broke into a distraught sob. "He's very evil, the incarnation of evil. Where he comes from, there are much worse things, pain and cruelty we can't conceive of, but here he is the absolute worst thing you can imagine." She shook as she talked. "You mustn't find him, do you understand? It's very important that you understand. When the girl is free of her nightmare, she won't see him again because he's trapped in that world, but if you find him before her, they'll kill you. Do you understand? You must know that; it's the most important thing."

"How do you know?"

The old woman curled up in her chair, hugging herself. "I don't know. She spoke to me. I woke up, and I knew. I don't know any more. I never want to see or hear from you or her again. I don't want to have anything more to do with you."

Ethan waited a few minutes for her to calm down.

Finally she looked up, herself again. "I'll walk you out."

They went out the door. The husband was nowhere to be seen. Outside, the four men were waiting without saying a word, vague shapes in the dim moonlight. The boss's light-blue eyes gleamed in the darkness. At an imperceptible nod from Rosita he came over submissively.

She squeezed his arm hard. "Martin. This man is either blessed or cursed, but there's nothing we can do about it. Nothing is to happen to him. Did you hear me, boy? Nothing is to happen to him."

They escorted him back to the hotel, where the reception was unattended and his key was on the desk. He took it and turned around, and the shadows disappeared. When he got back to his room, everything was where it should be. He went over to the telephone and found seven missed calls from Andrés. Surprised, he read the several messages he'd sent:

Don Ethan, I've tried calling but I can't reach you. CALL ME when you see this message.

Don Ethan, I hope you're well. If you don't answer, I'll call the police. Michelle has been attacked, she's been taken to the hospital. I don't know if she'll make it. I'm going over there but I can't reach you and I'm afraid they might have attacked you too.

5

Uncomfortable Truths

The bus station, with its aura of dust and diesel, looked inert to Ethan, in spite of the parade of passengers and luggage moving around him in a blur. In the end, Andrés had been unable to pick him up, and he found himself in the gray, worn-out station, suffering the fate of solitary travelers. But then he was approached by a gentleman of some bulk who introduced himself as Osvaldo. Ethan remembered his name; he was the taxi driver Andrés trusted. Typical of Andrés, he'd sent Osvaldo in his place with the keys for Ethan's next home. Now that Ethan was a little more familiar with the city, he guessed that it was on the opposite side of the city from Doña Maria's house, and the driver confirmed this. Unaware of the circumstances, Osvaldo asked him if he knew their mutual acquaintance through an NGO or whether he was there for business.

"We're working on something together."

Osvaldo accepted this naturally. Ethan's new neighborhood was almost entirely occupied by gringos and Europeans involved with various humanitarian projects. An almost foreign atmosphere had sprung up, so much so that at the nearby stores, one of which was run by an Italian couple, it was easier to get food from back home than anything local. Several bars had also sprung up to cater to the local community and a hip crowd from the city.

The difference was obvious right from the entrance, which was gated and monitored by a uniformed man stationed in a guardhouse. He'd been given advance notice of Ethan's arrival and asked for his passport to verify his identity. Once he'd been registered, he handed over the keys to the RAV4, which Andrés had left there the previous day. The property consisted of a quarter-mile main road flanked on either side by two-story buildings with slanted roofs. Each unit had a pair of parking spaces. The buildings were organized to maximize the number of potential occupants: they were split into two independent apartments. His belonged to the first floor beneath another that appeared to be empty. Osvaldo told him that this was normal given the rapid turnover of residents: the apartments were rented by the companies they worked for, and they kept up the leases even when they were empty. Andrés had shown excellent judgment. In addition to placing him in the district farthest away from Mara influence, he'd put him in the only spot in the city where he'd go unnoticed. As soon as Osvaldo left him, Ethan went inside and picked up his bags, which were on the bed. He took out his clothes and the gun. Then he showered and got ready to go right back out.

Throughout his return journey he'd kept in constant contact with Andrés, who explained what had happened to Michelle. In the end it had been a scare but not nearly as bad as they'd initially thought. A woman had found Michelle lying unconscious in an avenue and had called for help. When none of the passing cars had stopped, the passerby had jumped in front of a taxi. The taxi driver had swerved, thinking it might be a robbery or a panhandling bum. The cab had hit the woman and tried to drive off, but the passenger had seen what had happened and made the driver stop. The injuries to the Good Samaritan were actually more severe than Michelle's. Just another demonstration of the crazy way things worked in these parts.

Michelle hadn't suffered any broken bones and had asked to be discharged as soon as she recovered consciousness, but she'd been kept overnight under observation. Ethan and Andrés had gone back and forth about the details of picking up Michelle. At first they'd decided to go together, and then Andrés had said Michelle would leave on her own and would not be going back to her mother's. Finally, Michelle had agreed to wait for them, but then Andrés had said he needed to tend to his business, which he'd been neglecting of late. So now Ethan was on his way to the hospital. When he arrived, he found that it wasn't a hospital but a private clinic. Ethan was surprised at the quality of the facilities and wondered whether Andrés could afford all this. As Ethan came into the lobby, the receptionist acted as though she had been expecting him.

"A pleasure. Miss Michelle Orozco is almost ready to leave. If you like, you can take a seat, and I'll let her know you're here."

Ethan ignored her and went straight into the room where Michelle was waiting for him. When he opened the door, he found her asleep on the large bed, which wasn't surprising given the amount of sedatives in her system. She woke up groggy, and like back at the supermarket, he felt as though he were seeing the real Michelle: her face was swollen, her eyes bandaged, and her lips scratched. Michelle was defenseless without her makeup armor. There wasn't a hint of sensuality or coquettishness about her. She looked vulnerable, even bereft. Michelle opened her only good eye and wasn't at all upset that he was seeing her in that state. Nor did she seek refuge in self-pity. She smiled, revealing a gap in her teeth and emphasizing the swollen mouth covered in bruises and the scabs over her eye. Michelle wasn't smiling with her habitual, studied composure but with the humble happiness of a girl getting a treat. When she spoke with a kind of echo in her voice, Ethan realized that she was still stoned.

"Ethan!" She sat up clumsily, speaking with childish glee. "This is good, isn't it? It's good that this happened. I was so scared . . . but it's good for us."

Ethan tried to coax her up off the bed, not sure what she meant.

"It means that Michi is alive, doesn't it? I thought that when they were hitting me and while they were sewing me up here. They wouldn't be doing this if she wasn't alive. They're doing it because they're scared, because we're on the right track. At first I was terrified of what would happen to me, but when I realized that, I stopped caring. While I was lying on the ground and they were just kicking me, trying to finish me off, I didn't care. I couldn't even move. It was a very strange feeling: I tried to move my arms and legs so I could get up, but nothing happened. It was like I was dreaming. The people who saw me later thought that I'd lost my mind; it sounded as though they were speaking through a tube. When they brought me here, they thought that I'd passed out, but I could hear them talking. They were wondering whether I was going to die or not. I was happy because I knew that if the kidnappers weren't afraid, they wouldn't have done this to me. They would have just killed me. I didn't care because my girl is alive, and the only thing that scared me about dying was the idea that I'd never see her again."

Her happy, innocent words sank deep. Ethan stopped trying to get her off the bed and sat down next to her, took her hand, just nodding.

She went on, but her voice faded a little. "In the end, we never got together for you to tell me about your dreams."

"They're just dreams."

"But they aren't, are they? I believe you, you know."

At this, he put his other hand over hers. Ethan could see the bloodstains under her nails. One of them had almost come off—it almost certainly would in the next few days—but she didn't bother to hide them. She wasn't hiding anything. Behind the veil of wounds and bruises, she looked bright and clean.

"Talk to me. I know she spoke to you. Tell me about it, please."

For the next quarter of an hour, he tried in vain to provide a coherent account of what he'd experienced. He jumped from one dream to the next, mixing them up and allowing them to run together. He intentionally left out his meeting with Rosita and softened the worst parts of the nightmares to avoid giving too gloomy a picture. But Michelle begged him to tell her everything, and she took it well. She listened as though he were talking to her about a daughter who just happened to be living in another country. It was like he'd just been to visit her. Her eyes grew damp as he repeated the things she'd said. When he'd finished, all trace of joy had disappeared, and she was fighting back the tears.

"That's her. She loves you so much . . . she never forgot you. I wasn't a good mother; I didn't give her what she needed. I don't know why I do the things I do. I don't know why . . ."

She hugged him, and he gently stroked the back of her head.

"Why did she contact you, Ethan? Why didn't she speak to me? I want her to be happy—I never screamed at her; I never treated her badly—but I don't know how to make her happy. I don't know how to give her what she wants. I'm bad, Ethan. I'm a bad mother."

She buried her head in his neck to hide her tears, which began to flow like a swelling river. Eventually, a burst of hiccups indicated that her sobbing had reached a climax. Ethan felt that the only thing he could do was hug her while she drenched his shirt.

"You're not bad with her. We lived together. I've seen how you are with her," Ethan said. "I know what you're willing to do to get her back. Look at what's happened to you. Michi is alive, and we're going to get her back."

"I never paid her enough attention."

"Then you can fix that."

She drew back, revealing a face swollen even farther by her outburst. Her bandages were wet and wrinkled, and her nose was dark with bruising. Snot dripped from the tip. Instead of being ashamed, she broke into another smile and reached for a tissue. "I must look ridiculous. Between the cuts on your face and my bruises, we must make quite a pair."

"A pleasure to meet you, madam. You're looking very well."

She laughed again, and her voice recovered its earlier joy. "Thank you, Ethan. Thank you for being who you are. You've restored my hope. Only now it's more than hope. You've brought Michi back to me. She trusts you. Now I'm sure that I'll see her again, and it's all thanks to you. I love you so much, Ethan."

Michelle took hold of his face, and Ethan's gaze met that of her only good eye, which was bloodshot and bruised but still stared up at him in adoration. He'd never felt adoration from her before, the kind of adoration that she used to reserve for the goons who just used her and tossed her away. Back then, he'd have given anything to get her to look at him like that. He felt as though this was the first time he had ever truly known her. What he saw in her injured face was genuine beauty, the soul of a little girl afraid to grow old, happy in spite of her pain because he'd helped her to dream of her daughter. She may have had only one visible pupil, but it was still a wealth of contrasts, brimming over with gratitude and love. Michelle, moving clumsily as though her body were a stranger to her, leaned over and, ignoring the pinpricks of pain, covered his lips in tiny, dry little kisses that felt like the flapping of butterfly wings. Ethan allowed himself to be kissed but initially didn't respond. Then their mouths opened, and her tongue delved in deeply. The faint taste of blood from the assault came to him. She wrapped her good arm around him as best she could and clung to his body like a creeper, driven by a need to merge with him, to fuse them together so she could lose herself in his muscles. It was a need he'd never sensed in her before. They came together in a long kiss that began as intimacy and eventually became, for him anyway, an erotic experience.

She leaned back gently, and as she stroked his cheeks with her broken nails, she purred, "I love you, Ethan. I always wondered why I couldn't before, but now I know. I love you."

Doña Maria was ironing as she waited for her daughter to come home, listening to the romantic music she loved. As she lifted the sheets to fold them, she swayed her hips deftly to the beat. Leidy applauded her dancing.

"Let me help you."

"Oh, honey, don't worry. You've suffered enough. Now that Michelle's coming back, she'll help me with everything. You need to nurse your grief. Take a rest. You've looked after me so well over the past few days."

"It's the least I can do. You saved me; I couldn't be more grateful. If it weren't for Beto's love, I'd . . ." Leidy trailed off, and although her words had been filled with praise and flattery, her broken tone left no one in any doubt about the difficult moment she was going through.

Beto was curled up on the sofa next to her, checking out the soccer results, deaf to the conversation. He turned to Leidy. "Hey, love. Would you bring me a beer?"

"Of course, my king."

During a commercial, he opened the fresh can and addressed his mother in a childish, wheedling tone. "Mommy, when is Michelle getting back with the gringo? I'm scared about what he'll say when he sees Leidy and me."

"Don't worry, *m'hijo*; you have nothing to be afraid of. This is your home, and this is where you'll stay. If your sister has a problem with that, well . . . she has someone to take care of her, but who's going to cook for you and take care of you? Who else but me? And then there's poor Leidy. She's just been through a tragedy. She's lost everything."

"But you'll tell him that Leidy had nothing to do with what her family did, won't you?"

"Don't worry, *m'hijo*. While your girlfriend is in this house, she's like the second daughter I never had. Aren't you, honey?"

"Whatever you say, *señora*. I couldn't be more grateful to you. This is another home to me, better than my home . . ." She broke down in tears again, just as she had before.

"It's my pleasure, my pleasure. While I'm in charge of this house, it's yours. No one, *no one*, can say any different."

Beto went over to his girlfriend and perfunctorily brushed his lips against her cheek. Then, as though he'd done his duty, he let her go on washing the dishes and, while she cried into the sink, turned off the sports program, which had switched to basketball. He sat at the table with its white plastic tablecloth, picked up some pan dulce left over from breakfast, and ate it along with the beer.

"Mommy! Do you think they've had lunch?"

"They should have by now. I've made coffee for the men, and if Leidy has to make any more, it only takes a second. There's still some rice and chicken if anyone's hungry."

They were interrupted by the sound of an approaching engine, which came to a halt by the door. Doña Maria turned around in surprise. They waited a moment, and someone knocked on the door.

"They're early!"

"Shall I answer, Mommy?"

"No, *m'hijo*. That'll upset your sister. I'll go; you stay here. And you, Leidy, honey, go into the bedroom until we've talked things through."

Doña Maria unplugged the iron and carefully curled up the cable before going to the door. She walked unhurriedly, intentionally making the new arrivals wait. She wanted to show her disdain for Michelle, Andrés, and the gringo by delaying coming to the door. She wanted to force them to ring again. But they never did. Although she was determined not to let it show, this annoyed her because it meant that she couldn't be grumpy at their impatience.

But when she finally opened the door, it turned out not to be the guests she'd expected. Standing before her, taking up all the space between the doorway and the street, were a dozen or so young men standing in threatening postures, their faces held high, chests puffed out, shoulders pulled back, and faces grave, defiant, intimidating. Just over a foot away, so close she could almost smell his breath, was the leader of the pack, the one who just a moment ago had rung the bell so politely. The young man, who couldn't have been older than twenty-five, wore his hair closely shorn. His clearly visible skull revealed the scars and pock-marks of a life of violence and pain. To him, the only law that mattered was gang law. The young man smiled slowly as his hostess appeared, showing off his thin, chapped lips; bleeding, throbbing gums; and wide teeth blackened by tobacco, alcohol, and drugs. His empty eyes took her in, holding her in their gaze like a snake might a rodent. Maria knew exactly what this meant, but it was too late for her to do anything about it.

The leader's face was free of adornments other than a small moustache and a wisp of a beard under his lips. He didn't have any visible markings to show his allegiances, but his companions were another matter entirely. Dozens of cynical, jaded, bulging, reddened eyes, high on various substances, stared back at her, thirsty for violence and plunder. There were too many for her to take them all in.

Intricate tattoos crisscrossed their childish faces. A boy who couldn't have been older than fifteen had a giant twelve stretching from his chin to his forehead; another with just one real eye—the other was glass—had the letters *M* and *P* in slanted baroque text on his face. Behind them, another head had been turned almost completely black with superimposed drawings that created an unsettling effect. The motifs on the shoulders, chests, forearms, and hands merged together to create a bewildering medley of voices silently screaming in injected ink and labyrinthine, sinister ornamentation. It was a moving blob that, from a distance, looked as though it was vibrating fluidly but incoherently. They were proud of the stains on their pubescent torsos and made sure they could be seen by going shirtless or wearing white string vests. Almost as though it were a uniform, to a boy they were also dressed in low-slung pants with their underwear pulled up and almost unanimously wore the same classic model of Nike sneaker. Locals who weren't gang members knew that they were forbidden from wearing that model of shoe, at risk of death.

The leader pulled up his vest to reveal a brutal, recently finished conversation piece: an oval of blood filled entirely by tiny wounds, with geometric shapes layered on top. It ran across his chest and ribs to his belly button. The tattoo was so fresh that it gleamed, and some of the lines were still blurred by swelling. As he showed this to Maria for reasons she couldn't understand, he let out a high-pitched cackle. It was the closest thing she could imagine to hell.

"Good afternoon, madam. Is your son at home?"

Maria felt a rush of fear, and her knees began to buckle. She couldn't think what to say. In the kitchen, Beto quickly jumped out of his chair. Before they could react, without giving his mother a second thought, he fled desperately out the back. The group saw the movement behind Maria and set out in pursuit. Three of them climbed up the bars in the windows, and as Beto left the kitchen, he could already hear footsteps on the roof. The leader stepped through the doorway, irritably pushing down the old woman. Then he intentionally walked over her on his way inside. As he pressed the sole of his shoe into her mouth, he called out to the running fugitive in an amused tone.

"What's wrong, Beto? Don't you want to play?"

This was followed by several other jeers while the gang swarmed the house. Beto grabbed hold of the back fence and leaped over it in a single movement. In the neighboring patio he reached for the top of a wall and lifted one of his legs over, the momentum bringing the rest of his body with it. He'd made it onto the street in record time. And now he was running down a dirt alley. Not a sound crept out from the houses; the neighborhood he'd grown up in had become a desert with no hope of refuge. He looked all around him and eventually saw a patio he could turn into, wondering whether the people who lived there would try to stop him, help him, or stay locked inside. Deep down, he knew how this was going to go; he'd seen it many times before. No matter what happened, no one was going to come to his aid. He nimbly climbed the wall but stopped on top of it when a car he had noticed earlier pulled up by him, and from it emerged a kid with a graffiti-style tattoo on his eyebrows and a pair of strange drawings on his eyelids that made it look as though he'd gone blind.

"Stop, Beto! Don't be crazy!" he called.

Beto jumped down to the patio and went straight for a screen door, but someone was holding it shut from the inside.

"Let me in, please! Let me in!"

Through the flimsy walls he heard tearful voices begging him to stop; they had children inside; he had to leave. He stepped back, preparing to force his way in, but before he could start, he was grabbed from behind. The driver and his passenger had followed after him. He turned around and desperately kneed the first before climbing up him, his foot on the attacker's back and his hand on the other pursuer's shoulder, trying to get back to the wall. Then the second kid grabbed hold of his pants. Beto kicked twice, forcing him to let go, and fell headfirst onto the ground on the other side. He cushioned his fall with his hands, hurting his wrists, but in his panic he barely felt the pain. In front of him was an open car door, and if he was lucky, the keys would still be in the ignition.

Maria had stayed on the ground, watching her son climb the fence and then the next wall into the alley. He'd ducked out of sight before his pursuers could catch him. Half of the ones who had come into the house had gone back out in front. She was relieved and almost proud of how skillfully Beto had managed to get away. She could even ignore the pain in her hip. All she cared about was that the boy had escaped. It almost pleased her that the attackers had turned their attention to Leidy; as terrible as what they were about to do to her was, as much as it upset and shamed her, it would give her son more time.

By staying in the bedroom, Leidy had unwittingly put herself into a trap. She couldn't get out through the barred window, and the only other way out was through the living room, which was occupied by six excitable gang members. The strongest one broke the lock with a single shove, almost falling over with the momentum as well as the fact that he was being pushed from behind by the others. Leidy, crouched in a corner, screamed in fright, but the sound had the same effect as the call of prey did to a pack of hunters. She made to grab a weapon with which to defend herself, but all she could lay her hands on were clothes, a small table, and the bed, which she clumsily tried to use as a barricade. The goons piled on top of her. Then they grabbed her and dragged her out of the room. She struggled as best she could, but they carried her between them, holding each of her limbs as though they were planning to tear her apart. The last man greedily ripped open her blouse in search of her breasts, but she was wriggling too much for him to get them free. The struggle stirred up his friends still more.

"What a whore!"

"Oh, you're going to get fucked!"

"Beto was a piece of shit compared to me—you'll see!"

They threw her onto the kitchen table so they could keep her legs open more easily. She screamed for help, but it was useless: there was no one to hear, not even Maria, who preferred to keep to herself and put up with this barbarity for the sake of her baby boy. After all, Leidy was only paying for the sins of her family. Beto was innocent.

Leidy begged for mercy in high-pitched screams, squirming as hands violated her, hurting her, tearing off her blouse, and pulling down her shorts. They yanked off her bra and scratched and dug at her breasts. One of them contorted his body so he could bite her while the others urged him on.

"Hahahahahaha! Look at that ass!"

"Shake that ass!"

"Beto, what a guy!"

"What was he like in bed? Don't worry—we'll be better."

After her shorts, they pulled off her panties, which proved to be further motive for enthusiastic celebration. The one at the bottom of the hierarchy climbed up onto the table, driven by lust and his friends' encouragement. One of the table legs broke under the weight, tipping everyone onto the floor amid much hilarity. The fall hurt Leidy's back, and she lay in pain beneath a pile of bodies and gales of laughter.

Beto tried to stand up; his wrists were like jelly and burning. He thought they might be dislocated, but still he scurried quickly along the ground. He'd just managed to get upright when he was hit in the back by something pointy. It sank into him, causing fiery pain. The gang members who'd climbed up onto the roof had caught up with him. The first had leaped on top of him without much skill but plenty of accuracy, digging his knees into the boy's back. Beto fell facedown into the earth, and his mouth filled with dust. The hunter rolled away with the momentum of the jump and fell back, out of control. Beto was acting out of pure instinct, fighting to get back up, able to ignore the searing pain. He lifted his right knee to lever himself to his feet, but it was too late: another Mara fell onto his kneecap, shattering it to pieces. He collapsed and was soon surrounded by a forest of kicking legs. The first caught him in the neck, leaving him coughing and gasping for air. He curled up into the fetal position, and the blows rained down all over his body. Soon most of his nerve endings were senseless with pain. But then, the attack came to a sudden halt. He lay still. A few seconds passed before someone pressed down on his chest and pulled up his head by the hair so he could see. It was the assassin with the empty eye sockets, the one he'd kneed, crouching over Beto, thirsty for revenge. He asked his companions to pin down the boy's legs, not that he was putting up much resistance now; then he grabbed a nearby stone and smashed it against the boy's mouth.

"Look at me, you bastard! You don't want to look at me, you son of a bitch? Fucking hell, now I'm pissed!"

He brought the stone down again and again. Beto's nose was broken, his eyes were smashed in, and soon his entire face was reduced to a bloody pulp.

The group raping Leidy was pushing her onto Michelle's bed when footsteps on the roof distracted them. The guy who'd tracked down Beto appeared upside down on the other side of the barred window.

"Come outside—the kid's back!"

The younger gang members ran hurriedly, like kids at a birthday party, while the two oldest ones stayed behind, holding Leidy. The first pulled her hair, making her look up at the ceiling, while the other twisted her arm against her back until she screamed. They made her walk outside bloodied, bruised, and naked. They were met by Beto being driven along the street with improvised whips made out of branches and sticks. They beat him like an animal until he couldn't walk any farther. He was covered in blood from head to toe. Leidy saw him, but he was completely unrecognizable. His face had been utterly disfigured. The goons holding up each of their victims laughed uproariously.

"Hahahahaha! Look at your little boyfriend! Hahaha!"

"Hey, Beto, look at your girl! We're all going to fuck her! Hahaha!"

"And she'll enjoy it. I hear you're a little light."

"She'll never want to be with you again!"

One of the older Mara told the youngest of them to bring out the old lady. The kid went inside and dragged her out without even giving her a chance to get up, much to the amusement of the others.

"Look at your mommy, Beto. Look at her!"

Beto didn't react; his eyelids flickered, but it didn't look as though he could see anything.

"Whore lady, look at your son. He didn't tell you about Jonathan, whore. They both worked for people who pay us. It was terrible what they did to Jonathan, whore. If Jonathan dies, then that little fucker Beto is going to have to learn that you don't fuck with us . . . fuck, Charly, the doña isn't looking."

Charly pulled Maria's hair, pulling some of it out. Then he used a knife to lift her eyelids.

"Look! Look, old woman, or I'll cut your eyes so you'll never be able to close them again!"

Maria opened her eyes, and she couldn't take them off her son, who was as defenseless in the hands of these savages as an orphaned baby. His kneecaps were bent at unnatural angles, and he spurted out blood with every breath. He was an unmoving, unrecognizable mass sobbing silently.

"Look. This is our gift to you so you don't forget us." He raised his voice to address the whole neighborhood. *"Did you hear me, whore? Don't fuck with us!"*

They threw Beto around like a rag doll, pistol-whipping him in the mouth, leaving him spitting out shards of his teeth. Then they shoved the barrel right down to his tonsils until he started to gag with what little strength he had left. The gunman fired. The sound, slightly muffled by the boy's mouth, echoed around the streets that had gone silent with shame. For a second, the boy's cheeks glowed white and orange, making his flesh look like plastic while the rear of his head exploded into a shower of hairy crimson splatters that spread several feet around. Leidy screamed in horror, her anguish so keen that even some of the murderers were startled. Maria felt as though something had blocked her airways, preventing her from making even a whimper. At a sign from the leader, they let go of mother and son, and both fell limply to the ground. Maria tried feebly to go to him, but she felt as lifeless as him.

Ignoring Leidy, the leader got into the second car and made one last announcement to the unseen onlookers. "Don't you forget us, you sons of bitches! And you, old woman, remember that you have more children."

The teenagers guarding Leidy, who seemed to have screamed herself out and could barely stand, took advantage of her weak state to shove her into the first car while the others dispersed. Suddenly she seemed to realize what was going to happen to her, and she started to kick out without saying a word, just emitting a desperate moan. They found her struggles an annoying hindrance, and one of them responded with a powerful kick to the stomach that doubled her over. In that position, they shoved her onto the floor of the car as though she were a heavy package.

"Stop it, whore! You're going to go the same way soon enough, but first you're going to have some fun."

They disappeared, leaving behind only a tense silence, which settled all along the street together with the dust kicked up by the cars. Maria crawled over to her son's body and pulled him onto her chest. A spine-chilling howl began to emerge from her lips.

Neither Ethan nor Michelle knew what to do after their long kiss. Michelle was in too much pain and had to lie down, giving Ethan the perfect excuse to go out in search of a nurse. They left the clinic without mentioning what had happened and focused on the logistics of the investigation. However, the seed had been planted, and the shy, playful tension between the two of them increased with every accidental touch or inadvertent meeting of the eyes. But when they got to Michelle's neighborhood, she immediately saw that something was wrong. She pointed it out to Ethan, who was oblivious to the telltale signs. There wasn't a soul to be seen, no movement on the streets at all. The neighborhood appeared to have been seized by an invisible force.

"See?"

"I think so. It wasn't like this a few days ago."

"This isn't right. Oh God, I'm scared. Protect us, God Almighty, Blessed Virgin."

They didn't speak again. As they drove on through the unnatural silence, their apprehension grew. When the house came into view, they could tell it was open and deserted. And then they saw the devastating sight of a mother hugging the body of her son, sitting in a pool of his blood. Nobody had dared to come outside yet; no one had called the police or an ambulance. If they possibly could, they preferred to pretend that it hadn't happened at all. Maria was all alone, still holding Beto's bloody body and rocking him back and forth as though she were trying to lull him to sleep. A heartbreaking whimper could be heard filling the space around her. Ethan reached out for Michelle, who waved to him to stop without saying a word, guiding his hand to the gear shift. He did; he was stunned by the scene but was also trying to assess the situation. He turned to her, trying to decide what to do next, but the look of desperation and acceptance that met him left him with no doubt. Michelle looked back at him from deep within a strange void and kissed him in gratitude before opening the door. She walked toward her mother until Maria became aware of her presence.

"Don't come any closer! Concubine of Satan! This is all your fault! You had that fatherless child. How many daddies has she had? More than she can remember!"

Michelle didn't react to the insults. It was as though she was used to it, as though she'd heard them since she was a little girl. "Mommy, let me help you."

But the woman responded like a lioness protecting her cub. Her face was so full of rage that Michelle didn't move.

"*Back!* Look at my little boy . . . look what they did to him because of you! Because you can't take care of your own daughter. You do all this to us just because they took her from you!" She broke down and went back to rocking the boy, covering herself in his blood. "Look . . . look at my son . . ."

Ethan had stayed in the car so as not to intrude, but now he got out and called Andrés.

"Don Ethan, forgive me for not coming to pick you up. I can't talk right now, but—"

"Andrés, call the police. Beto has been killed at your mother's house. Come as soon as you can."

He hung up and tried to get Maria to stand up. "Get up—we're going inside."

Michelle, working on autopilot, picked up Beto's wallet, which had fallen a few feet away, and a sneaker that was lying in the middle of the road. She brought them over, ignoring her mother's insults. Maria pushed Ethan away.

"Go away! This isn't your home! *Get out!* I never want to see you again. She isn't my daughter! She isn't my daughter! Go back to your rich man's house! Go back to your boyfriend, the one who didn't want your daughter!"

Ethan couldn't understand her stream of invectives. It sounded like nonsense to him until Maria saw his confused expression and started to scream directly at him, spattering him with blood.

"She didn't tell you, did she? She lied to you like she does with everyone else. She didn't tell you that she lives with an engineer. A rich one! And she came to my house to fool you both. She told the other one that you were coming to help look for the girl, not so she could slobber all over you. And the moment you walked out the door, she went back to him! That's why she didn't want you to come to the hospital—so you wouldn't meet! Ask her. Let's see what lies she'll come up with next. She didn't tell you to make sure you'd come, and she told the boyfriend that you're a gringo detective, not her other boyfriend. Ask her where the money the other guy gave her is! She's a slut!"

Maria hocked up some saliva and spat at Michelle, who didn't react. She had bent down next to her brother in a daze and was carefully picking up the pieces of his skull, trying to keep them all together, then cleaning the blood from his face. She didn't seem to notice that she was getting blood all over her. Ethan put his hands on Michelle's shoulders, but she shook them off to stay with Beto while her mother reveled in the hatred that was the only thing keeping her going.

"That's my daughter! You never knew her! All she knows is evil! I've known that ever since she was a child. I told you. I always knew. Remember! Tell me if I'm lying! I always said it! I've always known—wrecking things is all she's good at. Just like she's done to us, her own family . . ."

Ethan grew sick of the tirade. He shook Michelle's good arm and pulled her up hard. She had broken down. Her good eye was teary, and she mumbled without looking at him.

"Leave me alone, please. I have to help her . . ."

Ignoring her, he pushed her toward the car, and she obeyed. He put her in the passenger seat, and she sat there vacantly, staring at the unmoving shape of her brother. She fastened her seat belt, still acting like an automaton. Ethan pulled out, watching her out of the corner of his eye. She stared straight ahead, letting the tears run down her face. The only thing Ethan could think to do was take her back to his apartment and let her shower so she could at least wash off the blood, but as he turned the first corner, she gently put her fingers on his hand.

"No, to the right," she murmured.

Michelle started to give him directions with light touches in one direction or the other. Ethan drove on robotically, and neither one of them said a word. Finally, they got to the financial district and then residential districts stalked by the paparazzi, where police vans with water cannons kept the peace on behalf of the upper class. They drove up to a brick wall with grooved columns and a twelve-foot-high triple-reinforced gate monitored by a security camera. She told him to stop, and Michelle poked her head out so they could identify her. Her skin was still spattered with blood, and a metallic voice spoke through the intercom.

"Do you need help? Would you like us to call an ambulance? Or the police?"

She demurely shook her head, and the main gate opened. The community was made up of detached houses placed in the middle of landscaped gardens. A hundred feet farther on, they stopped in front of a mansion built in a slightly garish neoclassical style. Two security guards came out of a lavish guard post and walked toward them with their hands on their weapons. A window opened from within the mansion, and a chubby older maid came running out, shocked by Michelle's appearance.

"*Señorita*! Bless me! Sir won't be home until this evening; would you like me to call him?"

Michelle looked at Ethan, not bothering to hide her shame or keep up the pretense. Ethan was unable to talk. His extremities were numb, and there was a lump in his throat. Before leaving him, Michelle said goodbye in a whisper.

"I won't ask you to forgive me. I won't ask you to do anything else for the girl." She got up and started to walk away before turning around. "It was all true, everything I said."

Then she walked on, being fussed over by the servant, who sent the guards back to their post. Ethan drove away completely stunned. He didn't know what to do or where to go. Eventually, he parked in front of his apartment, pleased to be where it seemed safe and comfortable. He went to a sports bar, the same kind one might find back in Florida, and sat down to watch a game, trying to relax. Andrés called him several times, but he answered with a text message apologizing and saying that he didn't want to talk. In addition to being hurt, angry, sad, and lost, he felt ridiculous. That was Michelle's magical power: he'd forgotten about that. She dusted each thrust of the knife in icing sugar and then came back to apologize, lifting him up higher and higher only for the fall to be that much more painful. Then she left him down there alone and rudderless. But he also told himself that this time had been different; this time he hadn't been the one waiting at home; he'd been the one to whom she'd whispered her words of submission, with whom she'd made crazy plans. After all these years, his role had changed. It was so much more depressing to see himself embrace her fantasies after all this time. He didn't dare share his anguish with anyone; it made him feel stupid and ashamed. He didn't even think of Ari. He was purposely avoiding that.

Andrés sent him several messages, which he answered out of politeness.

My sister just told me what happened. I knew the lie would end badly. Please forgive my part in it, I never should have allowed it to happen.

Andrés, all that matters is your brother and mother. The rest is nonsense. None of this is your fault. If she asked you to lie, you had no choice.

God forgive me but I have no tears to shed over my brother. I've suffered over him for too long. I watched him drift into the clutches of the Enemy and there was nothing I could do to save him. I'll understand if you don't want to continue your investigation. Thank you for everything you've done for us.

Of course I'll continue. I just need a day to rest.

Calvo contacted me. He gave me information but asked me not to say anything until he'd spoken to you.

Fine. If it's not urgent, we can discuss it tomorrow.

Later in the afternoon he got more calls from an unknown number, which he decided not to answer. Finally he received a text message.

Don Ethan, it's Adrian Calvo. I've heard. Please accept my condolences but it's important that we meet. I have what you're looking for. Call me on this number when you can.

Calvo knew how to push his buttons. Ethan finally decided to call him at the end of the day.

"Good afternoon, Don Ethan. You know, we started out almost like boyfriend and girlfriend, but now you're avoiding me."

"I'm sorry. I've been busy."

"I thought as much. I said how sorry I was, didn't I? Let's move on. There's a lot we need to discuss. Did you know that Leidy was hiding in Doña Maria's house?"

"I don't know anything about anything. Do you know where she is now?"

"For her sake, I hope she's no more. She was taken by the Doce; the best we can hope for her is for it to have been over quickly. The funeral is tomorrow."

"Hers?"

"Oh no, they'd have to find her for that. For Beto, and they'll also say something for Jonathan. They were good buddies. But you must know that. I hope to see you there."

"At Beto and Jonathan's funeral? You must be kidding."

"It sounds like it. I agree. But no. You can learn about our traditions."

"And say hello to Michelle and Maria while I'm at it?"

"Oh, they're not going. I certainly wouldn't bring you if the family were going."

"But of course the family is going. Why wouldn't they?"

"Now you're beginning to get the idea. The gang has forbidden them from coming. But we can; we're not locals. What you see there will teach you more than all our other activities put together. We won't get too close, just in case. It'll be worth your while—you'll see."

He opened his eyes and realized that he'd fallen asleep. He looked at his watch: almost half an hour had passed, and it would still be another half hour before the guy to whom he was going to make the handoff arrived. He rubbed his chin and was surprised by how long his beard had grown; he hadn't shaved in almost a week. Used to life on the road, he searched his bag for his brush and razor and went to the bathrooms, which he knew well. The buses went in both directions, but there weren't many people around at such an early hour. It was still before dawn. He went to the bathrooms on the platform; these were the ones the drivers used, so in addition to being empty, they were clean. The sinks were large, and a long mirror ran along the counter. They weren't covered in graffiti or lewd pictures, and they smelled of disinfectant. Just as he'd assumed, he was the only one using them, and he liked that. He had spread the foam over his face and started to shave when the door opened and a short man in a suit came in and walked past him to the toilet. Irritated by this intrusion, he went on, ignoring the man. The question came from the cubicle that the man had gone into. He thought he might be talking on the phone.

"Have you brought the merchandise?"

The man might be talking to him, but then it might also be a stupid coincidence. He went on shaving. The question didn't come again. He heard the toilet flush, and the stranger came back out. This time the stranger looked him in the eyes as he washed his hands in the sink farthest away from where he was shaving.

"I asked you if you've brought our merchandise."

The Beast looked into the man's cold gaze and answered firmly. "Don't talk to me. I don't know you."

"But I know you. Here's what we agreed." Without a hint of discretion he took a bulky envelope out of the inside pocket of his coat and threw it onto the counter. It fell onto the hair and soap, and the Beast had to be quick to stop it from getting wet. He glanced inside; there seemed to be the right amount of bills. Then he eyed up the man, who was standing still, staring at his reflection. Seeing this as an invitation, the Beast took out the money and counted it twice. It was all there. As he bent down to put it in his backpack, the man came right over to him.

"Now take me to the merchandise."

"Where's the gentleman I usually deal with?"

"That's none of your concern. I'm here. Take me to the merchandise."

"How do I know this isn't a trap?"

"I'm leaving now. If I leave the station without what you promised us, you'll be killed right here in the bathroom. What more do you need to know?"

Confused, the Beast led him through groups of travelers to the busy streets of the working-class neighborhood where the smells and voices mingled together until they seemed one and the same. This stranger seemed composed but made no effort to conceal his disdain for their surroundings, as if the air itself might stain his immaculate clothing. His shoes and pants cuffs were covered in orangey dust by the time they turned into a lot where dozens of articulated trucks were parked. Hidden at the back was the black trailer.

"She's in here. Did you come in a car?"

"No. I'll ride with you to the site where we make the exchange. You drive, and I'll give you directions. You must do exactly as I say."

The Beast, uncomfortable with taking orders, didn't object and allowed himself to be guided out of the crowded area into a more remote neighborhood that bordered slums. The danger in this area was palpable. They came to a stop in an abandoned lot containing a ruined building. An old factory for a product that had been forgotten. The man told him to switch off the engine, and they waited in silence. The Beast grew more and more nervous until the sound of eight wheels and eight blinding xenon headlights announced the arrival of a pair of Lexus RXs. They stopped on either side, and four or five shadows got out. They unceremoniously walked over to stand by the doors without bothering to say a word.

The Beast's passenger broke the silence but still didn't look at him. "Now you can hand over the merchandise."

The Beast warily climbed out of the cabin and went around to the tank, opened the latches, and removed the false bottom to release the semiconscious, dirty, sweating, bruised, and disheveled girl. Two of the shadows reached for her and helped her to stand while they untied her and removed the gag. As soon as they untied the rope around her knees, she collapsed, and they had to catch her. One of them held her gently, seeing to her comfort, while the other listened to her heartbeat and checked her vital signs.

The client ordered the Beast back into the cabin and told him to wait in his seat. He started to sweat, worried at what the little bitch might say. He'd restrained himself. He'd barely touched her. It was more than the pig deserved;

he should have had his way with her until she was dead. That was what she deserved, but now he found himself at the mercy of the lies she might tell these bastards. In spite of his repeated reassurances to himself, the truth was that he was afraid. He'd gone too far; he'd kept her in the tank longer than he'd needed to in revenge for her having made things difficult, and he knew that that wasn't right. He'd gotten carried away, but these bastards, these perverts who paid him to bring them little girls to do who knew what with, didn't know what he'd been through. He leaned over, trying to see what was going on in the side mirror. He could see the man he imagined was a doctor examining her back. The man walked over to the negotiator, saying something with a disappointed expression. Feeling the hairs on his skin stand on end, the Beast bent farther forward to get a better look, but his movement must have caught the attention of one of the guards because the man came over, took out something like a hammer, and smashed the glass. The Beast kept quiet. The voice sounded again next to him.

"She's not in good condition."

"If you know a better way of taking something like that from its home and crossing the continent, you're welcome to try. But if we use a truck, this is the only way."

"We warned you. The last one came in much better condition."

"That one was easier. This was a half-wild Indian. You have no idea where she lived."

The negotiator held up a finger to silence him. The Beast heard his frighten-ingly bland drawl. "We gave you two warnings. Hand back the money."

"You can't!"

"Give me back the money."

The Beast trembled in frustration, but he didn't dare argue. He reached into his bag and picked up the envelope. He was about to throw it onto the ground but was afraid they'd make him get out to pick it up. He decided to place it carefully in the man's hand. To his surprise, the man took out half the bills and gave back the rest.

"We won't accept any further failures. We'll have to decide whether to hire you again. Wait for our visit at your hideout."

"I'm not waiting anywhere. I have more orders to fill, things to do this week. A lot of clients."

"We'll check the merchandise. If the damage is superficial, we'll give you back the rest. The visit will occur in five days."

"What if I have to go, huh? What will you do then?"

The client turned around and walked back to the Lexus, ignoring him.

The Beast's blood boiled at the snub. Unable to control himself, he shouted through the window. "I can't wait! I have other jobs! Send me an email if you want to reach me! You'll work it out!"

"Five days," repeated the monotone voice.

The Beast didn't dare answer. He waited for them to leave and finally let out the rage he had been repressing for the last hour. "That fucking little bitch, fucking little bitch, fucking, fucking, fucking little bitch!"

He screamed and hit the steering wheel, cursing with all his might until his words started not to make sense anymore. But that didn't help. Choking on his own bile, he knew that if she'd been there at that moment, he would have ruined her. He'd have smashed her face in. But he was alone. They'd left him alone. They'd threatened him. The little shit had threatened him right there, in his own truck, and then taken half the payment he was due. The money he'd earned, the price they'd agreed on. Weren't they men of their word? Who was putting his ass on the line? He was. They owed him everything. He was the one who organized the trips. In a way, he'd invented them. Hadn't he? Without him they'd be unable to indulge their perverted desires. They couldn't do anything without him, and they dared to threaten him, to steal his money. He'd only failed once, just once in all these years, and even then the whore had survived. He'd told them she had a problem with her lungs or allergies. Whatever—it hadn't been his fault, and the next delivery had gone perfectly.

They were a bunch of fucking ingrates. They only dared to act like that because there were a lot of them. But that anal bastard, talking to him like that . . . *There aren't any real men left in the world*, the Beast said to himself, as he had so often. *There aren't any real men left in the world.* And he pulled out, savoring his hatred of everyone and everything. They weren't going to get rid of him. If they'd wanted to do that, they'd have done it there and then. They wouldn't have given him five days to get away, he reassured himself, trying to think strategically. They needed him. He was the only one who'd been able to organize all those trips without any trouble at the borders. Fucking whore. It was all her fault. If he ever got his hands on her, he'd make her pay for all the humiliation he'd suffered on this journey. It had been his worst ever, except for that asthmatic bitch. But he wouldn't get the chance; those girls never came back. And again he allowed the waves of hatred to crash down over his employers. They treated him like shit, as though they were better than him, but really they were worse. They lusted after little girls and didn't even dare to do it themselves. Why take all that trouble over those little whores? They didn't even have any tits. He could find better asses in any of the cities he passed through, in any park almost, and take them without having to go farther than a mile. Not to mention the fact that the parents would gladly sell them for a lot less money. These rich people had no idea what to do with their wealth. Europeans were like that. He'd known about them since he was a child: grasping, low-down, weak, fat, millionaire pigs. Inbreds who had plundered Latin America once and were now coming back to give free rein to their mysterious, twisted fantasies. How dare they presume to judge him like that? As though he were nothing. When he didn't need them anymore, he'd show them why he was known as the Beast. He'd do things to their wives and daughters right there in front of them. Things they'd never dreamed of in their mansions. He'd show them who was truly to be feared.

The morning was clear and sunny, but the air was full of dust, giving everything a cloudy complexion. Ethan had learned that this augured a sticky, dense, humid day. A circular, tropical day that provided a good metaphor for the society around him: always in a hurry but never getting anywhere. A society trapped in a secret war, whose forms changed with each new generation. He wondered if this land was destined to be violent until the end of time or if this was just a stage. It was like the tropics themselves: Were they stuck in a repetitive climate? Or were they in fact free and constantly changing in a never-ending orgy of natural renewal?

The cemetery grew out from the road. There was no paving or railings; you climbed up the bare stairs carved into the clay. The whimsical scene that greeted you at the top of the embankment was a favorite spot for walkers and courting couples: a sea of irregular tombstones and memorials in faded greens, blues, pinks, and yellows. This was an innocent, festive place that left no room for sadness.

A crowd had gathered in one corner. A wide range of clothing and tattoos was on display. Sitting on a small white stone laid for a child, Calvo was watching the proceedings from a distance. He hissed for Ethan to come over. Once they'd met up, he continued in a whisper: "Please accept my sincere condolences."

"You've already given me those," Ethan said.

"No, these are for Leidy. I'm truly sorry. My assistants tell me that she's been found."

The congregation was murmuring a song that came to them in fragments. Calvo tried to make it out.

> Sometimes it can be tough when a friend leaves
> and his soul heads for eternity.
> He's gone and won't be coming back;
> he's gone forever.
> His memory will remain,
> but now he's resting in peace.

"It's a song they sing," he said, unnecessarily.

The group stood still, drawing Doce symbols in the air during the recitation, which finished with a shared amen.

"This is for Jonathan, all for Jonathan. It's their way of taking control of the funeral."

Once the hymn was over, the ceremony leader, who was in a bright-white shirt and blue tie and had a Bible in his lap, started to speak passionately, like a television evangelist, making his sermon into a diatribe against violence. He railed against those who had lost sight of scripture and courageously condemned the Mara, expressing his pity for each and every one of them and describing them as wayward sheep. He decried their criminal activities and made sure that they knew how ashamed they should be. He talked up the Christian soul and begged them to show compassion and pity. Over and over again, he cited the peaceful example of Christ and the power of the church: the only solution was to turn the other cheek.

"Worthless!" he informed them. "Worthless! Joining a gang that only cares for the body when it's the soul that matters. Oh, the soul, my brothers! Only the Lord can account for the soul! Because everything we have is given to us by him! You can't turn your back on the Creator, just as you can't forget the love that Jesus Christ offers us. He who does not serve God serves the enemy! It is he! He who keeps you mired in poverty and suffering. It is he! He who plots harm, the harm you do to yourselves and those you love."

Ethan was impressed by the pastor's performance. He walked confidently through his congregation, pointing at them with an accusing finger while they stood with their heads bowed, though they continued to make their gang sign. It was their way of being submissive without giving up their principles. Ethan was amazed by their ability to combine religion with extreme violence. If there was something that the murderers and victims in this world shared, it was belief. The drug traffickers and the Mara sought his protection, justification, and consolation, just like the families of their victims, and they accepted the judgmental sermons of their priests, staring at the ground in exchange for being allowed to be a part of the religious community. But the moment they stepped off holy ground, they'd return to their criminal lives without a second thought. To them, God's love was compatible with whatever way of life one chose so long as blessings were given when they asked for them.

At some point during the sermon, Calvo lost interest, rolled a cigarette, and turned to Ethan. "You look a little run down. The tropics aren't agreeing with you. It happens. Some people can't get used to the sun. Are you using sunblock?"

"Yeah, slathering it on like mud. I'm trying to reduce the scarring. Apart from that, I'm not sleeping. And as you know very well, the climate has nothing to do with it."

"I don't know what to tell you. First you turn up as though you had an altercation with a cat, and then you disappear just when a crazed mob lynches Leidy's family. You're full of surprises."

"I read about it in the newspaper."

"To see if they left anything out? I have a journalist friend; if you want to share any more details, I'll pass them on."

"You're so sure I was there?"

"Ever since you arrived," Calvo said, "I've been nothing but good to you, and now you're treating me like this. You can accept my help or not, but don't take me for a fool. I knew as soon as I heard, but the witness statements confirmed it. I told you that those cuts on your face wouldn't help you to blend in. Maybe in a cane field . . ."

"If you already know all about it, you'll know that no one went there to kill anyone. The situation got out of hand. You can tell that to your friend; the press only mentioned the fire."

"Something tells me that the longer you're here, the more situations will get out of hand. Starting with mine."

"I don't think you have anything to worry about. You weren't involved."

"That's not how it seemed the other day. It was nice of you to send a warning through Andrés. But selling me out to strangers? That wasn't so nice."

"I knew you could deal with it. I assume I was right, but I still owe you. And I apologize, of course."

"I don't know what you thought you were doing, but I am grateful to you. On the one hand, you put me in danger, but on the other, you gave me an advantage. There's no need to thank me. I like to return generosity in kind."

"By bringing me here? It wouldn't have occurred to me."

"No, by keeping your ex alive."

"I don't understand."

"If she'd been at home, she'd be in there right now." He pointed at the coffin. "Along with her brother. We had to get her out of the way somehow."

Ethan bridled at this veiled confession. "What do you mean?"

"You know very well."

Reacting instinctively, Ethan turned to Calvo and grabbed hold of his neck, but just as quickly he remembered himself and let go. "That was your solution? You ordered them to beat her just to punish me?"

The detective didn't bat an eye. He smoothed out the wrinkles in his jacket. "No, that was the favor, not the punishment. It gave me a chance to negotiate for her life. But there had to be some kind of retaliation. Do you think they'd ever have been happy just to let her go? At least this way we were in control." He smiled sardonically. "It was only a minor beating, nothing to worry about. And it wasn't done by the Mara; otherwise she'd have been left unrecognizable. They told me that they only broke one tooth, and that was by accident. It's hard to get it exactly right . . ."

"So you didn't just allow it—you paid for the beating."

"If you had a better plan, you could have told me. It would have been a big help, but you weren't around."

"But you knew they were coming for Beto. You knew they were going to kill him, and you did nothing."

"I knew what was going to happen, and I did what I could. I find your indignation laughable. They were going to kill Michelle. You know now that she didn't spend the night there. As soon as you left, she went back to the engineer's house. By the way, I'm sorry you didn't know about that before. But they were going to kill her just the same. You and your friend Andrés's little street party really ruffled their feathers."

This was a bitter pill to take. Ethan knew that the detective was right, but it was still hard to accept. "Why didn't you pay for Beto?"

"You pay for what you can pay for, and I chose to save Michelle. Fortunately for us, the MP12 don't know anything about the daughter, and they don't care. That's why she wasn't important to them. They wanted to punish Jonathan's buddies for abandoning him, but if I hadn't intervened, she'd have met the same fate as the couple. There's always room for one more."

Ethan stood up and began to walk in circles, disgusted.

Calvo stopped him. "Calm down, my friend. Public displays of any kind aren't advisable here."

He discreetly nodded to the crowd gathered around the coffin. Their attention was still on the sermon, but they were hardly a safe distance away. Ethan sat down again, and the detective rolled another cigarette.

"That's much better. Look at them over there. They'll put up with the priest, but their eyes are open. We don't want them taking too much of an interest in us."

"So why are we here? You said it would be useful."

"I said that you'd learn something, and I'm sure you're smart enough to have kept your eyes open. See those kids? Look how clean and smartly dressed they are, in chinos, and the adults, the ones over thirty, they're the *pintos*, the bosses. They don't look like gang members, but none of them would think twice about killing you."

"I deal with gangs in the US."

"These are like them but on steroids—believe me. There are lots of ways to be a gang member, more than I can count. They don't always wander around with tattoos and their underwear showing. Murderers come in many different shapes and sizes. If they come for you, that's it."

"You really think this is useful?"

"Try to memorize their faces. It couldn't hurt."

"While they memorize mine."

"Yes, exactly. Look at it as though we've come to a fashionable bar, the kind of place where hipsters go to be . . . what's the word? *Cool.* We came to chat but also to see and be seen."

Ethan carefully scrutinized their faces. No one paid them any attention, or at least they didn't appear to.

"Have you sold me out?" Ethan said.

"My friend, how can you accuse me of something like that?"

"You brought me here so they can recognize me? Is that the punishment?"

"Well, that might be a more accurate description."

"So we're even?"

"Let's say it's part of the payment for Michelle."

"Giving me to them is what you paid for the beating?"

"No. They just want to see you, to put a face to the gringo. You must know that you've aroused their curiosity. It's part of the deal I offered to keep her in one piece."

Ethan sighed, taking all this in. "And all this because of Jonathan? I thought he didn't belong to the Mara."

"Neither did Beto. But there the Mara are, paying their respects while the family has been forbidden to come. This isn't about belonging; it's about ownership, territory. If Jonathan were Mara, I wouldn't have been able to buy Michelle."

The ceremony was coming to an end.

"Neither Jonathan nor Beto were Matapatria homies, but they both obeyed them and operated under their protection. And look what they did to one of them because of what happened to the other. It's a question of hierarchy. A lesson so no one forgets who's in control."

To Ethan's surprise, Calvo finished up with a congratulatory slap on the back. "But you should be happy, damn it."

Ethan stared at him in amazement as Calvo continued in a triumphant tone. "Well done. You were right, and I was wrong. Jonathan was an informant—he was the one who sold Michi's routine. My boys found that out. Good for you. How did you do it?"

"I was just following your advice."

"Hahaha! It came as quite a surprise. You're very good; you went under my radar and uncovered secrets I was unaware of. I don't know whether that's good or bad. But I congratulate you just the same. So someone paid for Michi, and the Doce gave it their blessing."

"At least we have something to go on. She was kidnapped."

"I didn't say she was kidnapped," Calvo said sternly. "I know that someone paid for information and the Mara knew about it."

"That's what you've found out? I knew that already. How do you know that they paid for the information but not the kidnapping?"

"I'm telling you everything I know. But I know something else that you'll find very interesting."

Ethan waited suspiciously.

"I have your villain. The man who paid Jonathan. A deputy police chief he and Leidy worked for. They spied on others before Michi, and guess what? They were all kidnapped."

He passed Ethan a handwritten note. Ethan took it curiously. It was a name. Calvo smiled, not that he ever really seemed to stop smiling.

"Nothing digital, no traces. If anyone asks, I have no idea where the piece of paper came from."

"An organized group?"

"So it would seem. There have been ten victims that we know of in three years. Seven paid the ransom and were returned. Three weren't. The deputy police chief has a deal with the Doce. I don't know how it works, but he doesn't pay for each kidnapping. That's why I never found a payment we could connect to her. Either he does jobs for them, or he pays a fixed fee. Even so, Michi doesn't seem to fit."

"She doesn't fit with those ten cases. We don't know how many more there might be or whether the chief had other informants."

"But that doesn't change my point. Our girl still doesn't fit. I shared all this with Andrés, but I held something back that I can tell you. Of those that came back, several were missing fingers. They seem like professionals, and tough ones, and time is still against you."

Ethan decided not to reveal that he'd already spoken with Andrés. "You told Andrés?"

"I asked him not to tell you, to let me do it."

"So what are we waiting for? Why aren't we following this guy?"

"Didn't you hear me? He's a policeman with an agreement with the Mara, the details of which are a mystery to me. And the way things stand, I'd say that I need to be careful they don't start thinking I'm getting a little too nosy for my own good." Calvo pointed to the young men who were now drifting out of the cemetery. "Getting that name wasn't easy. My life expectancy isn't looking too healthy right now."

"I thought that was what we paid for."

"That piece of paper is worth six times what you paid me. Stop complaining; this is my parting gift now that the contract's up."

"You mean that's it?"

"I was hired by the engineer. He's a good, trustworthy man. You know, I can say this now: when she moved in with him, she sent the girl to live with her grandmother. I'm sure she had her reasons. You know how it is. They're looking for a girlfriend, but when she arrives with an unexpected bonus, a lot of them run for the hills. Maybe she was waiting until he was good and committed . . . it's none of my business. Now do you understand my initial reservations? I said those things for a reason. The girl wasn't living with them when she disappeared. I imagine they hired me out of guilt."

Ethan struggled to process this flood of painful information. "When did all this happen?"

"Not long ago—maybe a couple of months? Yesterday, when the engineer went to visit Michelle, he decided that enough was enough. He summoned me and explained his priorities. He asked me if it was safer for her to give up the investigation, and I told him the truth: it is. It was stupid of me to get involved in the first place, but so far it's gone OK. Now things are beginning to look stickier. Now that the contract has been terminated, I feel better. I didn't like the look of where things were heading."

"But you're leaving me with a clue," Ethan said, holding up the scrap of paper.

"Like you said, that's what you paid me for. Listen, I don't know who's in charge, but from what I've seen, it seems as though you've been very intelligent to make sure that your left hand doesn't know what the right is doing. I think that's worked for you so far. But only so far. If you keep going and find them, if you fight them, catch them or kill them before they kill you. The Mara will have no mercy. There'll be no chance of a payoff or negotiation. You'll be dead, and so will everyone around you: Michelle, Andrés, and anyone else you're connected with. I like you. I'd be sorry to see you end up like that kid over there."

"I don't know what to thank you for and what not, Calvo. What do you get out of this?"

"Nothing. I thought that was obvious. This has all been a service, and it's been paid for. The Matapatria wanted to see what you look like, and so I showed you to them. You made trouble for me, but then your warning gave me enough time to work it out. Now I'm fulfilling the contract, and you have the name you were looking for. But I'm warning you: if you act on it, you're finished. We're even."

Everything seemed to fit. As far as Calvo was concerned, the conversation was over. He got up to take his leave.

"But why did you deal with Andrés?" Ethan asked. "He wasn't paying you. He had nothing to do with it."

"What does it matter? What matters is what you've got, what you know, and what you should know now."

Ethan wasn't satisfied with the answer. Why tell Andrés but forbid him to tell Ethan? It didn't add up. "Any final words of advice? What would you do if you were me?"

"Leave."

"You know I can't do that."

"You asked me for advice."

"How about you, Adrian? Could they pay you to find me?"

"That's not how the Mara work. But they could."

"And would you agree to do it?"

Calvo shrugged. Ethan stood up, and they said goodbye more like old friends than business associates. A flurry of questions still swirled around Ethan's head about Calvo and Andrés. Why give him the name knowing that it would be worthless to him?

"To find out who our source was!"

The detective turned around in confusion. "What?"

"That's why you told Andrés while I was gone. That's why you asked him not to tell me: to see who else he went to. To find out who the other guy was. Isn't it? They're looking for him too!"

Calvo smiled his smug smile and winked.

152

Ethan was sitting in his apartment in the dark. The telephone didn't ring. He reread the name written on the piece of paper. It meant nothing to him. Andrés must have given it to Suarez already, maybe days ago, while he was still at the beach, completely unaware of the web of intrigue being woven in his absence. Should he have stayed? Should he have ignored Lorena? She had turned out to be playing with him too. He was drinking beer, writing down the information he had and everything that had happened, trying to piece together everything in a way that made sense, looking for patterns. But all he'd put together was a puzzle in which Suarez was the missing piece, the one everyone was looking for. Was this a battle between two different families? And if so, who was he working for, and who was Adrian Calvo working for? Ethan felt that he was being swept along by events over which he had no control, hidden forces that were ready to change the face of the city, maybe even the entire country, to hold on to their power. But nothing that had happened led him to Michelle. It was as though the stories had crossed each other somewhere, but he'd taken the wrong fork. Was there any point in continuing to work from the pit into which he'd fallen, when he was unable to look at anything objectively? He said the name out loud. It meant nothing. Four people had died, and he hadn't achieved anything. What kind of madness might be unleashed if he went any further? Calvo had been suspiciously quick. It wasn't hard to see how this piece of paper could be a trap. But had it been laid by Calvo? What would Suarez say if they ever saw each other again? What action might Calvo take against Suarez, using him as an intermediary? And after that there was nothing. His ex-lover was telling him the same old lies, and he'd let himself be tangled up in them once again, just like old times. Just when he'd thought he was free. Her family was devastated, and Michi was gone. He kept trying to look at things from Ari's point of view. And doubting his own mental health. How could he have set out on this ridiculous quest just because of a few crazy dreams, dreams that he hadn't had again for weeks? And in the darkest part of his soul lurked the fear, which he couldn't admit even to himself, of what not dreaming of Michi might mean. It was as though all was lost. He thoughtfully dialed Andrés's number, knowing that doing so meant setting out on a dangerous path.

"Hello, Don Ethan. I've been praying for you, hoping that everything will work out and there'll be no more suffering."

"Hello, Andrés. How's your mother?"

"As well as can be imagined. She has her cross to bear; there's no point talking about it. I'd prefer to apologize for agreeing to hurt you with the sin of mendacity. I spend my nights praying that the harm I caused covering up my sister's lies leaves your heart untouched and corrupts mine instead. It was my fault. I ask your forgiveness just as I have of Christ."

"Andrés, you did nothing wrong. I don't even think Michelle did. She was just being cowardly, that's all. I should have guessed. I should have anticipated what was going to happen and saved your brother."

"My brother, God forgive him and accept him into his glory, chose his fate. And I share that sinner's fate."

"It's not your fault. You had nothing to do with it. You didn't grow up together; the only thing the two of you had in common was a mother. Your family was from Hungary, wasn't it?"

"On my mother's side. My father is from here."

"Yes, you shared a family, but he was raised by his father. You can't blame yourself for what happened to him."

"You know what they say. If there's no father at home, they'll find one on the street."

"You spoke about your father as though he were still alive. I thought he'd passed away."

"He may as well have. We haven't seen him in years. He had another family, and when my mother found out, she accepted it and went on living with him. He was the sinful one. But he couldn't accept it and left with the other lady, who was younger. You know how he beat me and how I escaped north. But it wasn't his fault; that's how he was. I never saw him again. How is your mother? I'm sorry not to have asked before."

"I went to see her recently—she's great. It's strange—with me, my father was the foreigner, but you got your nationality from your father. For some reason I always feel that you're from the land of your mother, not your father."

"I think you're right. We live where our mother brings us, not our father. It happens a lot; the men here are like that. Good men like you are hard to find. Your heart is as pure as my niece's, and if I were asked to sin again to save her, may God forgive me, but I'd do it."

"No, Andrés. I don't want you mixed up in this. Tell me what happened before I came. Please, tell me everything I still need to know. That's all I want."

"I told Don Calvo everything I know. He knows what I know. He laughed when Michelle told him that he had to hide it from you. He called her clever. The deception amused him."

"That sounds like him."

"I know—he's not trustworthy."

"How long has Michelle been with her boyfriend? Why didn't Michi live with them?"

"I don't know, Don Ethan. I only know what I've heard from the girl and my mother. He's one of the owners of the call center where she works. They started dating about six months ago. Michelle told us that at first she'd told him that the girl was her niece and then admitted that she was her daughter but claimed that she lived with our mother. That was a lie: they lived alone in an apartment, but she was afraid that he'd leave her. He asked her to move in with him, and she did, but little Michi was a problem. So my sister asked our mother to take Michi for a few months while she got settled in. She was going to persuade the engineer to take her daughter too. She said that he was very decent and rich and was going to give them a very good life."

"Why haven't you investigated the engineer? He should be on the list of suspects. What's his name?"

"Randall Gutiérrez Ochoa."

Ethan's heart almost leaped out of his chest. "What? You're kidding me!"

"No, that's his name, Don Ethan, but he has nothing to do with Randall the guitarist, the one you knew. He was called Randall Silva. It's a silly coincidence."

"You're fucking with me. I can't believe it."

"Yes, Michelle was worried about what you might think if you found out about that, but she also said that there was nothing she could do. He wasn't going to change his name. It's just a coincidence. The last I heard of the other Randall, he'd snuck back into the US, and that was five years ago."

"Fine, let's move on. It's nothing. Let's call him the engineer to avoid confusion. Why wasn't he a suspect? He comes into Michelle's life, separates her from her daughter, and then she's taken. Don't you think that's suspicious?"

"He's a good man. He hired and paid Calvo, the most expensive there is."

"Did Calvo investigate him?"

"I don't know. But Suarez did. He did it before you arrived, and he didn't find anything. He told me that he thought that the kidnappers were already following the girl. Michelle just made it easier for them when she sent Michi to live with my mother."

"About Suarez, Andrés . . ."

"I know you don't trust him."

"No, it's not that. But there's something strange about him. I don't know who he is. I don't know why . . ."

"I gave him the name Calvo gave us. He knows everything."

"I was sure you would have, but I wanted to discuss it with you. I'd like to meet with him."

"Whenever you like. I'll tell him, but now, if you're going to call him, to put your mind at rest, please listen: I've known him since before you were born. And if it was a choice between putting my life in your hands or his, forgive me, but I'd go to him first. I'll tell him, I promise, but he's a good man, the only one you can trust."

Once more, Ethan was stunned by his friend's blind faith. "Fine. I understand. I'll call him."

"And I'll tell him the next time I see him."

"Thank you, Andrés. Goodbye."

It wasn't hard to decide what his next step should be. He didn't really have a choice. Ethan decided to put his trust in Andrés's judgment about Suarez, as well as the fact that the Matapatria was desperate to find him. Now Suarez was his only lead, and whether he was on Ethan's side or setting a trap for him, Ethan would be ready for the former inspector. He took out the phone that tied them together and sent a text.

We need to talk. I'll follow your instructions. Let me know if you receive this.

He waited a few moments as though he were expecting an instant response. But then his thoughts got lost in the reflection on the screen, and he started to daydream. When he came back to reality, he threw the phone onto the bed. The moment he let go, the annoying device began its irritating ring.

"Hello, Suarez. I'm following your instructions, as you can see."

"Yes. So long as you follow my instructions exactly, everything will be fine."

"I wouldn't be so sure about that. Andrés gave you the name we uncovered, didn't he? It was a trap to lead them to you."

"Yes, it was. Your detective's goons followed him and slipped a tracking beacon onto him. I was watching from afar. But what they didn't know was that Andrés is wise, and he follows my instructions too. He used a phone no one knows about. But even if they'd bugged that, they'd still be going down a blind alley. I am pleased to inform you that my inquiries have been productive."

"Your inquiries into the name Calvo turned up, I imagine. So you went ahead on your own?"

"When an opportunity to make headway presents itself, it's a sin not to take it."

"But don't you think it might have been another trick, a way to catch you out?"

"No, not unless they also know that I have Jonathan's phone. Remember? All it took to unblock it was a piece of plastic. But I admit that the name was useful. His chat and message history allowed me to see who else they'd been in contact with and break the codes they use for their deals. I've learned that he has a team of four policemen under his command: extortion, kidnapping, and protection of certain drug traffickers. They're professionals but not very on the ball. They don't even know that Jonathan is dead, so they're not expecting any trouble. I was able to put together their routines without even having to put them under surveillance. They may never even find out about us. How much better can things get?"

Ethan was torn. The man's smug attitude, not to mention the fact that he seemed to do everything perfectly, were supremely annoying, but he also felt a grudging respect for what Suarez had achieved. "Yes, but you shouldn't have told Andrés about Jonathan. That was a fuckup."

"You can keep making petty arguments like a schoolboy or come with me to uncover them. Here's the situation: the gang is led by the guy and his girlfriend; the three others are lower ranked. The couple is the brains, and the others follow their orders. They rent a warehouse in a more or less abandoned industrial lot where I imagine they keep their victims. Since I've been following them, they've picked up a young woman, not more than twenty. They take turns watching her, but at night they leave her alone. That's how confident they are. They've beaten her and abused her, and last night the man guarding her raped her. He told her that she'd be in trouble if she told the others, but the fact that he's started taking liberties leads me to believe that they don't think they'll get the ransom and time's running out. The couple always comes to visit at dusk to bring groceries and settle accounts, but tomorrow he's on the day shift, and she's on the night one. There's a game on TV, so we won't be disturbed."

"What? What game?"

"Of course, you're a gringo. Soccer's not your thing. The national team is playing tomorrow—that's why she's taking the shift. The entire country will come to a halt. If we win, there'll be partying in the streets. If we lose, it'll be a funeral. Either the streets will be packed or empty, and both serve our purposes. I imagine that he'll come by to relieve her when it's over. Or maybe he'll go before so they can watch it together; either works. They're the ones we're interested in, and the soccer game will make sure that we don't get any unexpected visitors. If we go just before kickoff, we'll catch her on her own and wait for him, and if he's already there we'll just be saving time. We'll have until five in the morning before they're relieved."

Ethan didn't respond.

"What do you say?"

A shiver ran down Ethan's spine as he said, "We're not going to get a better chance, are we?"

"Precisely."

6

A Moment of Fury

When Ethan opened his eyes, he felt agitated and nervous. He couldn't remember the dream, but he knew that it had been related to his fears about what the coming night would hold in store for him. And death. Maybe it was he who had died. That could happen in dreams; they could go on even after you'd died. Maybe not. Maybe he'd killed someone. Whatever had happened, he'd woken up disoriented and annoyed, exhausted. At least nothing strange or supernatural had happened, which was both reassuring and disappointing.

He looked at his phone; it was almost an hour before he'd set the alarm to go off. Through the curtain he saw the morning birds in the predawn light and heard the sound of an engine or two in the distance. He turned over, trying not to waste the little time he had left to rest. He couldn't allow himself to be sleepy—today was the day. He had to stay relaxed. But his pulse was pounding. He spent five minutes lying there, his mind racing, and then decided to take a piss. Maybe he'd been woken up by his bladder. In the bathroom he heard a truck drive through the neighborhood, making a sad mechanical sound that went perfectly with the bleak horizon—today was the day. He went back to bed, still kidding himself that he'd be able to get back to sleep. But not for long. He reset the alarm for twenty-four hours later. *For when it's done*, whispered a silent, anxious voice. *Today is the day, and the alarm will wake up you or your killer, letting you know whether you've been successful. It'll all be out of your hands.* Successful or not, there could be no regrets because they didn't have a choice. Either they got the information and found themselves on the Mara hit list, or they lost to the kidnappers and probably got themselves killed in the process. However careful Suarez's planning was, they both accepted that a shoot-out was a very real possibility.

He went down to the main street just as the sun was peeking over the horizon. He wanted to have breakfast outside the apartment, which had begun to feel like a prison. On his way, he bought a fitness magazine to read but couldn't take in anything. Today was the day.

He wondered why he was getting so worked up. He'd been on dangerous missions like this before. He'd handled wild gunfights and organized arrests in the worst possible conditions, but now the stakes were so high and the potential results so unpleasant that he had no reason to be hopeful. He had good reason to fear their success as much as their failure. There was one outcome he was afraid of most of all, an unthinkable one that felt like a lead weight in his stomach: that Ethan and Suarez would break them, only to confirm that Michi was indeed dead. Then there'd be no reason for him to stay in the country any longer. He'd have to fly back with her blood forever on his hands.

The morning dragged on lazily, and he was unable to do anything productive. So he just walked through the city, weighted down by all of his burdens. Today was the day. He repeated the mantra compulsively. Today was the day. He thought about what Michi deserved and what she must have been through. There was an instinctive aspect to our relationship with children who depend on us, a kind of magical bond that helped us to focus and ignore logic. When he thought of Michi, he was overcome by a sense of responsibility and a need to protect her. The need to get her back and feel that she still had a future. It was Michi's future that was at stake, not his. He saw things with raw clarity: even if it was still possible to get her back by paying a ransom or by force, he'd be trading his life in return. Was it worth it? If he could get her back, he suddenly realized, if he could do it, then yes: it would be worth it. He'd swap places with her in a second, without thinking. And somehow that unexpected, suicidal impulse relaxed him. Today was the day.

He went back to the apartment and locked himself in, channel surfing, grateful that the apartment had cable. He could flick through the infinite range of networks indefinitely without ever taking in the image on the screen. Time stood still. Nothing happened. Several times he went to the window, and the blue sky shimmered and throbbed under the blinding sun. No matter how many times he went to look, it didn't change. The star appeared to be happy where it was, at its zenith, tormenting him, broiling the atmosphere, chasing away the shadows.

Ethan longed for and feared the designated hour in equal measure. Deciding that he'd allow the heat to drain him so he'd be forced to buy something, he went out again to walk in the sun—very unusual behavior in these parts. The guard greeted him with a dutiful smile, and he walked away from the gated community, distracted by the sights. When he got to the store, he forgot what he'd gone in there for. The establishment was small and claustrophobic, and the air grew thicker the farther inside he went, out of range of the fan on the wall, which appeared to be doing its job in the most lackluster way imaginable. The density of the atmosphere made him thirsty, and he went to the refrigerated drinks. Its fogged glass dripped so that it looked as though the machine itself was sweating. Inside, of course, the cans were warm.

He walked back, exhausted by the heat, its sheer spitefulness making him irritable. Crossing through the barrier into the private neighborhood, he answered the guard's offer—"I can have things brought to you, you know"—with a half smile. He locked himself back in his cell and collapsed in front of the TV to continue unseeing the shows. Then he found himself checking his gun but couldn't remember what line of thought had led him into it. He made himself go back to the TV after examining the fridge. That was when he remembered the other things he was supposed to have gotten at the store. He cradled the remote and remembered his endless arguments with Ari and how angry she got. He realized that at that moment all he wanted was for her to be there with him, scoffing at his grumpiness and the absurd way he judged people. He ached for Ari as though there were a hole inside of him. He couldn't help thinking that everything he'd done so far had been a mistake, a mistake he couldn't escape. A struggle was going on inside of him, and as much as he tried to avoid it, it centered on his fears that Ari wouldn't come back, that he'd lost her by going off on a wild-goose chase. He tried to reassure himself by thinking of ways he could bring this chapter of his life to an end and try to undo the damage he'd done. But he knew it was impossible.

Behind the curtain the sun began to go down. The light turned orange and the horizon purple. He emerged from a deep personal pit, regretting not having had a nap to clear his head. He yawned, stretched, showered, and headed for the meeting point.

Following Suarez's characteristically punctilious instructions, Ethan left the car in a parking lot with twenty-four-hour security and went into a nearby mall. He rode a service escalator that no one used down three flights to the rear loading bay. There, he waited five minutes to make sure that he wasn't being followed, went back up, and left through the food court among a crowd of families and couples. He crossed the street and turned down another, smaller, more solitary one, where he waited behind a row of dumpsters along with a group of bums, who eyed him warily. Suarez appeared in an unmarked minivan.

"I see it's a national habit to forget your plates."

"Good evening. I imagine that your detective takes similar precautions. He's a good professional. Do you like your apartment?"

"My apartment?"

"Yes, where you're sleeping now. You'll be safe there so long as you're not followed."

"Let me guess—you found it for me?"

"Andrés asked me to arrange it. There's no better place for you in the city. The Mara won't find it easy to get to you there. Not bad, hmmm?"

He'd been in Suarez's hands right from the start. He was fully involved in everything Andrés was. Maybe that was why he'd made the stupid mistake of telling him about Leidy. Maybe they really were as close as Andrés said. Ethan was forced to conclude that this was a good sign: if someone knew exactly where he was and he was still alive, that was all it could be. But he was still going to keep one eye on the former policeman.

"Well done. It was a good choice," Ethan said. "Have you planned how we're going in? I don't like to make things up on the fly."

"The girlfriend will be there, with him or without him. Definitely in the front area. They never move. They park their cars in front and go in and out of that door, but the warehouse has a rear entrance they don't bother securing. That's how we'll come at them. Are you a good shot?"

"Yes, but it's been a while."

"I don't think it'll be necessary, but we should be careful. If she's alone, we'll interrogate her. If they're together, we'll separate them and take turns. You know you can't speak, don't you?"

"This isn't my first time. No one will hear my accent. We're not going to make it easy for them."

"If you do speak long enough for them to recognize you, we need to shoot them there and then and make sure they're dead. Understand? It'll be them or us."

Ethan had met lost or angry souls who'd committed murder in fits of emotion, addicts driven to criminality by their habit, and gang members raised in violence and turned into rabid animals. He had fought with people he considered to be evil, people with perverse egos, and parasites willing to kill just to make themselves feel powerful. But all Suarez gave off was solitude and sadness. When he'd first met him, he'd thought he was a good man, a professor type who calmly defeated his opponents at chess. He never would have imagined him hurting a fly. But that same person had just suggested killing two people in cold blood. Planning with a mercenary's cold pragmatism, he hadn't thought twice. Suarez's judgments were purely practical; morals didn't come into it. *When you're fighting monsters, at what point do you have to become a monster yourself?*

"But killing them would be dangerous too. You know the consequences."

"Yes."

"The best scenario is to interrogate them without revealing our identities. We need to find out who their client is without their suspecting what we want."

"I'm sure that you've thought hard about it."

"I see it like this. Together with the list of victims we were given, I obtained several more, so we have more than a dozen. I'll ask them about each ransom, and if they tell us that one or two weren't a kidnapping, I'll ask them who their clients were, and that will lead us to the girl. God willing, they'll think what I want them to think: that we're a gang looking to move in on their territory. They won't suspect us of looking for a girl stolen from a poor family."

"It might be that they have money after all."

Suarez raised his eyebrows. "You'd know more about that than I do."

"Well, let's be optimistic. The motive wasn't money. What about Jonathan's death?"

"As I said, they haven't even heard about it, but I considered it. He was one of their informants, and all the cases we're going to ask them about are linked to him. The more we ask about, the more they're going to be thinking of a rival gang, not the girl."

"Still, it doesn't seem as though we have a choice."

"I don't know. This seems to be the best way to me. What worries me most is if we don't get them straightaway. There might be shooting. In that case, I have no idea what might happen."

Ethan nodded. *At what point do you have to become a monster yourself?*

They barely spoke during the remainder of the short drive, which took them out of the center and into the suburbs, where slums alternated with industrial estates. They were both lost in their own thoughts: the game was about to begin. After driving up some small hills, they found themselves looking down on a neglected industrial park. Suarez pointed to a building on a large lot about half a mile away. They methodically changed into entirely black outfits. Suarez handed Ethan a bulletproof vest, and they blacked out their eyes before pulling on balaclavas.

"Is there any trace of the other victims?"

"No, they know how to get rid of them."

"You don't think she's alive, do you?"

"You were sure she was."

"Not anymore."

Ethan checked his gun for the last time and watched Suarez walk around to the trunk, from which he took a case for a long-barreled firearm.

"You're bringing a shotgun?"

"Oh yes, a real beauty. Beretta, a modern classic. With a gas intake for different kinds of shot. It has a computer underneath that counts each shot . . ."

Ethan was surprised by Suarez's enthusiasm. Suarez, the emotionless hermit, completely lacking in human feeling or a sense of humor, was getting all worked up over a shotgun. Given what he thought of the man, Ethan couldn't help laughing. "You're really going to bring a hunting weapon? Wouldn't you rather something more . . . appropriate?"

"She's been with me for many years. She's good, reliable, and very quick. I'm very happy with her. She's my baby."

"Fine, fine." Ethan smiled sardonically.

"Yes, I know. You young people just want what you see in the movies. You want guns that look cool, like a Hollywood gangster. But then you have no idea how to use them, care for them, or even clean them."

"I've used a pistol and my short-barreled Remington all my life, and I've never had any trouble."

"Have you ever had to kill anyone?"

"I've been in some serious shootouts. I can handle myself."

"But what I'm asking is whether you've ever had to shoot a beaten man, knowing that he had to die. If you've ever looked anyone in the eyes before killing them. It's not the same as shooting into a cloud of dust when there's noise raging all around you, even if there is a cadaver behind it all."

He'd made fun of Suarez, and the bitter ex-cop was fighting back. Suarez was determined to have the last word one way or another, and he was always on firm ground because he didn't make things up or take gambles. His gaze was both hollow and deeply sincere.

"No. I've never executed anyone in cold blood, if that's what you mean."

"Well, you should prepare yourself. Is that your weapon?"

Ethan brandished the automatic. "Considering the fact that I've only been in the country a couple of weeks, this doesn't seem a bad option."

Suarez opened the cushioned case. Inside, in addition to the shotgun was an older stablemate: sawn off like a pump-action, with a filed-down muzzle and milled flutes. Suarez handed it over.

"You'll do better with this one. You won't have to look into anyone's eyes, just the smoke and dust. It's pretty powerful."

He handed Ethan a snub-nosed cartridge with green plastic casing. The tip had been scored hexagonally, while the end was bronze-colored metal.

"This is a Remington 12/89, an eighty-nine-millimeter super-magnum."

Ethan studied it, imagining the damage a cartridge like that could do. "I know it well. If we use this, anyone standing in front of us had better say their prayers."

"I pray that we won't have any trouble, but if there is any shooting, it'll be at close quarters, and this is my best friend for short-distance work. It has quite a kick, but I'm used to it. I hope you will be."

"I will be."

"You don't need to aim this one like a pistol."

"I won't need to aim it at all."

They walked over a weed-covered hillock to a run-down chain-link fence into which Suarez had at some point cut an opening. From there, the hill sloped down about fifteen feet to the building, from which a weak light shone. Crouching down, they surveyed the terrain. There was a pair of windows on each side where the offices must have been, with no other protection than fold-up shutters, a main gate for vehicles, and an entrance for pedestrians cut into the corrugated iron. At the end of a gravel path several feet away sat two black SUVs. Suarez pointed out, unnecessarily, that both the man and the woman were inside.

They waited a few minutes for night to fall completely and crept down the hill along a makeshift track. Once at the bottom, they slipped along the length of the warehouse, which was made from concrete blocks, until they got around to the back, where there was a metal door for the service entrance similar to the one around the front. As Suarez had already found on a scouting mission, the building hadn't been built with security in mind, and the kidnappers, who had grown overconfident after years of activity without a single hiccup, hadn't bothered to make any improvements. The lock was the kind you'd see on a garden gate and gave easily. Waving to his partner to stay quiet, Suarez opened the door little by little, and they poked their heads inside.

A large space stretched out in all directions beneath the metal roof twelve feet above with saw-toothed openings for skylights. In front of them was a four-foot-wide passage flanked by two seven-foot-high partition walls. They enclosed a small bathroom next to the door they'd opened and another three rooms placed where they'd seen the windows from outside. Suarez pointed to the second on the right and put his hands together at the wrists, as though they were tied up. Then he put his hand over his mouth like a gag. Ethan indicated that he understood: the kidnapping victim was in there.

At the other end of the passage, about fifteen feet along, was another half-open metal door that led into the warehouse's working area. Its frame stood out in the darkness. That was where the man and woman were. Some lights placed low down, perhaps table lamps they'd brought with them or light bulbs connected with extension cords, gave off a dirty yellow glow. At a sign from Suarez, they each advanced along the walls on either side, scouring the empty space for anything that might get in their way. The place hadn't been maintained for a long time; a thick layer of dirt had accumulated, and the passage was scattered with apparently abandoned objects: the frame of a chair, a bicycle, and lots of damp, grimy papers. The sliding windows that looked into each room revealed only a darker black. Suarez pointed, and Ethan saw the silhouette of the girl tied to both ends of the bed, lying still. Was she sleeping? Could her eyes, which must have grown used to the dark, see him? Trying to avoid any unforeseen consequences, Ethan stopped before he got to a strip of light coming from the door at the end of the hall. There was barely any sound on the other side, no voices at all. They listened harder and recognized the muffled, urgent, excitable sounds of a couple having sex. Suarez smiled, not like a voyeur but like someone who knew they'd arrived at exactly the right moment. Each man took a deep breath. Suarez looked to Ethan to make sure that he was ready. Ethan brandished the handcuffs in reply, and Suarez gave the signal.

A kick to the door sent it smashing against the wall with a bang, and they burst out from the darkness like something from their targets' worst nightmares.

"Back! Back! Get up, you bastard; then don't move!"

They moved farther into the room, pointing their guns at the lovers, who were dumbfounded and unable to react. Suddenly they had been confronted with a pair of monstrous, hooded shapes casting huge shadows onto the ceiling, filling the silent space with barked shouts that echoed around the huge metal shell, shrill, cold, and intimidating. As the sound bounced between the different surfaces, it grew almost inhuman.

The man froze while the woman opened her eyes in terror and fell back on the sofa where they'd been lying. The sofa was a cheap red one that stood next to a fold-out bed a few feet away. Other furniture included a table and fold-out chairs, a small portable stove, and a squat refrigerator connected by a mess of cables that also led to three standing lamps, the only lights in the room. The man stood up in his wrinkled shirt, obeying the orders of these howling ghosts.

"Behind your back! Hands behind your back! *Behind your back, you bastard!*"

Surrendering, he put his hands behind his back. He was watched by his companion, who was still on the sofa. She tried to put an arm across her chest, but this action was immediately answered with a shotgun barrel in the face.

"Stay still! Don't move!"

She meekly raised both hands, letting her breasts fall free. Ignoring her, Ethan handcuffed the man and kicked him to the ground, where he lay still. Both of the prisoners were familiar with armed raids and quietly obeyed the orders. With the man on the ground, Ethan turned to the woman and cuffed her in the same way, with her hands behind her back. Suarez grabbed the man by the legs and pulled him a few feet away to make room. Then he rested the gun barrel on his head to emphasize his orders not to move. Next, Ethan took out a cloth and shoved it into the woman's mouth before tying a gag over it. He grabbed her by the right elbow and led her to one of the chairs, making her sit down. Then he carefully tied her to the back.

When she was properly trussed up, he started to breathe more easily. His mask was damp with heavy breathing, and his heart was thumping in his chest. He allowed himself a moment to catch his breath. So far, everything had gone well. Then he looked at her naked chest and her frightened gaze and instinctively buttoned her blouse. For a moment he felt empathy for her, forgetting she was an unscrupulous criminal who had kidnapped, tortured, and killed innocent girls.

Ethan turned to the male prisoner, who was lying still with Suarez's gun to the back of the head, but he saw something he hadn't expected. Although his partner's face was obscured by his black camouflage, he was clearly unhappy. Suarez looked him in the eye and slowly shook his head as though something were wrong. Ethan was confused, but he decided to finish the job before asking any more questions. Without saying a word, they picked up the man and in the thick, dreamlike silence broken only by the squeaking of the chair legs and rustling of the rope, bound and gagged him as well. Then Suarez took out a roll of duct tape that Ethan hadn't noticed before and covered their eyes in several layers, letting it painfully glue to their eyelids. When he'd finished, they went back out to the rear, returning to the shadows, which fell slowly down from the ceiling to meet them. Once they'd gotten through the door, they disappeared completely. They walked down the gloomy passage and once they'd got to the service exit, took off their hoods so they could speak in whispers.

"What's wrong? You look upset."

"It's not him!"

"What?"

"It's not the deputy chief. It's one of the others."

"Who? One of the other policemen?"

"Yes! One of the underlings."

"Huh, fuck."

Suarez put his hand to his head and wandered away for a few feet before coming back. "Great. So she's fucking around behind his back."

"So it would seem."

"And we've arrived right in the middle of it. That's why they were so afraid when they saw us. They thought we might be him."

"I think so."

"They might even be relieved that we're not the boyfriend . . . but that won't help us. He probably doesn't know shit."

Suarez shrugged. He continued to walk around, growing more and more frustrated.

"I had them *bugged*! They switched shifts; the boyfriend was supposed to be here." The quintessential perfectionist, the mistake was driving him crazy. "I'll ask them why they switched shifts."

"And how will that help?"

"You're right."

In the distance, they heard something howling. Eventually, Ethan spoke. "Well, we have to go back. If we leave them alone too long, it'll seem stranger than it already is."

"But now we don't have the time we thought we had. We have until the boss gets here. Maybe when the game ends, in about an hour—I'm not sure. I didn't watch them all; I don't know if they're expecting him; I don't know if he's even coming. You understand? I don't know why he didn't come or if he's coming later."

"The only thing we know for sure is that those two weren't expecting anyone. That gives us an advantage. So now what do we do?"

"The guy won't know anything, that's for sure."

"What about her? She might still be useful to us."

"It was the boss we wanted, but she'll have to do."

"How do we play it? What if we say that we're here to free the girl who was kidnapped?"

"Then tomorrow they'll kill her whole family."

"Right, I wasn't thinking. We'd better stick with the plan, but now we really need to keep them separate."

"Now especially. She saw you do up her blouse; she won't be so afraid of you."

"I'll take the guy out into the passage and cover his ears too. You'll need to be quick."

"I will be."

"Give me a moment."

Ethan left a confused Suarez and went to the room where the kidnappers had put the victim. He put on the balaclava and cautiously crept inside, trying not to wake her, but after all the commotion she was obviously already awake. When his eyes got used to the dark, he could see her face. She was exhausted, dirty, and bruised, gagged with what looked like a sock, and her hands and feet were tied to the bed. Her ankles and wrists were covered in cuts and gashes, some of which looked infected. The girl shivered when she saw him, her eyes bulging, utterly confused by what was going on and scared that the worst was to come. Ethan went over and tried to convey reassurance, although his hurry, not to mention the balaclava, didn't help.

"We're going to set you free. Try to hold on a little longer."

He loosened the ropes on her legs, and she responded with a muffled groan of relief. Then he went back out into the passage, where Suarez was waiting, unhappy at his time wasting. Ethan gave him a defiant look.

"I had to. We couldn't leave her like that."

Then the two shadows went back to the couple, who'd spent several minutes in absolute limbo, blind and gagged with no idea what was going on. They were suffering the worst kind of fear: fear of the unknown.

"We're not going to kill you if we don't have to," Suarez said, removing the gag from the woman. "We don't have much time, so let's get this over with quick. I don't want any trouble, so don't bother screaming or making yourself difficult."

She felt the pressure on her mouth release and stretched the muscles a little before answering. "I . . . I'd like to thank you for behaving like gentlemen. My name is Johanna. I know there's no need for anything bad to happen. I only ask that you remember that we're human beings . . ."

Suarez looked at Ethan and clucked his tongue. Ethan nodded. Then he took hold of the tape wrapped around her head and pulled roughly, peeling it away mercilessly. It took hair, eyebrows, and a few eyelashes with it. Johanna screamed, and her lover shivered, shuffling nervously. At a sign from Suarez, Ethan lifted him up until he was on his feet with the chair still strapped to his back. He was forced to walk stooped over, almost on all fours, like a penitent pilgrim.

"Take him away. He won't want to see what's about to happen to his girl."

When he heard this, the man spun around, but Ethan nudged him with his gun, and he waddled along like a tortoise. Suarez returned his attention to the woman, who opened her throbbing eyes with some difficulty.

"Unless she's someone else's girl, of course."

When she heard this, Johanna's expression changed immediately.

"Look, honey, I don't know if you thought we were a pair of suckers, but the two other guys have left, and it's just you and me now, all alone. You know that I have no problem treating you any way I like, don't you? Tell me. Look at me, and tell me."

She didn't answer but stared defiantly back at Suarez.

Instead of using violence or threats, he just reached for the top of the balaclava and smoothly took it off in a single movement. "If that's the way you want it . . ."

"No!" Johanna looked away quickly and shut her eyes tight. "I didn't see you! You know I didn't see you!"

Suarez held her firmly, struggling to lift her chin from her chest. She squeezed her eyes so tightly shut that a drop of blood ran down from her shorn eyebrow. He addressed her again in his habitual monotone.

"I think we understand each other, don't we?"

She answered hoarsely in a near grunt that choked her a little. "The keys to the car are in my handbag. You'll find everything you want in there; that's where I keep the money. Take what you want and go."

Suarez hesitated a second before putting the balaclava back on and going over to the bag. He emptied it out and picked up the keys. Then he went out the front door and walked to the car. He checked the doors, the glove compartment, and the trunk before coming back with a pair of briefcases, the smaller of which contained a laptop. When he came back inside, he locked the door behind him and went back to the woman, who was waiting patiently.

"There's ten thousand dollars inside. That's my laptop and phone; you can keep them. You've won the lottery, but there's nothing else—there's no point going on with this farce."

Now that she had gotten over her initial fright, Suarez admired her calm professionalism. He knew that it would be easy to get precise information about Michi out of her in exchange for her freedom, but then that would seal the fate of her family and very probably his own along with it. He opened the larger briefcase, and the sight of the bills gave him an ambivalent sensation: it was a poisoned bounty that would only encourage the gang to come after them. But now that she'd told him about it, he couldn't leave it behind. He mused over this as he opened the other briefcase.

He turned on the computer and barked authoritatively, "The passwords."

"The email is Mimbura1983. The telephone unlocks with an L shape."

Suarez opened the email and checked the messages as he continued his thus-far simple interrogation. Following the plan, he asked about each victim in turn, all apart from Michi. Johanna couldn't remember the names but told him to open an Excel file, which documented each of them along with the money earned, saying he could have it along with the laptop. She even made a joke about her bad memory and how she had to write everything down so as not to get confused. It was as though she were talking about a shopping list or a work schedule. Finally, Suarez moved on to Michi and got the answer he expected: she remembered her because she was a recent job but not the sum they'd received.

"There's nothing written here."

"I must have forgotten. It happens sometimes."

"Who was the client?"

"What client?"

"Come on, honey. We know you do jobs to order. I want the list of clients."

"We . . . we don't have any clients."

"Aww . . . you're going to force me to get tough." Suarez put the laptop down on a chair, got up, and took hold of her hair.

"I don't know—I don't know—I don't know. It's Greivin, my boyfriend—he deals with the orders."

"And what do you do? Don't lie to me; we've been watching you. We know you're not a fool."

"I deal with the kids. I organize the surveillance, and then I arrange the pickup and transport if needed. But we barely get any orders: one every year or two. That's it. I don't know; we hardly do any."

"The pickup, right . . . what do you mean by *transport*?"

"If . . . if they don't come here or to the city . . ."

"You've taken someone from the city?"

"That girl."

"Why?"

"I don't know. We had a very rich client, and that's what they asked for."

"Go on."

"I don't know. It was on the instructions of some Europeans with a lot of money. Some lawyers who deal with Greivin. They came a few months ago and gave him the job. Money was no object; they gave us the job, and that was it."

"Go on."

"That was the job with the girl, and I don't know any more. I don't know why they wanted her."

"I don't care about the girl. I care about the client. How was she transported?"

"I don't know; they had their own transport guy. A shitty truck driver they work with. He's a strange guy—he travels around a lot. He told me that we might see each other again. That if he had more business for me, we could talk. He seemed to be trying to impress me. Said he was very important, but nobody paid him any attention. He said he took shadows across America, from one end to the other, that the continent belonged to him. He was very ugly, nasty. I didn't like him. I gave him the girl, and he took her away. I don't know where."

"I don't give a shit about him or the girl. I want the client."

"Greivin handled that, really."

Suarez examined her closely. She wasn't lying. "OK. The truck driver. How do you contact him?"

"By email. He says that he has a hideout in Colombia where he goes when he doesn't have any jobs. He wanted me to come visit him—you get the idea."

"Who's the client?"

"I don't know. *I told you.* Greivin knows them. I don't."

"Have they made any other orders?"

"No, they didn't want any more. It's just money, you know?"

Suarez looked at his watch. "Tell me about your other clients."

"What do you want to know? I've never dealt with them."

"Just like you told me before. I want all the information."

Johanna tried to share all the information she could think of with a willingness that amazed her captor, but he'd stopped listening. He knew what to look for on the computer. Finally, he found it: the conversation with the driver who'd taken Michi to another country.

"How many orders have you had in the past few years?"

"Well . . . about five or six. Yes, the girl was the sixth."

173

"Which of them?"

She listed them plainly, without a hint of shame, pity, or regret, like an office worker reciting a list of purchase orders. "And the girl the Europeans wanted."

"Fine, now let's talk money."

Ethan was waiting impatiently by the back door next to his charge, who was slumped in the chair, his chin on his chest, blinded, gagged, and with his ears muffled, straining to hear the sounds he imagined must be coming from the room in front. Nothing could possibly reach him, as the conversation never rose much above a murmur. Ethan was walking up and down, almost tempted to remove the gag just so he'd have someone to talk to. He wondered what they'd do with the victim before they left and how to ensure her safety. He was running through different possibilities when he heard a rumbling sound that soon grew louder until it was unmistakable: one, maybe two, vehicles were approaching. As soon as he heard it, the prisoner lifted his head like an eager dog. Ethan looked at him and listened hard; the guy knew that someone was coming, and he knew exactly who it was. Ethan's breath quickened, and the adrenaline started to pump in anticipation of what was to come. Keeping his eye on the prisoner, he walked carefully to the main door. Once there, he clearly heard the sound of two large vehicles.

Suarez closed the computer as soon as he heard the sound and immediately asked Johanna who it was.

"I don't know."

She clearly did know and had been trying to keep the conversation going until they got there. He quickly shoved the cloth back into her mouth and assessed the different options. A few moments later he saw Ethan appear in the passage. Ethan held up two fingers. Suarez answered by waving at him to go back: they had to cover the two entrances, as well as the hostages. Ethan nodded and went back down the passage.

Moving with extreme stealth, Ethan crouched down to avoid being caught in the headlights that shone through the windows as the cars pulled in to park. When he got to his prisoner, he put the gun to his forehead and hissed, "*Ssshhh.*" The prisoner nodded slowly.

Suarez considered his options. They had no idea how many people might come: Just two or three others? Or had they brought more? He knew that if he and Ethan became trapped in there, it would be a massacre. These people weren't going to trade the lives of their colleagues for safe passage. They'd rather see them all dead. The rumbling of the new arrivals' engines disappeared simultaneously, and the lights beaming across the passage turned off. Suarez quietly crept away from his captive, took the cushions off the sofa, and went over to a metal column to take cover. The silence was intense. He counted his steps, checking the ground for anything he might trip over, calculating the exact distance. He checked the sitting figure again; she hadn't moved. When he got to the column, which didn't protect him completely but was something at least, he set up his improvised sandbags and lay down behind them as best he could, aiming at the door. From then on the seconds seemed to pass slowly, like drops of oil, as he tried to work out what was happening outside.

Suarez listened for the sound of a fourth door closing, but it never came. It was the three others, the deputy chief and the other two underlings. Or at least that would make sense. Then he heard it: a fourth door. But an appreciable period of time had passed since the third. Were there several people in the back seat? No, they'd come out the two doors. Why the delay? It could be a fourth person, or they might have picked something up from a seat. If they had computers or some other package, that would explain it. Suarez felt his chest tightening, speculating on how many there might be.

He looked at Johanna, who was staring straight at the door, gagged and unmoving, as though she were trying to control it with her mind. She knew—he had no doubt about that. She knew, and he saw the sweat on her forehead. She had the information, and he could see her doing the same calculations as him, planning something to get her out of a desperate situation.

He wondered whether they might have found his car. They'd hidden it well, but these were professionals. He dismissed the paranoid thought from his mind: they weren't looking for him; there was no reason they would even notice it. The silence grew thicker still, heavy, almost tangible. It was broken by the double beep of a car being locked and then another one. Why had it taken them so long to lock up? He could hear voices growing louder. Suarez tried to focus on the number of footsteps, ignoring the conversation, which didn't tell him anything about how many there were. How far was it from the cars to the door? He tried to estimate the distance, step by step, the number of feet on the ground. How many people? It was impossible to tell. Johanna was still staring intensely, almost obsessively, at the door. Suddenly the footsteps came to a halt.

Ethan also heard the beeps from the cars. They were followed by two male voices talking and an indeterminate number of footsteps walking away from him. They were heading for the front door, which was only to be expected. Should he take advantage of that to go outside or wait there with the hostage? The tension grew as he heard them move farther away, until suddenly they stopped, and one of the voices could be heard behind him, next to the outer wall. It was coming through the grate in the room where the kidnapped girl was being kept.

There's no way they can know, Suarez said to himself. *They're not making any effort to hide; they can't know.* Their conversation seemed relaxed, unless it was a trick. He waited. Nothing. The silence was all encompassing.

The voice started up again near Ethan, who followed it with his gun all along the wall while still keeping the door covered. He traced out its path with the gun pointed at what he estimated would be the chest of a large man. The prisoner remained still. The voice moved away.

Nothing. Some footsteps and someone saying something. Something about coming back. Laughter. How many of them were there? The footsteps were very close. Something in Suarez's peripheral vision caught his eye. He saw Johanna rocking back and forth as though she were mentally disturbed. She was still staring at the door. She had started to make noise. Little by little she was getting the chair legs higher and higher, determinedly, making a clatter on the concrete floor. He wanted to motion to her to stop, but he knew it was useless; he couldn't stop her without making more noise. If they kept on talking outside, they wouldn't pay it any attention. Johanna was rocking as hard as she could, backward and forward. The chair creaked. They'd think it was just a normal sound. The clatter on the floor continued: tap, tap, tap. The chair creaked. The steps came up to the door and stopped. Tap, tap, tap. Louder and louder. Suarez looked at Johanna, the stupid bitch. Her whole being was focused on the movement. The chair was creaking a lot; the legs looked as though they were bending. Outside, they'd stopped talking. Suarez aimed at the door, or rather the space that would be there once it had opened. He heard a clinking sound. The chair almost tipped over. A key. He looked at his prisoner, who looked back with hatred in her eyes. A key slowly being inserted, each ridge slipping almost inaudibly into its slot. The chair buckled, and Johanna closed her eyes. The lock turned. The chair fell onto the floor with a bang, and she hit her head. The door began to open but stopped with the sound, revealing a thin vertical black line through which several bodies could be seen. Suarez didn't hesitate.

The interior of the warehouse exploded with a deafening roar accentuated by a metallic echo that expanded concussively into the space. Simultaneously, a flash burst from the end of the shotgun, blinding eyes that had grown used to the dark. Suarez was firing instinctively into the gap left by the half-open door, filling the metal with little dark holes. He fired again, and the second report merged with the echo of the first, making an earsplitting noise that was continued by the third and fourth shots. Anger, confusion, and chaos reigned. The door swung back against the frame again and again until it had almost been blown off. It was spattered with holes, giving it a moth-eaten look.

After the fifth shot he waited a second for the smoke to clear and his ears to stop humming. In all the noise he'd been unable to tell whether there'd been a scream, but he was sure he'd hit his target. Hoping to take advantage of the surprise attack, he left his shelter and ran to the door to finish them off before they had time to react, but in the general chaos he'd lost sight of Johanna, who'd managed to shake off the hastily tied gag.

Still deafened by the roar, she screamed with all her might, "He's going to the door! To the door!"

In reply a shot flew almost vertically from the outside up into the roof of the warehouse. Suarez dropped down and took shelter behind the column. The shot had obviously come from the ground. They might have been knocked down, but he'd lost the advantage. Two more wild shots accompanied the first, and Suarez crawled along the floor to avoid taking any more risks.

While the echo of the second shot could still be heard, Johanna shouted again. "There are two of them! Another's waiting by the back door!"

Suarez turned to her and fired twice at point-blank range, instinctively, without thinking. The shot ripped open her blouse, making it billow like a parachute as her body, tied to the chair, arched back, absorbing the force of the shot. Then it fell limply forward as tiny shards of fabric rained down over it. In answer, a full salvo spat back from outside, forcing Suarez to crawl into a safe place while the bullets clanged against the metal around him. This was followed by a hail of sparks and explosions that echoed around the metal walls. The volume of fire increased. Now there was more than one gunman, and Suarez had only a few shells left. He fired at the door again to give himself cover and thought of Ethan, who might not know what was happening. He heard a whispering followed by the sound of footsteps running away and shouted, praying that his partner would understand.

"Ethan: now! Now!"

Ethan tried to decide where best to position himself. If they came in, he'd have to cover Suarez from the passage, but if Suarez repelled them, he should take them on outside, before they had time to react. The two different paths crisscrossed in his mind's eye like rays of light. He had seconds to decide. He left his position and crawled to the room next to the one the hostage was in, the one that was closest to the cars. He listened hard and heard a weak dripping sound, as though from a faucet. He stopped in surprise. What was Suarez doing? Then he heard a bang, as though some furniture had fallen over. Following that, the passage lit up twice with flashes and roars, and he ran to the window. It had a screen, and when he opened it, he heard two shots from outside, shouting inside and out, people running around. He looked for the clasp to open the window but panicked and just forced it. Then he heard Suarez's shout.

"Ethan: now! Now!"

Fortunately, he'd anticipated his partner and fired blindly through the glass in the direction of the parking lot. The window was smashed into glinting smithereens. He waited a second to find a target, but when he couldn't see one, he fired again, more to cover Suarez than aiming at anything in particular. Ethan pulled the trigger, and the gun thundered into the night in an angry explosion of fire and powder. The explosion was so huge that he couldn't see if he'd hit anything.

Suarez heard Ethan's shots and took advantage of the time they gave him to hide behind the sofa and reload his shotgun. The space in front of him had grown calm once more, returning to the misleading but magnificent silence of the shadowy night. Nothing in Suarez's reduced field of vision was moving, but he strained his eyes, scanning for any sign of life. Nothing. Even the animals seemed to have gone quiet. His deafened ears were oblivious to the night breeze. Everything seemed to have frozen in time. In front of him, Johanna's inert body lay staring up at the ceiling as her blouse soaked up blood. He cursed her for having forced him to kill her and reassessed his situation, knowing that the open warehouse was unsafe. He tried to decide whether he should withdraw to the passage.

Silence fell upon the darkness once more, and Ethan looked out the window, trying to size up the situation. Everything had gone still. The area had returned to a state of tense silence. It had become a void, filled only by the sound of crickets chirping in the distance. In the darkness he made out the shapes of the cars but didn't detect any movement. He listened but heard nothing. Someone might be crawling along the ground, but he couldn't see where they were. Time crept on, slow and thick. Something was happening, but he couldn't tell what it was. His world had grown deceptively calm. He tried to decide whether to jump outside, but he knew that the move would be risky without cover. Then he heard running, leading him to believe that one of them had taken shelter among the cars, unless he'd hit them already. But that would be hoping for too much. He stayed still, believing he couldn't be seen, peering into the darkness in an unsuccessful attempt to make out the shapes. Then he heard the muffled sound of a car being unlocked and a door opening. He stepped forward and fired in an attempt to prevent the inevitable. Suddenly, brightness filled the room, glaring off the walls, lighting him up and blinding him at the same time. Ethan dropped to the floor, still seeing spots as he tried to avoid a couple of erratic shots that buzzed past his forehead. He crawled away from the window, blinking to clear his vision. The shotgun got lost somewhere along the way, but he made sure that he still had his pistol. There was more movement outside while he tried to find shelter. They were losing their initial advantage.

Suarez heard the shots and saw the passage light up. He realized that they'd returned to the cars. He wondered where to go. His and Ethan's position was rapidly getting worse, and there was nothing they could do about it.

Everything froze again. The parking lot outside was still completely dark apart from the two beams of light shining into the side of the warehouse. Now they were in a passive role; if the light hit them, they would be exposed. Fortunately the beams weren't wide. Now they were stuck in another hiatus that didn't work in their favor. There was nothing they could do but hide while their enemies took the initiative. Considering the risk presented by the large, unprotected space in front, Suarez decided to head for the central door, dragging the cushions with him like luggage he couldn't do without. From there he could cover both entrances, and Ethan could cover his back. If he stayed in the room, he'd be risking an ambush. He got to the threshold in time to see Ethan's shadow coming out of the lit room and crossing the passage, but he didn't dare to call to him. Where was the kid running off to? If he left the corridor, he'd be exposed on both sides. Was he a coward after all? As this thought came to him, he heard a new wave of shooting begin. It was all starting up again.

Ethan was pinned to the floor under the beams from the headlights, looking for the door while he regained his vision. To his left, he heard Suarez move. In front, he heard the muffled sound of a trunk opening. Whatever they had in there, it wasn't going to be good. He tried to think of a way to tip the scales in their favor. They didn't have much time, and the next attack would probably turn out badly for them. Without thinking too hard, he pulled himself out of the lit room in which he was trapped and slithered across the passage on his stomach to the other side so as to get back into the shadows. When he got to the rooms on the other side, he got up on all fours just before he saw Suarez next to the central door. Feeling safer, he took a deep breath.

Then all hell broke loose over their heads. A sheet of fire stunned their senses while the glass and walls were pockmarked with bullets, filling the space with spreading dust and smoke and reducing visibility to almost nil. The walls of the passage itself were ripped to shreds under the concussive fire. The bullets ripped through the entire building, embedding themselves in the opposite wall. Ethan was happy to have gotten out of there in time, although the bullets were still whistling around him, tearing through the inner walls as though they were made of paper. Trusting that the outer wall would protect him, he crouched under the window, another narrow sliding one that had been torn to shreds by the volley of fire.

Suarez covered his head with his hands, pressing himself as close to the ground as he could. The bullets streamed in and hit the passage, covering him in dust. He recognized the rat-a-tat of an AK-47 assault rifle, or the goat's horn, a favorite of drug dealers and other lowlifes, but he knew that this was just covering fire to keep them pinned down while the attackers planned the final assault. The sound of an engine gave him a clue as to what form that might take.

Ethan realized that the only way to turn things around was to go out and face them head-on. He knew it was risky, but he sensed that staying in the building would only court death. The shooting stopped again, and he took advantage of the lull to jump out the window, ignoring the shards of glass that stuck into him along the way. He fell behind the hidden facade, where the blanket of darkness was still undisturbed, a very different scene from the commotion and gunfire on the other side. He looked each way to make sure that no one else had decided to come around the back and saw that he was alone. He went around to the back door.

When the firing stopped, Suarez knew that they were ready to attack, and the noise of the engine seemed to echo his thoughts. He heard it rev while still in neutral until it charged forward with a devastating crash announcing the destruction to come. The 4x4 burst into the building, tearing away the door. It continued several feet, followed by a cloud of dust that blocked out everything before settling to make outlines visible once more. There was another brief pause, but that was then broken by indiscriminate fire from the Kalashnikov. Again, the main warehouse was filled with the hellfire of bullets and ricochets, and all Suarez could do was curl up in his sheltered position. He was sure he was safe until he found a way to respond. To the rear, another hail of bullets destroyed the back door, which buckled like a paper napkin once the lock had been blown away. The passage was now a horrific no-man's-land crisscrossed with bullets that crashed all over the warehouse in showers of stone, splinters, and metal shards, forcing him to crouch under the remains of the door, which was collapsing upon itself. Trapped between two lines of fire, blinded and suffocating, he turned as best he could toward the new threat, knowing that it would be the end of him.

Ethan heard the car smash through the main door and the rattling of the first wave of gunfire, followed a few beats later by footsteps running around to the door at the rear, where another volley of fire began with the screeching of bullets against metal and the creak as the iron sheeting buckled. From his position in the shadows he saw the attacker's shape and the flicker of sparks from the gun until he heard the door give way and crash loudly onto the floor. The attacker stepped inside. Ethan knew that this was his chance and followed him, firing as he went. The man was caught by surprise and tried to take cover while turning to fire at this new target. Suarez, however, still trapped in his fragile shelter, took the opportunity to fire all his remaining shells in that direction, almost blindly, still taking fire from the other side. He fired again and again until there was too much smoke to see anything. The gunman, caught in crossfire, was hit several times in the side and stumbled back outside, but Ethan was now in position and began shooting. The shots hit the ambushed man, and Ethan kept walking and firing. Like them, the man was wearing a Kevlar vest, making the blows painful but not deadly. Realizing this, Ethan aimed higher, between the man's eyes. The next shots went straight through his head, and the man fell before he could take another step. Meanwhile, Suarez was still holding out in the fetal position while withering fire rained down on him from the front. But then this salvo came to an end as well. Ethan was crouched down, breathing heavily, a few feet from the body, the stink of cordite in his nostrils, his throat bone dry. He was gasping, and when he held up his gun, he saw that he was trembling uncontrollably. Then he realized that another cease-fire had fallen. The silent night reasserted its dominance.

But things weren't yet calm: the reverberations from the shoot-out could still be felt, and no one dared move. The ringing in their ears maintained the illusion that the chaos was still going on, even though the night was now quiet. Nothing happened for almost a minute while the survivors waited for someone to make the next move. Ethan tried unsuccessfully to get control of his trembling body. This was the first time something like this had ever happened to him; it was as though he'd lost control of his hand. Finally, a shout rang out in the unnatural mist.

"Diego!"

But no one answered. The warehouse remained quiet for a few more seconds while Ethan and Suarez wondered what to do. Suarez slowly turned his shotgun toward the headlights, knowing that he had no more shells left, and Ethan, unseen in the shadows six feet away from the smoking corpse, recovered enough control over his body to identify the new threat and reload the gun as stealthily as he could.

Unexpectedly, as they planned the next move, the 4x4's wheels started to spin again, and it reversed, struggling to escape the surrounding structure, which made a creaking sound like a chain about to snap. Finally, it forced its way out like an animal breaking free from a trap, and they heard it circle around in the dirt, change gears, and then drive alongside the building before speeding down the dirt track toward the main road, briefly lighting up Ethan in its headlights. A second later, it was just a pair of red dots disappearing off into the dark. This development took them both by surprise. Ethan stepped back into the passage.

Everything was quiet now, although the ringing in his ears wouldn't stop. Behind him, the body was bent over its weapon. Inside, the dust and smoke floated in whimsical shapes, making it even harder to see; in front of him was the kidnapper they'd captured, still tied to his chair but lying on the ground. He'd been hit by fire from his colleagues. Moving on from him, they saw some of the partition walls now barely existed anymore while those still standing were riddled with bullet holes. The door in the center was hanging on one hinge, torn to pieces. Suarez was still crouching under it like a cat. Ethan mimed to him to stay still and walked through the dense atmosphere to where he was. He came out of the larger part of the warehouse, which was just as dark and misty as the rest, and looked at the ruined door in the darkness. While Suarez stood up, Ethan went outside and found the results of the first shotgun barrage: another body lying about twelve feet from the door, its stomach blown open. It looked as though the man must have dragged himself along the ground before dying. Ethan walked around the perimeter, checking every nook and cranny, before coming back into the parking lot. The remaining cars were shot up. Using the light on his phone, he saw a trail of blood that stopped where the fleeing SUV had been. Behind him, he heard Suarez coming over, dusting himself down, and proudly reloading the shotgun.

"That's why the bastard escaped. You got him."

"Or you did."

"One of us at least."

"How badly was he hurt?"

"Judging from the way he was driving, not badly. But there's blood; we definitely got him. Four dead bodies and not a scratch on us. I think we may have used up all our luck for the next few years."

"I hope that we won't have to test it like that again. Do you know who they were?"

"Of course, the rest of the gang. It was the deputy chief who got away. The way I see it, they came for a group meeting, and when he saw that he was the last one standing, and wounded, too, he decided to beat feet. He was the most dangerous one to leave alive."

"The good news is that he doesn't know who we are."

"Yes, and that's why we need to get out of here right away."

"You're right."

"You saved me. You did well—thank you."

Ethan didn't reply. He was humbled and gratified by the compliment, like a child being praised by his teacher. But Suarez wasn't done. He pointed to the man who'd dragged himself away from the front door.

"He's still alive."

Ethan looked at the unmoving body. "Did you see his stomach? He won't last long."

"Sure, but we can't take the risk. Go and see if the girl's still alive. I'll take care of this."

Ethan nodded and walked to the back entrance to pick up the weapon he'd dropped. Suarez strode over to the last survivor, who appeared to be unconscious. He peered down at him with disgust, then gave him a push, but the man didn't react. "Hey, you."

The man couldn't hear him. Suarez lifted the barrel of the shotgun, which was still red hot, and put it against the man's eyebrow, burning the skin. The wounded man, woken by the terrible pain, opened his eyes in bewilderment. He had no idea what was going on.

"Hey, rapist. It's easy to abuse little girls, isn't it? You motherfucker. Listen to me."

The dying man, faint from blood loss, tried to say something, but it only came out as shapeless wheezing.

Suarez put the barrel against the man's nose and stood up to give himself some space. "I wanted you to know."

Ethan heard the shot while he stepped into the makeshift cell, fearing the worst. To his surprise, however, he found the mattress tipped over with the girl still tied up, lying unmoving but safe beneath the mattress with no obvious wounds. He untied her ankles, and she curled up in pain and fear. When he released her, her face twisted up in absolute terror. Sweat, dirt, and dried blood had accumulated on her bedraggled clothing and above the gag, which Ethan removed with brief words of comfort so as to avoid giving himself away.

"Don't worry; they're dead."

The girl burst into tears, trembling as she got up. She clung to his hands but didn't open her mouth. Ethan realized that her terror hadn't just made her cry; the bottom half of her clothing was soaked through. He put the mattress back on the bed and sat her shivering body down before going back into the front room to take a bottle of water from the fridge. He gave it to her. On his way, he saw Suarez head off toward his vehicle. A few minutes later, he parked by the door to pick up the briefcases with the money and the computer. The girl allowed herself to be led into the back seat, where she collapsed in exhaustion. They pulled away and took her into the city without saying a word. The car floated over the silent, empty freeway as though in a dream, until the first traffic lights brought them back to reality. Suarez coughed and murmured.

"We lost."

Ethan didn't say a word, but he nudged Suarez's shoulder, wondering how he could possibly say that after everything that had happened. Then he thought he saw a smile beneath the mask.

"The game."

He pointed to the streets, which were pregnant with silent bitterness. Ethan smiled too. Suarez stopped the car at a corner two blocks away from the public attorney's office.

Turning to the girl, he said, "This is the most trustworthy public official in the country; you'll be safe with them. Go there, and tell them everything that's happened. They'll help you."

She got out, still bewildered. Unable to believe what had happened, she didn't even manage to thank them. Or, for that matter, say anything at all. She stumbled for a few feet and turned back toward them like a frightened puppy, but they waved to her to go on. She nodded and obeyed like a sleepwalker. When she'd made it halfway there, the two officers guarding the building saw the state she was in and ran to help. Before they got to her, Suarez pulled away with a screech of rubber, and they disappeared in the opposite direction. Suarez told Ethan that he would take him back to his house. He could pick up the car tomorrow. Then they remained silent for the rest of the ride. Ethan didn't know whether it was because he was still trying to take in what had happened or because he hadn't yet even begun to. He tried to remember what he had been thinking about, but he couldn't. It was as though he'd been empty for the entire journey, as vacant as the light of the passing streetlamps. Suarez pulled up outside the gated compound. Ethan got out, still dressed fully in black but with his face clean and uncovered. Suarez said goodbye with a slight nod, like a work colleague, but Ethan couldn't allow it to end so coldly.

"What a night, Suarez. Hey . . . you can come in if you like. I'm sure I have something to eat."

"Many thanks, but we need to check ourselves for wounds and see to your arm. It's covered in glass."

"You never stop, do you?" Ethan got back into the vehicle, and they passed through the gate.

"We need to copy everything and then destroy the originals," Ethan said. "If they have a way of tracking them, we're screwed."

In the kitchen, they looked around and found some bread, cheese, and a couple of beers, but Suarez refused with uncharacteristic friendliness. Ethan felt as though a completely different person were standing in front of him.

"Are you a member of Andrés's church?"

"No. Just that I can't drink. I drank a lot for a long time—I'm an alcoholic."

"Ah, OK. I'm sorry. I put my foot in it."

"No, you didn't know. And it's appropriate; it was an excellent raid. One of the hardest nights of my life. You were a very good comrade in arms."

"Thank you. I . . . admire what you've done. I don't know why you've done it, but clearly you're a great detective, and I've known a few."

Suarez carefully patted Ethan down, looking for internal damage. Strangely, after he'd seen to his partner and treated several of his wounds, he wouldn't allow Ethan to return the favor. Ethan put it down to Latin machismo.

"I lost my family years ago," Suarez said with unexpected candor. "Andrés is the only friend I have left. He helped me when all I did was drink, and in his infinite generosity and patience, he picked me up off the street time after time. I owe my new life to him. Of course I have to help find his niece. I'd rescue her from hell if I have to, because that's exactly what he rescued me from."

With each new revelation, Ethan was able to build a much fuller picture of this mysterious man.

"I have to confess: at first I didn't want to work with you. I only agreed because Andrés insisted."

"Don't worry—I didn't like the idea either. And I understand. I mean, I know how you see gringos, and some of my fellow countrymen ruin our reputation, chasing after drugs and whores."

"It wasn't because you're a gringo. I work alone. It's hard to trust someone else. It's not gringos that worry me. Have you seen the way our young people talk? They say *issue* instead of *problema, fuck* when they're surprised . . . it comes naturally to them. They want to be like you and scorn our traditions. That's what worries me, not the gringos. You won the war, but we're still losing."

"When did we fight a war?"

"The culture wars. And when you've won the battle for culture, you can impose your thinking on everyone else."

"I think the same in English and Spanish. I don't feel that one is dominant over the other."

"You've never been to the indigenous reserves. You've never seen an entire people forced to do all their paperwork or study their history in someone else's language. It changes everything. It's the enslavement of everything that is truly theirs. That's true colonization, the colonization of thoughts and language. Young people learn from your films, music, and myths. That's why they think you won the war against Hitler at Normandy."

"Normandy was very important."

"The Russians won that war, but you don't hear about it because no one reads Russian except for Russians. Normandy was a joke, a very bloody joke. Like all the jokes governments play on us. The lives of all of us here in Central America are a joke played on us by your government. Our blood is the primary raw material that goes into your drugs. Our poverty serves industries owned by billionaires, but our grandchildren will study the story of it in English. And they'll believe what they're told."

"So it's all our fault? I've studied what I could about Latin America, and I still don't understand it. But one thing I've learned is that it's easier to see yourself as a victim than fight back. Maybe we're too obsessed with success, but you spend your lives afraid of achieving it."

"I think you're right about that. I don't understand it either. Latin America is too big. There are too many different Latin Americas—there's even a lot of different Central Americas, and it's just a tiny strip of land. And then there's the Caribbean, the islands, each with their own world and accent." Suarez paused, trying to get his thoughts in order. "Well . . . listen. It's like this: if Central America were a residential condo, then Panama, say, would be the *nouveau riche* guy. No one knows where the money came from, but one day the bastard turns up in a brand-new car with gold chains dangling from his neck. Costa Rica is an old lady from a good family fallen on hard times. She goes to Mass every Sunday and looks down on the rest. Nicaragua is a guy who had a difficult childhood. All of them were abused as children. Nicaragua was a talented kid who looked as though he might amount to something but ended up as the town drunk, staggering everywhere and challenging everyone to a fight. El Salvador was the runt of the litter who had to learn to defend himself when his family was murdered before his very eyes. Now he's the neighborhood thug. Honduras is the wife of a domestic abuser who still defends her husband to the hilt, and Guatemala is a quiet, humble worker putting in long hours and tolerating his boss's mistreatment without complaining. They all have indigenous, Spanish, and lots of other different kinds of blood, but the more indigenous they have, the more they despise it. They're ashamed of it."

"How about Belize? People always forget about it."

"Belize is the black man who lives at the end of the street and smokes pot all day. He's also the one who sells to gringos. It's a staging area for drug trafficking. Everyone knows about it, but no one's going to do anything. Here's another home truth: each different part of the Caribbean is an independent state with its own language and culture. The different Caribbeans have more in common with each other than their own countries. But that's just what I think. A lot of people will tell you different."

"You don't speak as though you're from here."

"None of us are, not really."

"Except for the indigenous people."

"You should visit their land. It's not easy: they're surly and mistrustful, the legacy of victimhood. You don't know anything about them; no one does until they go there. Nobody sees how they're treated. They're isolated, reviled, impoverished, alcohol dependent. Genocide dressed up as counterrevolution is a recurring theme. But why is it a revolution just to ask for the same rights as everyone else? During the civil wars, it doesn't matter who's fighting who—they always get killed. Gringo companies like the Fruit Company did experiments on them as though they were animals. And this was thirty years ago, not five centuries. Lots of people complain about the conquistadors, but then they spend their lives trying to prove they're white. It's the lie we live: we claim to distinguish between one thing and another, but nobody here is just one thing. We're not indigenous or Spanish: we don't fit any specific heritage. Here, people act as though the Spanish came, stole everything, got onto a ship, and left. Then we appeared out of nowhere, with no interest in anything, not even who we are."

After a brief silence, Suarez turned the conversation back to the case and the information he'd found: a legal firm they knew nothing about and a truck driver who'd taken Michi out of the country.

"Johanna contacted him by email. We have the password, and he has no way of knowing that she's dead."

"That's right, but we also have the hard drive and the telephone. In all that, I'm sure we can find something to lead us back to the law firm. That seems easier than finding a truck driver who's God knows where. Also, they're more likely to know the client. But there's one thing I've been thinking about since we left: What will the deputy chief do? His friends have been killed, his money's been stolen, and his business has been ruined."

"I don't know, but I wouldn't want to be him right now."

They laughed mirthlessly.

"The only thing I know for sure is that if he's smart, we won't be able to find him. His friends are dead, and the girl is going to identify them as her captors. It'll be a huge scandal. The way I see it, unless he's extremely powerful, he's fucked. I don't think it's in anyone's interests for him to stay out of prison."

Ethan walked around the small living room, plotting their next move. "So we're going after the lawyers?"

"You can if you like. I'd rather try with the truck driver."

"You're going to look for him even though you don't know what country he's in?"

"To me, the difference is that we have him and not the others. I understand that to you every border is a new world, but I think there's a good chance. It's not so hard for me."

"Are you saying that you're going to look for him on your own?"

"I have my contacts. What do you think?"

"Split up? I'm not sure that's a good idea."

"Given what we have to gain, I think we should try. Think of this cash as new funding for the investigation. Now we've got plenty of money but not much time. What if you can't find the firm? Or I can't track down the trucker? I don't think we have a choice."

Given the course things were taking, Ethan told Suarez about Ari and suggested making her their remote contact. With each of them in a different region, she could coordinate with them more easily. Suarez agreed. Ethan wrote Ari an email to let her know, and Suarez left.

It was early morning, and the events of the previous night began to take a toll on Ethan. His imagination was stuffed full of images and voices from the night before, and they were all screaming at him at once, competing for his attention. He relived the flashes of light, the noise of each shot, the gunman turning toward him, the bullets hitting the gunman, and then the gunman falling back with his eyes still on Ethan. His arms had been stretched out on the ground, like Christ on the cross. He tried to wash it all off in the shower, but he knew that the night wouldn't stand for it. It would be with him for a long time.

Suarez, sticking to the discipline that had kept him going for years, woke up at five in the morning, just as the sun was coming up over the horizon. He made himself some toast and sat down to watch the news. It had long been something of an addiction for him, giving him a false sensation of control, as though he were forewarned. Deep down he knew it was a game, but he still kept it up. When he went out, he'd be two steps ahead of his fellow pedestrians, just the way he liked it.

That morning, he watched his programs even more closely, waiting in vain for a report on the incident. It might be too soon, or it might be that there wouldn't be anything; it was just as likely to be overlooked. It was completely out of his hands, depending more on the deputy chief's contacts and what favors he might be able to call in. Once he'd finished his first scan of the news, he showered, ate some more, and walked around the patio he shared with his neighbors, studying the perimeter and inspecting traps only he knew about. Someone had jumped over the wall behind the Marquez house and crossed the garden, leaving certain signs that only he could detect. Upon closer, discreet examination, he saw that they'd gone to the front door. There was no sign of it having been forced, but the key had scratched the paint and wood. No doubt the son had come back drunk again and either mistakenly, or for some other reason, had crossed several different properties before recognizing his parents' house.

After his patrol, he came back and collected his mail. Then he resumed his monitoring of the news but still didn't turn up anything. At seven thirty he lay down to read until sleep overcame him. At nine he came out of his doze and went straight back to the news channels. After another fruitless scan but feeling refreshed, he started to examine the hard drive in detail. It was a veritable gold mine of information about previous kidnappings, but there was nothing of interest to his case. Johanna had set up a database for all the information about her clients that she believed to be relevant: the ransom, the days each victim had spent in captivity next to some macabre deliveries highlighted in bold: finger, finger, ear. The final column was for the sum obtained or a NO in red followed by coordinates he tried to pinpoint on a map. But what he thought would be simple was not. He couldn't make heads or tails of them. So he contacted Ari.

To his surprise, the answer came back almost instantly in a precise and organized way. Ari sent him a series of screen grabs for each of the coordinates he'd sent, confirming his suspicion that they were all scattered around an area not far from the warehouse where they'd found the girl. In order to avoid repetition and anticipate possible discovery, Johanna had recorded where they'd buried the dead bodies from unsuccessful operations. They didn't need maps or signs anymore; with a simple cell phone they could keep records that dated back years. Like every tool, new technologies were amoral: they facilitated activities both good and bad. Underneath every cross was the unfortunate victim of a kidnapping whose ransom had never been paid, people who'd just disappeared one day and had never been heard from again. Looking at this scattered chart of anonymous graves made Suarez anxious. Suddenly his breathing grew labored; he needed to get some air. He got up to go out but found that this was a mistake. His legs buckled under him, and he fell to the floor as the room spun around. He placed his knees and elbows on the floor and curled up until he recovered control. Then he used the table to pull himself back up and went to the kitchen. *A fainting fit. It was just a fainting fit—I need sugar.*

By midday, when it was obvious that the news that he and Ethan had created wasn't going to be reported that day, he sat down in front of the outdated computer. He signed in to an email account that would never be used by its deceased owner again. After spending a long time trying to think of the best approach to take and studying Johanna's curt style very closely, he decided upon a brief email that he thought mimicked her exactly. And so he made the first move:

> From: Mimbura1983@ . . .
> To: Latinbeast32@ . . .
> Subject: New job
>
> Hello again. All well? Have a new job for a different client that I think might interest you. Let me know when you're free to discuss it.
>
> Best

The next morning, Suarez found that he'd received an answer as predictable as it was concise:

> From: latinbeast32@
> To: Mimbura1983@
> Subject: Re: New job
>
> I'm not interestd in a new cliant. Thanx.

But Suarez had anticipated a rejection. He just had to copy and paste the reply he'd prepared.

> From: Mimbura1983@ . . .
> To: Latinbeast32@ . . .
> Subject: Re: Re: New job
>
> It's our oldest client. We can vouch for them. We trust them completely. They've never moved merchandise to another country and don't know how. We told them that you're the

best and they're willing to pay 50% more than for the girl. Please tell me if you're interested, it would be very good for us. We'd be very grateful. If you take it, more goodies will be coming your way in the future.

Best

Adrian Calvo walked through groups of stuck-up, fashionable youths who didn't give him a second glance. His response to their snub was to shamelessly stare at the legs of the female students in their tights and cutoff shorts. People were so used to it that only a couple of the girls noticed, walking off hand in hand, muttering about the dirty old man. The rest just put up with him, mistaking him for a professor or janitor. He went to the dirty, nearly deserted cafeteria, where the waitress was watching a soap opera, completely oblivious to anything else. Only two of the tables were occupied; Michelle sat at the one farthest away. Calvo was amazed to see that she didn't stand out at all among the much younger students. *And neither do her legs*, he chortled to himself.

"Madam."

"Good afternoon, Don Adrian. Thank you for coming. I'm surprised you chose this place. The Faculty of Architecture cafeteria?"

"In the private university too. No one could possibly expect to find us here. But I was surprised by your message. I heard about the incident. You seem to have recovered well."

"Thank you. There's still some pain, but the worst is over."

"These gang kids are violent bastards," Calvo said, pretending to be outraged. "What did you want? I'd like to get this over with quickly. It's not healthy for me to be seen in your company, as pleasant as it is. If my wife knew . . ."

Michelle ignored both the compliment and the bad joke. But she did take note of her new status as a pariah. "I haven't heard from Ethan, and I'm worried."

"If you'll forgive me for saying so, I think that the gentleman needed time to think. He seemed upset."

"This has nothing to do with us. I'm worried about his safety."

"An admirable sentiment and one that I share."

"But you're not on the case anymore. Randall stopped paying you."

"So he did. I see that he isn't hiding anything from you. A good man, your engineer. He seems to have taken it well. I mean both of you have."

"I can pay you too. I want you to protect Ethan—I don't care how much it costs." Michelle's face was inscrutable and unsettling.

"You couldn't afford it."

"I'll pay whatever it costs. I'll find a way."

"You don't understand. Not even the engineer could afford it. I came to meet you as a courtesy. Have you been reading the newspapers or watching TV?"

Calvo put a tabloid he'd brought with him down on the table. The front page had a prurient four-column story with a photo of a curvy woman in a thong and high heels showing off her generous bust and buttocks. She was introduced to readers as "Samaris the market beauty." Above it was a completely unrelated report with a large red banner headline: "Corrupt Policemen Gunned Down." Accompanying the lovely Samaris was a photograph of the kidnappers' industrial warehouse. It had now been cordoned off and was crawling with police.

"I like this newspaper. It doesn't go for subtlety, but it knows its stuff. The article mentions a girl they had trapped in there and lists the horrible things they did. They obviously made them up because the girl didn't make a statement, but they know what they're doing; their sales prove that. This is the most-read front page in the country."

"Of course I've seen it. But they said that this was a gang dispute."

"Some dispute. A gang executing cops? And then setting their victim free? They wouldn't have the guts. This wasn't a gang. This is the work of your Ethan. These were the bastards who took Michi, and he found them. Who was behind it and where they sent her I couldn't say. You know, like a Greek once said, 'The only thing I know for sure is that I don't know anything.'"

Michelle couldn't help tearing up. She put on a pair of sunglasses. "Ethan . . . killed those people?"

"He has a partner who hides himself very well. I wonder who he might be . . . therefore I am. How does it go?"

"What are you talking about?" Michelle said, utterly confused.

"Yes, that's how it goes: 'The only thing I know for sure is that I don't know a thing, but I think, and therefore I am.' That's very good—do you get it? I think; therefore I am. Something to ponder."

"You were telling me that Ethan killed those policemen."

"Don't go around telling everyone. I mean, the less people know, the longer our gringo will stay alive."

"Three? They killed three people?"

"Four. The guy's good. I wonder how he managed it. Aren't you happy? He took revenge on the people who took your daughter. And now he must know what happened. If he hasn't called you yet, I suppose it's because he is tracking her down. I wouldn't have bet a cent on him, but he had his own ideas, and he put them to good use. See? I think; therefore I am. Ethan knows what to think. Congratulations. That's all I can tell you."

"How do you know it was him?"

"Oh, that . . . let's just say that I know."

"Now I need you more than ever. I need you to protect him. Nothing can happen to him. Did you hear me? Tell me what it will cost. I'll pay anything."

"You don't understand. You can't pay me. No one could. I warned him, and he went ahead anyway. The Doce are going to execute him. The criminals he got rid of paid their dues, and debts like that are collected in blood. You saw their price for Jonathan—who knows what the bill will be now? I can't save your Ethan, and I don't know anyone who can."

"Someone must be able to!"

Calvo hid behind a cynical grin, refusing to offer a solution.

"Who can I go to?"

"No one I know."

"Ethan won't answer my messages."

"He doesn't want to put you in danger. However, from the looks of you, you're riding the storm pretty well."

Michelle revealed her eyes, which were now black with running mascara. "Not really."

Calvo smiled at some double entendre she didn't understand. "The bloodshed has to be paid for. He knew that and decided to make the sacrifice. He'd do it happily so long as it means rescuing the girl. If I got involved, they'd kill me too."

"No, it can't be. It can't be."

"Either that or put him on a plane and get the seat next to him. Because if they can't find him, they'll come for you. Go. Today, tomorrow at the latest. I don't think you'll get much more time than that. And not with the girl, obviously; you can't afford to wait for her."

As he signed into the email account again, the only thing that came as a surprise to Suarez was how predictable people could be.

From: Latinbeast32@ . . .
To: Mimbura1983@ . . .
Subject: Re: Re: Re: New job

OK. send me all info and ill look at it i'm free on tuzday, i'll look at it when i arrive and if i'm interstd i'll let you know on wenzday.

It disgusted him to be dealing with such a despicable excuse for a man, but he reminded himself that he was a professional. He had been dealing with trash like this for as long as he could remember. He implemented his plan with bureaucratic patience: he telephoned his Panamanian contact and was immediately entangled in a long conversation about the good old days that may never have actually happened. Then he succinctly outlined what he needed: a truck driver who smuggled children across the continent, of uncertain nationality but who had a hideout in Colombia, where he was heading right now, arriving on Tuesday. He needed him found beforehand. He had gleaned a little more information from Johanna's computer: the state where he was hiding, that he'd be crossing the border from the south but hadn't gotten there yet, and thanks to Ari, an IP address. They discussed the difficulties involved, not just in finding the truck driver but also in arranging Suarez's passage and supplying him with a weapon. The man soon started to get nervous and asked for more time—there was no way he could get all that information before Tuesday—but Suarez knew him well and let him go on. Embarking upon a long diatribe full of excuses, his friend entered into a spiral of frustration that fed on its own arguments. By the end he was almost shouting: There was no way he could help Suarez; why didn't he go find someone else to do his dirty work? Suddenly, however, he remembered that he knew a top guy in customs who could check to see whether the guy was in Colombia, and once they'd established the route, they could ask for it to be traced, an internal, unofficial request, off the books. It would be an interdepartmental favor, but then the police would be able to track him, and the Colombian police force was reliable enough for Suarez to assume that they'd do it competently. He then breathed a big sigh of relief and started to list the different things they'd need to do to make sure that the tracking went well, asking again, almost as though for the record, whether Suarez wouldn't prefer that they issue an arrest warrant. But Suarez didn't answer that either. Then the monologue continued before transforming into an entertaining succession of funny stories and shared anecdotes that went on for almost another hour, as it always had for as long as the two had known each other. Once they'd said goodbye, Suarez went back to the computer and typed out an answer in the name of a woman who'd died several days before.

From: Mimbura1983@ . . .
To: Latinbeast32@ . . .
Subject: Re: Re: Re: Re: New job

If you agree, we need your current license plates, chassis number and trailer model to do the paperwork. Attached is a form for you to fill out.

Best

Three days later, Suarez was wondering whether he'd made a mistake. Perhaps the truck driver was smarter than Suarez had given him credit for, or maybe he'd tried to contact Johanna by a different means and had worked out that he was being set up. If so, Suarez tried to think whether there was any way it could lead back to him, but there were no worries on that score: he'd always used Johanna's address and telephone. So Suarez went back to thinking how they might catch the intermediary if he didn't send the requested documents. He considered the different options, and the only one that seemed likely was the weak, very risky lead of the deputy chief. He didn't have much faith in that line of inquiry. He wondered how Ethan was doing: obsessed with his own investigations, he hadn't been in contact. He was worried that his search might put him on the Doce's radar and told himself that he needed to talk to Ethan and make sure he was covering his tracks when, as though in answer to his prayers, a response came that would define his next steps.

From: Latinbeast32@ . . .
To: Mimbura1983@ . . .
Subject: Re: Re: Re: Re: Re: New job

Info recuested atatched

Suarez downloaded the file, checked it, and forwarded it to his contact. Then he called him to speed things along. The man got to work, promising that they'd move fast. Suarez packed, excited like a gambler before a big race. Just over an hour later, he received the report: they'd made a positive ID. A full update would arrive in a day or two. Together with the confirmation came a number and a code for obtaining a weapon once he arrived. It was expensive but reliable. Suarez thanked his friend, as he had so often, and bought a ticket for the first flight, full of hope and expectation. He had forgotten all about Ethan.

The date had gone well, and Ari had had a good time, but by the time she got home, she was feeling even more lonely. She decided that she had to move out; the house had become an empty shell. She felt a sadness settle upon her, not just because Ethan had gone but because of how different she felt from "normal" people. She grieved for the most stable period of her life, the only time when she'd ever been happy.

When the doorbell got her out of bed, the last thing she expected was to be faced with the hulking form of Bear on crutches. He was still wrapped up in bandages, providing a marked contrast to the silhouette of Candy, who was small enough to fit into Ari's purse. Although she saw them almost every day, there was something suspicious about the couple just dropping by like this.

"Hi, guys . . . what a surprise. You should have let me know you were coming. Come in; don't just stand there."

"Hi, honey. Sorry to come by like this. We need to talk."

"Hi, Ari, f-forgive me. It's my fault. I asked Candy to come. I didn't want to talk over the phone."

"Well, come in, damn it. What's wrong? You're making me nervous."

"Michelle wrote to us."

"To you? What's got into her now? I'm still in touch with Ethan. Isn't she getting enough attention already? What, now she's jealous?"

"How long has it been since you spoke?"

"A couple of days maybe. I'm talking to his partner there, but I don't think the gorgeous Michelle knows him."

Ari had begun to enjoy her spitefulness, but Candy held up her hand, brusquely cutting her off.

"She wants to talk to you. She asked us to come on her behalf."

"Well, I hope you told her to go to hell. Straight to hell."

"Ari. You need to listen to her."

7

Stolen Confessions

Ethan woke up a little before dawn. For once, he felt good and well rested. He went straight to the computer and found Ari online. They caught up. She told him that his strange old buzzard of a partner had contacted her, and they said goodbye. Then Ethan got straight onto his own line of inquiry. The shoot-out had caused a major scandal. Journalists were taking advantage of it to attack the government and vested interests; the terms *ignominy*, *shame*, *purge*, and *cleaning house* had become commonplace. Rumors were multiplying and growing wilder and wilder, often disguised as leaks from supposedly verified sources. The only real truth was that the nerves of the security forces, public institutions, and the media itself were frayed. The latter's crusade was little more than payback for a thousand historical slights. By now, he knew that he was doomed, just as Calvo had warned him. He just didn't know how many days he had left to solve the case and get out alive. He didn't expect Suarez to make any progress with his investigation, and working on his own again, he arranged to meet with Andrés to give him an update before insisting that for his own good, he didn't follow Ethan down the dark path along which he was heading.

The property was large but neglected. No one grew anything there, and weeds had spread over the fence, the path, and up the walls, blurring the distinction between garden and jungle. Which was just how it should be. Sinister, like him. Dark, like his soul. The undergrowth was so thick you couldn't walk through it. It hid the lair of the black-headed beast, a cave in which to take refuge after claiming yet another innocent life, somewhere to muffle their final screams, which thrilled and frightened him in equal measure. The Beast cherished the bloody garment in his hand, which would be kept with the others so he could masturbate over it later or flagellate himself with it.

The sickly, inevitable feeling that came after violence was always bittersweet. Like sexual desire, it devoured everything before it even began, transforming the pain of others into pleasure, stirring his hunger for sacrifice. The world was a rabid, lusty animal that existed to satisfy the powerful. There was only one choice: you could either be the executioner or be the victim. He was driven to stain innocence, ruin beauty, and pollute purity, but when it was all over, a feeling of emptiness and an inexplicable anxiety cloaked him; sometimes he even felt guilty. He was forced to seek refuge, disappearing into this dominion, which was rough, dirty, and insidious, the same as him.

He headed toward the front door with the afternoon sun on his back, his purple silhouette getting bigger on the wooden boards, drunk not so much on alcohol as frustration at finding himself forced to wait on the bastards who were coming tomorrow. At least they'd be bringing his money. He had forgotten his earlier fears. He knew he'd be safe: they needed him and would give him back his fee. They must have earned it doing business even more horrible than his own. Then he'd be able to spend the money on whatever lordly whim came to him in his lewd magnificence. The Beast would use it to punish several bitches. He wouldn't kill them: it would be consensual, or so they'd think when it began. Not by the time it was over. And then he'd pay what they'd agreed on so as to further shame them. The Beast was still brimming over with resentment after the slights he'd suffered, and he wouldn't stop until he'd worked it out by unleashing his rage on defenseless creatures.

When he opened the door, he didn't notice the grooves in the lock. There was no reason to suspect that he had been spied on, analyzed, and dissected. But when he set foot inside, he instinctively sensed that something was wrong. Nothing had changed, but he knew. He could smell it. He listened hard and quietly walked to the kitchen, looking for the gun he kept taped to the bottom of a drawer. But what he found surprised him even more. A miserable old man waiting for him next to the sink, drinking coffee that he had clearly taken from the Beast's own cupboard.

The old man nodded curtly, holding up the mug. "Do you mind?"

In that moment, the Beast swore that he would kill him. He was going to grab this spindly little son of a bitch and end him in a way that . . . but the greeting was just a distraction from the other hand, which was carrying a Taser. The electric shock hit him before he could react, immobilizing him and knocking him to the ground. The Beast collapsed in a heap but remained conscious, angry but nullified, swearing that . . . the second shock, jarringly painful, wiped his mind blank. A second later he passed out.

When they were together, Ethan tried to give Andrés a credible reason for them not to see each other anymore. The honest Christian's humble nature accepted what Ethan had to say without complaint. Ever since Jonathan's death and its even more tragic consequences, Andrés hadn't argued or asked any questions. He was willing to do whatever his two partners told him, always ready to be useful and fulfill his self-imposed penitence. So he waited patiently while Ethan tangled himself up in a confused web of reason and delusion. Eventually Andrés had the chance to change the topic.

"Don Ethan, I wanted to talk to you truthfully about my friend Oliver Suarez."

"That's the first time I've heard his first name. That's Suarez for you. Don't worry; there's no need to explain."

"I know that sometimes he can be an enigmatic so-and-so, but I think you need to know—"

"I said don't worry about it. I have no more doubts about him. I trust him as much as you do."

"You need to know who he is. Forgive me if I'm being naive. I respect what you say; you're always right. But you need to know him and understand, especially now that you're leaving. I'm going to try and find him now before he leaves—God willing I won't be too late and he won't have left yet. Oliver can't go chasing an evil man who takes little girls. Oliver mustn't."

Ethan listened to this veiled criticism expectantly.

"Fine, go on."

The Beast woke up tied to a chair, gagged, his mouth covered in duct tape. He tried to flex his muscles and found that he was completely immobilized. Not much time must have passed: if this nobody was working alone, he must have worked quickly. His hands were down by his butt, touching something metal. They were cuffed, but when he tried to move them to consider ways to escape, he felt a tug on his ankles: his feet had been tucked under the chair and tied to his wrists, making any movement absolutely impossible. Someone must have helped the old cripple. He felt an acute pain in his little fingers, which had been tied up tightly enough to cut off the circulation. He realized that they were swollen—they must already have turned purplish—and began to worry about just who it was that had caught him like this. Who had sent the old bastard? He thought it might be a cruel joke, some sadistic humor before he was eliminated. His fears grew through him like vines. He listed the different gangs who might be candidates: the PCC in Brazil, also the Urabeños, the Paisas, or the Rastrojos, but none of them had any grudges against him. He'd completed all his jobs satisfactorily, and none of his clients had complained. The vines spread to his lungs, and he started to have trouble breathing. Then there were the European clients. He was under their protection; everyone knew that. But after the last drop-off, they were the only ones to have complained. If they wanted to punish him, there was nothing to be done. They had told him to wait, and he, like the moron he was, had waited for them like a lamb for slaughter instead of disappearing with the money. It all fit perfectly; it was so fucking obvious. They'd lied to him about when they'd come, and then they'd arrived twenty-four hours early. He wasn't getting enough oxygen. There was no negotiating with them, no way out. They were the worst of the worst. *Oh my God*, he begged to himself, *let me talk to them—let me explain.* It was unfair, so fucking unfair, after he'd been so faithful to them for so many years. *Just because of a little oversight.* He heard a noise in the next room, and his throat constricted even more. *Oh my God, my God, just once, please, listen to me this once . . .* Then he stopped kidding himself. *At least let it be quick . . .* the TV. It was the TV. He tried to listen. Someone was changing the channel. Maybe he was wrong. They wouldn't do this. His alveoli relaxed and expanded; his airways cleared. He took a deep breath. *If it wasn't them*—he breathed out—*then who?* No organized gang would dare with the protection he had. He tried to picture the guy who'd attacked him. What kind of a joke was this? He laughed at his earlier fears. The old man had taken him by surprise;

otherwise he'd have just smashed his face in. He'd have skinned his soul. No one in their right mind would send a flea-bitten wretch to get rid of the Beast, especially not the Europeans. Those people had no sense of humor. Of course it wasn't an organized group—what was he thinking? This was obviously somebody working on their own or thieves, but thieves would have killed him or taken whatever was there and left him tied up. No one would have tied him up like this unless they were idiots who'd seen too many films and thought that he had hidden treasure. Considering the state of the truck and house, only a crazy man would suspect he was rich. Plus, whoever had tied him up, as he found every time he tried to get free, knew what they were doing. Now it all made sense. It was obvious. A professional. He went back to his earlier supposition: the guy had to be working independently, but he still didn't understand why. Finally, a few minutes later, the television was turned off, and he heard someone walk slowly out of the house. There were no other sounds. The Beast appeared to be alone. The same slow footsteps came back to the screen door and up the three steps. The wood creaked as he approached. The Beast didn't turn his head, but when his captor arrived, the Beast studied him surreptitiously. His surprise and relief grew: it was the same spindly, defenseless old man. He looked like a farmer with that moustache. But he was still suspicious. This walking skeleton couldn't be working alone. The man seemed pleased to see him awake.

"Aha, you've come to. I thought that I was going to have to throw a bucket of water over you. I've had a look around. I like it. You chose a good spot to get away from it all. That's a big fucking help. You can scream as much as you like, and no one would ever hear you. But you know that already, don't you? This is very you."

The Beast still couldn't believe it. This mangy dog was talking as though he were alone, but that couldn't be, unless he was a stinking peasant, the father of one of the girls he'd taken. But that was even more ridiculous. A peasant wouldn't have tied him up like this. The Beast started to worry that this idiot had tied his little fingers too tight. It might damage his circulatory system, and he didn't want to have that kind of trouble just because of an illiterate *indio*. On top of everything, the bastard came over with that careful walk of his and painfully tore the tape from his mouth. The Beast spit out the gag and cried out, more in anger than pain. The man looked at him in surprise.

"It doesn't take much to make you scream."

"Who are you with, old man?"

"I'm on my own. Can't you see that?"

"I don't believe you. Tell me what you want, and I'll see what I can do, but first you need to loosen the ropes on my fingers. I might get a hematoma, and then I won't be able to help you."

The bastard, who seemed to be getting dumber all the time, didn't answer. Instead, he grabbed a chair and sat down in front of him. "Huh, I thought I'd been quite gentle."

"Well, it's time to stop fucking around. Let's get this over with. If you behave, when I get out of here, I'll leave you alone, but if you mess with me, when your friends set me free, I won't forget you."

"Now, why wouldn't you believe me?"

The Beast looked into the man's eyes. His own coldness and lack of empathy made him an excellent judge of when someone was lying to him. This asshole didn't appear to be lying at all. "You've been working alone the whole time?"

"Why would I lie?"

The Beast realized that it was going to be easier to get out of there than he thought. Some dumbass idiot had taken him by surprise. It was his craziness that made him unpredictable. The first blow always counted twice, but now his advantage was over. If he'd seen him in time, things would be very different, and even so he didn't think it would be too much trouble to get away. He just had to get him to release his little fingers, which were beginning to throb quite painfully.

"Fine, I believe you. Now tell me what you want, and we'll get this over with. When I'm set free, I'll give you some money and forget everything. OK? I don't have much—I'm just a humble truck driver—but please take everything I have. From what I can see, you need it more than I do."

"How much do you have?"

"About a thousand dollars. A little less because I put gas in the truck."

"And where is it?"

"First, you have to loosen my fingers. They're hurting, and I can't think like this," he answered with the innocence of a child.

"But you're not in a position to ask for anything."

"If I help you, you need to help me."

He was met with a look of disbelief. "But you're in no position to ask for anything—you're tied up."

Now he was sure that this guy was demented. How did you deal with crazy people? On the one hand, he was reassured, but on the other he was a little worried. He knew that madmen sometimes did the unexpected. There was a chance that this man couldn't tell the difference between right and wrong. But he didn't seem so bad. The Beast had to talk him into letting him go, and then he'd show him who the Beast really was.

"Sure, I'm tied up, but it's hurting me. You're causing me pain, and I haven't done anything to you. I want to help, but I can't. Please, I'm begging you, from one Christian to another, untie my fingers, and I'll tell you where to find the little I have."

"But I don't care about your money."

Just as he'd suspected, the bastard really was crazy. He wondered how a nut like this could have found him. He was starting to get annoyed, but he knew that he had to stay calm and take control of the conversation. "Fine, fine. Then what do you want? I'll help you in whatever way I can. Just loosen these fingers, and we'll be even—then I'll help you."

"I want you to tell me all about the girl you took to Brazil two months ago."

Finally, he was showing his cards. He must be the granddaddy of one of the packages, the last one from Central America, from the looks of things. Now everything really did make sense. He was relieved that he hadn't lost his patience because now things were more complicated. The little old man had clearly been driven mad by the absence of his little piglet. That made him hard to handle but also gave the Beast more of a chance: all he had to do was convince the man of his innocence, and then, once he was set free, he'd show this fool some real danger.

Andrés took a sip of water and gulped it down. He seemed to be having difficulty starting his story.

"Oliver and I have known each other since we were children. I can remember when Michelle was born, not Beto because I'd left home by then, but not when I met Oliver. It was too long ago. He was always with me, since we were babies, maybe. He was always like a big brother to me."

Ethan was growing impatient with Andrés's peculiar narrative style and his tendency to stray from the point, but he knew that he had no choice but to be patient and listen to the story.

"Yes, when we were kids, we were inseparable; we'd go down to the river and throw stones at the kids on the other side. Oliver was clever and strong, and he defended me when I was still little. You know about my father—he wasn't a good man, and so we spent all day outside. We didn't go to school much either, although Oliver's father made him study and pass his exams. My father didn't care. He hit me and drank like all the men, but Oliver's father was strange. He was an old-fashioned man, a real one. He didn't spend all day in bars like my father, although he did drink at home. He was a large, hairy, angry man. He wanted his children to get out of there and locked them in their rooms to make sure that they studied. He sat there with them even though he couldn't read. And he used to share his hooch with them so they'd get used to it. He wanted them to grow into men as soon as possible. When one of them came home with good grades from the teacher, they all got drunk and celebrated. I used to go with them. He wanted me to drink too. He was scary when he was drunk. He was the kind of man who really put the fear of God into you. So I drank with them, and then my daddy would hit me and call me a pathetic drunk. But Oliver was already drinking with his father, and in that house they began before ten, every day. The mother didn't say anything because God only gave her boys, and it was a house of men. His father knew how to raise them, not that he made it easy. Still, the brothers all grew up to be strong and brave. But like father, like son: they were also surly to a fault."

Ethan took advantage of this pause to try to speed things along, partly so Andrés would get to the point and partly because he was unsettled by these raw, painful memories. "I'm very sorry to hear all this, but you don't need to share it with me. I know that Suarez—"

"Forgive me, Don Ethan. I know that I can't talk as well as you educated men. I'm sorry if you find these stories boring, but it's very important, so important . . ."

"Fine, go on."

"Oliver suffered the most. He wasn't a good student. He was strong and brave like his father. He made himself the boss of all the kids in the street, and they all, even the older ones, obeyed him, but his father . . . whenever he heard that he'd skipped classes . . . he went to see the teacher every week to check up on him. Every Friday, he waited at home to punish Oliver for skipping school, and every Friday Oliver knew what awaited him. He spent Saturday and Sunday in bed; that was how badly the man beat him. Then he'd give him alcohol to help him through it. The mother cared for him as best she could and cried every time the father took off his belt. The brothers studied hard when they saw what happened to Oliver, but he didn't—he studied less and less, and then he had to face the brute and his punishments. When they let him go on Monday, he wouldn't go to school; he'd go down to the river to fight the kids on the other side. He barely felt their punches: no one could hit as hard as his daddy. But you won't believe what happened next. Doña Asunción, our teacher, began to lie to his daddy to protect him, because she was genuinely worried that he'd end up killing the boy: 'One of these days, he'll go too far,' she used to say. Doña Asunción was a saint."

"I'm sorry to interrupt, but why didn't the teacher go to the police?" Ethan asked, surprised how the story had drawn him in. "I know that things were hard. It's not as though you could go to social services, but the police . . ."

"That was how the world was, Don Ethan. You might not understand, but that was how things were," Andrés said, clearly saddened by this reality. "Doña Asunción knew that I was Oliver's best friend, and she asked me to persuade him to go see her after school. That woman, who was the most generous soul I have ever come across on the face of the earth, convinced Oliver to go visit her. I went, too, after hours if he wanted, whenever he could, so she could teach him. She'd taken pity on him. Oliver, who only agreed to go if I went with him, started to learn little by little. As you know, he's very intelligent, very bright, and he soon caught on. So she'd lie to his father about how often his son went to school, and then he'd pass his exams, and I swear by everything that's sacred he passed when a lot of others didn't because Oliver learned everything so quickly. He even did homework and brought it to the teacher, and his daddy was more relaxed at home, although he never fully trusted his son. Because they were so much alike—he knew exactly what the boy was capable of. He never stopped checking up on him, but he wasn't as violent as before.

"So we got through primary school, and as you know, halfway through high school I set out for the States, and they sent me back. I worked for a few years and did everything I could to save up enough to return. During those years, because I didn't want to go back to my mother and Beto's father, I lived with Oliver. He took me in. He lived with one girl after another and rented an apartment with money he made here and there, on the street mostly. But he'd got a taste for learning, and he was always asking questions. That was around the time he started really thinking about becoming a policeman. I stayed with him, but he wouldn't let me pay him any rent unless he needed it. He always had his nose in a book. He used to say that he owed his education to Doña Asunción. His daddy was a bastard, but the good woman had saved him. But we do terrible things when we stray from the path of the Lord. That pure soul, that generous woman who had all the grace of our Savior, was murdered by her own husband when she was an old woman.

"I was getting ready to leave again. Oliver, meanwhile, had avoided getting into drugs but knew lots of people on the street and also used to hang out at the policemen's bar. The police knew him and told him to get ready for the exam because of course he was going to pass, and they needed men like him. So he went for it. After he'd joined the force, some people called him a traitor, a sellout. They said he'd be buried upright, but he didn't care. So he became a policeman, and his career went well, even though he continued to drink. Like his daddy, he drank more at home than anywhere else, although he went to the bar with his colleagues of course. I left the country again, and he got married, and they had their first child, Tavo, then another who died very young, followed by another, a girl: Patricia, the apple of her father's eye. He loved that girl so much. She was everything to him, and he did everything he could for her. She was lovely, pretty, and well behaved. A delight. To cut a long story short, there was a five-year gap between Tavo and Patricia, and in that time I'd married too and was named her godfather. We'd always stayed in touch, writing to each other and sending Christmas cards, asking after each other's families. He kept me up to date with things at home, and I told him about the people who'd left. He even helped Michelle to come to the US. He paid for her ticket, saying she could pay him back later. And the same went for his children. I would have gladly taken them in, in the States and raised them along with mine. I would have cared for them as though they were my own. My wife knew that and accepted it."

"But they never went," Ethan said. "You would've mentioned them to me."

"And that is the real tragedy of Oliver's life. His children."

The Beast examined his adversary and identified his weak spot. He was a good man: arrogant and confused but generous. He had no idea what he'd gotten himself into, and that made him easy to manipulate. The first thing the Beast had learned on his path to becoming who he was now was how to ape the behavior of good people to get them to trust him. No one could blame him; that was just how predators learned to feed themselves. He'd draw him in, fool him. Good people's weakness was their innocence.

"I want you to tell me everything you know about the girl you took to Brazil two months ago."

"Oh, Jesus, that's awful. I don't know who you're looking for, but you're way off. I don't know what lies you've been told, but I've never been involved in anything like that. You have the wrong man. But I'll help you to find him! You hear? If you let me go, I'll show you my passport, and you'll see that I have never in my life been to Brazil, only Colombia. Colombia's all I need. This beautiful country is very large."

"But you're not Colombian."

"I've lived here for many years. I left my home country in search of an opportunity in this beautiful land, and they welcomed me. I haven't left since then except to visit my family. You don't know how much I miss them, from the bottom of my heart. I imagine that the girl you're talking about is a part of your family, and if you let me go, I'll try to help you. We'll both go looking for the scoundrel, especially if he's a truck driver like me. I know all of them around here. We'll find him in a second."

"Tell me about the girl."

"But I swear on the blessed Virgin . . . listen: look me in the eye. Look at me, for the love of our Lord on the cross. I swear on my mother's life, and I love her more than anything. I swear by the sacred heart of the Virgin that I have no idea what you're talking about . . . I'll do everything I can to help you because I can see that you're a good man, and I want to do something to help. If something like that happened to my family, I don't know what I'd do."

To the Beast's exasperation, the idiot's only answer was a rude yawn. A yawn that he would make him pay for when the time came. The moron stretched before repeating with exaggerated irritation.

"Look, I know I've got the right man. Just to make things clear, so we don't waste any more time, your friend Johanna has been dead for over a week. I wrote the last emails you received from her."

Now the Beast was truly stunned. He blinked a couple of times before answering. "Wh-who? You're making a huge mistake. I don't know anyone called Johanna—I d-don't . . . I don't know what I can say to convince you, but really, I promise you that you're wrong. If you let me go, I assure you that I'll help you with everything you need."

Suarez, moving exceedingly slowly, took a piece of paper from his shirt pocket, unfolded it, and read out the last few emails, which hit the Beast like a slap to the face.

"I swear to you by God I don't understand what's going on. Are those letters?"

"They're your emails. You sent them to me—you should recognize them."

"But I don't have a computer; check if you like. Look everywhere. I don't know how to use them—I don't have any of that stuff. You've made a mistake, do you see? Let me tell you something that'll help us both: I understand. I've put myself in your shoes, and I know that you're doing this for the right reasons, but you're wrong, and it's easy for me to prove that to you. Look around. Search the house—search everywhere. You won't find any computers or your grand-daughter or anything."

Suarez replied with a sigh of annoyance. "Listen, we're going in circles. Let me make it easy for you. Of course I'm going to let you go, and then I'll leave, and you'll never see me again, but you have to tell me everything you know about the girl. She's not my granddaughter. I've been paid to find her."

"They're paying you? So you're a professional. Well then, you'll know by now that I'm just a humble driver trying to live his life without stepping on anyone's toes."

"Listen, I think maybe you might be right. It would be best if I found your computer and maybe any paperwork you have related to the girls. Where is it?"

"Please, just look around, and you'll see I'm right. You're making a big mis-take with an honorable man who—"

But Suarez didn't seem very interested in their conversation. He left the room, heading for the kitchen. He came back almost immediately with a couple of dishcloths and the Beast's toolbox. *His* toolbox!

"What are you going to do with that? Take it with you if you like."

Suarez answered distractedly as he looked inside, paying more attention to the objects than their conversation. "Well, I searched the place from top to bottom, and what do you know? You're telling the truth. I didn't find anything."

"Because there's nothing to find—because I'm not lying. Why don't you let me go? Or at least my little fingers. They're hurting very badly."

Instead of that, Suarez, who seemed to have forgotten all about the box, brought over a damp, rolled-up dishcloth. The Beast closed his mouth and moved his head away, knowing that if he was prevented from talking, it would be easier for the man to objectify him. His many years of experience as a kidnapper had taught him that it was the worst thing that could happen to a victim: it reduced them to speechless bodies devoid of humanity. The perfect puppets with which to fulfill their tormentors' desires. The memory almost made him feel better. Suddenly the situation seemed to have turned in his favor. His captor appeared to give up. Winning back the initiative made him feel strong, but then he saw the man come back with a chisel, and before the Beast could ask what he was planning to do with it, the man had pulled back his hair with one hand and used the other to shove the gouge between his teeth and lever them open. Frightened by this unexpected turn of events, not to mention the pain, he opened his mouth to stop the man doing any more damage.

"OK! OK! Fine, I'll open up—don't hurt me. When you realize that you're hurting an innoce—"

Suarez wouldn't let him finish. He shoved the damp cloth into his mouth. It leaked water every time he bit down, giving the Beast an unpleasant choking sensation that made him gag, forcing him to keep his jaw almost completely straight. Then Suarez tied the gag viciously tight so that it cut into his cheeks and tightened the restraints around his thighs almost as tight as the rope around his little fingers. He put his face right under the man's nose and spoke to him once again in a measured tone that was rapidly turning colder and colder. The old man's breath stank of alcohol.

"I see that you still don't get it, so I'm going to have to teach you a lesson. I have all the time in the world to get what I want, and you're going to help me. That God you keep mentioning knows very well that you're going to help me. And when you do, I'll let you go free. Meanwhile, however, you're going to be afraid of me, and that's how I'll know that you're really helping me."

He picked up the toolbox again. The Beast was unnerved by the unnatural sound of the last phrase. He was afraid that the man might be suffering from delusions of grandeur and let things get out of control while the Beast grew more and more vulnerable. Suarez turned around with a hammer and chisel, and the Beast instinctively shut his mouth, making himself swallow water again before he opened it.

"It's not that I care about the noise. Screaming is a release; that's why we do it. You're about to find out how nasty it is when you can't."

As he spoke, he placed the chisel upon the medial meniscus of his captive's right knee. "I'm sorry for doing it like this, but I don't want to miss."

Then he calmly brought the hammer down as hard as he could. It hit the chisel full on, and the tool sank between the two bones in the joint until they separated. The knee came apart with a pain as sharp and intense as anything the Beast had ever felt, but his scream was thwarted: his tongue was pressed down by the cloth, and the pressure from his jaws sent more water down his throat. This created a sensation that was absolutely new to him: the need to cough blocked by the flow of water. He started to squirm in panic. Overcome with animal fear, he was scared that he'd choke to death. Then Suarez cut off the gag, helped him to take out the cloth, and then went on unperturbed.

"It feels like you're drowning, but without the cloth, it isn't real; it's just fear. Now, I'm going to get your computer from the truck while you think things over. The more you help me, the easier this will be on you. Thus far, you'll just have a limp for the rest of your life. I don't know whether you'll be able to drive."

Then the Beast was alone, with the chisel still sticking out of his leg. It was right in the gap, which grew wider with every involuntary contraction. He was filled with primeval fear. *My God*, he thought. *He's sick, crazy—how am I going to get out of this one?*

Andrés paused to take another sip of water before returning to his story.

"After I left, Oliver's career with the police went well. He knew the streets, and he joined the Criminal Brigade. You probably haven't heard of it."

Ethan shook his head.

"It was a special elite force. They worked against organized gangs and the like. During the dictatorship they played a major role in the repression. Oliver was very useful to them. He had contacts. He never told me what they did during the early years, but I know they went to indigenous reserves, supposedly to quell uprisings. All he said was that it was soul destroying. His exact words: *soul destroying*. They did things that could only be done if you didn't have a soul. Sadly, that was a fair description of almost all of his colleagues. He went back to the capital and asked to be transferred to a desk job, but he was too useful to them. Although they never sent him back to the reserves, he stayed in the field for the rest of his career. He took refuge with his beloved Patricia, but Tavo grew up stubborn and angry, just like him. He was a troublemaker. That was when Oliver began to lose his way like his father, but he didn't want to turn out that way, so rather than lay a hand on his boy, he went out into the street and gave some miscreant a beating. But there was no saving Tavo. Now that Oliver had gone up in the world, they went to live in an expensive condo and started mingling in wealthier circles: with captains, lawyers, and public attorneys. You could get ahead quickly in the Criminal Brigade. The nature of the job meant you had power. When peace and democracy returned, Oliver was well set up, and he sent the boy to the best private schools. But the kid wasn't interested.

"Patricia, in contrast, was his polar opposite. The girl was like a Disney princess, always dressed in pink and purple. She wanted to be a ballerina, and she took music lessons. I don't remember what instrument, but she was good. She was the perfect daughter, the kind any father would want. You should have seen the photos he sent, and she also got top grades at school. Her teachers predicted that the girl would go far. She was an example for all the other children.

"But that's not to say that Oliver didn't love Tavo. Of course he did, more than anything, and the boy made him suffer as a father has never suffered. He had to restrain himself to keep from hurting him, but the boy just got worse and worse. When he went to high school, he started to mix with a bad crowd. One of them was the son of the public prosecutor or something. That kid was bad news, a little thug. He started to get mixed up in drugs; he'd tried everything before he'd even turned eighteen. Oliver wanted to send Tavo to boarding school, but his mother wouldn't hear of it. The thug kid was twenty-one when Tavo wasn't yet eighteen, and Patricia had only just turned thirteen. The older kid took a liking to her and came on to her shamelessly when Oliver wasn't around. He was terrified of Oliver, so he waited until he was out of the house before coming over. And the little shit of a brother, instead of protecting her, was attracted to the older boy's rebellious nature. He wanted to be his best friend. Poor Patricia. Oliver never told me this, but I heard when I got back. The poor, innocent girl was dazzled by all the attention. The kid would turn up in a brand-new convertible bringing gifts and making promises, and she allowed herself to be seduced. She was just a little girl in love, but the kid was already letting Satan talk through him.

"So one weekend, the parents went to a wedding at the beach, but their children didn't have to go because they had exams. Tavo had become such a good-for-nothing that they weren't expecting him to pass anything. That very weekend Oliver went on and on to his wife about setting him straight before he did something really terrible, and she finally agreed. They came back planning on sending him to a boarding school outside the country, even if they had to sell everything to pay for it. Accounts of what happened next vary—even Oliver still has his doubts—but when they got back, both children had gone. The maid had been there with them, and she swore on everything that was holy that they were still there on Saturday, which was her day off. But when she and the parents came back on Sunday, the apartment was empty.

"The first thing they did was look for them in the condo building, running from one apartment to another. Then they and the security guards searched the public areas. Oliver got into his car and searched the whole area while the mother called all their friends' houses, but no one knew anything. Both children had told their friends that they were going to the beach with their parents. Oliver spoke to his police friends, and they organized a major search, but it didn't turn up anything. When they searched the apartment, they found that the pair had packed clothes and stolen credit cards, money, and jewels. Tavo, who'd learned from his dad, had used the cards to take as much money as he could from the ATMs two days in a row and then had disappeared. On the CCTV recordings, he looked to be acting alone, but it was enough to issue an APB for burglary as well as a missing person report. Patricia had disappeared completely. Oliver always said that she'd been kidnapped, that her brother had sold her for drugs and forced her to go, but later I heard from her friends that the evidence pointed to her leaving voluntarily. The guards hadn't seen her leave and hadn't noticed any strange cars, so they must have planned ahead and jumped over the wall in the middle of the night. No one had heard anything.

"That same night, deeply anxious, Oliver put two and two together and went to the public prosecutor's house. All hell broke loose. You should have heard the different accounts of the scene. The guards at the house were unable to stop him coming in and throwing around all kinds of accusations. He demanded to know the whereabouts of their son: he knew he was responsible and swore that he'd kill him if he didn't return his daughter safe and sound right away. There was a huge commotion; people said that he was drunk, very drunk. Eventually his colleagues came and tried to calm him down, saying they'd look for them together. You can imagine what effect the terrible things the public prosecutor—or judge, I don't remember what he was—said back, saying that no one could insult his son like that and especially not threaten him like a gangster. Worse, he said that his son didn't live with them anymore, that he was a good boy who'd been living on his own for two years. They had lunch every Saturday; he had his own business. He'd sweet-talked his parents into thinking that he was the perfect son!

"Oliver told me several years later that that was the worst mistake he'd ever made. He'd never been so lost, crazy, or distraught. The feeling never went away. He never found out what happened to Patricia. She was never seen again."

The Beast had no idea how much time passed before he heard the returning footsteps. The pain had died down a little into waves that rose up from his leg in peaks and troughs, clouding his mind so he couldn't think clearly. He hadn't wasted his time crying out, but now he realized that he hadn't used it to make a plan either. He was simply trying to process his confusion and the bleak scenario. Suarez sat down in front of him, ignoring the pool of blood forming under the Beast's leg.

"You were right. I didn't find anything."

The Beast started to talk, but his voice broke. "I . . . I told you. Please, you're making a mistake. Don't hurt me anymore. I forgive you, but—"

Suarez shoved the cloth back in his mouth, which the Beast snapped shut before he could get it halfway in. However, when he saw the gouge, he opened up again in terror.

Suarez praised him. "That's better. That's the way to do it. Now I don't care if you talk anymore. You only tell lies."

The Beast shook his head anxiously.

"The lies are why I'm gagging you. I just need to know once and for all: Are you going to help me?"

The Beast nodded, trembling.

"Where do you keep the computer and the girls' papers?"

The Beast shrugged and made guttural noises that sounded as though he were asking a question back. Suarez pushed down on the chisel, causing more pain, which only grew more intense when he roughly took it out again.

"*Uuuuuuuuuuuuuuuuuuuurrrrrrrrrrrrrrrrrrrrrggggggggggggggghhhhh!*"

"This is only going to get worse for you until you realize that you have the power to stop it."

As Suarez spoke, he freed the Beast's little fingers by cutting the cords around them. The relief mingled with the fire raging in his knee, which he could feel more clearly now that the throbbing in his fingers had subsided. Meanwhile, Suarez was rummaging around in the toolbox. He was clearly allowing the tools he found to determine his next move. He came up with wire cutters.

"I don't know if this will work. I'd rather have a pair of . . . what do you call them? Shears."

The Beast felt him place the wire cutters at the base of his little finger, just as he was beginning to feel it again, and when he realized what was about to happen, he shook his head as hard as he could, lifting his tongue in desperation but choking on the cloth. The more liquid he swallowed, the more room was left in his mouth. Suarez ignored him and got ready to make the cut, although it turned out to be much harder than he'd expected. He pressed down with both hands and got through the flesh easily, releasing more spurts of dense, dark blood, but the bone itself refused to snap. He ignored the moans and shudders of the Beast as he tried to wriggle free from his ordeal and focused on his work with all the concentration of a born perfectionist.

"You're not going to get the better of me," he mumbled, clearly referring to the bone rather than the Beast, to whom he wasn't paying the least bit of attention.

Suarez took a break for a few seconds and inspected the red marks the handle had made on his hands. Then he returned to his task with renewed vigor. This time he concentrated on the joint between the second and third knuckle, assuming that this would make the task easier. He proved to be correct: the blade cut through fairly easily. There was a loud popping sound, indicating that he'd severed the joint, and with some satisfaction he managed to work the final third of the finger free until it fell to the floor. The victim's expression of horror and despair as his body shook in spasms didn't seem to bother him at all. He took the cloth out of the Beast's mouth again.

"That was harder than I thought. I'm going to have to wet the cloth again."

The Beast didn't answer. He could only gasp as the waves of pain spread up from his knee and finger with every heartbeat. He was finding it hard to think rationally.

"Now, let me explain again: I'm not going to leave you alone until you tell me what I want to know. As soon as you do, I'll let you go."

The Beast raised his puffy head. "B-but I'm innocent . . ."

"Then I'll keep going until you die. It's up to you."

"No, no, no, stop, stop. I haven't done anything to anyone, but I'll tell you whatever you want. Just stop, please."

"Very good—it seems that we finally understand one another."

"Promise that you'll let me go? That I'll walk away?"

"Why would I lie?"

"I swear I won't do anything. I just want to get out of here."

"You don't know who I am."

"Yes, that's true. It's true. I don't know you."

"Where's the computer? Where's the information about the girls?"

"Please, please, I just want to explain. I'll tell you, but first I want to explain."

Suarez immediately shoved the cloth back in his mouth. The Beast, stunned, tried to say something, pleading with his tormentor to stop for a moment, to listen for the love of God. He'd said that he was going to help. Why this again? To his horror, Suarez picked up the chisel again, sizing up the other knee.

"I told you. I've come to teach you a lesson. You need to obey. If I ask you a question, you answer that question. Do you understand?"

The Beast nodded as hard as he could, his eyes bulging as they tried to find a hint of compassion in those of the other man.

"I think you understand."

The Beast nodded his head in desperate hope.

Suarez picked up the chisel. "But this time, that understanding has come too late."

Ethan was speechless. He gulped and nodded to Andrés to continue with his story.

"Oliver always remembers that night. He was very drunk, but he swears he can remember every minute as though he were reliving it. He still wakes up thinking that he's back there and goes to bed still agonizing over it."

"How long ago did this happen?"

"I'm not sure. Thirteen, fifteen years ago? Patricia would be almost thirty by now. Oliver was always hard on himself, saying that he'd been stupid. If only he hadn't gone to look for the kid at his parents' house. If only he'd put out a search for the car's license plates, they'd have found him in time. But it wasn't God's will; he slipped away. Also, his colleagues told me that the kid had already had a day or more to get across the border. That along with his money and contacts and if the girl was willing, there was nothing they could have done. But who knows whether he would have had time to cross the border, if thanks to God Almighty she could have returned alive. We'll never know.

"Oliver spent that night in jail, but the kid's parents tried to get in touch with their son the next day. They didn't want to bother him so late at night, so that's why they waited. But the next day they couldn't reach him. They sent some officers to his apartment, worried that Oliver might have hurt him even though he was locked up and didn't have the address. The agents found lots of drugs and some of the girl's things. That was terrible for everyone. The parents, as you can imagine, were humiliated. They didn't press charges, but they didn't apologize either, and Oliver was still suspended for a month. The double life the kid had been living for the past few years came to light. He was mixed up in drug dealing, and they tried their best to find him—really they did. By then, I'd heard about it and bought a ticket to fly back. I offered him my support. You have no idea the state he was in, God take pity on him, but he didn't want any help. He tried to go it alone. It was as though he was sleepwalking all the time. Suddenly he was talking to himself and coming to conclusions that I couldn't follow. We went from one place to another, talking to the worst kind of people. You can't imagine; his colleagues let him do what he wanted, acting like a policeman even though he wasn't anymore. Sometimes, one of them came along to help. It was a horrible, depressing time. I remember it now with a deep pain in my heart and pray that the people I saw no longer suffer that life of pain and sin. The worst came when we found Tavo. Because we did find him. That boy was in such a sorry state. It had only been a month, but he was completely hooked. He'd become a junkie, a shadow of himself. That was when the Mara were just starting to establish themselves, and it was hard to find them. They were run by deported gang leaders and former guerillas. It was easy for them to move a boy around without the cops ever finding out. But they didn't just attract the poor; *fresas* like that nasty rich kid soon began to see them as the next cool thing and got involved in their business. That silly boy Tavo, who was high all the time, had wanted to join him and become a narco, and he was willing to do anything to do it, even sell out his sister. But he was at least smart enough to realize that he had to disappear, or his father would kill him. The other kid sent him to join his homeboys, and soon the boy realized that this wasn't a fun adventure after all. He got scared, but he was even more scared of his father. He became an addict and started working for them as a hawk. But Oliver had contacts, and they eventually found him. So we went to see him. I've never been more afraid in my life, Don Ethan—it was like venturing into hell. We were awaited by a cohort of demons. I entrusted my life to God. Oliver and I went with two of his colleagues, his closest friends on the police force. They knew the gangsters. I went, unarmed, surrounded by boys. They were just children led astray by the evil one. If any of those kids had been taught the ways of the Lord, they would be no different from our own children. The memory pains me so: Oliver's face when he saw Tavo. He'd promised the gangsters that he would respect him. Nothing was supposed to happen to him. It was the only reason they agreed to let him see Tavo, even though the boy didn't want to meet, but in the end he was in no position to argue. You should have seen his face and the boy's: he knelt in front of his father the moment he saw him. I think he peed himself. Then he started to beg forgiveness: 'Forgive me; forgive me, Father—I didn't know.' Then he started to cry. He had debased himself, and when his comrades saw that, they were a little disgusted and disowned him. Oliver couldn't stand it anymore. He went for him. The hatred with which he grabbed the boy, his own flesh and blood . . . he started to curse and beat him. He would have killed the boy on the spot if we hadn't intervened. The three of us jumped on top of him, trying to get him to stop, but we couldn't. He knocked him flat with the first punch, and the other boys just stood by. They didn't care. One of them laughed and shouted, 'Thirteen!' and they all laughed and watched like it was all a big joke. That was when I learned that *thirteen* meant thirteen seconds. It's the test they put you through when you join the Mara: they gang up on you for a thirteen-second beating. Imagine the evil that taught those poor innocents such a thing. They started to count the seconds while Oliver asked the boy questions that he couldn't answer because of the beating he was receiving. Oliver hit him harder than I've ever seen, unleashing all the beatings he'd held back since the boy was little. Everything he'd kept repressed inside and all the ones his own father had given him. I heard him say that he regretted not having hit the boy when there might have been the chance of setting him straight. But I can assure you that laying hands on children doesn't solve anything. A tree watered with beatings grows up crooked. Meanwhile, the gangsters all shouted together, 'Six, seven . . . ,' and we tried to separate them. The kid told us everything he knew in the hope it would stop his father, but it didn't make any difference. Oliver wasn't even listening.

"But it didn't matter because that sorry excuse for a brother didn't know what had happened to his sister. He and his sister, who was head over heels in love with the other kid, had agreed to run away together. They'd made their plans and escaped, just as we thought. On Sunday they had still been together, but by Monday morning Tavo had gone to the gangsters' headquarters and started his new life there. The other kid had left with Patricia. He'd said that he'd left the country, that he had his own plane, and Tavo realized that he'd been used. He never heard from Patricia because they'd left her in the hotel they'd gone to that first night. He thought he'd see her again and they'd make the journey together. While he'd been there, the kid had respected her. He swore that to his father on everything that was holy. While he had been with them, the girl's virginity was intact—they hadn't even kissed. At her age she was just happy to be with the boy she was in love with. She was happy holding hands. The more the boy said to his father, the harder his father hit him. You can't imagine how terrible it was to see that disfigured face until the boy finally stopped talking, and we had to drag Oliver away as best we could. Poor Tavo was left lying on the ground. The boy cried, and the others laughed. I think that it's the worst memory of my life."

He woke from a strange, agitated, allusive dream. He was back in the same room. He felt a throbbing pain in his temples and cold sweat running down his neck. Then the waves of pain began to flow from his two knees and his little finger.

His mouth was open, and he was able to breathe, so he started to take great, gasping breaths that rose up from his stomach. His body was wet down to his groin, and he could see the remains of vomit dribbling down his shirt. For now, he thought with a sigh of relief, he was alone.

Suarez spilled a little of the whiskey. He was concerned that he might have drunk too much, too fast. He finished the little the Beast had left and looked for more, disappointed in himself. Tired, he moved from the kitchen to the bathroom, where he turned on the shower to clear his head. As he toweled off, he felt a lump in his throat. Sometimes he had second thoughts about what he was doing. Sometimes he was horrified at himself. Then he went back to the lair, the hidden room where he'd found the trophies: clothes, necklaces, all of which were bloodstained. They had belonged to at least twelve different women. There were also photographs of terrified teenagers, their fear of death captured forever. Maybe there were more, maybe fourteen. He used the discovery to revive his hatred. He drank more. Now that he was refreshed, a new idea came to him. He opened the medicine cabinet, where, next to a couple of expired pill bottles, he found the medicinal alcohol and opened it.

The Beast saw the demon reappear. He now looked a little more confused and agitated, but he was colder than ever.

"You pissed yourself, threw up, and passed out. I think it was because the cloth was choking you, but don't worry; it's only been five minutes. I have relieved you of the cloth. I think that we now understand each other. You only have to answer my questions, and then you can talk about whatever you want. You'll never walk properly again . . . maybe you can get an operation. Who knows? And you can forget about driving, not with two ruined knees. Also, you're missing a piece of your finger."

"It's . . . it's in the right water tank, under the cabin. There's a false bottom. Half of it is hidden."

"See how easy that was? Thank you so very much. I'll go get it." He disappeared, pleased at his success, humming a bolero to himself.

The Beast wasn't sure what he'd said. Only that it meant relief. He thought that he might have told the truth. Some unconscious part of him had answered, working on autopilot. Then he worried that he might have made a mistake— maybe he hadn't hid it in there because he'd been making a delivery. Maybe he'd hid it in the false roof in the cabin. He was terrified, like a small child afraid of some terrible punishment. He almost called out to the man to let him know, but he was also afraid to anger him. He wanted to say that he'd made a mistake, that it hadn't been on purpose, that he just wanted to help—he'd help; it wasn't on purpose, he swore . . . the footsteps came back up the stairs one by one. The floorboards creaked closer and closer to his chair, and with each creak, panic, terror, and pain coursed through him. Without realizing it, he started to sob.

Suarez smugly came back in with the computer tucked under his arm. He looked for a socket and plugged it in before turning it on.

"See how much easier it is this way? If you keep helping me, soon it'll all be over, and you'll be free."

In the face of his torturer's bonhomie, the Beast felt the tension break him. He started to sob harder. Suarez looked up for a moment and turned unsympathetically back to the computer. He asked his prisoner for each password as they came up, and the Beast obediently gave them to him one by one. The man logged into his emails and looked into every folder.

"How many girls have you taken in the past few years?"

"F-f-for me?"

Suarez took note of this answer but didn't react. "For the people who pay you."

"The clients?"

"The clients."

"I—I don't know . . . about two a year, sometimes one, sometimes three. At first it was a different client."

"How long ago?"

"I don't know. Ten years, I think."

"And then?"

"Then they disappeared. They told some others about me, and the first ones stopped calling."

"Who were they?"

"I don't know. I met the first through the owner of a strip club. He knew me well and asked me if he could pass them my telephone number. Then a woman called and told me what they wanted."

"And what was that?"

"To take asses from one country to another. Other drivers do it. Sometimes they need to move girls from one club to another without anyone knowing."

"Why?"

"I don't know; they were whores. No one gave a shit about them. Because they'd pissed someone off or someone had bought them, maybe. I just took them from one place to another."

"From one club to another?"

"Yes. Just that. I never hurt anyone—I promise."

"And you don't work for the pimps anymore?"

"No, once I got offered two jobs at the same time and took the one with the girl for the Europeans because they paid better. You know how people are: the others stopped giving me jobs. So I stayed with the Europeans."

"And they pay you enough to live on?"

"I do other things, not just work for them. But yes, I could live on what they pay me."

"How do they contact you?"

"They . . . may I say something that isn't the answer?"

"Yes, you may."

"My knees hurt very badly. It's hard to talk. I'm very thirsty. Could you give me something to ease the pain? Something to drink? I'm not asking you to let me go; I just need something for the pain."

"No. Later, when it's all over, they'll give you tranquilizers, but you don't get anything until we've finished."

"Wh-what was the question?"

"How did they contact you?"

"I don't know. They were clients of the other guys, I think. One day the woman called and told me that some Europeans who lived in the south of Brazil needed a driver they could trust for some work. Different work. They'd told them about me and asked if I was interested. I said that I was, and then they called me and said that they'd be in touch by email. That was the only contact I'd have with them. They sent me an email with the girl they wanted, saying where to pick her up and where I had to take her. And just like that, I had to wait in a bus station or a public place they decided on. It was always near Curitiba, but the location was just to trick me; I know that. Then they come to the truck, and I hand the girl over. They pay me, and that's it."

"Why do you say it was to trick you?"

"They don't keep them there. They take them to a small town about four hours farther south. They go all the way to Santa Catarina. They don't know that I know. I found out."

"Fine, now tell me the place."

Suarez's questions were now lackluster; he was concentrating on the screen, going through the emails. It took him half an hour, during which the Beast didn't dare speak so as not to break his concentration.

"But there's only three years here. You didn't work with them before that?"

"Yes, but they changed the email account and told me that I had to use that one. They sent it to me with the password and everything, and I closed the other one. I've forgotten what it was."

"Five girls, one after Michelle."

"You're looking for Michelle? I remember her well. I didn't do anything bad to her. She was very quiet. And I don't think they do anything bad either—they're like an adoption network or something . . . I can tell you where I took her."

"I've got that from your email already. Why do some girls come with photos of the house and the family name while others just have some coordinates?"

"With some I just do deliveries. Their contacts pick up the package themselves. That was how it was with Michelle. I just had to pick her up. But in some countries they don't have any contacts, and if it was easy, they'd tell me to get them and give me a bonus."

"And they pay you well."

"Not that much. It's not . . . it means food on the table. Life is hard. I swear. If I didn't have to . . . I feel very sorry for them. I don't like to think about it, but if it weren't me, someone else would do it . . ."

"Then all you know is in these emails. You don't know who they are or why they're looking for little girls."

"No, I've told you everything I know. You can go now. You don't have to untie me if you don't want; just call an ambulance. Please, I'm begging you—they can get me out of this, and you'll be long gone. I only ask that you make the call in front of me so that I know you really did it, or you can hand me the phone. I won't tell them anything—I promise. I'm so thirsty."

"What about the other girls?"

"What other girls? There aren't any more. I promise."

By way of an answer, Suarez got up with his now-habitual callousness and went back over with the gouge and the dripping cloth.

"*No!* Nonononono! I told you everything! No! *No, no, no, no! Please!*"

Suarez grabbed him as hard as he could, but the man started to shake his head from one side to the other, gritting his teeth. Irritated, Suarez dropped the cloth and started to stab the point at his lips, aiming for the gums but cutting him all over his face. Eventually, the terrorized Beast stopped.

"Enough, stop, please! I won't move! No more, no more, please! No more!"

But Suarez ignored him and went on even when he opened his now-bloody mouth voluntarily. He dug the point into the top of his victim's mouth, above the incisors, and started trying to lever them out. To his surprise, however, one of the teeth below broke first with a horrible cracking sound. The Beast let out an inhuman wail and renewed his attempts to defend himself. Suarez picked the cloth up from the floor and shoved it back in his mouth, the water mixing with the spurting blood. After gagging him, he walked up and down in annoyance, trying to decide what to do next.

"I told you, you fucker. Don't lie to me again. You're making it so difficult. Now, you see, the worst is yet to come."

And before a pair of horrified eyes that revealed both pain and panic, he picked up the hammer, slightly uncertain. He hesitated for a little while, unsure what to do with it. Then, when the idea finally came to him, he kicked over the chair, sending the Beast's head smashing against the floor. He cut the ropes away from the ankles and wrists and forced the legs straight with a terrifying crack of broken, unnatural-looking joints. Suarez took off the man's shoes and pinned his feet to the ground.

"You may not know that the hands and feet have more nerve endings than the rest of the body. But you soon will."

He put the soles against the ground, leaving the toenails exposed. Then he lifted the hammer as his victim, muffled by the cloth, let out a wild, high-pitched, rodentlike squeal.

Andrés went on with the rest of the story more easily, as though he'd rid himself of a burden he'd been carrying for many years. He enjoyed the relief of finally having gotten something painful off his chest.

"Lord knows I wanted to stay with Oliver for as long as I could. I offered him everything I had, all the help he could want. I even suggested he come back with me, though I knew it was useless. I had to go back for work. I'd used up all my vacation time, and my family was waiting for me. I left for the States, dealing with the sorrow of someone abandoning a soul they know needs them." Now his voice began to break, and he had to take a few moments before going on. "After that, I only know what I was told by other people, but it's not much, and it's all bad. Tavo soon turned up shot to death, whether in a shoot-out with another gang, simply to escape his life, or killed by his father, we don't know. I was told that Oliver started hitting the bottle even harder. Soon his wife left him, and they never saw each other again. He rejoined the force, but now he was obsessed with his daughter; it was all he could think about. Even so, he never heard from her again. A year later they found the horrible kid in Panama. He hadn't lasted long; he'd continued playing at being a narco until he crossed someone, and they gave him a Colombian necktie. Do you know what that is?"

"Yes."

"Well, that. Oliver went there, but he was unable to find her. He had his contacts and wasted a lot of time and money, but he never told anyone what he saw or did. He came back empty handed. After that he was suspended several times, and his colleagues covered for him, as did his superiors because, they say, of what he knew from his years in the Criminal Brigade. Eventually, they gave him an office to sleep in until he was pensioned off. By then he was refusing to talk to me or anyone else. I think he just wanted to die. But then we came back, and I went to look for him. You can't imagine the state he was in or how he was living. At first I don't think he even recognized me, but I prayed hard to God for strength and started to go to see him after work. Finally, I persuaded him to visit us at home and then to stay the night. He was living in a motel; it wasn't good for him. Then he started to come to church with me, although he never came to believe in anything again. That's what he told me at least, but my wife and I prayed for him every night, and if a man is good, God must listen even if he isn't pious because God knows and forgives all. After many months he eventually agreed to move in with us. At night we could hear him crying in his bedroom. Our hearts were filled with grief, but we prayed to God to give him succor, and in the end he heard us. I told him that if he wanted to stay with us, he had to stop drinking. So he started to go to the meetings."

Ethan couldn't believe his ears. "Andrés, you took him into your home? A drunk? With your wife and children there?"

"My children stayed in the States—you know they live there. They were grown by then. And my wife and I had to help someone in need. Oliver always took care of me and helped me. He took me into his home when I had nothing. And the Lord says that we must share and give food to the hungry and drink to the thirsty. If I had abandoned him, what would that make me? Cain, that's who I'd be, Don Ethan."

"I wasn't criticizing you. I'm in awe."

"After a while he rented a house, and although his life had lost all its spark, at least he'd started to live it again. That, Don Ethan, is why he wanted to help us and why, although I know he can be difficult and he sometimes comes off crazy with his obsessions about security and everything, he's the best man you could ever hope to meet. We can't let him relive his past. The enemy is waiting to exploit his weakness and make him fall back into his old ways."

But when they went to see Suarez, he'd left a few hours before. What was to come was now inevitable. These were the moments that defined their fate: one's entire life could be decided by a matter of a few hours. The destinies of both Suarez and the Beast were fixed during the conversation between Andrés and Ethan, because it happened then and not before.

Suarez came out of the bathroom. He'd wet his hair several times to wake himself up, but he was fading. Each splash of water revived him a little, but the effect was lessening every time. The small bottle of alcohol was now nearly empty. *Just a sip more*, he told himself. He was afraid of getting careless and leaving behind clues. He filled a bucket with cold water, went back into the living room, and put it on the floor. Slumped in the chair, his legs free and twisted like a vine, his bare feet tenderized by the hammer, his toes missing a couple of nails, and his bloody hands, one of which was missing part of its little finger, tied behind his back, the Beast was panting. His mouth gaped open, his lips were torn apart, and his eyeballs rolled back into his skull, as though he was asleep. Suarez went over and poured the bucket over him. The Beast woke back up immediately and choked and coughed several times. He started trying to get away, but Suarez ignored him. He was concentrating on removing the sheets of plastic he'd placed on the floor and putting them in trash bags. Then he started to scrub the floor before the blood, which had spread a long way, congealed and left a permanent mark. He wasn't satisfied with his efforts.

"Hmmm. We're going to have to cover that up with something."

He thoughtfully spread out some new sheets and then dragged the body on top as though he were moving furniture. The Beast passively allowed himself to be moved, moaning in pain. Once the cleaning routine was complete for the second time, Suarez looked down at his shirt with a frown, unbuttoned it, and threw it away with the rest of the trash.

"Look, it's all covered in shit. Oh dear!" He looked at his body with genuine surprise. His string vest was also spattered in different shades of crimson. "Oh dear, you've ruined my vest too! I'll have to change later."

Under the cotton was a once-toned but now very run-down body. It was wide shouldered, but his chest was drooping, and he had a slight belly that stuck out over his lower half. This provided a contrast to spindly arms that didn't appear to have any musculature at all. Of course, his audience was entirely oblivious to all this, struggling as he was to stay lucid amid the different sources of pain and constant fear that accompanied each of his captor's movements. His torturer appeared to be behaving erratically, ever more drunk and unpredictable. Suarez approached again but this time without any of the tools. Nonetheless, the Beast recoiled at what might be in store, the terrible mystery of what might come next.

"Listen, are you tired? I am. Things have been much more difficult than they needed to be, haven't they? You need to accept the fact that I know who you are, and there's no point denying it anymore. The only thing you're achieving by denying it is to make things worse. I've already got all the information I needed about this case, but now I need to know about the others. I'm going to ask you a question, and if you protest your innocence again and say you know nothing, I'll cut off your thumbs. Right now you can still pick things up. After that, you won't be able to. You'll be like a dog, which doesn't have a thumb. That's what they call opposable apprehension. Do you understand?"

The Beast, who had instinctively closed his fists around his thumbs even though he knew it was futile, nodded hard.

"Fine. So I'll ask again: How many girls have you attacked? How many women have you raped and killed in your life? Not for the clients, for yourself. I know what you do—don't give me any shit."

The tortured man didn't answer for a few moments. Before he could speak, tears came to his eyes. "I—I . . . I . . ."

Suarez was generous.

"Yes, yes, it's easy, isn't it? You're getting there. You're on the way to the truth. See? It's hard to learn, but if you do what I say, it'll make up for all the suffering. When you let it all out, you'll be free, and your suffering will be over."

"I . . . don't know how many I've attacked. I try to forget afterward. It's not me; it's the demon that takes possession of me. I try to fight it, but I can't. Then I feel so sorry and want to disappear from the world. I don't want to remember, so I never counted."

"Yes, I understand. But how many have you killed? That's not the kind of thing you forget."

"I . . . I . . ." Before answering, he looked into Suarez's questioning face and gave in. "Two," he said, starting to cry in earnest. "I killed two, but they were mistakes, accidents—I never meant to. They were accidents . . ."

"Of course, of course. I know how things can happen. You see? Now your suffering is going to come to an end because you're telling the truth, and I'm going to let you go. Now I want you to give me their names and where you killed them. And where you left the bodies. That's not the kind of thing you forget either. Is it? You know that as well as I do. Their names are somewhere in there. Come on—tell me."

The Beast hesitated. He wasn't sure; now he was worried that sharing the information might get him in trouble with the police.

After a tense silence, Suarez carefully put the cloth back into his mouth. "Tsk, tsk, tsk. I gave you a chance, but you took too long. You know it's your fault, don't you?"

The Beast wriggled around and tried to protect his hands.

"I don't want to do this, but you're forcing my hand. You're making me do things I don't want to do."

The Beast tried to get up in vain. Suarez took a firm hold of his head.

"Listen, I don't want you to lose your way on the path to the truth, so I have to punish you. It's your fault; you know that. I want you to think about what you've done so you can learn from it. I'm going to cut off your left thumb. It's the hand you don't use so much, and if you tell me what I want to know, your other one will be safe. But you must remember that lying or refusing to speak is the wrong way to go. Lies won't get you anywhere."

Ethan determinedly continued his methodical search, convinced that the lack of news from Suarez meant that he'd met a dead end. One of the things that he'd learned in his time as an investigator was that people revealed much more about themselves on social networks than they thought. Even very basic security precautions were forgotten the moment they turned on the screen. With Johanna's WhatsApp and Facebook accounts, he was able to completely reconstruct the lives of almost all her contacts: work, home, relatives. He augmented this information with data from other networks. In most cases he was able to get useful information just by typing their names into a search engine. Investigations that used to take weeks and required a lot of movement and risk now just took a few days sitting in his bedroom. So in spite of his apparent lack of progress, he kept on cross-referencing his information and searching through thousands of conversations, messages, and posts. Ethan knew that he wasn't looking for a well-lit road but rather a flash of light that might appear at any time. And so, after he'd spent four days typing in different names and staring at deathly dull profiles, his patience was rewarded. In some photographs of a party, someone he recognized from a couple of comments by Johanna's boyfriend about a payment they hadn't been able to track down appeared: Marlon Figueroa, who identified himself as a lawyer. He seemed to have a relationship with her but not since the dates Johanna had given them for Michi. Several comments on different walls about the pleasure of doing business and bad inside jokes led Ethan to believe that this lawyer was a promising candidate. A visit to his LinkedIn account identified him as assistant at the firm Smit & Betancourt and provided a work address. The profile also said that he was the representative of "important European businesses" whose activity had begun in the city just a few months ago. After having had to rule out dozens of other suspects, Ethan was jubilant. This was the thrill of success.

Suarez forwarded the emails with the information he'd obtained to Ethan and Ari. Names, photographs, and in some cases, the addresses of families with the same rendezvous location, always in the state of Paraná, near to Curitiba with no obvious link to the much smaller town that the Beast claimed was where his employers, "Europeans from the north, like Fins or Greeks, one of those countries where they have gays," lived. It worried him to hear that they kept an eye on the email account. When they discovered that he'd disappeared, they'd soon make the connection to the emails he'd exchanged with Johanna, and then it wouldn't take them long to work out that she was dead. He was amazed at the idiocy of the bastard—telling her to contact him via a channel monitored by third parties—but still, he assumed that he had plenty of time. After the recent delivery they might not need him again for several months. By then, it would be too late.

Suarez thought about his victim and the torture he was inflicting upon him. He hadn't thought that he'd be able to do it. It scared him to find out that he was still capable of such savagery. He thought that he'd reformed. But he didn't regret his actions or what he still might do in the future. Everything this piece of shit, this low-down scum who didn't deserve to breathe, said reminded him of his past. Every lie and excuse, every protest of innocence, every plea for mercy made Suarez want—*need*—to see him suffer more. Every pleading word, every scream of terror goaded him into unleashing all the anguish that had built up within him over the years. We all have an assassin sleeping inside us. It's better not to wake him up.

He stood up and realized that it was dawn. He'd been up all night. He was exhausted and would have to wrap things up pretty soon. In his tired state, he might make basic errors, and although he knew that it was unlikely, there was a remote chance that someone might come by. He came out of the kitchen and walked back to the living room, where the specimen awaited him. The tipped-over chair was to one side while the toolbox was on the table. Five feet away, the Beast's deformed body had gotten free of its restraints, and now he was trying to crawl to the exit. Given his condition—broken knees and elbows, amputated thumbs and little fingers, and four toes smashed in—Suarez wasn't particularly worried about him getting away. These were skills he'd been taught a long time ago. With his hands tied behind his back and limbs dislocated, the victim looked like a huge worm. He even left a crimson trail along the wooden floor. Suarez walked over and put a foot on his head.

"What have we said about escaping?"

He heard the inhuman moan, and a smell reached his nose. He'd pissed himself. Again. He bent down and unblocked the Beast's mouth.

"This time, I'll give you another chance. How many girls was it? How many girls have you abused in your life, and how many have you killed?"

The Beast, his mouth in pain, his body falling to pieces, mumbled as though he were stoned. "I don't know. I told you. Dozens, hundreds maybe, but I killed eighteen. I know that for sure. I'll never forget them. It's an impulse, like a force I can't control. I know it's wrong. If you let me go, I'll go to a doctor. I'll tell the police so they can put me in jail. I'll do therapy to get cured. I swear on everything that's sacred, please—I'll pay for what I've done. I've given you all my money."

"Twelve thousand dollars. You lied about that too."

"But not anymore! I told you that's all I know. I've given you my money— that's all I can do. You have to let me go. You promised."

Suarez knelt down in front of him and took his head in his hands. "Why do you keep kidding yourself, you coward? I now believe you completely, but you know very well that I lied to you too."

The Beast, so close to this strangely intimate but cold, objective man whose breath stank of alcohol, started to cry in despair. "I-I told you everything. I helped you. Why? Why did you do this to me? Why did you make me believe I could be set free?"

"I've already explained this to you, but you didn't believe me. I came here to teach you a lesson. I had to show you what those poor girls went through. You had to feel what they felt: the disorientation and denial. They believed that they would be safe if they went along with it. The realization that it was all a lie only makes everything worse. You had to learn about denial and anger, impotence and desperation, but above all horror and fear. The horror of what is still to come, fear because we still haven't finished. And terror, which I see in your eyes when you hear me speak: the terror of knowing that you're going to die. That's why I'm here. Everything you never bothered to think about before. You needed to learn about the suffering they went through. Take it as life's final lesson. And after going through all that, you're going to die. I'm going to witness you shitting yourself with fear when you discover that even your ability to breathe has been taken away from you. When you realize that there's nothing to be done. You're going to be reduced to nothing. The only thing you have to look forward to now is the sight of me enjoying myself as I make all this happen."

The Beast sobbed uncontrollably, bloody mucus running from his nose. His brain had frozen up in terror now that the end was nigh. Suarez quieted him so he could go on.

"We're getting to the end. I need to tidy up and leave. Just so you know, I'm going to wrap you up in those plastic sheets and dump you close to your trailer where I've made a little hole to bury you in. It's good that your yard is a jungle. No one's ever going to fucking well find you. It's not big, but you'll fit nicely, all smashed up like you are. There'll be plenty of air trapped in the plastic and nothing you can do. Your lungs will keep on filling until the last breath. You have no control over that. You'll see. Get ready: that's when you'll really be clinging on to life. I'll sit and wait for you to go. I wanted you to have a really good understanding of what's going to happen. I don't want you to miss a thing. The important part is that you know all this so you'll be prepared for everything that awaits you. As you know, I'm in no hurry."

The SUV bounced along the steep, curving road, spitting out rocks on either side. The bodyguards looked disinterestedly out the windows, their view filtered by their sunglasses and the layer of dust that had gathered on the glass. When they finally got to their destination, they stopped and honked twice. When this was met with no response, they got out. A tall, thin, pale blond dressed in a full suit as though he were on his way to an office meeting rather than a wasteland in the Colombian outback took out a packet of cigarettes but before lighting one asked permission of the man in the back seat.

"Do you mind, Don Armando?"

"Not at all, so long as it's outside."

When he heard this, the driver got out as well, dressed similarly, but he had dark hair, a thick head, a square jaw, and a broad back; he was built like an athlete, but his movements were rough and clumsy. They both opened the gate. The tall man cradled his tobacco as the car passed through the barrier and drove onto the property. He followed them, inhaling with pleasure. A hundred and fifty feet on, they came to the house, and the driver asked him for a cigarette. They climbed up onto the porch and knocked on the door. They waited, knocked some more, and started to call out.

"Hello? Helloooo! We've come to see you! We have your money!"

They let another minute pass with no response. Eventually they tried the door and found, to their surprise, that it wasn't locked. They went inside, and the passenger looked at his cell phone in annoyance. After going through some emails, he murmured, "Idiot," and got out to join his employees.

"Don't waste your time. He's not here."

"His truck's parked out back."

"Fine, then his truck's here, but he isn't. Let's take that as a bad sign. We're not going to stomp around in there messing with the evidence."

"Evidence of what, sir?"

"I don't know; that's why we can't mess it up. I'd rather have someone who knows what they're doing go through it. Call the Bloodhound."

"He can't have escaped. He wouldn't be that stupid."

"That's what I want to find out. Let's get out of here and keep watch until the Bloodhound arrives."

"But sir, he's in Brazil. He'd have to—"

"Tell him to come! *Now!*"

Cowed, they ran back to the car, making sure to open the door for him first.

"Of course, Don Armando, right away."

8

Colônia Liberdade

The Volkswagen Touareg drove up to the fence, shielded from the house by rows of trees. When the dust had settled, a strikingly styled man got out. In his bespoke three-piece Harris Tweed suit with its perfectly folded pocket square, the mauve tie, and oxford shoes, he looked like some distant relation of Dorian Gray, just as handsome but slightly taller. He had mahogany hair, a milky complexion, and youthful athleticism that belied his delicate appearance. He quickly surveyed the terrain before remarking caustically to the front window, "They were here yesterday?"

The driver, who was a little flustered, poked his head out and nodded. Careful not to sweat all over his outfit, the fresh-faced dandy got back into the car, next to his employer, to whom he didn't say a word. He didn't feel that he owed any explanations to the people who had hired him. It was more important to examine the terrain. He haughtily instructed them to move on.

"What are we waiting for? We're not going to find anything here. Armando, I congratulate you on the diligence with which you besmirched the scene with your footprints. Whoever was here before you will be very grateful. One would hardly describe it as German efficiency. But then, you're Argentinian, I believe?"

"My parents were German. I am Argentinian. I come from proud Aryan blood."

After driving on, they repeated the ritual, trying as best they could not to aggravate the tension that already existed between the two men. One of them was the head of security, the other a freelance adventurer. Before entering the cabin, the Bloodhound shared a cigarette with the others, who regarded him with a certain amount of awe. Then he went inside to perform his examination alone so no one else could contaminate the scene: he walked around the patio, circled the parked trailer twice, and bent down under the radiator. Throughout, he took great care not to muddy his pants or shoes. Armando was staring at his telephone in the car when a voice through the window made him jump. The young man enjoyed catching people out like that.

"My dear *Sicherheitschef*, will you please accompany me?"

Armando reluctantly got out and walked to the Beast's truck.

"His truck?" the Bloodhound asked.

"Yes. This is the one he used to deliver the latest package: last week."

"And you believe he ran away?"

"We think that it's a possibility. I was hoping that you would tell me."

"He might have left without his truck."

"In fact, that would be the smartest way to do it."

"But you wouldn't bet on it, hmmmm?"

"He's not the smartest man I've ever met."

"I suggest that we start talking about him in the past tense, just to get used to the idea." He grimaced. "The door is shut, the keys are in the bowl, and everything is neatly stowed away. Nothing seems out of place. Did he use the water tank to transport the package? You can clearly see two different layers of dust, one of which is much thinner than the other. It was opened very recently, and the person who opened it had to feel for the handle. We'll get an excellent haul of fingerprints off it."

"Whose fingerprints?"

"Whoever was with him. He wasn't alone."

They walked up the steps to the kitchen, the lithe tracker pointing out different clues as they went. When they got to the living room, he dramatically pulled back a thick, old, red woolen rug to reveal a portion of the floor. There was no change in color, as one would expect if it had been covered for a significant period of time. To Armando's annoyance, the Bloodhound lit another cigarette, but his employer didn't object.

"I think it's quite clear: he was killed. He was ambushed by one or two people; maybe there was a fight or he was tortured. The wood soaked up a lot of blood, which they then had to clean and cover with the rug. They must have found it in the second bedroom. They were good. It looks as though it was always here."

He knelt down onto the floor, which he caressed lovingly.

"Mightn't this be his work?" Armando asked. "What if he brought back one of his 'indulgences'?"

"This is nothing like the rape of a young woman. I'm afraid that you're down one driver. Blood, blows with a heavy object, cuts. Bleeding. He might have been attacked with a knife and hammer, but if so, it would be odd for it all to be concentrated in one corner. If he'd died quickly, with the cleanup coming soon after, the blood wouldn't have soaked in so much. That takes time. They might also have left the body to search the area. Once they'd finished, they might have come back to get rid of the body and clean up the crime scene. If you give me a few hours and bring me a few tools, I can tell you what happened more precisely."

"I don't care how it happened. How sure are you that he was killed?"

"Very. Either it was him or the other guy, but I'm betting on him. About . . . here, someone was hit hard by a hammer, and they bled—a lot." The Bloodhound pointed to the dents in the wood. "And . . ." He started to sniff around; he'd detected a scent. His sudden reaction did justice to his nickname. He smiled at his own perspicacity. "A nail, or a piece of it at least."

He immediately started to search for dents in the floorboards, which were scattered around at regular intervals, some of them triangular, some flat and square. His bottom eyelids drew up involuntarily. "You don't fight sitting down."

He got up and walked around the table, which was large and flanked by six chairs. He counted them and then inspected each one closely, paying special attention to the feet. Then he homed in on one of them, stroking the sides. "He may have been tied to this chair, although I couldn't say for sure. After that he didn't fight and was sitting down. Do you trust him to be discreet?"

Armando answered this with a derisive snort.

"Then take care. He was sitting down, and something was done to him. I don't know what, but they were rough. The blood flowed in longitudinal lines. Outside, you can see where a heavy object has been rested. I imagine he was wrapped up in plastic or something waterproof that then leaked, like an ink stain on paper. This wasn't random or improvised. I'd say that they lay in wait for him and were very careful. One or two men, no more than that. Not much space, not much movement, few clues. If it was two people, one kept watch while the other went to work on him. That's how I would have done it. You should be looking for a pair."

Now that this conclusion had been reached, Armando shared some information he'd been holding back. "We found some emails he exchanged with the group that abducted a Central American girl. They just came out and asked for his information so they could track him down, and he sent it to them like the idiot he was. When we tried to contact them to find out what they were up to, we found out that they'd been dead for weeks. Someone got rid of them and assumed their identity."

"And now you have a parked truck, an empty hovel, and a disappeared man. I bet we'll find him buried out back or in the stream. There are plenty of excellent places to hide a body. Whoever did this seems to have been quite competent. They didn't leave any obvious prints or make any big mistakes. But they must have been in a hurry. There are plenty of clues in the gaps and corners, plus the visible marks on the floor where they put the rug down."

"Do you think we'll be able to track them down?"

"I think that while we're wasting our time here looking for that bastard's remains, your enemies are in Sao Paulo looking for the colony. If they haven't found it already, that is. You need to warn them. What will you do? Move the girls?"

"That, of course, is none of your concern."

The office building was in the financial district, the capital's newest neighborhood. Ironically, it wasn't far from Calvo's office. Visitors were welcomed by a rotating door, and the spacious lobby left ample room for patrons of the two buffet restaurants at the back, most of whom were employees of the offices above. Ethan leaned on the bar from a spot that gave him an excellent view of the ground floor. He sized up his options, which were many; he hadn't seen any security apart from the two guards watching the entrance with shotguns. It would be easy to slip up the stairs or get into the elevators along with the crowd. Emboldened, he decided to try visiting the floor where the office was located. But when he looked at the board with the directory of businesses, Smit & Betancourt wasn't there. Surprised, he went to the information desk to ask the receptionist. As soon as she heard his accent, the girl started getting flirtatious, but still, she had no idea what he was talking about. She was new and hadn't heard the name since she'd started working there. Keen to make a good impression, she asked him to wait for a moment and went off to consult her supervisor, who she said had been there for years. Two minutes later a pompous man was quickly explaining that the business he was asking about had only used their facilities for three months, even though they'd paid a deposit for six. They'd never really moved in to the office and only used it for occasional meetings. When Ethan asked when they'd left, he found that it was on the very day he'd arrived in the country, ten days after the kidnapping. Ethan left the building with a sense of frustration and the receptionist's telephone number.

Brazil was a continent unto itself. It was an oft-repeated cliché, but you couldn't really understand it until you'd been there. The general image of Brazil was the postcard one of endless beaches flanked by skyscrapers with idyllic, jungle-covered mountains looming in the background. For many, Brazil was still Rio de Janeiro, samba, and the Amazon. But Suarez, who'd been there before, marveled at how the landscape changed as he drove through the south in his rented car. He was dressed in his best tourist outfit, brandishing a guidebook as his alibi. He drove for hours through featureless grassy plains and undulating hills that reminded him of the Pacific coast. He was looking for a town with a population of fewer than thirty thousand inhabitants known, like most of the state, for its tranquility and, more distinctly, for the German heritage of many of the locals, most of whom had emigrated at the beginning of the Cold War. He couldn't help but be surprised by the gradual disappearance of black and darker-skinned people the closer he got. The south of Brazil held many surprises for the uninitiated, the biggest of which awaited him on his arrival. He had lunch in the local capital surrounded by signs in German. After lunch he passed several run-down farms before his long journey came to an end, heralded by a flashing sign telling him to reduce his speed before he got into the town. To his left was a Protestant church. The smooth asphalt road gave way to rural ruts. When he got to the town center, however, the infrastructure suddenly improved to what he considered "first world" quality: unblemished traffic circles, cobbled streets, and notably better housing with tiled roofs instead of the more typical metal sheeting. But the transformation stretched to more than the materials used. The design and decor also took on characteristics that he, who'd never been across the Atlantic, associated with Bavaria. The neat, orderly town exhaled peace and quiet from every stone. The signs for restaurants, some of which were illustrated with rosy-cheeked Tyroleans, invited their customers to enjoy traditional Alpine fare. His amazement increased when he got to the hotel, which was built like a Swiss guesthouse: three whitewashed stories with balconies, artisanal red beams, and similarly styled wood fittings. The exceptionally polite receptionist, who loved his town, informed Suarez that 90 percent of the population was of German origin. It had been founded by Prussian colonists in the nineteenth century, and German was still the official language. The population in this part of Brazil was bilingual, speaking both German and Portuguese, while you were as likely to come across a black person as you were in Austria. At the end of his exceedingly friendly introduction, the receptionist suggested seeing the natural wonders of the surrounding area and even an amusement park. Suarez, who knew his history, was intrigued, excited, and concerned by these revelations. He had been warmly welcomed into one of the safest and most peaceful parts of Latin America, but the area also hid a terrible secret.

The house belonging to Marlon Figueroa, the link between the deputy chief and the ghost firm, was in a middle-class neighborhood with public streets supervised by guard posts on every corner and signs that declared that the neighborhood was organized against crime. But it wasn't as luxurious as one might imagine for someone who moved in those circles. Or perhaps Figueroa was just a small fish who helped keep the shoal moving, feeding on the scraps left by sharks like the deputy chief. Ethan studied the cozy little house protected by a fence that was mostly for show and decided to stake it out to see who else lived there. By the second day, he realized that something was wrong: nobody had come in or out. The house appeared to be empty. Given the circumstances, he decided that he'd risk breaking in at night so as not to attract the attention of the guards sitting in their little wooden boxes. In the dark, it was easy enough for him to walk over and unlock the gate. Once in the garden he listened hard but couldn't hear a sound. The house was completely dark. He checked the guard post on the corner, which showed just as few signs of life, and applied himself to the lock. It was easy enough to force. He opened the door carefully, lifting it a little so that it wouldn't make a sound scraping against the floor. When Ethan went inside, he was met with a terrible, nauseating smell. Gagging, he closed the door and pulled his shirt over his nose to block out the stink. Before going on, he went into the kitchen to find a cloth, wet it, and wrapped that over his nose. The stench grew more powerful the farther on he went, until he got to the door at the end of the hall, which was half-open. He pushed it. Just as he'd suspected, he found a rotting body on the bed. Dead for an indeterminate number of days, it was stretched out as though it didn't have a care in the world. Its teeth glowed in the weak light from the streetlamp. The morbid grin seemed as though it was mocking Ethan, smug in the knowledge that its secrets would never be revealed. Ethan explored the room, the grin following him around with its obnoxious grimace. He thought, *I know; you don't have to rub my nose in it.* He went into the bathroom in search of deodorant but couldn't find any. He covered a towel in scented soap and wrapped that around his face in the hopes of making the rest of the search bearable.

After checking in and getting settled, Suarez set about trying to make friends with the locals. He toured the family-oriented oasis, keeping an eye out for anything that might lead him to what he was looking for, but he met only dead ends.

It wasn't until the end of the second day that one of his exploratory drives took him to a community set slightly apart from the town. He entered a small forest on a well-kept dirt road whose entrance was signaled by an anachronistic garden. On the other side of the woods was a concrete wall with fake columns that flanked the road for half a mile, ending in a large set of double doors and a neoclassical roof with a sign in German and Portuguese. Suarez slowed down to study it, but all he saw was an intercom and several security cameras monitoring the entrance. Not wanting to give himself away, he didn't stop, though he memorized the name so he could write it down as soon as he got away from the estate, which went on for another half mile. This concerned him. A fortified compound in one of the safest states in the country. It had a cool, impersonal feel, not dissimilar to that of a prison. He wondered how many people lived there and why it didn't appear on any maps or traffic signs. It seemed to have been forgotten entirely. There must have been a reason for all this secrecy. He stopped at the first grocery store he came to and decided to try sharing his discovery with the shopkeeper in the hopes of getting some answers.

"What's that strange castle down the road? Do you know it?"

"Castle? Haha, you won't find many castles around here, I don't think."

"Yes, down a path, just over a mile. It has a *very* long wall. The signs say that it's called Colônia Liberdade. Why would anyone want to spend their time locked up in a place like that when it's so lovely here?"

The storekeeper's expression changed, and she stopped laughing. "Oh yes, the residence. Well, you know, people. They live there and don't bother anyone. Everyone's home is their castle; they can do what they want. Is that all?"

"Oh, this, too, please. Thank you."

Suarez headed back to the hotel, deciding not to say anything to the concierge or any of the other people he'd met. Instead, after a brief rest he got back into the car and returned to the capital, where he'd had lunch on the day he arrived. Colônia Liberdade. He didn't need to write it down; he knew that he'd remember it.

Just before dawn, Ethan finished his search and left the tomb before the sunlight exposed him. The guard was asleep. He crossed a small park to where he'd parked the car and drove back to the apartment, looking forward to a shower and some rest before deciding his next steps. The people who had organized the kidnapping had been careful to cover their tracks, and all the leads he'd found had apparently been unceremoniously cut off. The only thing left to investigate was the origins of the ghost law firm, for which he'd need some help. But he wasn't very optimistic; Figueroa had probably eliminated any records that might lead Ethan to his bosses before they'd tied up that last loose end and left him rotting away in bed.

Suarez wasted his money and much of his sobriety in the wood-and-corrugated-iron dives that lined the sides of the roads, looking for someone who might be useful or at least somewhere that had the right mood. He wandered through seriously dangerous neighborhoods, ignoring the rude, challenging stares of the local toughs. At some point he realized that his mind was a little clouded, and he splashed water on his face but refused to admit that he was in no condition to drive. He got the barmen talking, asking them about different towns and the countryside. Then he'd inquire about company, asking if they knew anyone who could get him something special for a party. Two ignored him, one threw him out, and the other went on and on and forgot the original question. The loud music made conversation difficult. His fellow customers were solitary visitors of an age similar to his, groups of men and the odd woman, who was always accompanied. The spaces were dark, sordid, and lit by fairy lights, with maybe a karaoke screen hanging from a wall, some mirrors, or a few colored spotlights sweeping the dance floor, which was almost always empty. In one of them, a curvy dancer in a skirt halfway down her thigh and a top that left most of her breasts exposed was sitting on top of a drunk, sweaty local several decades older than her. She waited for him to go to the bathroom before she gave Suarez a rather unsubtle look as she ran her palms underneath her tights, giving him a peek of her underwear. He left his drink unfinished and got out of the bar as fast as he could. He knew the type: it turned her on to goad her man into fights. He couldn't afford to make a scene. He sat in the car and waited for the attendant to come over. The attendant was an old man whose life consisted of sitting in front of the bar and watching the cars for fifty cents apiece. But this one looked at him differently. He leaned on the window.

"You got it, didn't you?"

Suarez was beginning to forget his Portuguese. "Here you go, old man. Two *reais*. Thanks."

The decrepit attendant didn't take the money. He just held his gaze, arousing Suarez's curiosity.

"You didn't like the *mina*?"

"I'm not Argentinian. And I don't like getting into fights over nothing."

"It's dangerous around here, my friend. You could get hurt."

The two of them sized each other up in silence. The music was still playing loudly, and the dust in the parking lot bounced along with the bass. Suarez was uncomfortable. He felt drunk and wasn't certain of his reflexes. Keeping his eyes locked on the old man's, he felt for his hand and closed it around the coins. "Thank you."

But the old man grabbed his wrist. "What are you looking for?"

"Nothing you can help me with."

"You've been wandering around all night. I saw you asking the others—try me."

"I'm not looking for anything. I don't want girls or boys or to party. I'm fine for tonight."

But the old man wouldn't let go; instead he squeezed harder. Suarez felt in his jacket for the Taser.

The attendant appeared to read his mind and let go. He tried to smile, unsuccessfully. "Try me. I can help you."

Suarez sighed and took a chance. "Colônia Liberdade."

The cadaverous face broke into an amused smile. The music from the bar pounded into their skulls. "Hah! Hahaha. See, man? I can help you. What do you want from the fortress?"

"Information."

"A few people around here work there. They're strange people. Cleaning, gardening. How did you know to come here?"

"I didn't. I was fishing."

"And how can I help you?"

"I need someone who knows it from the inside. Give me good news, and I'll give you a good handful of *reais*."

Red, green, yellow, and blue light slipped through the gaps in the planks that made up the wall of the bar, giving his contact's face a strange hue. The effect grew more ghostly as he bared his gums. "Oh, I'll help you, man. I'll help you—you'll see."

Ethan had breakfast at a traditional café where tourists mingled with office workers having quick midmorning coffees. He was trying to outline his strategy. All his work had been for nothing. He'd run out of time and contacts, and he didn't think that Suarez was doing anything useful at the other end of the continent. He knew that every move he made increased the danger he was in, and he tried to decide what to do as he flipped through a newspaper. It brought some worrying news: the police had found the deputy chief, or rather his mutilated body. After the scandal kicked up by the press, they seemed to be working quickly to bury a death for which they were partly responsible. But Ethan knew what it meant for him. The Mara were cleaning house. He went back to his apartment to have a shower, intending to move to another city or farther still. He had to find Suarez so they could plot their next moves together.

Lost in these thoughts at the entrance to his compound, he quickly became annoyed when the guard didn't lift the barrier. Irritated that he'd fallen asleep, Ethan looked for him through the window, but the boy, who said hello to him every day, didn't move from his seat. Before Ethan could call out, the boy leaned forward in the window and gestured discreetly to Ethan not to make a sound. He was clearly agitated and continued the mime act by shaking his head several times with harrowed, pleading eyes. Ethan, who had been exhausted just a moment before, felt the adrenaline begin to flow in his chest and his pulse accelerate. He knew what was happening. For a moment, nothing could be heard other than the chirping of tropical birds. In the shade of the buildings, the two men silently communicated with each other. Ethan took a deep breath and nodded toward his apartment while the boy, upset but pleased to have been understood, nodded gravely. Ethan thought he saw tears glinting in his eyes. Without answering, he put his hand to his chest in thanks and reversed out, trying not to rev the engine. He turned the car around, knowing that he wouldn't be able to go back. He'd have to make do with the clothes and money he had on him. Fortunately, he always kept his passport with him.

The bar was decorated with framed black-and-white photographs from the fifties. Over time, they had grown speckled with damp and complicated formations of petrified mold. These were accompanied by pages from magazines and newspapers, the ones from the seventies in saturated colors. There were also photos of customers, the older ones developed traditionally while the latest ones were printouts. It was a form of fame apparently available to anyone who wanted it. Thanks to the obstinacy of the original owner, now deceased, the bar had never been refurbished, and after many years of decline, the trend for nostalgia had made it popular again. The regulars were now joined by young people huddled around devices and traditional dishes, drinking fashionable liqueurs like Jägermeister.

At one of the tables, which had old-fashioned metal legs and imitation marble surfaces lending the place even more authenticity, Suarez was sharing a beer with a small, sun-wizened old man in overalls that identified him as a gardener. Suarez had been asking questions and buying beers for quite a while. This was their third attempt to meet, not because his informant was reluctant but because he'd intentionally missed the first two appointments at the two other places they'd set so he could watch for any signs of betrayal. It was difficult for him to delay like that, but Suarez was now sure that the man was clean. When they finally did meet, it hadn't been difficult for him to earn his trust. The man didn't like his employers at the colony. He'd worked for them for years, well over a decade, and set about complaining almost immediately. The beer made him even more talkative.

"So they have their own security system?"

"Oh my, the system! They have their own police, with dogs and uniforms."

"They go on patrol?"

"Why? Nothing ever happens there, but if there's a problem, they handle it themselves. The real police don't get involved. Of course not! I've never seen them there, and it's not for want of trying."

"What do you mean? They don't let them in?"

"It's like the tree, the tree that fell down. It was . . . over ten years ago. I remember because I hadn't been there very long, but there was a storm. Oh my, the storm! One of the worst I've ever seen, with lots of thunder and lightning. The sky turned white, and the lightning hit some swings behind one of the houses, in the back lot. I don't know why the boy was there, whether he'd run away from his parents or they'd lost sight of him. Oh, the boy! You should have seen what it did to him: all twisted and black, and there was a terrible smell, like chicken but sweeter. Very strong, horrible."

"What about the police?"

"The police came to investigate, but they wouldn't let them in. Take that, police! Hahahahaha!" The man broke into a cackle as though he were the one to have defied the authorities. "Oh, the police! They made them stay outside—can you believe it? They let the ambulance in to take the boy away, but they wouldn't let the police accompany it. They argued for a long time at the door—I saw them—and then they called for more cars on the radio. They weren't happy about not being let in! But the men at the gate stood there. They wouldn't get out of the way, and in the end the ambulance left, and the police left with it. They stayed for as long as they could, but then they had to go. You should have seen their faces! Hahahaha!"

"So when do you see the private police?"

"Oh! Almost never. I don't know where they come from, but I've heard an alarm go off when a branch falls or a group of kids tries to jump over the wall, and then they come running. Oh, they're scary! Those big barking dogs and the poor kids . . . once they get frightened off, they don't come back."

"They have an alarm all around the perimeter?"

"What else? And television cameras. And I'm pretty sure that they're the kind that see in the night because they move when I leave."

Suarez was listening carefully, leaning back in his chair as he mulled over what to do next. The gardener, emboldened, went on chattering.

"But the gardens are great, the best you'll see. And then there's the store. They have their own store! I don't know what it sells, cheeses and food from Europe. They're very strange; they never meet up with anyone, but you'd never guess it. They speak Portuguese! Ha! Portuguese! To order around the gardeners. They speak it very well! But they don't like it . . ." The gardener suddenly went quiet.

Suarez realized that something had happened. Without turning around, he asked, "What is it? What's wrong?"

"It's them—it's them." The gardener blinked nervously, and his hand started to shake. But from where the old man was sitting, he couldn't see the entrance, so he couldn't have seen anyone come in.

"Where are they?"

"It's them—it's them. They're coming. They don't like us to talk. They're coming—they're coming."

The poor man started to hyperventilate. Suarez turned around, following his line of sight. A side window with net curtains looked out onto the field that served as the bar's parking lot. His own car was there, but now two large SUVs were parking. Suarez turned to his companion, who was scared like a small child about to be punished.

"It's them. They're coming to the bar."

"Don't look at them; look at me. Look at me!" He grabbed the man's wrist to get his attention. "That's better. Who are they?"

"They're from the colony. Some men from the colony."

"Why are you scared? We're not doing anything wrong."

"Oh, I don't know; I don't know. They don't like us talking to strangers. Oh! Now what do I do?"

"Look at me. You're not doing anything wrong. Do those cars belong to their security? The ones you told me about?"

"Yes, oh dear, that's them."

"Fine. Listen: you haven't done anything; there's no reason to worry. I'm going to go to the bathroom, and when I come out, I'll leave. You have every right to drink a beer; there's nothing they can object to. They haven't seen us together, and they won't. OK?"

The gardener didn't answer. Suarez stood up while the vehicles parked. He squeezed the gardener's forearm to get his attention again. "OK?"

The gardener nodded dubiously. Suarez walked to the bathrooms, which were behind the storage area, at the back. He locked the door behind him and sought out a window. He had no idea how they'd tracked him down, but however it was, his informant's face had told him everything he needed to know. They were after him, and he could no longer trust his anonymity to protect him. He was concerned by how frightened the man had been. Suarez climbed up onto the toilet to get to the tank above. It was an old-fashioned cistern with a pull flush, a large porcelain basin about half a meter below the ceiling connected to the bowl by twisted lead pipes. He stood on the seat to push himself up and drop the telephone inside. It disappeared with a splash. Next he pulled back the plastic curtain and slid the translucent window open. Bars. The window was completely blocked by bars.

Ethan took a rest at a gas station. His situation seemed hopeless. Deciding to play his last card, he dialed a number, and a familiar voice answered.

"It's my good friend Ethan! My, this is a surprise. Not necessarily a nice one, but definitely a surprise. Don't get me wrong; you know that I like you, but whenever we speak, it seems as though you're determined to bring me bad news."

"Hi, Adrian. Don't worry; I understand. I'm calling because I need your help."

"I'm all ears."

"How much time do I have?"

Calvo chuckled. "What kind of a question is that? That's always for God to decide—you're no different."

"The girl was taken out of Central America by a truck driver. I don't know where. He was given the job by a law firm called Smit and Betancourt, but it's disappeared, and I'd bet that if you go through the records, you'll find that they've managed to erase the name of the founding partner. I don't think there's any way to track them. There was a possible link, an assistant called Marlon Figueroa, but he's dead. They see to every detail."

"Why are you telling me this?"

"Because it might be the only information you don't have."

"Why don't you come here? Or we could meet for lunch? If you have new information, I'd be delighted to help you again. I can pick you up if you like—where are you?"

Calvo didn't seem surprised, doubtful, or confused. He didn't even sound curious.

Ethan gulped and felt his throat tighten. "Are you going to sell me out?"

"Hahaha! I would never do a thing like that. That's not who I am, my friend."

"This morning, someone was waiting for me at my apartment. Do you know where it is? The Mara don't search for people; that's not what they do. We talked about this, remember? Someone must have led them to it."

He could hear Calvo breathing calmly on the other end of the line.

"I'm asking you to do me one last favor. How long do I have?"

The silence stretched on. The tension was electric.

Calvo cleared his throat and said, "Wait."

Ethan heard some footsteps on the carpet and a door closing. Then the voice returned.

"I don't know why I hold you in such high esteem. I think it's because you're so straightforward. You can't be this blunt, not in this line of work. You should have searched your car. You must have suspected that it had a tracking device. Why didn't you think of that, detective?"

Ethan felt deeply stupid. "I don't know."

"I think that you're concentrating hard on just a few very specific things. That's good, very good. But you neglect others. I am, however, very impressed with how you dealt with the kidnappers—well done. I don't know how you did it."

"How long have you known?"

"My God, Ethan . . . you're like a bull in a china shop. Ever since my friends on the force asked me to take a look at your massacre. You know how it is: for delicate questions like that, you can never have too many eyes."

"Are you going to hunt me down, Adrian?"

"Let's do two things. First, pretend that this conversation never happened. We can't meet in person, or I'll have to hand you in. Don't worry about the GPS; they only asked for the address, and now they have it. The battery ran out a few days ago, and we didn't replace it. I don't know where you are, and I don't want to know."

"How long do I have?"

"Not long at all. Head straight for the airport; don't delay. I don't know whether you'll make it. They're probably watching the roads. I warned you. In places like this where everything happens in the shadows, things only get really dangerous when they come out into the light. As far as they're concerned, you're a dead man. It's just a matter of time."

Suarez knew he had to act fast and, making sure that he couldn't be seen, slipped from the bathroom to the storeroom, which was shielded by the kitchen. It was a run-down space with metal shelves and two cold chambers with a door for deliveries at the back. That was what he was looking for. Before crossing the room to head outside, he checked his gun and the Taser. Night was falling. There was only a thin strip of blue left, and it was rapidly being eaten up by the darkness. On the other side of the restaurant, which took up an entire block, he would try to creep past a few one-story houses and make it to a taxi rank he'd noticed earlier. There was no way he could get the car back; it was parked to the side. He'd have to wait for his pursuers to give up or move on. He ruled out going back to the hotel until he could work out what had given him away. He was lost in these considerations when he felt something like a burning needle run through his right shoulder, immobilizing his arm with a piercing, sharp, throbbing pain. He hadn't felt this sensation for a long time, since he was a young man. It was followed by a bang that sounded like a firecracker, a shot from an old-fashioned, low-caliber weapon. Suarez felt himself thrown forward. He fell and pushed himself into a roll, ignoring the pain, and got up to run. He quickly looked back behind him before ducking between two houses and saw the youthful, gloating face of a young man dressed like his great-grandfather. It was like something out of a practical joke or a nightmare, but the pain in his shoulder was a forceful reminder that this was really happening. The danger was very real.

The young man observed him with a hunter's air of superiority, smiling. He called out in a strong central European accent. "They have no idea, do they, old man? You almost got away. But we're smarter than them, and I'm smarter than you."

Suarez sped up to get to the taxis and save his life. The Bloodhound, pleased with himself, turned to the restaurant, where the mercenaries were coming out, having heard the shot. He waved his Swiss 7.65-caliber Luger P-08, a collector's item that had become his pride and joy. He used it only on special occasions. He pointed them in the direction the target had run off in. After seeing him push down the bar for the rear exit, he'd known that his prey was right handed, and with the wounded shoulder, it was increasingly unlikely he'd be a good shot.

"What are you waiting for? Bring the cars! I've stung him, and now we have a runner. We need to truss his feet."

As was usual after midday at this latitude, the sky was filled with dark storm clouds. The light dimmed, as in an eclipse. Ethan was driving along, looking for *flanelinhas,* friendly if shady characters who charged car owners to "take care" of their vehicles while they were parked but who usually disappeared until the owners returned to pick them up so they could claim their tip and offer unnecessary and often counterproductive help pulling out. But now there were none to be found. The street was deserted, and Ethan couldn't see anyone among the parked cars. Then he heard a voice behind him.

"Is that your car?"

One of a pair of barely pubescent girls with no tattoos or other sign of gang affiliation had spoken with poorly concealed malice. Ethan just answered with a curt yes before getting in quickly. They started to giggle. One ran to the corner while the other tried to keep the conversation going.

"It's very nice."

Ethan ignored her and pulled out, driving to the end of the street. As far as he knew, he was well outside the Doce's zone of influence, much closer to their enemies, the Diecisiete, but these girls seemed more than suspicious. He pressed down on the gas when a Nissan appeared at the end of the street to block his way. He reversed, but a Hyundai was coming toward him from the other end. He knew that he had only a few seconds until they came alongside and that they were most likely carrying automatic weapons. The only reason they hadn't already started firing was that they wanted to catch him alive, and that option was worse than a quick death. He made sure that his safety belt was fastened and did the only thing he could, pumping the gas, pushing the pistons and revving the engine as much as he could before releasing the brake. The engine roared like a furious animal. He rocketed toward the car that blocked his way, surprising its occupants, who tried to get out the other side. They were too slow. Ethan's growling car smacked hard against the side, spinning the other car around like a top. Ethan felt himself thrown forward into the steering wheel before the momentum rocked him back again. Everything around him was a blur until he came to a halt. He'd lost track of where he was and which direction he was facing. He tried unsuccessfully to focus. The colors had begun to run into one another, creating a strange feeling of unreality. He couldn't understand what he was looking at but pressed down on the gas again, and the car limped up onto the sidewalk. He slowly recovered his bearings and shook his head several times, praying that the radiator had survived the impact. In front of him he saw a large avenue and tried to head for it. In the rearview mirror he saw that the Nissan had tipped over onto one side. Two kids were walking around like zombies. He managed to get onto the main road and drive on with his crumpled hood, looking for a way out. He saw a line of waiting taxis 150 feet from a traffic circle; he parked illegally and ran to the first taxi, where he slumped into the back seat.

"Airport, please."

The taxi driver, who'd seen him get out of the wrecked car, couldn't understand what was going on.

"Just like that, sir?"

"I . . . I've been attacked. Quickly, please."

"Man . . . you don't want to go to the police station?"

"The airport. Airport, please."

Only now did Ethan realize that his forehead was wet. He was bleeding. "Do you have a handkerchief?"

"Don't you want to go to a hospital?" the driver said, looking very worried. "I'll take you to the hospital."

"They're coming! To the airport!"

When he heard these mysterious but threatening words, the driver forgot his concerns and headed straight for the freeway without asking any more questions. A couple of thunderclaps rumbled in the sky.

Suarez made his way between backyards, his back to the main path and his shoulder throbbing, until he got to the taxi rank in the small square. There wasn't a taxi to be seen. Clutching his wounded arm, he searched for something he could use as a sling. He went one way and then the other without seeing any sign of life. Given that he couldn't escape, he took out his gun and crossed the empty traffic circle to hide in a copse next to the road. He soon found that he'd chosen well. The two black, military-style cars were driving down both sides of the road and turned around to wait for him to come out. His only option was to go farther into the woods to make them follow on foot and maybe, he thought, go back to the restaurant if he went right to pick up his car or at least seek safety in the crowd. He ran as best he could, swaying to balance his wounded arm. He did not look back, though he heard the engines stop. Six pursuers got out to track him, and the Bloodhound was quick to work out where he'd gone.

"Point your headlights at the trees! At the trees, you idiots! Didn't you hear me?"

They turned the front of the car at the copse and lit up the undergrowth, exposing Suarez's moving silhouette. When he realized he'd been discovered, he turned around to shoot with his left hand, hoping more to keep them at bay than to actually hit anything. With no particular target, the bullet screeched through the air a few feet above their heads, much to the delight of the Bloodhound. It confirmed that he'd been right. He stopped his men before they could respond.

"They want him alive! Alive! Be careful!"

Armando emerged from the second SUV. Ever since sending for the Bloodhound in Colombia, he'd stayed with him as he tracked this man down.

"Do we have him?"

"We have him. It's definitely him."

"I thought there were two of them."

"Not here. If he has a partner somewhere else, we'll find him. We just need a few hours alone with this one. I don't care how tough he might be—he'll talk."

"I hope so. So far your work has lived up to your reputation. Long may that continue."

The Bloodhound glared at him. "So long as your clumsy oafs don't get in the way."

Armando whistled to his men. "Take him alive!"

Ethan's vision finally cleared once the storm clouds had blocked out the buildings. He was beginning to calm down. He'd only just managed to escape. He was lucky that he still had his passport and credit card. The rain began to fall with the dense fury of the tropics, slowing them down and reducing visibility to a few feet. The bunched traffic drove on cautiously. They passed several accidents. He didn't know what he'd do in the terminal, but for now he was relaxed, as though getting there was his only goal. Once inside, with airport security around him, he'd have time to sit and think. He could even sleep on it. He saw the transit halls as a sanctuary where time stood still.

"It's stopping."

The taxi driver said something. Ethan came out of his daze, wondering whether it had anything to do with what he had been thinking. "Huh?"

"It's all snarled up. Look."

In front of them all three lanes were blocked by rows of cars, apparently stopped by the aggressive downpour. People were wiping condensation from the windshields. The shortwave radio gurgled messages only the driver could understand.

"Listen: it's gridlock. I don't know what kind of hurry you're in, but there's no fucking way. We're not going to get there. I'm sorry, but there's no way."

"What happened?"

As they spoke, they were swallowed up by the traffic jam, surrounded by exhaust pipes busily belching out fumes.

"The bastards! The girl on the radio says that a bus has been shot up ahead. Just over there. That's why there's a jam. See what it's come to? Just the same as how they attacked you. It's getting impossible to live in this country. They say to be careful because the gangsters have started to walk among the cars. Not even the army can deal with this, you know?"

This news horrified Ethan. He knew what was happening. The Doce would think nothing of shooting up a bus; for them it was just a show of strength. They were reminding everyone who was in charge. They weren't just going to let him go. The gangsters were searching the cars. It was just a matter of minutes before they found him.

"I need to get out. I have to go."

"You can't get out here, in the middle of a traffic jam. In this rain!"

Ethan paid him double the fare. "If the gangsters ask, I wasn't here."

This terrified the good man, who made no effort to stop Ethan. The sight of a passenger getting out in a downpour came as a surprise to the other drivers, who watched as he stepped onto the berm, jumped the wall, and disappeared into the curtain of rain. Farther on, he arrived at a smaller two-way road scattered with potholes with no sidewalks. People around here didn't walk anywhere. He went on walking for twenty minutes, getting thoroughly soaked before the clouds started to clear and the rain stopped. It was as though a gigantic showerhead had been floating over the city. The dividing line between the sheet of water and the now-clear sky was very clearly defined: it seemed almost solid. You could hop in and out of it if you wanted. Surrounded by a cloud of mist as the water evaporated in the heat, he came to a shallow pit placed to one side, as though the asphalt had run out, with a metal post that had once borne a sign. A disheveled-looking woman was sitting next to it, eyeing him warily. Ethan approached her.

"Is this the bus stop?"

The woman nodded, still staring at him rudely, as though she'd never seen anything like him in her life.

"Do you know if it'll be long?"

She shrugged. Ethan smiled, thanking her for her help, and sat down a few feet away. He didn't know what to do next. Seek refuge at the embassy? He didn't know what he was going to do, where the bus would take him, or how long it would take, but at least he'd be getting away. That was as far ahead as he could plan.

Suarez saw his shadow cast ahead of him in the headlights, stretched out like an expressionist painting or a child's drawing, and heard footsteps coming closer in the undergrowth. They were closing the net around him. He knew that his chances were growing slimmer every second. He saw a light flashing through the branches. The restaurant. If he made it there, they wouldn't be able to kill him in public. The police might already be there to investigate the commotion. He leaned on a tree and started firing again to stop them, sow confusion, and attract attention. Firing in a semicircle, he achieved his objective, which was to get his pursuers to lie flat on the ground. The fact that they weren't firing back gave him an advantage. He knew that that was all he could hope for with his left hand and switched hands. Although his right arm was wounded, he was still better with it at close range. He set out running as fast as he could with the gun pressed against his chest. He'd made a gap for himself, and his confidence grew. He could see the restaurant through the tree trunks.

They'd all thrown themselves to the ground at the first sound of gunfire, like cowardly little girls. Gunfire from a cripple. It took only the most basic training to see that the bullets weren't being aimed; he was more likely to hit a cow than them. The Bloodhound despised these men. He despised their ignorance, their idiocy, their cowardice. But he appreciated the courage of his prey. He was surprised at how skillfully he'd managed to get out of a tight situation, his determination not to give up and to keep them at bay. He admired the inoffensive guise he'd assumed. It was a matter of respect. In fact, he said to himself, if it was only the others chasing him, he'd have a real chance of getting away. But the Bloodhound was with them. He felt sorry for the man. The Bloodhound didn't let his prey get away.

He rearranged some leaves to protect his pants and knelt on the ground in a stylized pose, looking for a forty-five-degree angle on Suarez, his left arm hovering just above his left knee. He held his breath for a few seconds and focused on his target, a target that was running with one arm across his chest to ease the pain, waving the other around unconvincingly, as though to scare them. He fixed the man in his sights and calculated the length of his stride. Instead of aiming at the legs, he opted for the neck. This was the beauty of small-caliber guns that the goons behind him would never understand. He assessed the speed, distance, and momentum; fell into rhythm with his target's strides; noted the heavy breathing; anticipated the next step; and pulled the trigger. The others were butchers: all they knew was brute force dealt out at point-blank range, while he was a surgeon who made precise incisions with a scalpel. He extracted organs, then disinfected and sealed the wound. His seven millimeter was all he needed.

The bullet hit Suarez in the neck and went straight through, clean as a whistle, cutting his spinal cord without touching his trachea so he could keep breathing and thus still distribute oxygen across his agitated body.

Suarez suddenly lost control and felt himself float forward on momentum. He could no longer feel his feet; it was as though they'd ceased to exist. He fell forward like a puppet whose strings had suddenly been cut.

Contrary to Ethan's expectations, the bus didn't head into the center of the city. On the way, it went through two more showers, and the sky remained cloudy. It approached the far south, where the neighborhoods were extremely poor and always under the control of one gang or another. He went to the bus driver and asked where the end of the line was, but the address didn't mean anything to him. Then he tried to decide whether to get out immediately or stay and wait for the bus to go through a safer area. He grew more paranoid as he saw passengers getting off and on, exchanging glances that may or may not have been casual. All their conversations seemed to be about him. Eventually he decided to ask about a taxi stand and was informed that there was one at the end of the line.

To his surprise, a rotund woman in thick glasses and a floral dress joined him for the last part of the journey. He returned her warm smile out of politeness; she was sitting so close that he was a little uncomfortable. He could feel her sweaty flank touching him, and then she leaned in even closer and took his arm.

"Good afternoon, *m'hijo*. Were you looking for a taxi?"

Ethan stammered a confused reply. She smiled, but he thought that she was signaling something to him with her eyes. They flickered forward at the driver, who was tapping into his phone at the red lights. In his bewildered state, he didn't know whether she was trying to tell him something in code or was just a bored housewife. When he saw the square in the distance, she crossed his forehead as she murmured a prayer and got up, pulling on his arm.

"May God bless you and keep you."

"I'm sorry?"

"Come."

She headed for the exit, trying to drag him with her. He resisted uncertainly.

"But . . . this isn't my stop."

Maintaining a smile that seemed increasingly forced, she tugged harder, glancing up at the driver, who was watching them closely in the rearview mirror. Ethan decided to go along with her, and they got out together. The bus pulled away behind them, the wheels covering them in dust. Amid the cloud she looked at him grave faced and pointed to a side alley.

"Take that street; the taxis are at the end. Sometimes there are even a couple of cops. Don't take the square, *m'hijo*—they'll catch you before you're halfway across."

She crossed his forehead again and bade him farewell with a blessing. Ethan didn't have any idea where she'd come from or why she was helping him, if she was, but decided to take her advice and ran down the alley she'd pointed to. At the end of the street, the bus got to its final stop, and he noticed agitated movement around it. He ran over brush and rubble until he crossed another street leading out from the square. Then he saw a dozen or more armed and tattooed young men running toward him. He ran as fast as he could, until his lungs were bursting, and came out onto a wider, firmer street where he saw three taxis parked to the side. They were all empty, with drivers nowhere to be seen. He kept going, forcing himself to the limits of his endurance, leaving the wasteland behind him. There was nowhere for him to go—he had no plan or hope of finding somewhere to hide. His only remaining option was rapid flight. He ran on, his lungs burning, his throat gasping down air while another rain shower fell, making him skid on the slippery surface, the steam billowing off his body. Now he looked like a pale comet, not unlike his pursuers, who were getting closer with every step. Ethan wasn't thinking. He just kept running, grateful for the refreshing shower. He didn't care if he fell—he was alive with effort and survival instinct, alive for as long as his feet would carry him. At the end of the street he saw a figure next to a barrier, a dark-blue blur in a cap. He couldn't believe it: the man was holding a gun. In front of him was a policeman with a gun that was pointed at him. In the unrelenting rain, which dripped down from his visor like a miniature waterfall, his eyes peering through the screen of water, the blur called out to him.

"Stop, sir! Freeze!"

Ethan couldn't believe it; he refused to accept that this was happening. He threw himself at the policeman to knock him down, but the officer fired before he got there. The bullet whistled past his temple and stopped him in his tracks while in the painful lapse during which their gazes met, the sound of the pack approaching from behind caught up with them. The eyes of the officer seemed to beg forgiveness, but Ethan didn't have any time for that. He felt himself swamped by the roar of the horde of pursuers. They fell upon him like a swarm of locusts. Before he caught sight of them, he felt a powerful blow at his back, which he recognized as a flying kick, and found himself knocked to the ground, where the blows came raining down onto his stomach. He curled up while his grunting aggressors surrounded him, and through the water, which had merged with the attackers into a huge, overpowering wave of violence, he heard the voice of the man who had been responsible for his capture.

"I'm sorry, sir, so sorry . . ."

The Bloodhound watched the body drop and noticed the weapon fall from the hand to land somewhere among the weeds and ferns. He raised his hand to stop the pursuers, who obeyed his orders like trained dogs. Then he brushed the dirt from his knee, making sure not to stain his tailored tweed, and cautiously approached his immobilized prey. The man's head was buried in the undergrowth while his left arm stretched out in search of the Beretta it had lost. He kept his weapon trained on the man, looking for signs of life. The crumpled jacket made it difficult to tell whether he was breathing. Now that the man was unarmed, the Bloodhound was concerned with keeping him alive. It bothered him to think that his immaculate shot might be ruined by the poor physical condition of an inferior man. He'd be blamed for a death that had nothing to do with his aim and everything to do with a deficient specimen. His admiration for the tenacity of his rival in the face of his own superior genes increased even further.

When he got to the body, he knelt down and felt for a pulse in the carotid artery. His face lit up. Spurts of blood were gently, rhythmically being fed into the brain that the Bloodhound needed functioning in order to interrogate this man. He put his Luger down on the grass and got ready to turn over the body when he caught sight of a dark shape about six feet away, obscured by the undergrowth. It was black with yellow reflective strips that gleamed more like plastic than metal. He came to the realization in the same moment as he turned over his victim's inert body. It wasn't a gun; it was a Taser. The fugitive hadn't thrown away the gun he'd been firing but a Taser that he must also have been carrying. He must have switched hands as he ran with his arms across his chest. He'd clung on to the gun in his right hand, which was still resting underneath his breast. He saw that it was still stiff and useless but that enough tension was left to pull the trigger of a gun Suarez cherished as though it were his only possession. Before the Bloodhound could react, his eyes met those of his executioner. The barrel roared, and a close-range bullet obliterated his nose, knocking him backward and taking off the top of his head. Due to some incomprehensible reflex, his legs kicked out uselessly while he lifted his left hand to cover the hole in his head, as though he were ashamed of it. As the Bloodhound's life snuffed out, the hand slapped roughly against his cheek, a slapstick topper to the joke that had been played on him.

As soon as they heard the report and saw their leader fall, the rest of the team started to fire at Suarez, whose body shuddered like a rag doll until Armando, the head of security, forced them to stop.

"Back, back, you fools! I want him alive! They need him alive!"

The flustered boss ran toward the two bodies. The Bloodhound was lying still, and just a few feet away, Suarez was vomiting blood. He'd dropped the gun, and it was all his immobilized hand could do to make a final effort to beckon him closer with a pair of fingers.

Intrigued, with the barrel of his gun pointed at the man's forehead, the head of security went over to listen to what the dying man had to say.

"H . . . h . . ."

"What?"

Armando stepped back, convinced that he wouldn't get anything out of him when a brief grimace that might have been a smile spread across Suarez's face.

"Ha . . . ha . . . I was smarter."

And with that final effort, his eyes went blank, and the muscles in his neck relaxed, letting his head bounce lifelessly to one side. Armando stood up angrily and gave him a pointless kick to vent his frustration.

"Shit! Shit! This can't be happening." His tone shifted from anger to fear. "Oh my God. They're going to crucify me."

The rest of the goons surrounded the two bodies, but none of them went any farther, stunned and almost drunk on the image of the young tracker lying supine with a hand over his mouth and a scorched hole where his nose should have been. A black circle gaped morbidly in his skull. They murmured in nervous awe, as though they were in the presence of the supernatural.

"He's dead."

"The Bloodhound's dead."

After the initial shock, more thoughts came spilling out.

"The old man's luck's ran out."

"The network won't put up with any more delays."

"What about the Schwindts? How are the Bloodhound's brothers going to react?"

"Yeah, when they find out . . ."

"They won't do a thing without the network's permission. Everyone obeys the network."

"Their youngest brother has been killed. They won't forgive that easily."

"The old man's more powerful than you think. They've been letting him do what he wants for forty years."

"That was before. Now the other four will come, and if half of what they say about them is true, the old man is dead meat. We all are."

"Not that he has long left anyway."

Armando took back control so ruthlessly that they started running around as fast as they could, cowed by his anger.

"What the hell are you doing? Get rid of the bodies! We need to clean up this mess as soon as possible!"

They sheepishly scurried off in different directions, cleaning up the scene with eager efficiency, bringing buckets of water to wash away the blood. Soon there was no sign that they'd ever been there. That was when a phone call was made to the local police telling them they could come to take witness statements and look for nonexistent clues to a crime that they'd soon dismiss as a fabrication made up by local drunks.

9

Lights in the Distance

The flight was comfortable, but when Ari, exhausted by the stress of the last few days, opened her eyes, having been woken up by the landing announcement, it seemed to mark a passage from her real life to a weird new present. She was about to set foot in a land that was in many ways like a new world. This reality belonged to Ethan. Suddenly it seemed as though nothing she'd experienced only a few hours ago existed: now there was only the inexplicable, disturbing dream of her ex-boyfriend, and somehow she'd been dragged into it. Her stomach cramped up; she hadn't been able to eat since breakfast, but there was something she needed to get rid of, to vent.

The immigration official wished her a pleasant stay with his best smile while the policemen in customs politely asked for her form and welcomed her with a nod. In spite of the way she was being treated, anger continued to build up inside of her. She knew what awaited her in the arrivals hall, and the closer she got, the more irritable she became. The sensor opened the doors, and across several dozen heads belonging to waiting relatives and friends, she immediately identified that false pose, the fake smile. Standing behind the barrier, demanding the attention of everyone present as though she were the star of the film rather than a bit-part player, Michelle was just as superficial and full of artifice as Ari remembered. She was wearing a flimsy blouse and a dark skirt that suggested a degree of discretion. Ari interpreted this as false modesty, an attempt to be demure that was forgotten when you arrived at the high heels. Then there was her neck, tilted at an angle like a vulnerable princess, calculated to attract the flies that swarmed around her in spite of her feigned indifference. Her face was concealed behind enormous round sunglasses.

With her eyes hidden like that, she had no idea when Michelle had caught sight of her in the crowd. Nothing perceptible changed in her expression, but the tension she was under could be seen in her limbs. The woman's hesitation over whether to greet her was palpable, and Ari enjoyed that. It made her feel powerful. Eventually, Michelle stepped forward, trying unsuccessfully to act naturally, but she still felt obliged to play host. After clearing her throat, she spoke in a quiet, insecure voice.

"Hello, Ari. Thank you so much for coming. You can't imagine how grateful I am."

Ari refused to touch her, as though she were some kind of reptile. "Where's Ethan?"

"I haven't heard from him for days."

"Well then, let's find him."

"Yes, of course."

They left the airport and walked to the parking lot. Michelle clicked her key fob, and the lights of a basic Korean car flashed. It was decorated with stickers emulating bullet holes while the blue belly of a galactic lizard stretched over LED worms.

"This is your car? Are you fucking with me? Because if you are . . ."

"It belonged to my brother. I paid for it, but it was his."

"Your little brother?"

"Yes."

Ethan had told Ari what had happened to Beto, and she didn't say any more. Sitting in the passenger's seat, she fastened the seat belt, which was decorated with bullets. On the freeway she looked over at the clogged lanes of traffic heading in the opposite direction. Pushed to one side was the bullet-hole-ridden carcass of a bus.

"Yesterday, a bus was attacked on its way to the airport. It was awful. They killed the driver, and lots of people were wounded. Then the thugs spread out everywhere searching the cars. There was a huge traffic jam. It was chaos. It's lucky you didn't arrive yesterday."

"Searching the cars? What were they looking for?"

"The news says that it was a battle between the gangs. But we never know what really goes on."

Michelle left the car in a guarded parking lot before the two women headed for the apartment where Ari would be staying. They went through a gate into a depressing gray building, an unpleasant place: dirty and dangerous, kind of like a sleazy motel, the last thing Ari would expect from this stuck-up little bitch. She assumed that this was another of the queen of deception's little tricks. But Michelle took out the keys matter-of-factly: if she was faking it, she was doing it well.

They entered an apartment with damp walls that consisted of a run-down living room with a TV mounted to the wall, two plastic chairs, a two-seat sofa, and a kitchenette. Through a two-foot-long hallway was a bedroom that turned out to be slightly more habitable, with a small bathroom and shower. A barred window faced out onto the corridor. Michelle seemed embarrassed as she meekly showed Ari around.

"I'm sorry—it's not very nice. I'm staying here while I look for a place."

"You sleep here?"

"It doesn't look very nice, but it's quiet."

"And you want me to stay here too? Where?"

"You'll sleep here."

Michelle put Ari's bags in the only bedroom and sat down on the bed, bouncing to show that it was comfortable.

Ari wrinkled her nose. "You want us to sleep together?"

"No! I'll sleep in the living room. I always do when I have visitors."

Ari went back into the living room. She couldn't see any cots, and the sofa definitely didn't pull out. There was no way you could spend a night on it without tweaking your back. "What visitors? You just moved in."

"I've already spent a couple of nights on the sofa. I like it."

Ari walked around the apartment again and grew more annoyed. She rounded on Michelle. Suddenly everything was starting to make sense.

"I thought you lived with an engineer."

"We're not together anymore."

"Since when?"

"Well, he didn't want me to look for Ethan. He thought it was too dangerous."

Ari looked upon her with new eyes. Suddenly she remembered that Michelle had recently been beaten half to death. She went over and tried to take off her sunglasses, but Michelle wouldn't let her.

"What are you doing?"

"If we're going to stay in the same apartment, you're going to have to take them off sooner or later."

Michelle obediently dropped her hands and removed the glasses. One of Michelle's eyelids was still swollen, and there was still bruising visible under the foundation. Ari thought that one or two of the bruises might be more recent still, but she didn't say anything.

"I'm not sleeping here, and neither are you. We're going to a hotel."

Michelle was tired and depressed. Since the beginning of this hellish experience, she'd lost everything: her daughter, the rest of her family, boyfriend, friends. She'd almost been killed. She had nothing left. She was broken.

"But . . ."

"Let's go."

They went to a modern area close to the tourist attractions, parked, and went the rest of the way on foot. Several cars honked at them as they passed by. The first time, it made Ari jump, thinking it was a warning, but when she looked inside the car, all she saw was a smiling jerk pleased to have caught her attention. This happened three times, one of which with the added touch of a shout about sucking a *pusota*. Michelle just ignored it. For her, it was an everyday occurrence.

Ari grew annoyed. "I see it's the same everywhere."

"No, it's much worse here."

Ari felt a sense of solidarity. "Yeah, it seems as though it happens much more here, doesn't it?"

They checked in to a midrange hotel with all the proper facilities, and after unpacking, Ari took a shower. Michelle was amazed to see Ari put on a tracksuit and sneakers. She stared open mouthed.

"I needed that. So where are we going?"

"Andrés gave me the keys to Ethan's apartment. He hasn't seen him in days either. We thought you'd want to go there, but he wants us to wait for him. He doesn't think it's safe for us to start the search on our own."

Ari smiled sardonically. "Andrés is going to protect us? Anyway, if you've searched it already, I'm not going to find anything."

"Searched it? Of course not."

"You haven't been inside?"

"We don't know where Ethan is, but he hasn't been kidnapped. He might be hiding; that's what he said to Andrés. We can't go into his home without permission."

Ari was stunned into a few moments' silence. "You're incredible . . . of course he won't mind. Let's go to the apartment. Where is it?"

"We're close by."

"Then we'll walk. I'd prefer that after the plane. I need to stretch my legs."

Ethan came to with an icy splash of fear and aggression. A bucket of cold water had been thrown over his head, waking him up from a horrible dream that merged with the reality of the cloth over his face. He felt as though he were choking or drowning, lying prone with his hands tied behind his back. He started to spin around desperately. His struggles were met by a brief chorus of laughter. Eventually, he managed to sit up and found that he was on a concrete floor. With each movement, he felt a horrible pain in his chest that almost caused him to fall back down. He couldn't help but moan: his ribs were throbbing while waves of pain moved through every part of his body. Eventually, he was able to shake the cloth from his eyes and was met with the sight of three half-naked young men with tattoos all over their bodies: shapes and symbols from a mythology they'd invented themselves. They mocked him with disdain. It was easy to see the children hiding behind the shield of ink; it acted as a kind of armor to protect a soft, sensitive underbelly that they now imagined was untouchable. These street kids had sealed off their humanity through acts of violence against themselves. Living the hellish *vida loca* had turned them into demons. The apparent leader, who had toned arms, a muscled chest, and a cigarette between his lips, seemed calm and in control. He walked over to Ethan and slowly, delicately, with evident pleasure stubbed out his cigarette on Ethan's nipple. Ethan screamed and felt his mouth fill with blood. His ribs stuck into his lungs, making it difficult to breathe. He had to move his legs like a crab to find a posture that, while certainly not comfortable, was at least bearable. The kid, who was barely of legal voting age, strutted around him while more young men appeared, attracted by his cries of pain. It was as though they wriggled out of the woodwork. At first Ethan thought he was in a warehouse like the one the kidnappers had used, but he soon learned from the way his screams echoed around that it was a smaller building. They'd probably taken him to a destroyer house. There might even be local residents living nearby, like in Doña Maria's neighborhood. People who could hear his screams but would just lock themselves in and turn up the TV. Ethan had become a kind of giant insect spinning around on his back, surrounded by a crowd that now numbered over twenty and was still growing.

"Fucking hell, it's about time," barked the leader. "Who's paying you, you piece of shit? You'll be paid for your work. You're done."

His comrades laughed, but Ethan wasn't able to answer.

Ari and Michelle walked up to the guard post outside the condo. The guard met them enthusiastically until they told him where they were going. Suddenly he wasn't so talkative, mumbling something about it not being allowed, permits and other vague excuses. They called Andrés. When Andrés threatened to lodge a complaint with the guard's boss, the guard backed down and slunk back into his hut.

They walked up to the apartment, confused by the guard's reaction until they got inside. The lock had been forced and the place had been trashed for no apparent reason. Nothing seemed to have been stolen; furniture and lamps had been covered in clothes while other things were in pieces. Even Ethan's bags had been torn up and covered in something that smelled very much like urine. The graffiti on the walls told them that he'd been threatened. Michelle was horrified and couldn't stop herself from crying, but Ari took it all in stride. She told her companion to calm down. She picked up the largest suitcase, turned it over, and inspected the stitching at the bottom. Then she ran her finger down the seam until she found the bump she'd been looking for and used a kitchen knife to open it up. Inside, well hidden, was the money they'd taken from the kidnappers. She showed it to Michelle, not in triumph but certainly with determination.

"Put it away somewhere, and we'll call Andrés and the owners of the apartment. Someone needs to explain this mess to them. Don't worry—this is a good sign."

"Ethan's alive?"

"Or at least that they haven't found him."

After some negotiations, Andrés and the owners agreed to meet there and leave the women out of the police report. The deal was that the owners would agree not to say anything about the two investigators in return for their not casting aspersions on the security of the complex. Although she already had a pretty good idea, Ari asked Michelle to give her a detailed history of the case so far. Ethan had told her about Calvo, but Suarez had warned her off him. Michelle, however, confirmed her suspicions that he was their only possible line of inquiry. His office had closed for the day, so they couldn't consult with him until the next morning. The best thing to do was go back to the hotel and rest.

"OK, we'll wait. Ethan told me about him. He deals with the Mara. Let's try him—he must know something."

"But we don't have a contract with him anymore."

"But I have money, which can be much more persuasive. Tomorrow, before we go see him, we need to find a sporting goods store."

"Sporting goods?"

"That's right."

Ethan felt like the main attraction at a circus. They'd even set up a kind of stage for the freak to be put on display. The ringmaster was keeping up a constant patter, calling on his comrades to step right up and take a good look. To the prisoner's surprise, he was making no effort to interrogate him.

"Fuck you, man. You're going to sing. When the *pozolero* gets here, you're going to wish you'd never been born. You're going to tell him everything, right down to the first time you ever jacked off, you motherfucker."

This brought an admiring shiver and exclamations of surprise from the audience. Pleased with this reaction, the gangster repeated himself. This time, though, he was addressing his men.

"Fuck me, the *pozolero*. They're bringing the *pozolero* just for you, you fucker."

"I thought the *pozolero* worked for the Diecisiete?" said a voice.

"Fucker, you don't know shit."

"Hey, that's just what they say, man!"

"Look, you piece of shit, the *pozolero* is the *pozolero*. He's a fucking magician, a magician. You have to fucking pay him—he'll work for anyone if they pay."

"So he's a sellout!"

"Motherfucker, shut the fuck up! Who's going to mess with him? You?"

The audience enjoyed the public put-down. The only thing keeping Ethan awake was the pain. He struggled not to pass out, afraid it would mean certain death.

"Yeah, man! I'll fuck with him. For the Doce!"

"Don't fuck around—you don't know shit. Wait till you see him. You'll shit your pants. You'll see, bitch."

He turned to Ethan, who could barely see him. "Gringo, you're shit out of luck. You know why they call him the *pozolero*?"

"Because he turns you into *pozol*, man!"

There was general laughter. Ethan knew *pozol* was a corn-based soup. Gangs often used acid to get rid of their enemies. It was a favorite method of the toughest cartels. The Mara must have decided that that was how they were going to deal with him. First, they'd get all the information they could; then they'd make an example of him.

"Yeah, that's right! They're going to *pozoliar* you, man. And they're not going to kill you first. Motherfucker, I saw it once, and I threw up. You can't believe how they scream, bitch. Even when they don't got a mouth no more. You'll see, bitches, and you won't forget it. They didn't even call him. He put out word that if we found the gringo, he'd take care of him. Weeks ago. No one's allowed to touch him."

The emboldened pack started to chant in unison, not unlike the crowd at a soccer match: "Po-zo-lero! Po-zo-lero!" Ethan tried to look around through blood-soaked eyes. He stared back at this grotesque gathering of pubescent psychopaths who were braying for his blood. He realized that Michi wasn't the only child to have disappeared. All these kids—hardened murderers, proud rapists, pitiless aggressors willing to commit great acts of cruelty on behalf of their gang—were just lost little boys. He was surrounded by faces that may have been prematurely aged and hardened by their lifestyle but still belonged to children who had known nothing but abuse from the moment they were born. Ethan couldn't bring himself to hate them in spite of the way they were treating him. They were the real lost boys, brutalized right from birth, made this way by their own people, like the babies carried by the girls they took as their partners, whose faces were tattooed with the same symbols. These girls all knew what it was like to be raped by a relative; they all trusted their future to a life as slaves of the

Mara. Their babies would be condemned to the same fate they'd suffered because when you'd only ever lived in hell, that was all you knew.

Adrian Calvo leaned back in his chair and looked out at the city through the window. He'd seen the violence increase over the past few decades, but he'd always managed to stay above it. From where he was, the figures moving around below looked like toys. He couldn't help thinking that they were all at his beck and call. Deep down he hated arrogance and delusions of superiority, but he felt that this thought was justified. He'd known generals, landowners, and dictators who boasted about how they terrorized their citizens, and now there were criminal gangs who wanted to act like oligarchs. The violence and cruelty were always the same. He'd learned that the look of power never changed, only how you got hold of it. That was his greatest skill, the one that had kept him alive and allowed him to prosper. It was why he had a driver but was still able to walk to his old block to see Doña Amelia, the old woman who'd been making tortillas in the street for the last thirty years. He made sure to have lunch there regularly so he'd never forget who he was or where he'd come from. Every time he went through a difficult experience, every time the Mara threatened him and he was able to deal with it, he allowed himself the luxury of looking down at the rest of the city from on high, telling himself that he was above it all. Not in a snobbish or elitist way. It was about survival. There was no doubt about that.

The Doce gangsters had captured their gringo, and he was back on good terms with them. Did he feel bad about that? Certainly. In spite of everything he'd been through, Calvo still maintained a clear sense of right and wrong, and although it never interfered with pragmatic concerns, it hurt every time he violated it. The gringo was a good person, without a trace of malice. He'd warned the man and explained the consequences of his actions. Once again, Calvo had survived when others hadn't. He went to his minifridge, which was nestled in a cherrywood cupboard, and covered the base of a tumbler with ice to enjoy a glass of Johnnie Walker Blue Label. This was his reward for successful business deals, be they palatable or otherwise.

Then he heard the commotion. It sounded as though it was coming from right outside. But it couldn't be. He felt his adrenaline begin to flow. He heard someone run across the carpet, and then it was over as soon as it had begun. He went to the intercom and buzzed his secretary, but she didn't answer. Then he opened the drawer in his desk and took out his gun, although he knew that if they really had come for him, it wouldn't do him any good. He tucked it into his belt behind his back and went to the door, wondering what could possibly have gone wrong and whether he should call his wife to say goodbye before he opened the door. Then he banished morbid thoughts. He'd survived prison during the dictatorship, avoided the death squads, and sat down with the heads of the worst Mara factions. If he couldn't get through whatever awaited him out there, he didn't deserve to.

Before he exposed himself, he reflected that he hadn't heard any gunshots, which was a hopeful sign. Maybe it was a kidnapping. Maybe they were coming only to take him away. If that was the case, it might be worth barricading himself in and calling the police. Then he remembered his assistants and what would happen to them if he didn't come out. He couldn't hide himself away; his life wasn't worth all of theirs. He worked up his courage and stepped out into the open only to be greeted with one of the most welcome surprises of his life. A couple of his employees' desks were smashed to pieces while they themselves lay in the rubble. Two of them were trying to get back up while the other two were knocked out cold. At the reception desk, his secretary was kneeling down like a turtle with her hands over her head. Presiding over the chaos, in the process of kicking over another desk, was a young woman armed with a baseball bat. She glared at him, speaking near-perfect Spanish in a terrible accent.

"The things you can do with a bat," she said, nodding to her weapon. Then she threw it toward him, not trying to hurt him but to distract him while she went for a gun she'd seen on the ground. Calvo stepped back a little as he watched the bat put a dent in his door. Then he found that the girl was pointing the gun at him. She didn't look to be in the mood for jokes. But he was.

"Hello. Hmmm . . . you must be Ari."

Ari walked toward him decisively, keeping the gun trained on him.

He smiled. "How much is Ethan paying you? I don't know why he didn't just send you first."

She kept walking toward him without saying a word and pointed the gun in his face at point-blank range.

He pushed it away with a finger. "Don't bother. It's not loaded. We don't keep loaded weapons in the office."

Ari looked annoyed and dropped the gun. Before he could react, she grabbed his right thumb, and he suddenly found himself with his arm twisted behind his back, his elbow bent almost to the breaking point, and his face against the doorframe.

"My, you're good. Do you do outside work?"

Ari searched him, took out his Glock, and pressed it against his cheek. "This one's loaded."

"Yes, it is. Be careful—it's sensitive."

"Where's Ethan? Who has him?"

"I don't know."

"Pick up your phone, and call whoever you have to. Right now. Then you're coming with me to get him."

"Don't take this the wrong way, but if the Mara have him, he'll be dead by now. And we'll be next."

"You're next, whatever happens."

"Wow, what a girl. I just set that up for you, didn't I? Well, Ethan certainly has good taste in women."

Ari didn't understand much of what the man was saying or his jolly attitude, but she could tell that she wouldn't be able to force him to do anything. She let him go and stood back.

Rubbing his arm, he spoke to his secretary. "Ángeles. Would you be good enough to bring a couple of coffees?" Then he turned back to Ari. "Black, I imagine? We're in the land of coffee. Sugar or sweetener?" He nodded to his secretary, who stood up, her hair a mess, and went to the kitchen with as much dignity as she could muster. "Send the guys to the doctor to see if they've hurt themselves. Except for Wilmer; I think I'll be needing him. And would you mind calling the super to see if there's any way we can salvage this mess? Please? Thank you so much. Doña Ari, please come into my office. Ah! Before I forget . . ."

Ari waited warily as he went through his pockets.

"Here's my card. Adrian Calvo, at your service."

All Ethan knew was that he'd been dragged into a cellar. He'd lost consciousness along the way, but that hadn't mollified his captors. They'd just rolled him along in a barrel to make things easier. Every time something touched his skin, he felt a sharp pain, while his broken ribs meant that he was uncomfortable both sitting up and lying down. In his confused state, he found it hard to take in the gravity of the situation. Although he knew what was going to happen, it didn't seem as though it was going to happen to him. The situation was completely unreal, a series of random, unconnected events. Suddenly he found himself presented with the three leading members of the gang. The chorus must have disappeared at some point. So what they were planning to do to him was either too horrible or too exclusive for the others. In a sudden moment of clarity, he realized that they were more nervous than he was.

Finally, an echoing sound announced the *pozolero*'s arrival. He was a beast even these savages feared. That was all Ethan needed to know. After the overture, he emerged from the shadows like a dark colossus, gleaming in the weak light. The three gangsters, trembling like scared little kids, knelt down before him. Ethan, resigned to his fate, had no qualms about looking straight at him. His eyes met those of a living sculpture, the jet-black embodiment of cold, stony, demonic indifference set off by albino irises that bored straight into his soul. Ethan had seen them before. For a second, their eyes made a ghostly connection, and Ethan realized why the executioner had insisted on dealing with him himself. The *pozolero* saw that he'd been recognized, and his gaze was snuffed out like a candle. He walked toward Ethan, kicking his fawning admirers out of the way. They obediently scurried to the side. Then he gently took hold of Ethan and tried to stand him up, but the beaten man could only moan and mumble.

"No . . . I can't . . ."

The Mara observed warily, unsure what was going on. The *pozolero* lifted Ethan and carried him to the only chair in the basement, where he was a little more comfortable. Eventually, the three gang leaders lifted their heads, unnerved by this gentle treatment. Ethan, aware of an irony that was beyond them, tried to laugh, but the snort he produced sounded more like a cough. The *pozolero* was Martín, Rosita's Caribbean right-hand man, the one who had escorted him back to her hut. Ever since their experience at the beach, Ethan had been under his protection. He knew that he'd never get to the bottom of the complex web of relationships that governed this strange universe, nor the bizarre ethics of its inhabitants. All he knew right now was that that web had saved his life. Martín, the *pozolero*, stood between him and his executioners. They had no idea how to react.

The talkative one stood up hesitantly. "So . . . what's going on?"

Martín bared his teeth and answered in a growl that sounded as though it came from hell itself. "This foreigner has been blessed by Rosita the witch. He can't be harmed. I told you. You've sinned by hurting him! He mustn't be profaned. Under no circumstances can he die. Now your job will be to save him. I'll talk to whoever I need to. You just do what I say!"

The three Mara couldn't believe their ears. They just stared at him open mouthed before looking to each other for answers.

The second-in-command shrugged. "Is this . . . fuck me, is this a joke?"

After her little display, Calvo quickly came to an understanding with Ari.

"So let's see if I've got it right. Your plan is to storm Mara territory, guns blazing, shooting everything in sight until you find Ethan? Is that right?"

Ari nodded slowly to indicate that that was indeed what she had in mind.

Calvo poured himself another drink. "I'm getting a better idea of how you work as a team. He does the planning, doesn't he?"

Ari knew he was making fun of her, and she wasn't in the mood for it. "What's wrong? Are you afraid?"

"Oh, I'm always afraid, my dear. Don't underestimate fear; it's a useful emotion. We evolved from the monkeys that managed to escape. The brave ones were eaten by tigers. By the way, Ángeles tells me that Doña Michelle is still waiting down in the lobby. Why don't we invite her up?"

"She can go fuck herself."

"I see you've picked up the local lingo too."

This warrior possessed a quality that Calvo knew was as rare as it was valuable: a determination that wasn't going to let moral qualms, or anything else, get in the way. He was surprised by how different she was from Ethan. Where he was noble to a fault, she had a wild resolve to achieve her goal, and she wasn't about to waste time on strategy or planning. Such an attitude could get her in serious trouble if she didn't have anyone to guide her, but at the end of the day, he'd much rather have her on his side than as an enemy.

"Let me tell you what I can do for you. One of my boys is going to find out where they're holding Ethan. It won't be easy, and it's very dangerous, especially for me. Your partner has got me into some tricky situations. Let's just say that I won't be thanked for bringing him up again, but at least I'll be able to say that I did everything I could. My opinion is that he's already dead, but it can't hurt to try. My fee will be two thousand dollars, in cash, right now."

"You're going to charge two thousand dollars for picking up the phone?"

"It doesn't seem fair, does it? Listen, I've spent the past forty years working for justice, and it scares me a little more every day. It's a creature with nothing but a mouth and an ass, and when you're standing in front of it, you have no idea whether it's going to swallow you whole or shit all over you. It is very much against my better judgment that I try to achieve justice for you, but you must at least give me my due. I'm putting my neck on the line. Two thousand dollars is a bargain. Also, when you go off to get yourself killed, you'll think of that money and say to yourself, 'At least Calvo has it instead of these bastards.'" He pressed down on the intercom. "Doña Ángeles, would you be so kind as to show Wilmer into my office, please?"

Ari left the office, and before she could sit down, she heard Michelle's hysterical voice in the corridor. Her surprise at seeing her was tempered by the resentful expression of Ángeles, who, hair now back in place, offered her a coffee. Before Michelle could answer, Calvo's office door opened again to reveal Calvo looking confused and thoughtful. They rushed toward him, fearing the worst.

"What's wrong? Where is he?"

He raised his eyebrows as though he hadn't been expecting them. Apparently his brief meeting had made him forget about everything else. Behind him, Wilmer, his assistant, mimed an apology. Calvo pulled himself together and addressed them.

"They say that he's alive and relatively unharmed. They're willing to set him free, today. They wanted five thousand dollars, but we negotiated it down to three."

They couldn't understand why he seemed so upset. "But that's good, isn't it?"

His face was grave and worry stricken. "The condition is that I have to pick him up myself. Alone. Wilmer is the contact. He deals with them, but they won't accept him this time. I have to go right now; they're waiting for me."

The women went silent. Behind him, Wilmer seemed just as upset. The Mara didn't play games like this. This wasn't their kind of deal. There might well turn out to be no one to pick up, but if Calvo didn't go, they'd come looking for him.

"But it might be true," Michelle said. "What if it's true?"

"Even if he were alive, even if they did let him go, the Mara don't let someone live without claiming another in exchange. Let's hope that he is alive. At least then you'll get him back. There's your justice for you. It's eaten me alive."

Calvo left without saying goodbye. He was stunned, distraught, a dead man walking.

Michelle and Ari had been waiting for an hour. They were together but very much alone. They didn't say a word: each was lost in her own world. Ari was inscrutable, like a sphinx. Michelle glanced at her surreptitiously but couldn't guess at what she was thinking. For her part she was trying to find a way to escape her despair, to avoid the darkness that was eating her up inside. She'd lost everything, and she was the only one to blame. Her decisions had ruined her life and those of the people around her, just like her mother had always warned her. She had always known that she was selfish and reckless. The only explanation for all this was that she was being punished for her evil ways. But she couldn't understand why other innocent people had to pay for her sins, why her affronts to the Lord led to the suffering of others. She wanted to pray to God to put her in their place, as she had several times before, but her prayers had never been answered: she wasn't a good Christian. She didn't deserve it. She knew why God was hurting others instead of her: to show her what a cowardly, despicable person she was. It had always been that way. What would happen when they left the building with just another failure under their belt? Ari already hated her. She'd go back home to grieve. What about her? What should her punishment be? One path, from which there was no return, became apparent to her. She was already lost, the consequences . . .

She was jolted out of these dark thoughts by the sound of her phone. She felt ashamed, as though someone could read her innermost thoughts. It was Andrés.

"Michelle! Michelle, get over here." He was jubilant. "Ethan is in the hospital. He's fine—he's been sedated, but he's fine!"

Upon hearing this unexpected news, hope suddenly flooded back into her. She was surprised by her next question. "What about the detective? Do you know where Adrian Calvo is?"

"Here, celebrating. He's brought a bottle of champagne."

Calvo had bought lottery tickets and was rubbing them on Ethan's back. Ethan himself was still feeling dopey. Calvo brandished them in his sleepy face.

"They're tickets for tomorrow's draw. Don't be stingy; share a little. I've never met anyone like you, and you can't let opportunities like these go to waste."

In Ethan's blurred vision, he saw the shapes of two women coming toward him. If his eyes weren't deceiving him, Michelle and Ari were standing there, together. He blinked and rubbed his eyes, trying to work out what was real and what was a drug-induced hallucination. But nothing changed. Michelle and Ari were looking down at him bashfully, afraid to disturb him. They were right there, next to the bed.

"Oh . . . then I must be dead . . ."

Ari hugged him, and he felt something sink into his soul. She touched his scars in concern, as though she were worried that they'd open again. Michelle stood aside to give them some space while Calvo had characteristically appeared out of nowhere with several bottles of wine and was giving out glasses.

"You only have a few cracked ribs. You're tough, my friend. I've spoken to your travel insurers. Things were getting ugly. But with my office's statement and the accounts of a couple of police officers who specialize in tourists, we worked out our differences. The witness described an assault, a carjacking, and a brutal beating. They rescued you in partnership with my team. The case file has been issued. But there was one condition: you have to go home tomorrow so they can keep you under observation. They don't want any more mishaps."

Ethan sat up in alarm, disoriented. "I can't go home! They can't—I can't stop now."

Ari reacted indignantly. He had nearly been killed, and now he was talking about going on as though it were all a big adventure. They got into a heated argument in English. Calvo tried to calm the girl before they came to blows. A nurse asked visitors to leave the room, and Michelle left without even having been able to say hello. It was an hour before anyone was allowed back in. This time, Ari went alone. She stood there with her arms crossed while Ethan, struggling to come to terms with the situation, apologized.

"Ari, I'm sorry. This is all a lot to take in. I . . . I can't . . . I can't stop now. I . . . why? Why . . . I've just realized how strange it is that you're here. I'm so happy to see you, but I don't understand. How . . . why are you here?"

Ari tried to compose herself before answering. "Because you were going to get yourself killed, you idiot. Because Michelle called me. Because Suarez was worried." She started to stammer. "Because I had to. I . . ." She sighed and gulped, and her voice started to break. She decided to change the subject, telling him what Suarez had relayed to her. She told him about the Beast, his employers, and where he was headed in Brazil. The news renewed Ethan's hope. "Suarez has made progress. He's found a place called Liberdade—he thinks it might be where they orchestrated everything from. He's on his own. I need to meet him there. There's no time to waste, and you have several weeks of recovery time ahead of you. Months maybe. I can't wait. This is a case, Ethan. It's not about your ego. It's bigger than you."

Ethan felt his throat constricting and couldn't get his thoughts straight. He put his face in his hands and asked Ari to forgive him for everything. He kept apologizing. Under the effects of the tranquilizers, he started to repeat himself, again and again, as though it were a mantra.

When she saw him looking so vulnerable, Ari was moved to hug him. But it didn't come easily. She bent down and pulled his hands away. "Hey!"

Ethan blinked and sighed, as though he'd just woken up. He pulled himself together. "No . . . I'm not in any condition to help."

Ari coughed. "There's something else. I saw something in the information that Suarez gave me that affects both Michelle and Michi. Something very important. I don't know what to do about it."

They spoke for hours, and although there was no physical contact, they reconnected, rediscovering an intimacy that they hadn't shared in months. Neither of them mentioned it for fear of ruining the magic. Ari left at the end of visiting hours. Michelle had been waiting outside all that time with stoical patience. Again, she left without seeing Ethan.

The next morning Michelle came back, left her name, and waited, but the nurses never delivered an invitation from him to come in. She was left waiting, stuck in the hallway. She spent several hours in a plastic chair until Ethan was put onto a gurney and wheeled into an ambulance. She saw him pass by, flanked by the paramedics, but he never looked at her. Then she got up and walked outside to follow him to the airport along with Andrés and Ari. She never got close enough to say a word.

Yarlín tried to stay awake, but she knew she wouldn't be able to. The drugs were always too strong. She wanted to scream and cry: she missed her mother, but she contained herself. The darkness sucked her into nowhere. Or always to the same place. She was moving again, this time down a long corridor. It looked strange, like on a spaceship. *A hospital,* she thought, trying to remember every detail so she could tell her parents about it later when she was allowed to go home. In front of her was a wall with posters of Disney princesses. She liked them. She was in a large room decorated in pinks and purples with a row of shiny beds on each side and a play area with a cushioned floor that had every toy she ever could have dreamed of, including a Cinderella's castle big enough for her to fit into. It even had a little table and two chairs inside. She'd been here before, but she couldn't remember if it had been real or in a dream. All this distracted her from her sadness until the voice of another little girl made her jump.

"Hi, Yarlín."

She scurried for cover in the castle, hiding behind the table.

"Don't be afraid. You were in my dreams too; that's how I know you."

Somehow, Yarlín felt as though she wasn't alone anymore. Someone was there who understood her. It was the first time she'd felt that way since they'd locked her up. "Are you sick too?"

"We're not sick. Don't believe them. They're keeping us for some reason. They say they're good, but their boss is bad. Do you know the Grandfather? He's bad. He's not here, but I've seen him. He's very old, older than anyone else in the world, but I don't think he knows that."

Yarlín didn't understand what the other girl was saying, but she didn't care very much. She was much more curious about her new companion and poked her head up above the plastic battlements. The girl was older than she was.

"When I dream of him, it's like he has one eye, but I know he doesn't. Have you dreamed of an old man with one eye?"

Yarlín, deeply intrigued, shook her head. "I'm very happy to see you. I hated being alone."

The image grew blurry.

Outside, a maid as chubby and rosy as a Rubens model was doing her daily round, wobbling along the corridor. Looking through the window, she was shocked to see the little girl lying awake in the storybook bed. She came back along the corridor and went inside, speaking in a bright, friendly voice. "Good evening, my darling. What are you doing up so late? Didn't they give you your medicine? Did you have a nightmare?"

The girl, who was older than Yarlín, turned to her with disconcerting confidence.

"No, it wasn't a nightmare. There's another girl. There's definitely another girl. I've seen her."

Her caretaker gulped. "How can there be another girl? You're alone—you know that you can't see anyone. You have a contagious disease."

The girl gave a firm, aggressive response. "There's another girl. Her name is Yarlín, and she was stolen from her parents in a country called Colombia. Just like I was stolen from my mommy. She's been brought here. I saw her in the game room."

"H-how can you have seen her? You never left the room. You must be confused—"

"We spoke in her dream. Her name is Yarlín, and she was stolen."

Her expression took on an almost adult air. The nanny went pale and took a step backward. "D-don't worry, Michi—it was just a nightmare, honey. I'm going to get some help, and we'll see what we can do to fix this. I'm going right now, Michi. You just wait here."

10

Ratlines

The Vatican is of course the largest organization involved in the illegal movement of emigrants . . . The justification for its participation includes a desire to ensure the spread across Europe and Latin America of people who, regardless of their other political beliefs, are anti-Communist and pro-Catholic . . . Large groups of German Nazis still come to Italy to obtain false documents and visas and then leave immediately from Genoa or Barcelona, heading for Latin America.

Memorandum by Vincent La Vista, the US military attaché in Rome, sent to Herbert J. Cummings, dated May 15, 1947. The document was sealed as top secret but was declassified in 1984.

Genoa, 1947

The war had finished two years earlier, but many party leaders were still on the run. For Walter Stobert, however, the flight had begun twelve years before in a city to which he'd never returned: Vienna. After the fall of Berlin, he'd gotten lucky. When he'd been captured by American soldiers together with members of the *Volkssturm*, the initial chaos and his fortuitous lack of a tattoo had seen him taken for an ordinary militiaman and freed before winter. The Allies barely documented their investigations, and the lack of food at the teeming detention camps made them more generous and permissive than they would have liked.

Once he was free, he'd wanted to return to Austria but believed that the risk of living under the Soviet occupation was too great. He'd tried his luck in a village south of Munich, where he'd spent some time working as a baker. Although there had been bombing, the battle lines had never pushed this far south, and the communities of those who remained faithful to the fallen regime were much stronger, better organized, and harder to detect than elsewhere. Throughout 1946, he'd heard rumors about *Die Spinne*, a local network helping former Nazis to flee, and the Nuremberg Trials had convinced him, like many others, that leaving Europe altogether was the only way he could be safe.

Tormented by nightmares, he was always grateful to see the dawn so he could work next to the oven and warm a body that only seemed to be getting colder and colder. Eventually, in early 1947, a successful call had been made, and he'd been visited by a customer he'd never seen before.

Dressed in an olive-green fedora and a trench coat with an empty sleeve sewed to one side, the man had stretched out his good arm and said just one word. "Odessa."

After Ethan passed through security, Andrés, Michelle, and Ari sat in the airport cafeteria for a while as though the delay would ease the pain of separation. They watched the planes taking off and landing and wondered which was his. Andrés asked Ari, very respectfully, whether her place shouldn't be with her boyfriend so she could take care of him at such a difficult time. Ari took a deep breath and counted to ten before answering that they'd both decided that she would be more useful looking for Michi. She didn't bother to mention that they weren't a couple anymore, thanks to Andrés's lovely sister. Instead, she abruptly said goodbye and walked off with Michelle. Andrés knew nothing of her contact with Suarez, and she preferred to keep it that way. The poor evangelist begged them to keep him informed.

On their way back, Ari didn't say a word, and Michelle didn't need to ask to know that something was worrying her. Finally, she asked if they could go to a Denny's along the way. After ordering, they were swallowed by a silent, expectant bubble.

"What's next? What do we do now?" Michelle finally asked. "Tell me what I can do."

Ari drank some water and spoke in English, worried that her Spanish wasn't up to it. "I spoke to Ethan. He wanted to talk to you himself, but that was stupid: he was leaving. I don't know where to begin . . . have you heard from Michi's father? I mean, are you still in touch?"

Michelle hesitated for several long seconds before answering. "Yes, a little. What's wrong?"

Ari uncertainly scratched her chin. "I suppose you know something about the other detective helping you. Not Calvo."

Michelle nodded anxiously.

"He's now in Brazil. Michi's father is Brazilian, isn't he?"

Michelle reared up like a frightened cat. "What are you getting at? That it was him?" She smiled bitterly. "That's impossible. You don't know—"

"Listen to me. Michi isn't the only girl to have disappeared. This was the work of a network. We have records of other kidnappings, and the victims are always girls. I knew Michi's father's name through Ethan. Suarez didn't, so he couldn't tie the two together." She handed Michelle some papers. "The files were pretty disorganized; some of them only had a photo of the girl while others had family information. His name is Henrique Teixera, right?"

Michelle nodded quickly.

"He's listed as the father on at least four birth certificates. They're official documents, not private letters or forgeries. He's the father of at least four of these girls in different countries in Latin America."

Michelle's mouth opened wide. She looked around her as though she didn't know where she was and began to hyperventilate.

Walter Stobert's life was austere and methodical. He woke up very early in the morning to work at the oven, and by midmorning, when he'd made his batches, he always joined the team of volunteers clearing rubble from houses and roads. They collected scrap iron and tried to restore a vestige of normality to the area. Silently, he worked side by side with widows, old people, and cripples, exhausted and guilty. They wouldn't allow themselves to cry or show any sign of weakness, just as they'd been taught. They were trying to dispel the harrowing memories as soon as they could. The locals admired his strength and the tireless energy that appeared to course through him, and nobody asked any questions. Nobody ever asked any questions.

A large, matronly woman from Berlin with a determined mien and a limp appreciated the way he gave his all and served him generous portions of broth during their brief moments of respite. She sat next to him, and they both wolfed down the soup and stale bread he brought with him without saying a word. When she gave him his bowl and came back to collect it, their only moment of physical contact, she shivered at the cold touch of a stranger who never seemed to get warm, not even when he was dripping with sweat.

Walter had forgotten what heat was. Hard as he tried, he was unable to imagine it, like a blind man trying to conceive of color. He could put his hand in the fire in the oven, and only when the skin had started to crisp did he feel a slight tingling. He had acquired several serious burns on his forearm that way. Since that night in Vienna, twelve years ago, he'd lost all sense of his own temperature. The gradual change had been imperceptible when he'd been in the East, but by the time he'd gotten back, it was stark. It was a strange trait for which he had become renowned, one that haunted his brain like an obsession. His life had become a struggle against the cold and fear that had settled inside of him. He was afraid of the cold; he thought it would be the end of him. He was afraid of going to sleep, of dreaming. Dreaming most of all, because he didn't want to become trapped in the strange dream in which he lived. He slept only four hours each night; he didn't need any more. He took refuge in his routine, hiding from the occupying armies, the situation in Europe, and himself.

One spring morning in 1947, employing the same distant but effective practicality that had defined his anonymous existence there, he gathered the few things he wanted to keep and, not bothering saying goodbye to anyone, set out for the south. The first leg was an eighteen-mile trek by foot to meet his first contact. He had been taken in by the clandestine Odessa network.

Michelle was wandering around the parking lot in a daze. After paying the bill, Ari ran after her worriedly. Michelle had almost stumbled into a crosswalk, and a car braked, honking angrily. She stood staring blankly at it while the driver shouted misogynist insults. Ari caught up with her and pulled her back.

"Michelle! Michelle, I know that this is a shock, but you have to tell me how to find him. We need to talk to Henrique. He's the only one who'll know."

Michelle gave her a confused look and walked to her car. She leaned on the hood and seemed to come to. Then she answered in Spanish. "He was . . . Beto loved it . . . his car was his favorite thing in the world." Michelle smiled to herself. "Beto and Henrique. That's ironic. I'd never have suspected. They never met. Henrique never took the trouble to meet him. He said . . . he said that he was going to take us away with him . . ." Her voice broke, and a new sense of resolve hardened in her eyes. She turned to Ari with dry lips and spoke in English. "What about Ethan? Did he know?"

"I told him."

"And he let you tell me?"

"Ethan could barely speak."

"He let you tell me? Ethan knew, but he left."

"Michelle, I know how you feel, but—"

Michelle broke down. "You have no idea how I feel! No idea!"

Passersby slowed down to watch.

"You're telling me that my daughter, my little daughter, is part of a production line? That Henrique was making them all over the continent? That she's just one of many? And Ethan wasn't man enough to tell me himself? I waited for him for hours! I thought he loved her!"

Ari didn't know how to calm Michelle, whether it was best to get her moving or to keep talking. She wasn't good in situations like this, and deep down she hated Ethan for not being there, even though she'd insisted that he go.

Michelle walked around in a circle, then again, saying something to herself. She glared at Ari. "She isn't a product; she has a light. She has a light!" She got into the car, and her face grew redder and redder. "She's special, you understand? She's special!"

Now several of the customers and waiters from the restaurant had come out to the parking lot, eagerly observing the women. It was like a private soap opera, although they couldn't understand what they were saying. Ari, who treasured her privacy, was made more uncomfortable by the onlookers than Michelle's reaction. Michelle just ignored them all and drove off. Ari, stunned, watched her drive onto the freeway. She waited until the crowd dispersed and, summoning all the dignity she had left, went back inside to shelter from the sun.

The journey was hard and fraught with danger. On the first night, Stobert slept in a barn. The second was spent in the open air, but things got better when he crossed the border into Austria, where he was taken in by a Franciscan monastery whose residents helped him get to Italy. They crossed the Brenner Pass and finally left the Alps behind with Stobert naively anticipating Mediterranean warmth. No one asked any questions on the journey. No one asked anything in postwar Europe. There weren't any answers.

A few miles from the coast he met with a contact in a room at a rural inn and learned how he would make the last leg of his journey. He'd wait north of Genoa for a few days in a transition camp set up by W. Rauff until his documentation came through. After considering several different destinations used by former soldiers, including Egypt, Lebanon, and Syria, he opted for the South Atlantic: Argentina. There was a large German community in the country, and capital had flowed there since the surrender. This, in addition to Eva Perón's tour through Europe, where she'd met the pope, seemed to create a very favorable environment for emigration.

Four days later, he received a white passport bearing the International Red Cross stamp. He examined it thoroughly: it was genuine. The Catholic Church had started to wield its influence in decisions related to the status of political refugees, and the Red Cross was issuing hundreds of letters of transit without checking backgrounds, simply trusting the Vatican's word. His last step was to visit the Argentine consulate, where he immediately received a visa and ID card. From then on he'd be known as Fausto Aspiazi.

Finally, on October 3, he set out for Buenos Aires as a second-class passenger on the steamer *Veneto*. He wouldn't return to Europe for thirty years.

Armando, the head of security at Colônia Liberdade, got out of the Mercedes along with Lucas N., the head of administration, and his bodyguards. In front of them was the imposing skyscraper that housed the headquarters of Schwindt Worldwide in Geneva. Schwindt was one of the largest private security companies in the world, but it had also branched out into legal services of every kind. The intimidating architecture had the intended effect: they went to their meeting cowed and subservient. They were politely led to the twenty-second floor and placed in a thirty-by-ten-foot room with a one-piece glass-and-cast-iron table that seated twenty people. A friendly secretary offered them drinks and left them alone for a quarter of an hour. Lucas and Armando were a bundle of nerves but didn't dare say a word in case they were being recorded. They hadn't been informed of the purpose for the meeting, but there was no way they could have refused. Ever since the Bloodhound's death, they'd been expecting some form of retribution, and they were the highest-ranking members of the organization after the Grandfather, who was untouchable. They didn't know what to expect. Armando just prayed that the infamous Schwindt brothers wouldn't be there in person. Eventually, a series of executives came in and occupied some of the empty seats. Finally, a woman about forty years of age in a smart Armani suit with a blonde ponytail came in, and those already in the room stood up. She took a prominent position and started the introductions in clear-spoken, diplomatic French. They would continue to speak in the same language for the rest of the conversation, which required a considerable effort on the part of their two guests.

"Allow me to welcome you on behalf of Schwindt Security, a subsidiary of Schwindt Worldwide. Let me introduce you to our representatives: the distinguished lawyer Barnes, from the firm Barnes and Barnes, and the distinguished Mister Trujillo, the Geneva representative of Smit and Betancourt, a firm that has provided legal services for us over the past few years."

The guests nodded nervously.

"On the other side we have representatives from our Department of International Relations and my personal assistant, Miss Barraud. I am Monique Lombard, director of Schwindt Security."

Armando started to stammer an introduction of his own, but the woman cut him off abruptly.

"We will shortly be joined by the owners of our company, the Schwindt brothers. We'll wait for them."

A heavy silence fell over those present. It lasted for another ten minutes of pure torment for the foreigners, who were still afraid to say anything, even to each other. But their discomfort was dispelled when a hand-crafted mahogany door opened at the other end of the room, and each of the Schwindt brothers came in, escorted by an assistant to the end of the table. The eldest, in dark glasses with gray hair, presided over the meeting; the two next in line wore tailored suits just like their employees; and the fourth, who looked to be in his thirties, was dressed informally in a leather jacket that must have been worth thousands of euros. He took the last free seat. Between them and the others was a gap that made the atmosphere even more ominous. None of them said a word. At some imperceptible signal, Monique Lombard got up and walked over to the president, her steps ringing out in the oppressive silence. The president whispered something in her ear. She nodded and spoke.

"The owner reminds you that you have been invited to a meeting of the highest level, attended by the leaders of the business group, when ordinarily your community wouldn't deserve the attention of a regional director. This is in deference to our longstanding relations with your leader, Fausto Aspiazi, and so we must ask why he has not attended in person."

"As, uh . . . we said in our messages, we are grateful for the opportunity to explain what happened in person," Lucas said, his words echoing around the pristine walls as though he was talking on a mountainside. "We are determined to cooperate fully, but our mentor's advanced age and frailty—"

Monique went back to her seat before he'd finished, stomping her high heels on the floor to drown him out.

The uncomfortable silence fell back over the room until the three eldest brothers stood up and left through the same door they'd come in by. The fourth stayed in his seat. The snub undermined the morale of Armando and Lucas, who shrank back into themselves.

Finally, the brother who was left, whom they'd heard described as the Jackal, spoke. "Now we're on equal terms."

Misiones, 1951

Since the beginning of the war, Buenos Aires had been swarming with spies, and although life was much easier for the fugitives who had flooded in, they weren't entirely home free. Anxiety was a constant. Stobert, now known as Fausto Aspiazi, tried to use his educational credentials to find work at a German school but was unsuccessful. Life in the city shredded his nerves, and he decided to leave. A large number of families were moving south, to Bariloche, while others headed for the Sierras of Córdoba, where the landscape was reminiscent of the Alps. But he decided to go to the jungle, near the border with Paraguay and

Brazil, which had several small German communities. He wouldn't be missed. He'd never fully integrated, and although he was welcome at meetings, he had always been withdrawn and distant. However, he was also possessed of a strange magnetism; it had had an effect on several women, and he seemed to find it easy to get under people's skin, and this aroused suspicion. Well aware of this, he decided that it was best to isolate himself and avoid social interaction as much as possible. He yearned for solitude and warmth and continued to suffer from his inexplicable affliction. He was caught on an obsessive treadmill from which he couldn't get off, as though only movement could keep his fears at bay.

When he got off the bus in Misiones, the temperature was sweltering, and the air was humid. The man who met him was amused by his attire: "You're wearing a coat in the jungle?"

After allowing the contempt of the three absent Schwindts to sink in, the director, Monique Lombard, addressed the foreigners.

"We have discovered serious irregularities in the agreed-upon service contract with your institution in Brazil. These were the direct cause for the death of Stefan Schwindt, the director of operations at said location." She picked up an iPad and started to read from it. "Stefan was apparently asked to undertake a tracking job without the knowledge of the firm, which has specialists who could well have done the job in his stead. This job then took him back to Brazil with the aforementioned consequences and, given the nature of the information gathered, on absolutely illegal terms."

Armando leaned forward, visibly furious to discover that they'd been led into an ambush. "These were contract extensions anticipated, agreed to, and charged for by Mr. Stefan Schwindt, who was acting in the name of the company," Lucas said, trying to achieve mutual understanding. "We don't know how he communicated with the company internally, but as was explained in the memorandum—"

"Which was wholly inadequate," Monique interrupted.

Her lawyers backed her up.

"We may take legal measures to close down your facilities."

"And cease all commercial activity."

"We don't understand," Lucas said. "We offered our apologies and expressed our willingness to negotiate the necessary compensation on your terms. We are the first to lament the loss of such a close collaborator, but it was an obvious risk that he fully accepted of his own free will. Your firm has supported our colony for decades; you can't—"

"That was a significant time ago. This tragic incident is just the last straw of a situation that has long been in decline. Right now, we can see only one acceptable way out."

The Jackal, who hadn't been listening to a word, now chipped in. "We want the old man."

The two foreigners stared at each other in disbelief.

Monique went on. "It's the only viable solution. This event has just accelerated matters. The . . . shall we call them *eccentricities* of your leader could be overlooked when he had ties to dictatorships during the Cold War and might even be of interest to one or two New Age hippies, but such people disappeared twenty years ago. For some time, large companies in the network have expressed their discomfort with characters like him, and the fear that a scandal might come to light and damage the reputation of large commercial brands far outweighs the value of the services he purports to offer, which are, of course, deeply out of date. Now is the time to turn the page and choose someone more suitable. Someone more in tune with the times, not a remnant of ideologies from the past century. That person may well be sitting in this room with us right now."

"He's very old, isn't he?" said one of the lawyers. "They say that he's over ninety—he can't have long left. We just want to see him while he's still alive. We're only anticipating the inevitable."

"This is a sham! That's why you wanted him to come here! But he's smarter than you. You want to buy us off with his job? You simply don't understand. You can't do that; you don't understand his power. He can do terrifying things. He . . . has access to worlds you can't imagine. You've never seen . . . I've seen what he can do."

"We're not interested in your superstitions. For some time several of our clients have been interested in his more . . . esoteric activities. One or two internationally renowned families are willing to pay unseemly sums to have him. That's how it is: the network doesn't want him anymore, but there are others that do."

"He has faithful followers willing to die for him. You don't know how far they're willing to go."

"It's the same in every cult. We know how to handle them."

"What if we reject your offer?" Lucas asked.

The Jackal ran his tongue over his teeth and spoke for the third and last time. "It wasn't an offer."

The four-year experience in Misiones resulted in an epiphany that would change his life. He alternated manual labor with the occasional German class for the children of immigrants, and although the nightmares remained the same, he found some relief in the area where he was living. The jungle temperature appeared if not to reduce the cold in his body to at least slow down its progress, giving him temporary respite. The changes this brought with it—his beard grew longer, and his features matured—allowed him to devote more time to studying himself, a pastime facilitated by the long hours he spent awake at night in the remote cabin in which he lived. He was the only one to keep his stove on all year round. He came to entertain the notion that perhaps his loss of temperature wasn't a symptom of imminent death, as he'd assumed thus far, but of abnormal longevity.

His teaching revealed skills within him that he'd not been aware of previously. Due to a lack of stimuli, they'd never manifested themselves before. The incredible ease with which his pupils learned German and the passion even the most dull-witted among them displayed during his lessons made him famous. Soon he had more pupils than he could handle. Before the year was out, it was his only occupation, and he dedicated himself to it obsessively. With nothing else in his life, plus his short sleep cycle, he was able to spend ten or twelve hours a day on his work to meet the needs of his clients. It wasn't just German; his miraculous gift applied to every subject. He seemed to cast a spell on his students. Grateful families gave him gifts, and he rejected offers from far-off schools, much to the delight of the local residents, who knew that even for all the hours he worked, his income couldn't compare to what he'd receive at a school in the city. But Stobert didn't care about money or success. Surprised by his genius, he experimented and learned. He found that he didn't need to use a teaching plan; he just had to read a page to fix it into the mind of a pupil, so long as he was looking them in the eye. He came to call the extraordinary process *fixing*.

For two years his sway over his pupils grew to an extent that even he found unsettling. He learned that if he spent enough time and effort, their will could be bent to his whims like soft reeds, simply because of the murky charisma that had become apparent in Buenos Aires but that he had never been able to take advantage of before. These remote villages provided the perfect environment in which to exercise it in the form of classes. With each new class he taught, he expanded on the spell of his leadership, eventually taking on a kind of messianic air. But he had yet to learn the consequences of his game. The more he developed, the more powerful his nightmares and sense of imminent horror grew. He woke up in the night vomiting, aware of a tangible presence glaring at him through the void with burning eyes. He knew that he was powerless against it. Meanwhile, some of the parents became wary while others decided to confront him outright: they didn't like the way in which their children blindly accepted his opinions or the way they adored him in spite of the cold touch, "like a dry fish," which had frightened them at first.

During his first argument with a couple of parents, he decided to put himself to the test. He bluntly declared that their children were improved thanks to him and they shouldn't doubt his methods. The husband, a tough former paratrooper, was enraged by his insolence and knocked down Stobert, swearing that his son would never see this fraud again. The wife, however, knelt down to help him. She was gentle and understanding. He speculated that during their brief conversation, he'd had time to bend only her to his will. He savored the sensation of blood flowing through his teeth even though he knew that his credit with these guinea pigs had run out.

His grand opportunity came in 1955, on the eve of the fall of Perón, and he seized it with both hands. Friedrich, now known as Federico, a former aide-de-camp who had become a smuggler in Brazil, told Stobert about a Mennonite colony looking for a teacher of their faith. They'd heard of him. He knew immediately that this was his destiny. Eager to try his luck in an innocent community, he quickly made contact, claiming to be an Anabaptist. As a final exercise before he left, he decided to leave a gift for the father who'd punched him. He took the man's son's best friend aside and, focusing all his will in his gaze, gave him a compass. He told the boy over and over again that he wasn't giving it to him:

the boy was stealing it. When the boy saw his friend, he'd grow extremely angry and plunge it into his eye. He'd never understand why.

The boy's silence told him that the suggestion had been successfully implanted.

Calvo pulled on his jacket as he headed for the lobby. His assistants were sharing a pair of boards placed on top of temporary stands while they waited for the new furniture to arrive.

"Did you hear me, boys? Isn't anyone going to lunch? I'm telling you none of you had better come back late. Come on—let's go; let's go . . ."

Like a mother duck rounding up her chicks, he bustled the four of them, two of whom were still clearly suffering from the effects of Ari's attack, out the door.

"When you're out on assignment, you claim that you don't have time to eat, but now that you do, you're just gossiping away. I'm going home for lunch, but I want you all here when I get back."

Ángeles hung up the intercom and interjected. "Forgive me, Don Adrian. Miss Ari is coming up."

Calvo turned around in annoyance. "That girl never calls ahead. Didn't you tell her that we were going out for lunch?"

Ángeles shrugged.

"Fine, fine. You all go. I'll wait for her here. You wait, too, if you wouldn't mind, Ángeles."

The chrome elevator opened, and Ari got out, walking past Calvo's staff, who kept their eyes down. Distracted by her anger, she ignored them. Calvo awaited her with his best smile.

"What an unexpected surprise . . . how can I help you? I thought we'd wrapped up all our business. You know, we were just going out to lunch. You only just—"

"I'm sorry. Michelle ditched me on the road, and I realized that I didn't have her phone or address, and all my things are there, including my passport. I found a taxi, but this address is the only one I have." She showed him the card he'd given her a couple of days before. "I've come to ask you to help me get back."

Calvo rubbed his forehead.

"Ángeles, could you let my wife know that I won't be coming back for lunch? And please try to track down Doña Michelle. Tell her that we'll wait for her here." He put his hand on Ari's shoulder. "Come into my office. You know the way, of course. It's the one with the broken door."

To Calvo's surprise, once inside Ari succinctly outlined the progress they'd made in the case: the transport network, the Brazilian connection, the colony, and her plan to meet up with her contact. She told him everything, except for Suarez's identity. Calvo noted down every detail admiringly.

"This friend of yours fascinates me. I can't remember ever seeing such good work. But you're not telling me this just to pass the time, are you? What do you need from me, my good Ari?"

"I haven't heard from him for two days. He hasn't answered my emails or logged on to WhatsApp. He's disappeared."

"I see. You're afraid that he might have gone too far on his own."

Ari seemed upset.

"I understand." He started to sing a salsa. "'You baited your hook wrong and caught a shark instead of a sardine . . .' Forget it. So what can I do? I can't see how I can be of any use."

"I'm going to Brazil. And if something has happened to my contact, I'll need more help. Not there but here. Do you have any contacts in Brazil?"

Calvo whistled before saying, "My dear, Brazil isn't like saying . . . Costa Rica. Brazil is a continent. It's as though you were asking about all of Europe. I'm flattered by your trust, but any contact I might be able to offer you in Brazil would be worse than nothing. I'm not that powerful. To begin with, you should be concentrating on Santa Catarina, not all of Brazil. But then there's also the internet—one doesn't have to meet people in person. My boys can try to find out anything you need found out, but I can't promise anything. Would you like me to look for your friend?"

"I want someone to help me find him and the girl. I have to fly there right away."

"A detective?"

"No, the investigation is finished. I know where to find them. I need someone who'll break in with me. Someone with weapons. I need a hit man."

Calvo whistled again. "I'd forgotten that you're never interested in anything trivial. You want a mercenary? I can do that here, but so far away—"

He was interrupted by Ángeles on the intercom. "Don Adrian. Doña Michelle is here."

"How wonderful; the whole family's back together. Would you mind ordering us some sandwiches and one for yourself, Ángeles? I don't know about you, but I'm starving."

Santa Catarina, 1955

The community received Stobert with the curiosity, interest, and wariness of isolated, insecure rural folk who had refused to change their ways, or their clothes, since their arrival eighty years earlier. He decided that they urgently required his leadership. The coldness of his skin was now unpleasant to the touch, but his charisma had only grown more compelling while his confidence in his abilities made him feel invulnerable. In the first week, he found them defensive and mistrustful. However, they would never have dared to expel him so soon, not without justification at least, and that was all the time he needed. It irked him that there was a town so nearby. The smuggler had told him that two former comrades, who'd arrived in '45, lived there. He asked the smuggler to be discreet, worried that if his former affiliations became known, the Mennonites might not like it. They agreed that he'd keep his true identity secret from the Germans. It took him a month to win over the congregation, and he set his sights on an attractive young woman. Initially, she found him repulsive, but she had no idea that she didn't stand a chance. He didn't give her much thought or even desire her—he just saw her as a way into the social life of the community. At first he concentrated on her parents before eventually breaking her will.

And yet his presence didn't go as unnoticed as he'd hoped. One morning, while he was out on a walk through the forest, two men in uniform crossed his path and greeted him in Portuguese. He hadn't come across police or soldiers until then, and their presence upset him. He smiled at them and continued on his way, but one of them asked a question he didn't understand. He tried to gesture that he didn't know Portuguese, but they stayed where they were. The one who had asked the question gave an order to his inferior, who quickly marched off. Once they were alone, Stobert was surprised to hear the man address him in excellent, heavily accented German.

"You may not speak Portuguese, but don't worry. I like your language. I learned it from my grandfather; he was from Bavaria. My father and family honor their history. My name is Marcelo Rocha, and I'm the head of the federal police here. I was informed of your arrival and thought that I'd introduce myself. Not much happens in this province."

"Thank you. It's a pleasure. I'm on my way home, if you'll excuse me."

"Fausto Aspiazi."

"Yes, that's my name."

"A strange name for someone who only speaks German."

"I was nationalized in Argentina. I came before the war."

"Aha . . . well, it's been a pleasure."

Stobert tried to walk away, but the officer stayed where he was.

"And yet you haven't visited our compatriots in the town."

"I . . . don't know them."

"Aha . . . they arrived after the war."

Stobert shrugged, and Marcelo apologized. "Maybe you don't share their opinions."

"I have no way of knowing."

"I, however, think that they have something important to say. There are a lot of black men around here, you know. Also Indians and more and more Jews. Greater Brazil is in danger. Prussian colonists built this area: before, it was just a wasteland. I honor the memory of my grandfather and his people. I admire you."

"I don't know what to tell you; I'm just trying to help some decent Christians."

Marcelo lit a cigar and inhaled deeply before going on. "Difficult times are coming, and when they do, there'll be no second chances. Watch the young people. The Zionists are playing their cards. One day they'll come for you. You and your colleagues. You have the look of a leader; you may well subjugate the dirt eaters, but the moment will come when you'd do well to have a partner. My question is: Can Brazil count on you?"

Stobert was hesitant, disconcerted. Eventually he nodded, and the chief of police tapped out his cigar ash and smiled before walking away. "I'm glad about that, Aspiazi. The day is coming when we'll have to choose sides. If you need me, you know where to find me."

He said goodbye with a raised arm.

This unsettling meeting stayed with Stobert for some time. He began to take notice of how young people had started to behave. Ever since the end of the war, the global balance of power had changed: ideas such as the purity of race were now an anathema, and the ubiquity of the cinema served as a loudspeaker for the new world power, the United States, which was molding the world according to its own mythology. European culture had all but disappeared, and what was left, an erratic intellectual class with disturbing sympathy for left-wing causes, worried him even more. For the moment, this land was still isolated from these trends, but they'd arrive. You could hear it beginning on the radio: they'd started playing the black music they called jazz. Marcelo knew another war was coming.

Half a year later, the wedding was held. It was the last step on Stobert's path to becoming a full member of the congregation. He was now the new German teacher at the Colônia Irmãos Menonitas, but this was only the beginning.

Now that Michelle and Ari were standing in the same room, the atmosphere became electric. To Calvo's surprise, the drama he'd been expecting didn't materialize. Michelle addressed Ari in conciliatory English.

"I went back to find you at Denny's, but you'd gone. I needed time to think."

Ari didn't answer. She didn't know how to deal with situations like this. Calvo only understood the odd word.

Michelle sat down next to Ari and handed over a sheet of paper. "I got two plane tickets, flying in four days. I'll have spoken to Henrique by then. The last I heard, he was living in Joinville."

Ari looked at it incredulously and answered in Spanish. "What? I'm going alone."

But this time Michelle wasn't prepared to be passive. She ripped the piece of paper out of Ari's hand. Her voice wavered with emotion. "She's my daughter. You and Ethan have no right to keep what you find out from me or to treat me like an idiot. You hear me? You don't know Henrique; the only one who's going to speak to him is me. Understand? You don't have to come with me. We can say goodbye right now if you like."

Emotions ran high for several minutes. Ari didn't understand much of what Michelle had said, but she got the gist loud and clear.

Calvo was torn between his curiosity and his desire to be anywhere but there. Eventually he decided to play intermediary. "Doña Michelle, it's none of my business how you decide to proceed, but a moment ago Doña Ari was asking me for help finding someone to help her to find your daughter in Brazil. I don't know whether . . . you'd like to continue along those lines?" He tried to meet both women's eyes. "Yes? Fine, so you're going to Joinville—is that in Santa Catalina?" He looked it up on his phone. "Yes, it is. It's a fairly large town; that'll help. Doña Ari, the town where your contact disappeared isn't far from there. It might be a good base of operations."

Michelle looked up in alarm. "Who disappeared?"

Calvo sighed. "Couldn't you have spoken before coming to see me? That secret detective of yours has disappeared, and Doña Ari has quite sensibly asked me to find her some help before the both of you disappear along with him. Which reminds me: we haven't yet discussed my fees."

Ari flared her nostrils in annoyance. Michelle added nothing, waiting for her to reply.

"A week ago I paid you two thousand dollars for a phone call. Whatever. How much is it now?"

"Don't be like that. You paid me to bring Ethan back to you, and I delivered him safe and sound, at not inconsiderable risk to my life. You can't have forgotten so soon, can you? Nonetheless, I shan't charge you for this work; we've been through a lot together, and as you say, you've already paid me something. Let's just say that this one's on the house so long as you can clear up one last little matter for me."

Ari and Michelle waited, intrigued.

"It's simple. Tell me the name of your contact. You won't be able to search for him *and* the girl. If he's still alive, that is. But maybe I can."

Ari's strength began to waver, but Michelle stood firm, speaking with a resolution her companions had never seen in her before.

"Go to hell. Using blackmail to get information you're not a good enough detective to find out on your own. Come on—we'll find another way."

Calvo stood up with a conciliatory expression. "Doña Michelle: wait, please. I didn't mean to upset you." In the blink of an eye, Michelle had dispelled the deep irony that Ari and Ethan had had to put up with since the beginning. "Don't take it the wrong way. I'm not looking for revenge or to hand him over to the Mara. No one cares about him except for me. He's too good; he's brilliant." Calvo's voice was infused with admiration. "He's managed to go under everyone's radar like a ghost. I want to meet him and, if he agrees, to work with him. He's incredible. And if he's in trouble, what better way to help him? I don't mean to be pessimistic, but if a genius like that, after what he did here, has failed there, you could well be heading into the mouth of hell. Let me help you. I'll give you all the logistical support I can. You know that you need me. Can't you see that it's in my interest? I want the bastard close to me. What do you say? It's a gift!" Calvo flashed his supercilious smile.

"I just want you to help him," Ari said.

Calvo nodded with childish eagerness. "And if I break my word, Ari will kill me. Don't you have a feeling of déjà vu?"

In the elevator, Michelle had just one thing to say to Ari. "My daughter is unique. You don't know her. She's special, not just one of many spawned by a son of a bitch. Get it? Fuck your information! I'm a failure—I know that—but she . . . she's unique."

Then she returned to icy silence. Over the next few days she would limit herself to a distant politeness that Ari didn't dare to intrude upon. Now it was she who allowed herself to be guided. She'd judged Michelle harshly before, but, as she reluctantly had to admit, this woman was beginning to demand a little respect.

Angela, the new bride, did honor to her name in her plain dress—frills were not well regarded in the community—and told her friends that she was marrying a good man even though he might appear cool, physically and emotionally. They were pleased that she was happy, not that there was any joy in her face, and congratulated her on her union with someone who was clearly a teacher of souls while she was just a humble rib. This concept, which Stobert had patiently and persistently worked to implant within her, became fixed in the young woman's mind. He would be a great shepherd for her people.

The wedding night was a more disagreeable trial than she had expected. Although they kept their nightshirts on the whole time and he was done quickly and efficiently, the coldness in his body passed through the sturdy fabric, creating an unpleasant sensation. Stobert told her that they'd sleep in separate beds, and she was very grateful to him for this. The first few months passed quietly, and their physical encounters were few and short lived. For this she thanked God because she couldn't bear to touch him, although this made her feel extremely guilty. A subconscious manifestation of her wish to atone took the form of a fantasy about how her husband would shepherd his flock, and she told him about it one evening over dinner. He reacted with feigned surprise: it was true that the Mennonites elected their minister among the community, but he had to be nominated and voted for after a period of prayer and consideration. Neither of them, for fear of incurring the sin of pride, could put his name forward.

Months later they were visited by Friedrich, Federico the Traveler. He had come under the premise of giving them a gift along with his congratulations, but Stobert saw something in his manner and took him aside. Once they were alone, he saw that the smuggler was beside himself with fear.

"I'm finished, finished! I have to get out of here, disappear." His eyes wandered the room in search of something that wasn't there. "None of us are safe . . ."

"Friedrich, calm down. What's happened?"

"I saw her at the reception. The bitch didn't take her eyes off me. At first I wondered if she was a prostitute, but her eyes were frightening, off putting. I got away from her for a moment, and when I turned around, she'd gone, like a ghost. The whore! She was a fucking ghost from the past . . ."

"What do you mean?"

"She had a tattoo, Walter. She was a fucking Jew. It took me a while to understand, and by then she'd gone. There are more and more of them coming each year, like a plague. They're fleeing from Europe, and they help each other to hide in South America like cockroaches."

"You were in Brazil?"

"Yes, here. In Florianópolis. I was in a hotel. I'd been invited to a reception—"

"You idiot! Have you forgotten your discipline, your oath? How could you have gone to a public event like that? How did you know her? Do you think she recognized you?"

"How should I know? She might have been on any of those wagons or trucks. Do you think I take the trouble to notice livestock? Who can tell? But she . . . those eyes . . ."

"You may have compromised all of us," Stobert said as he paced, trying to come up with a plan while Friedrich stopped pitying himself.

"I need to warn the two comrades in town. We need to leave the province. Go north or to Sao Paulo maybe . . ."

"No, don't warn anyone. I'm going to try to fix this. Wait here, and most important of all, don't talk to anyone. If your idiocy gets back to Odessa, they might not be so generous."

Four hours before their flight, Ari and Michelle met with Calvo, who'd asked them to give him as much time as possible for his investigation. He met them with his habitual warmth and was surprised by the subtle change of roles; it seemed as though Ari was now waiting for Michelle's approval before they made their decisions. He held up some glasses of champagne to toast with.

"Ladies, it seems that this might be the last time I see you before you go. I hope that it won't be long before we meet again and that it will be under better circumstances. I toast to your success. For my part, I have good and bad news. The bad news is related to your partner. We checked hotel reservations and the airports, but nothing came up. Maybe Suarez is traveling under a false name. But we did find a report by a car-rental company. It seems that he didn't find it so easy to forge a credit card and had to rent a car under his real name. A few days ago they found the car in a river, and when they looked for him, they could find no record of his entry or exit from the country. The police washed their hands of it, saying that he must have duplicated his ID card, and the agency is in dispute with the insurance company because they refuse to pay for it. This wasn't very difficult to find out: it appeared in the local press. It's the kind of story people like—morbid and mysterious with the tang of a conspiracy. You just have to know a little Portuguese."

"That's bad news."

"The worst. According to the press, he stayed in the town you mentioned, which is in what they call Europe Valley, very close to an old colony of German immigrants: Protestants or Lutherans or what have you."

"Colônia Liberdade?"

"None other," Calvo said, smiling smugly. "My boys checked it out, but they seem to be quite a discreet group. There's no trace of them on the internet except for government records of title deeds and wills. It seems that they're also mentioned in a book a journalist wrote about collaborators with the dictatorship forty years ago. Later on, a case was opened into the disappearance of several opposition figures, but it was then summarily closed, and there was a big scandal. In the end, people just forgot. But why not take a guess at the law firm that represents them? Smit and Betancourt. They don't like people talking about them."

Ari pursed her lips bitterly. "Suarez didn't deserve to go that way."

"I'm as sorry as you are, but I'm more worried about the two of you meeting a similar fate. My advice would be not to go to the town under any circumstances. For that, I've got you your hit man. People call him Caimão; I don't know his real name. He's originally from Joinville. We made contact with him through an escort and bodyguard agency. He organizes security for concerts and events, but they gave us a good account of his other activities. Unfortunately, I can't offer you any direct guarantees because I don't know him, but he's the surest thing I can find. He's well regarded; they say that he's reliable, loyal to the person paying him, and fearless. He can get his hands on weapons, and he seems serious. If you're interested, he knows that you're going, the general nature of the job, and that you don't speak Portuguese. It seems that he can speak English; he deals with a lot of musicians from overseas."

Ari and Michelle were grateful for his help. Ari even gave him a brief hug. Once they'd gone, Calvo was filled with a vague sense of melancholy and wondered when it was he'd developed affection for these people. After all, they'd caused him nothing but trouble.

Stobert rode his bicycle around the small county capital, trying to get his thoughts in order. He kept coming up with plans, but they always fell apart before he could get anywhere. Brief moments of inspiration flashed in his mind, only to be snuffed out almost immediately. All of his ideas were either useless or misguided. That damned Friedrich had ruined his life. After twenty years living as a fugitive, Stobert had made a potential future for himself, and now it had been jeopardized by an idiotic mistake. He was consumed by frustration and hatred. How could he overcome this challenge? Could he find the Jewish woman and try to influence her? His methods of persuasion needed time, effort, and some degree of predisposition. He didn't think it was possible. Suddenly he was feeling as anxious as he had in Argentina. Then he heard a whisper. He braked and looked around. He was alone. He was possessed by the same irrational panic with which he woke up every day and went on pedaling, afraid to look back, as though something real might materialize on the sidewalk. It was the first time his night terrors had intruded upon his waking hours.

At the police station he was unable to make himself understood in Portuguese, but when he mentioned Marcelo's name, he was led up to an upper floor where he waited half an hour. When Marcelo came back and saw him sitting there, his face lit up. He had the German where he wanted him.

"I still don't know Portuguese."

"Better that way. It's always a pleasure to practice my German."

"You warned me about the Zionists. I've come to see you because I need your help."

This made the chief of police sit up. "Have you had any contact with them? I make it a point of principle to get to know the Jewish communities under my jurisdiction."

"I haven't. An old comrade may have, and not in your jurisdiction but in Florianópolis, in a hotel. I've written down the name."

"And how can I help you with that?"

"I wanted to consult with you. Would it be possible to find out if anyone has filed a false report? Libel against a citizen, making up falsehoods about his past?"

"To the police?"

"I'm also worried that they might have contacted organizations overseas."

"That would require making an international call, and they'll certainly have a record of it at the hotel. From the way you're asking, I can tell that this is an urgent matter. Wait outside; I'll make some inquiries."

Stobert thanked him and waited in a damp room with dirty windows. He started to shiver. His anxiety grew as the cold crept through him. Then he found a hot plate in a rickety cupboard. Feeling even more afraid, he turned it on and looked around to make sure he was alone. The resistor shook and spluttered before it glowed red. Nobody could see him. His shivering grew more violent. Nobody was around. He put his palm on the burning surface.

Marcelo opened the door and immediately started sniffing. "How strange; did you burn yourself?"

Stobert went into the office, ignoring the question.

"I made my inquiries. The report you mention . . . could it have been made by a woman?"

"Yes, I believe that's the case we're talking about."

"I spoke to the local police. You're lucky that our network is so widespread. We talked about failed romances, the twisted revenge of women scorned. We agreed that racial issues only aggravate matters. I suggested that the woman's malice might be accentuated by the resentment, avarice, and villainy of the Jews. A Semite looking to redeem her blood by mixing it with Aryan stock. Isn't that the story you came to tell me about?"

Stobert maintained a prudent silence.

"Say it, Aspiazi, damn it. I've been waiting for a year. I know that you haven't come to me for selfish reasons. I know that you're helping someone else—and your altruism does you honor—but you must be honest if you wish to earn my trust."

His wait for an answer spread like a cloud between them, a cloud that swept Stobert off firm ground, where Marcelo stood waiting with a scornful smile. Marcelo was the sole possessor of a light at the end of the tunnel. The only light that could guide him. But it would also expose him.

"The Jewish race is a cancer on the earth. They're the origin of evil because they are governed by hatred. Their driver is envy, and their method is to copy superior races and steal their culture."

Marcelo repressed a shiver and lit a cigarette. "I have friends in high places who will be very pleased to hear that we've come to an understanding. Friends who might be able to help us in the future. Friends whom you will help for the common good. It is true that a damned Jew has denounced a refugee, accusing him of being a war criminal."

"Slander, of course."

"We're not here to judge him but her. What worries me is the fact that a plague like hers might spread. We have no record of her making any overseas contacts, but she requested that the report be sent on to the Israeli embassy. They've frozen that channel for the moment, but clearly the case will be investigated and more information uncovered."

"What can be done about it?"

"There's nothing we can do as officers of the law, but if the woman filing the report were to disappear, there'd be no reason to proceed further with the case. Of course, we must make sure that she disappears entirely."

"And how do we make sure of that?"

"I have been informed in detail of the hotel where she's staying, a luxury place that only the richest can afford. The lady is traveling alone and generally goes to dinner at the same place every night, at the same time. It's a lonely walk of about a mile and a half around a deep gully. At dusk, the dew makes the loose stones slippery, and the path becomes dangerous. Several people have been lost there, careless tourists especially. The local government knows they need to put up railings, but for now there's only a warning sign."

"From this moment on, I pledge myself to you as a gentleman, just as you have pledged yourself to me."

Andrés willingly drove Ari and Michelle to the airport, just as he had with Ethan. He said goodbye with unaccustomed emotion, upsetting the women a little. He told them that he loved them and supported them wholeheartedly; he'd never been so intimate with his sister before. He also thanked Ari for her generous support. They said goodbye to him with a wrench in their stomachs and gave him big hugs.

Since they'd boarded the plane to Brazil, Ari had noticed a different kind of fragility in Michelle. It was as though she needed to get away from her homeland to be herself again. Michelle asked for three glasses of wine to bolster her courage as she faced ghosts only she could see. Halfway through the flight, once she was drunk enough, she embarked upon a mumbled tale in a mixture of English and Spanish. At no point did she ever look at Ari.

"I was born into a very poor family. I know that when I say that to someone in the first world, they don't understand. Our poverty is different. My dad was a bad person—that's why Andrés escaped. Then my dad left, and my mom got together with my stepfather. They made Beto, and then he left too." Michelle sighed and let a tear fall. "My mom may not have been a good mother, but she always let me go to school. I was pretty and got harassed a lot . . . other girls my age already had boyfriends and got pregnant, but I never went out with anyone. I wanted to study. I wanted to get away like Andrés did. He always helped me, and all I dreamed about was getting away. I was lucky that my mother let me study. Other mothers didn't. I got good grades, better each time, and I wasn't afraid of boys because I'd seen worse at home. That was why I concentrated on studying and dreaming of going to join Andrés one day, of living on the other side. I dreamed that one day I would be happy."

Ari didn't let the sympathy she was beginning to feel show.

"Then one day he appeared at the school gates. He had dark hair, but he looked European, which was where his family was from. He was very handsome, stunning, and he had a way about him. He spoke Spanish very well, almost like a native, but with a Brazilian accent. I thought he was romantic and mysterious, like a traveler who knew everything about life. He always wore designer clothes and a sports watch and carried a BlackBerry around with him. At the time that was what rich people used: I'd never seen one before. The girls said that he was the son of a diplomat, although we knew that couldn't be true. But then again, who knew? I'd just turned seventeen, and I was either going to leave the country or find a job and pay my way through university; either option was fine. I don't remember how I met him, whether someone introduced us or not, but he pursued me right from the start. My friends said it was because I was so pretty—others said it was because I was asking for it. Whatever the reason, he'd come to pick me up from school in his Lexus, in front of all my friends. He'd get out to open the door for me. He promised me that I was his only love and that I would have his love and heart forever. He said that he'd die if he couldn't see me every day and . . ."

Michelle's head was bowed, and she didn't wipe away the tears that fell slowly onto her knees.

"I was seventeen, and he was twenty-five, at the least. I wore my school uniform because they were the only clothes I had. When he kissed me, he became the whole world. I didn't want anything but him. He could take me where he liked, and I'd serve and bless him for the rest of my life. When I got pregnant, I was terrified that my mother would beat me to death, but he stood in front of her like a gentleman and told her that he'd take care of it. Then he gave her five hundred dollars 'to get clothes for the christening.' I felt terrible, but I told myself every day that I should be happy, that I had a guy who loved me even after I became pregnant. I'd seen my friends' boyfriends run off at the first hint of trouble. But this was a real man who took responsibility and brought me gifts. But I still felt bad because I knew it was all my fault. I'd been stupid. He'd asked me to make love without protection because he said that condoms were for prostitutes, not for people in love. But I still could have gone on the pill. At school people started to say that I'd done it on purpose to trap my man. They applauded me for it. He took care of me, told me that I was his baby, said I was what he wanted most in the world, and made me all kinds of promises. He said that we'd get married . . . it was probably the happiest time of my life. But still I cried every night because I felt so sad and everyone called me a mistress and a gold digger. I asked him to marry me, and he said he would, but he wanted to have a special wedding so everyone could see me as the angel I was . . . he wanted me to be the most beautiful bride in the world, but I didn't want to get married after the baby was born and especially not with a huge belly, which was already beginning to show . . . he just kept making promises . . . swearing to me that everything would be fine and he'd take care of everything and make me his queen. He took me to the best gynecologists to do the tests and tried to take me out of school, but I didn't want that. Then one day, at five months I think, I did a test that showed that it was definitely a girl, and he made the doctor say it a thousand times and show him on the ultrasound. He said that he'd pay what it took to make sure . . . he kept saying, 'My love, my sweet love, my princess' and how happy he was that it was a girl; a girl was what he'd wanted. And then he went off to pay the bill while I got dressed, and . . . it was one of the saddest experiences of my life. I sat down to wait for him, full of hope, waiting to hug him and especially for him to hug me and give me strength because I was feeling that it was all too much for me . . . but he never came back. That's exactly how it happened. I went out into the hall and sat down to wait for him. I sat there for half an hour, calm at first but then getting more and more worried. I started to get embarrassed because the nurses kept passing by again and again, smiling at me with other couples, older women who looked at me . . . I was dying of shame and getting very worried because I was so confused, but I didn't dare move just in case he came back . . . I didn't even dare to go to the bathroom until eventually a nurse who'd passed me an hour ago came by and asked, 'Are you waiting for someone?' I wanted to die. I felt my face burning up and told her that I was waiting for my boyfriend: he'd gone to pay for the examination. She seemed confused but told me that she'd come with me to the cashier, and the cashier told me that the guy I was talking about had paid an hour ago and left. She'd seen him get into his car and leave . . . I've never been so embarrassed in my life . . . I didn't have any money, just my ID card and my clothes . . . I didn't know what to do, so I lied and told them that he'd gone to get something and must have forgotten about me but that he'd be coming back. They asked me if I'd like to wait in the waiting room—I'd be able to see him come back from there—but I said, 'No, I'd rather go outside, but thank you.' Then the nurse said that she'd go with me. She asked if I had any money . . . she gave me a bill, saying that it was just for while I waited, in case I needed something. I wanted a hole to swallow me up, but I said thank you and that I'd give it back when he came. She told me not to worry. But even then I didn't go; I stayed on another two hours waiting in the parking lot outside, like an idiot, watching the cars come and go. I didn't know what to do. I tried to think of every possible reason why he might have left, hoping that he'd come back, thinking hard, fantasizing. In the end I saw the nurse coming off her shift and hid behind a car so she wouldn't see me. It was night, and the street was emptying out. When I saw her go home, I realized that he wasn't coming back. The money the nurse had given me was enough for the bus back home."

Stobert didn't come up with a strategy—he just improvised, trying to keep all the lies he'd told straight, lies that might send him to prison or, at best, ruin his standing in the community. He'd ordered his wife to keep Friedrich in their cabin in secret and then had come back to sneak him away to Florianópolis. Still, he knew that the rumors would spread, and if he didn't justify his absence beforehand, he was finished. Although they'd dealt with their accuser, he was still in danger.

The hills rose translucent and ghostly in the waxing moonlight. That was how he'd always remember them: he'd never see them again. The deed had been bitter, clumsy, dirty, and horrible. The woman had screamed and cried hysterically, her nightmare having suddenly and unexpectedly returned. She'd cursed them and pleaded for her life. During the struggle she'd lost her bra, so she'd fallen half-naked into the gorge, coming to rest in a grotesque, indecent posture.

It was almost midnight, and they still had forty miles ahead of them when Friedrich pulled over, saying that he needed to stretch his legs. The truth was that he was still trembling. He was driving like a drunkard. The coward hadn't failed just to thank Stobert for his help; it looked as though he might run off at any moment. "It's not like it was before," he'd said. "Things have changed." Friedrich had grown soft—he'd shown that with his receptions and expensive hotels. He'd become bourgeois and could no longer be trusted. He smoked cigarette after cigarette with shaking hands and grumbled about getting back into the car. Stobert was disgusted by his former comrade. Disgusted and ashamed. In his annoyance an idea came to him. It wasn't, however, a structured response. He didn't plan his next step; it was spontaneous. He knew this might be his last chance to get rid of someone who had become a dangerous liability. Stobert took the belt from his trench coat and wrapped it around his fists. Friedrich couldn't be trusted.

Michelle had stopped again to cough and clear her throat. But there was no complaint in her voice.

"Henrique never came back. I was left alone, and then my life really did go to hell. The next day, when he didn't come to pick me up at school, everyone knew. I could feel them all talking about me. My mom was the worst—she called me names, said I was disgraced, and blamed me for everything. I'd driven him away . . . I had to leave school and find work because she said that she wasn't going to support another mouth to feed at home if I didn't contribute anything. Then Michi was born, and we never had any contact with him. Well, we did once. Before the birth, I looked for him like crazy, and only then did I realize that I had no way of finding him. He had always taken the lead. He took me to a rented loft in the city, and we always took his car. I didn't know how to get there, and my friends who knew him didn't know how to find him either. He'd changed his phone number and just disappeared. That was how easy it was back then. But I kept on looking. I even found his apartment, but of course he didn't live there anymore. The doorman told me that he'd rented it before we met and left it the day after the examination, but he did have another number to reach him on. I called him then and there. By then I was eight months pregnant, and the only examinations I'd done were the public health ones, which were poor quality. I couldn't afford any better . . . I walked around in my school uniform and a belly twice the size of my body . . . I was very young and felt so unhappy and alone. I called him, and when I heard his voice, I started to cry. I didn't know why. I wasn't capable of feeling joy or sadness or hatred—I just cried. He recognized me, but he didn't hang up. He just offered a vague explanation and asked me where I was so he could come pick me up. I don't know; I can't remember very well. He gave some kind of explanation that I chose to believe and repeated the same old promises, even more this time. He was going to send lots of money home just to show how committed he was. I wanted to see him right away and told him to come: that was what I needed, not money. He told me that he wasn't in town but he'd be there the next day . . . just to show he meant it, he'd send me money that very afternoon. I went home. I had no choice. I didn't know what to do or how to react . . . and so I waited again, until I fell asleep. That was the last time we were in contact. When I called him the next day, the number had been changed. After I gave birth, I found work. When Michi was a little less than two years old, I was able to leave my mother's house, and when Andrés asked me to join him in the States, I went right away. Andrés was always the only one who ever helped me. That's my story."

Ari was speechless. Her companion blew her nose.

"A few years later, some people I knew gave me an address in Florianópolis, the capital of Santa Catarina. He'd stayed in touch with the people she knew—he hadn't tried to disappear from the face of the earth, but he had ditched me like a dog. At seventeen years old I didn't have the tools to find him. And what good was that address? All I knew about him was that he was a con man who'd used me and abandoned me. I wrote him a letter, pouring out everything I felt. I don't know if he ever got it, but at least it helped me to get over the ordeal. A long time later, about three years ago, I suddenly got an email from him apologizing. It was so strange—it didn't sound like it came from the same person. He said that he regretted his actions and had really loved me and worried about me but at the time he had no control over his life. He asked me for my address so he could send money to help the girl. He wanted to take responsibility for his actions. I sent it to him and started to receive fifty or a hundred dollars every two or three months, and he always let me know when it was coming. I asked our mutual acquaintances, and they said they never saw him anymore. He'd gone to live in Joinville and joined a Pentecostal congregation, the Universal Church of the Celestial Kingdom, and they'd not seen him again. He still sends me a little money, I suppose whenever he can. After I left the other day, I wrote to him, but he didn't answer. I found the Joinville church on the organization's website. The main service is on Saturdays, and the faithful are obliged to attend. If he's still with them, he'll be there."

Ari just nodded. She didn't know what to say.

"I've brought Michi's passport. If we find her, we'll need it to get her out of the country. And this." Michelle handed over a sealed, stamped document. "I've thought about what might happen, because of what happened to Beto and me. We don't know where this will end, and . . . it's a notarized statement in which I name you Michi's legal guardian. It's just us. I don't know if Ethan will come back, and I was afraid to think of what would happen if something happened to me. She can't be with a father who never loved her or even knew her. I'm sorry for not telling you before; it's just insurance. I don't want Michi to be alone ever again."

Ari tried to reassure her, but her voice gave her away. All she managed was a weak "Of course."

Angela woke up when she heard him come back in the middle of the night. She got up to make him a snack or warm up water for him to bathe, but what she saw turned her stomach inside out. Faithful to the restrained traditions of her church, she didn't make a sound and ran straight over to help him: he had obviously been the victim of a violent attack. Neither of them said a word. She undressed him, filled several buckets with water, and calmly and carefully washed away the dried blood and mud, cleaning, dressing, and covering each wound. Once she was done she saw that most of the wounds were superficial, and the only ones that would be visible once he'd dressed would be the scratches and bruising around his eye.

Stobert was oblivious to his wife's attentions. It was as though he hadn't yet arrived home. The rational part of him knew that the situation had become worse and he had no way out, but his mind was still tied up in a knot he couldn't unravel. He couldn't remember what his subsequent actions had been even though he'd driven forty miles with the body lying next to him. He knew that he'd wiped away the fingerprints and dragged him back into the car, but he couldn't recall a single part of the journey. He could easily recite the route he'd taken as though he'd learned it by rote, but it made no emotional impact upon him, like a story he'd read in an imaginary book. His spirit returned again and again to the warmth of Friedrich's head against his forehead, the hair in his mouth, and the tension of the belt, which had felt as though it was about to break. The idea that amazed him in that memory was the fear, their terror, and the dying man's incredible strength. The shared fear: a monstrous communion. Friedrich's fear had somehow spread to him. The whole ordeal now seemed nothing more than a blind struggle of which only the scratches, the gasping, and his wounds were real. He'd never felt anything so intense before, and he never would again. From that moment on, his obsession with repeating the experience would grow more and more desperate with each failed attempt. He was sure that it hadn't been transmitted through touch but via a sense unknown to science, a sense that had helped him to chart his victim in detail: the violence of the spasms, the limbs like roaring motors, all depicted in his mind without ever truly touching him. He knew that it hadn't been a random feeling or a false memory. Friedrich had died fighting: his flailing punches, the thrusting knees, the nails digging into his face. Stobert had been bonded to him in panic, afraid to let him go, worried that the belt would snap or that his painful act of survival would fail. It was like some inhuman sexual act.

It was Stobert's body that had won the battle, not him. Animal panic had strengthened his muscles and made him immune to the pain of a nail gouging his eye. It was his body that had stayed firm until the claws had gone limp, their heat fading into the air, scalding him just before the man's life ebbed away completely. And there was the other voice, like the whisper on the path, that had rejoiced in an unintelligible language, making them both suffer. The voice that had revealed both fears, the one he knew well and Friedrich's terror in asphyxia. The voice, he knew, had opened a channel between them just to share the horror of the absurdity, the emptiness of death. Just to show him. Until Friedrich's strength had failed and he'd gone limp and heavy, letting go like an empty wrapper collapsing in on itself, a bag leaking into the sea. The voice had pushed him until he'd lost his self-control. And all on a whim. Just to enhance the terror that now would never leave him.

Stobert had cleaned the seat, laid the body out, driven along with it, and left the car in town before walking back to the colony. He'd come up with a story that he knew no one would believe. The locals would find the dead body and come for him, but none of this stuck in his memory. All that came back to him was a never-ending death, like the prelude to his own hell. It went on forever.

Stobert didn't sleep. He was obsessed with the brief sensation of warmth that he'd felt after more than twenty years of feeling nothing but cold. Reality returned with the sun, determined to make him pay for his mistakes. Now, his premises looked flimsy; nothing of what he'd planned seemed likely to work, as though he'd been drunk when he'd come up with it.

Angela woke up before dawn and dutifully made him breakfast without asking a single question. Exhausted, starving, and red eyed, he asked her to call a meeting of the community elders first thing that morning, before news of his nocturnal movements reached them from other sources. Resigned to his fate, he decided to press ahead with his plan, if only to win some time with which to get away.

When he was sitting in front of the elders in the large, empty hall, he began his tale just as he'd originally planned, even though it was filled with holes and inconsistencies that he couldn't explain. He told them again that he and Federico were devout Christians. His friend had come to him for advice, having discovered that their fellow countrymen in the town were fugitive war criminals, and he was afraid for his life. Stobert knew that most of the German colonies overseas had supported the Nazis and so had no idea how these supposed wise men might react, but he rolled the dice, trusting that his gift for persuasion would help tip the balance in his favor. To his relief, he was right. These Christians, who had little idea of what had happened and had even less experience of mendacity, saw no reason not to believe him. They were horrified by the term *war criminal*. They asked where Federico was, and he asked forgiveness in both their names for failing to share such a terrible truth before now, saying that it was Federico who had asked him to remain silent so he could confront the two evildoers alone. Guided by his faith in God, he had been confident that he would make them see the error of their ways. Of course, these people weren't naive enough to believe that it would end well. Shocked, they immediately sent a cart into town to find out what had happened and, if necessary, contact the authorities.

Stobert was amazed at his initial success. He calculated that the trip and commotion would give him a couple of hours to disappear, assuming that Marcelo wouldn't make much effort to find him. After all, it was in his interests to keep things quiet as well. At the last moment he realized that he should have ditched the body and hidden the car. He could have used it to get away. He went to his cabin to get hold of a knife and thought about stealing a horse but decided against it so as not to give the Mennonites a reason to chase him.

However, events didn't play out as he'd expected. Just as he was getting ready to leave, the only police car in the area appeared on the main drive, kicking up dust on either side and attracting the attention of children and the elderly, who'd barely ever seen such a vehicle before. The car was being towed along behind it. Stobert stopped, knowing that there was no point even trying to escape. The patrol car's doors opened, and Marcelo stepped out with a pair of officers. They came over, and Marcelo greeted him with surprising friendliness.

"Good morning, Aspiazi. We keep seeming to run into each other."

"I'm afraid that I don't understand."

The colony residents watched them curiously. Angela's face appeared alongside the others, but she stayed quiet.

"We met the cart on its way to town. They told us what you'd told them. It was a great help."

"I still don't understand."

"A cowherd came across the body of your acquaintance Federico, the smuggler, as she was taking out her livestock this morning. They called us from the town phone, and when we arrived, your two compatriots, with whom I know you have no contact, had disappeared. With your statement—which, if you please, we'll take down at the station—we can clear everything up and issue an order for their arrest."

His neighbors listened on in amazement. He couldn't believe it; somehow he'd become a hero. For want of a better idea, he'd left the body near the Germans' house with the vague, ridiculous intention of blaming the crime on them, simply because they were close by. The former soldiers, whose senses were more attuned than farmers', had been the first to find it. They'd seen it as a Zionist threat: the area was no longer safe, and their military discipline had helped them to get away before anyone woke up. They'd disappeared without a trace.

When Marcelo questioned him, Stobert changed his story accordingly. Just as Stobert had imagined, no arrest order was issued. No one cared. The exile would be laid to rest in one of many anonymous graves.

Following this sequence of events—the spiritual guidance requested and given to his friend, the respect for his determination, the secret he'd kept, and the moral values he'd demonstrated—the council informed Stobert that he was under consideration as a candidate for pastor. He was invited to give a sermon to the congregation. In the most absurd way, his moment had arrived.

The main gate of Colônia Liberdade opened, revealing what lay behind it: a two-lane drive leading to a small plaza where the original entrance had been. Lucas and Armando's car drove on and turned left toward the community center, where the houses of the main families were located along with the different meeting rooms, the church, and the school. These buildings surrounded the incredible glass construction that had been the leader's residence for many years. In the distance, the profile of the old hospital, which was now abandoned, could be seen.

The construction consisted of two floors, the lower one surrounded by dark brick walls decorated with childish murals while the top one, which could be accessed by interior stairs, held the Grandfather's greenhouse residence. The strange design was fully intentional: the greenhouse was built over the boiler room that served the entire complex, thus enhancing the heating, just as Fausto Aspiazi had required. In the 1980s, when he'd given up his pastoral work, he'd moved his office there and had barely left in the past fifteen years. Since then, his staff had made obligatory visits and the children attended a weekly class to keep his influence alive, but even so it wasn't what it had been. The youngest among them hated going to the big glass sauna.

Armando and Lucas prepared themselves as best they could to withstand the heat and opened the misted glass door. Inside, lush vegetation pressed up against the roof, and a swarm of insects fell upon anyone who entered but ignored their benefactor. The condensation could grow so concentrated that it sometimes fell like rain. A barely discernible path led through the undergrowth into the central space, which appeared to have been set up as a minihospital. From the damp bed, a weak figure with a drip connected to his arm pushed a walker to an office desk. Once there, he fell into an executive chair with a grunt. Walter Stobert, or Fausto Aspiazi, awaited them. His body was little more than a skeleton draped in aged skin, and his bony fingers trembled under their own weight. It looked as though his flesh had outlived itself. His skull was covered in spots and the odd gray hair while his eyes, blinded by cataracts, still seemed to bore into everything they looked at. He lifted his head, shuddered, and turned occasionally, as though listening to an invisible voice. Sometimes it made him laugh while at others he appeared afraid. These were the moments that his followers most feared, when he seemed to have forgotten they were there. Now his reedy, barely audible voice welcomed them in German, the only language allowed in his presence. In spite of the muggy atmosphere, he exhaled mist with every breath, as though he were on the frozen tundra.

"Come in, my children. Come in—don't just stand there. I was anxious to hear from you."

Having just returned from Geneva, they were both on the brink of fainting. Lucas, as the senior party, gave his report as they'd agreed, saying that the brothers had come to an agreement and the youngest would be coming in a few weeks to sign it on behalf of the company. Their master blinked a couple of times, unusually slowly. His eyelids couldn't close completely anymore, and a milky glow, like the insides of mussel shells, was always visible. When he opened them again, the translucent, rough, cataract-infused surface seemed to light up in a smile. His thin, dry cardboard lips separated to reveal empty gums trailing with saliva. He gestured to them that they could go. When Armando stood up, Stobert stopped him.

"Not you, my child. Not you."

When they were alone, his happy grimace returned. "I have her. Fortune has finally smiled on me. One of the two is the girl."

"Are you sure?"

"There won't be any more girls. One of them is the answer."

"I visited them before coming; they were still sedated."

"I know. Of course I know that, you fool."

Armando bowed his head, avoiding the old man's eyes. He knew very well what Stobert was capable of. He'd seen men tear out their own tongues under the noiseless influence of those eyes. His master sat up in his seat and readjusted the rug he'd draped over his lap.

"What happened at the meeting?"

Armando hesitated. He gulped, knowing that whatever side he chose now would come at a price. But really he didn't have a choice; he hadn't had a will of his own for years.

"We . . . we've run out of time, sir. We've been betrayed."

The skull fixed on a brugmansia, a bunch of orange flowers that hung down like bells, providing a frame for a spider's web.

"How strange . . . fate usually seems to align itself one way, either for us or against us. But now some events appear to be affecting others that don't seem related at all." He pointed to the plant. "Remind me the name of that plant."

317

"Angel's bells or trumpets. My father called them the Queens of the Night."

"A lovely name. They must be prepared and administered to the two girls." For a moment the old man grew excited. "They visited each other in their dreams. Do you understand, my son? One girl found the other! They spoke to one another." He laughed, emitting a cloud of mist. "After all these years I finally have an answer. One of them is the conduit, but we don't know which one. We have to prepare them both. What do I care about these betrayals if I can make the transit? It might all be related after all. We must hurry. Who was at the meeting?"

"The . . . the brothers."

"All four of them? The eldest too?"

"Yes, they were all there."

"Then it's true. Ingrates. I remember when they were children. Their grandfather and I were close. He built his empire. His son learned from him and respected me, but he died young, and the grandsons . . . they inherited it all but understand nothing. They're just spoiled children, corrupted by capital. For shame!"

"We no longer have the support of the network. There are powerful figures willing to pay for you."

"That's nothing new. There have been for years. Stupid nouveau riche, arrogant apprentice sorcerers who think that they can obtain my powers if they lock me up like a freak. Bastards!"

"The Schwindts have taken on the job. The one they call the Jackal is coming for you."

"Aha, the ritual of the true name. You see, my son? They mislearned that from their grandfather as well. A name must be earned by deeds, it must be given by a superior, and it must be kept secret. No one knows the name of the eldest."

"I didn't think he had one."

"Of course he does! And that's why he deserves it. The others are just nicknames: the Mastiff, well, just look at him . . . the Bloodhound—I doubt he deserved it if he got himself killed. And this one, the Jackal: I don't think he even did anything to earn it. Do you know where it came from? From a fictional assassination attempt on de Gaulle! From a film! Ridiculous. When does he arrive?"

"We don't know yet. If . . . if they find out that I warned you . . . if . . ."

"Fool! You know you have much more to fear from me. They won't get to me! It'll cost them more blood than they can possibly imagine. I simply need to make the transit. After that, I'll be free . . . and so will you. I'll give you your freedom. Now go."

And Stobert was left on his own once more, surrounded by his ghosts.

Colônia Liberdade, 1964

Over the next decade, things settled down. After Stobert's first sermon he found that his powers were increasing, and soon nobody would dare to challenge him. His path was set, and his word became law, but his temperature continued to fall, and the voice leaped out of his dreams to torment him as it saw fit, whenever he was least expecting it. Stobert knew that there were times when he wasn't alone. There was nothing more frightening than that. Over eight years, Angela gave him two children, and her youthful, healthy body withered away, leaving her prematurely aged. She had been taught never to reveal her fear of her partner. Now nobody in the community seemed to see him for what he was.

After 1960, when the capture of Adolf Eichmann was reported internationally, Stobert began to pay special attention to youth movements. The Zionist influence was increasing, just as Marcelo had predicted. Even more degenerate music was being imported, and rumors of social change were spreading across the underground. Ever-larger groups of wealthy children were flirting with the counterculture and challenging the status quo while even in his own realm a group appeared that sought to support indigenous rights: they shared food, studied their farming methods, and even planned to build a school for them. Many of the faithful came to him in an uproar, but others sympathized. They spoke of the basic values of Christianity, equality, and sharing; they talked about returning the land to the original inhabitants, updating God's message. But he knew that subversive ideas lay behind their reasonable-sounding arguments. Messages of love spread the disease of socialism like a virus.

Eventually, in 1964, Marcelo came to see him. It was time to call in a favor: "Do you remember my warning? You've seen them with their guitars and protests, undermining society. They're becoming a problem. No one wants another Cuba. Everything's ready. Now is the time to get involved."

Stobert accepted his role and solemnly prepared for what he believed was the most important sermon of his life. Thus far, he'd managed to control his flock, but never before had he forced them to violate their moral compass. He started by praising the work of the new arrivals.

"We have all heard that these visitors have come on a charitable mission to help the unfortunate. I have heard that too. And I also see, my children, because nothing must escape the eyes of the pastor. And I am pleased. I am pleased to see goodness with no ulterior motive. Commitment with no expectation of reward. Our Christian duty is to help the needy, to give water to the thirsty and food to the hungry. That is charity, my children. It is not simply just but necessary in the eyes of God. But who are we to say what else is necessary? I ask you, what books does he who works with his hands need to read? What books can help him more than the sacred book, which has always shown us the way and must always be provided? I ask you: What other philosophy does one need to work the land? What thinking other than the true way must be imprinted upon the souls of our children at school? Is it not arrogance dressed up as charity to impose one's thinking upon others? I say to you: How does the savage benefit from the harsh gift of studies that only corrupt their happy innocence? What new enlightenment can strange ideas, which are focused on undermining the established order, an order created under the auspices of our Father, possibly offer? These false promises of equality cannot conceal their origin, which is none other than envy! Envy of what our bountiful God has granted to us in his infinite generosity and what we have earned in accordance with his teachings. Envy that makes them long for what they have no right to. I know that well, my children. I know them."

His congregation started to mumble in protest. Several eyes glared at him, trusting that they wouldn't be detected in the crowd.

"And what is the source of that envy if not pride? To declare oneself a possessor of something that can only be handed out by divine grace. Only the Holy Ghost may determine the established Celestial Order! Or are you curious about these different ideas, these strange teachings?"

He pointed his finger at his accusers, forcing some to look away in shame. "Avarice! Their only goal, concealed behind their flowery words, is not to share but to take away your possessions for their own benefit. Or have your Indians returned the help you have given them by loaning them your land?"

Now he pointed at those who had been most involved, until the rest of the congregation began to stare at them accusingly.

"Anger! They can only achieve their objectives through confrontation. Have not rifts opened up among you? Has not the seed of discord been sown among you?" He addressed the elders who arbitrated the arguments caused by this new movement. "Lust! You have seen them live in sin, even if you prefer not to mention it. And what do you think the consequences will be if their demands are met? They'll set up house with your daughters . . ."

He looked toward the mothers, who crossed themselves or even covered their ears. "Without the holy sacrament! They will be damned!" He repeated the word until the upset mothers started to nod. "And sloth! None of the ends they pursue are sought with the sweat of their backs. They want to take them from the good flock. From you, my children."

He stopped to catch his breath, offering brief respite to his terrified congregation. "These are all capital sins. A doctrine based upon the capital sins!"

His voice echoed around the silent hall. "We know what their ideas will lead to, the damage caused by their slander, the lies that have, as I well know, deceived several of our brothers, taking advantage of their trusting hearts."

He sought out those who had most fallen under the sway of the peaceful revolutionaries. But no head was raised. Below him there was only shame and fear. Another war had begun, and war did not allow for dissent.

"We know what it is that they truly want. Shall we allow their teachings to continue to pollute the simple spirit of these indigenous peoples? Shall we allow them to poison their childish minds? Not only must we protect our possessions, not only must we defend the natural order of things; it is also our duty to protect innocent happiness. It is time to speak of both our good and theirs, that of all the communities of the children of God. It is time to denounce the dangers that stalk us, hiding under the cloak of false goodwill. Our enemy is not the freedom or justice they hypocritically promise, my children. Our enemy is not their school, because we are committed believers in education: it is not for nothing that I have been your teacher. Our enemy hides behind terms such as *reason* and *science*, which they pervert to their own ends, for there is no reason but the word of God and no science without his will. Who is our true enemy, my children? Communism!"

A large number of the congregation crossed themselves at the mere mention of the word.

"This is the ignominy that lurks behind these generous words! Deceit! And the only way to combat it is to treat it as the weed that it is, to rip it out from the ground by the roots!"

Commotion spread throughout the crowd, but Stobert quieted them with raised arms.

"Now is the time to act, I tell you! It is time to work with the forces of order however we can! And to commune with God's truth just as he has taught us. That is why in the difficult tests to come, we cannot sit on our hands. That is why as part of our humble service to the Almighty, we must change the name of this community, giving ourselves up to the task that God the Father demands of us, declaring the goodness that shall be required during the sacrifices to come. And so, in his divine bounty, we shall be renamed *Colônia Liberdade!*"

The sheep clapped. They assumed the name as their own and rejected the creed of those who were now their enemies, unaware of the true extent of the concessions they were making.

A week later there was a coup d'état in Brazil, and when the first executions were announced, no one raised any objection or asked any questions. Within just a few weeks the building that the first colonists had built as a hospital would be repurposed as an illegal detention center. Stobert was now powerful enough to remold the religious community in his own image. The isolation of the young was agreed so as to prevent contamination from the outside world; fences were put up, followed by barriers and eventually walls with a guard put on the gates. Dissidents from across the nation were taken to the compound in windowless vehicles. After interrogation, they were buried in the cellars.

Soon, militia, patrols, and private security would follow. Angela, who was the first to suffer from Stobert's so-called heat diet, died in 1968. She was spared the worst of it: the militarization, disappearances, and discipline. Stobert's strict regime was combined with his experimentation on children, who grew up living in terror of his punishments, especially what would become known as his "cold hugs."

In 1976, he was overseeing the construction of his greenhouse when he got the most unsettling news he'd received since arriving in South America.

"Excuse me, master. A gentleman has been asking for you. He arrived in a Mercedes. He looks very rich."

"And he hasn't introduced himself? Let him wait!"

"We told him that you couldn't see him, but he just laughed. He said that he had no idea who Fausto Aspiazi was, and he didn't care. He's come to see Walter Stobert. He said that his name was Helmut Schwindt. Apparently you were friends many years ago."

Stobert's stomach turned a somersault. "What did you say?"

"He says to remind you of Vienna 1935. He says he has answers."

The silvery belly of the plane became a mirror reflecting the glaring sunlight. Andrés was going home, pleased that everyone had finally left. A vague melancholy settled inside him. It was just the void left by absent friends and family. As he left the terminal thinking about his ruined family, the likelihood of his niece being found alive, and the light the girl had always given off, he knew that he regretted nothing. All the suffering had been worth it. She would do more for humanity than the two people who'd been killed for selling her out would have done combined. They were just like Judas and his thirty pieces of silver. He was beset by doubt about this line of thinking, wondering whether it was compatible with his beliefs. Who was he to decide who was worthy of life and who wasn't? Who decided who was wise or righteous, who was better? Better in what way? Better because they were good, he said to himself, but deep down he knew that such definitions were relative. Even his rote answer to everything, "It's in God's hands," seemed insufficient given what had happened over the past few weeks. People made choices, and they were often bad ones. He knew that if he asked anyone he knew, they'd establish priorities: family first, the people I love, then those who are like me . . . That was it, he thought. Life had taught him that that was where it always began: with people who were similar to oneself. He'd spent enough time as an immigrant to understand that. It didn't matter where you went—that was the heart of it, as though we were nothing but a herd, a pack, or a pride.

Then he smiled to himself: *I think I know who can decide; the person who sacrifices himself can make the decision. When you give your life on behalf of the most deserving, then you have nothing to lose. There can be no deceit, lies, or selfishness.*

That was what our Lord did on the cross. From the cross he showed us who must live and die, and if I follow him, my choice shall always be the right one. More relaxed now, at peace with himself, he parked the car in its usual spot and went to visit his most recently opened store, knowing that he'd done the right thing. And although he felt terrible for his wife and children, they were well prepared. He had paved the way for them while little Michelle's life was only just beginning. The girl still had to learn, but she could do good—he knew that she would do good. Beto and Jonathan had embraced evil and would be punished for their sins. Play with fire . . . he, meanwhile, may have tried to do good, but he hadn't lived well enough, not enough to earn forgiveness, and that was what gave him most satisfaction about what he was doing. His final act had been to make things right, to help the needy and follow his conscience. Now that it had been made, he rejoiced in his choice. He had secretly called Don Adrian and found out about the plans of the evil horde known as the Mara: they would make his sister and niece pay; that much had been decided. If they couldn't touch Ethan, then they'd go for the people close to him. Their wrath was implacable, and they never forgot. He knew this, and he couldn't allow it. Even Calvo hadn't been sure what he was offering: it had taken him a long time to catch on and even longer to accept it.

Sometime later, the door to the shop opened, and a pair of girls dressed in gang clothing, youngsters no older than fifteen, came in. It upset him to see them starting so young, innocents dragged down into their pit of hatred and pain. Who had decided that he must die? A kid their age or an adult who had only known death for his entire life? A villain who chose between life and death depending on who was most like him or maybe, when it came to his fellow gang members, on just a passing whim. Filled with a sudden bout of empathy for these sheep in wolves' clothing, Andrés got up from his chair and walked over to them, raising his right hand as a symbol of forgiveness and mercy. "You still have time to reject Satan."

The girls exchanged a knowing glance and started to laugh with adolescent hysteria. The laughter separated them from the dull world of adults. He realized that they were the same as the others: they decided who deserved to live and who must die. It didn't matter who had given the order. Still laughing at him, they took automatic pistols out from their sweatpants and aimed at Andrés, who stood indifferently, looking down at them with a paternal expression. They fired six shots into his hand, mouth, and body, blinking with each discharge. After seeing the inert body fall, they fired one final shot to wipe out his face, removing his last human attribute so he would be remembered like that: an empty, featureless John Doe, nothing but orphaned flesh and blood. A victim, like them, of the *vida loca*. They emptied out the cash register and left to report to their boss, feeling nothing but pleasure at having completed a mission. They'd gotten rid of an old man whose final moments of pity they'd already forgotten.

11

Secret Societies

"Suffer no more" was just one of the slogans of the Universal Church of the Celestial Kingdom, but it had become the most famous. Research had told Ari and Michelle that it was a controversial community that had been accused of being a cult and ejected from the Union of Evangelical Churches, of which Andrés's church formed part. But it was only one of many amid the chaotic mixture of cults and blurred doctrines that had proliferated in the Americas. The church's history was plagued with accusations of money laundering and fraud across several different countries, but it had nonetheless been able to influence presidential elections and was expanding exponentially across the globe. Its followers now numbered in the millions.

After finding a discreet apartment that was less exposed and cheaper than a hotel, they bought food and SIM cards and prepared for their journey. Michelle's stress levels rose, as though she were about to take an exam. She struggled to choose an outfit and grew extremely tense, sometimes so much that she started to physically shake. She spent hours getting dressed, and Ari noticed that she'd covered a nervous rash with makeup.

Once they got out into the street, they paid no attention to their new surroundings; they went straight for the local church. They found it easily enough: it was prominently situated on a main road in front of a modern bus station. The two-story building was right in the middle of the block, but its brick facade suggested a vague neoclassical influence, with reflective glass windows and an immense atrium with four Doric columns that immediately caught the eye, making it stand out from its neighbors. The two women stepped into the atrium, where they were welcomed by several very friendly members of the church wearing white shirts, red ties, and beaming smiles. The timetable for the services was pinned to a notice board. They were held almost every hour under the guise of seminars on happiness and how to triumph with titles like "Congress for Success," "Meeting to Cure Body and Soul," and so on throughout the week. Ari and Michelle were overwhelmed by the different options. They smiled at their hosts and stepped outside in order to talk privately.

"They sound like movie titles. What shall we do? When will he come?"

"I don't know. What if he doesn't come on Saturdays?"

"Then we have no choice but to come every day until we find him. Let's go back inside."

The congregation members came over again. They were just as friendly as before but now more curious. "Boa tarde, irmãs. É a primeira vez de vocês?"

Ari didn't understand a word and kept her mouth shut.

Michelle answered in Spanish, but she was flustered and sounded like a teenager. "We're traveling, but we didn't want to miss a service. So we came . . ."

The answer seemed to arouse more curiosity, although everyone remained relaxed. What were they doing there if they didn't speak Portuguese?

Meanwhile Ari instinctively trusted her bad pronunciation. "Suffer no more!"

The ushers' faces lit up while those farther off repeated the phrase in watery, Portuguese-inflected Spanish.

"Suffer no more! Suffer no more! God be praised!"

They were enveloped in a wave of empathy and acceptance. Faith didn't need communication.

Ari and Michelle went to the church every day that week. Rather than helping Michelle to relax, the repetition made her even more nervous. She vomited before each visit while her skin seemed to age visibly and her personality withdrew into itself. This, paradoxically, appeared to endear them to their fellow churchgoers, especially after they'd contributed to the collection, not that they had much choice given that it was requested a quarter of an hour after they'd stepped through the door and then again an average of three times per session.

The first surprise was the hall, which was more like an auditorium than a church. It was an airy, double-heighted construction with a ceramic floor, white walls, and a false ceiling with neon lights and hundreds of red chairs that were always filled, flanked by hundreds of other churchgoers who'd arrived later and had to stand. Michelle scanned the crowd, looking for a particular face while staying anonymous herself, which wasn't easy. Meanwhile, Ari was forced to observe what was going on without understanding a word. At first she was just bored, but she soon grew irritated. The pattern was replicated again and again. There were no decorations other than a fake stained glass window and a plastic pulpit with a blue LED cross. A raised stage was constantly being crisscrossed by church employees leading believers to and fro, serving the pastor, handling the public, and preparing the offerings, which could be made by cash in velvet bags or by card. Michelle and Ari ended up paying an average of thirty dollars per service. Apparently, this ensured that they'd avoid any further scrutiny.

The pastor, who dressed either in white or in gray pinstripe pants, always seemed to announce something important on his arrival; then he read a phrase from a book that Ari assumed was a Bible. He never moved away from the pulpit but, like on a talk show, invited those present to come up on stage to share their experiences. Images were projected on a screen, and every twenty minutes, a social issue was introduced as an excuse to ask for more contributions, ostensibly to pay for more churches, provide help to poor communities, or to support women and children in need. Every request had a goal, just as every instructive lesson had a protagonist. The first was an ordinary-looking man in a striped shirt who desultorily described the marijuana addiction that had brought him there. The sinner droned on like a bureaucrat listing municipal regulations while the pastor added the spice with questions, thoughts, and exclamations, all of which were applauded by his audience. Eventually the pastor deemed the sinner saved and proved it by making him smell the contents of a bag. The regretful man stepped back, stating in his monotone voice that he couldn't stand it—he didn't know what it was, but it made him sick. To general amazement, the pastor announced that it was marijuana. Thanks to prayer, the addict could no longer stand it.

The ceremonies turned out to be a series of miracles and payments punctuated with musical performances that occasionally spurred spasmodic dancing in the front rows. A young woman overcame terminal cancer, a dull office worker got a wonderful job, a single mother won back her partner, while a serial seducer gave up his lovers and now celebrated a life in Christ. The boundaries between religion and magic show appeared to have been torn down.

Ari soon saw the reason for the church's success. Its promise was transactional: the more one paid, the greater the benefits would be. On the third day, she heard something called "the theology of prosperity." She became increasingly frustrated, but she did nothing.

Their fourth visit was on a Saturday. Ari, now very annoyed, expected a new set of hokey miracles, but this time the congregation was much larger than on the previous days. The pastor solemnly announced that the devil lurked among them. After her intensive linguistic immersion, Ari was picking up a lot more. She knew that she hadn't misheard. The pastor was accusing someone, and the hair on the back of her neck stood on end. Had they been found out? To her relief, the same pastor, taking a calculating, defiant pose, invited the demon to show himself. Four women of different ages stood up amid general murmuring and were led by members of the leadership to the stage.

The moment he called them, the possessed started to walk along, gesturing frantically, with bestial expressions, staring up at the ceiling, more or less as one would imagine a possessed person might act. Although they were supposedly controlled by the devil himself, they seemed happy to wait quietly at the back of the stage as the pastor interviewed them one by one, microphone in hand. The interviewees waved their arms and bodies around, shook their heads back and forth, and answered the questions in deep voices, amid demoniacal laughter. Providing polite answers to each question, they dutifully explained how and when they had taken hold of their victim (led astray by an evil lover or through pagan practices) and their objective (to cause suffering, disease, and death among the young) and then allowed themselves to be exorcized with surprising passivity, especially the one who'd just seen three demons have the same thing done to them. Together with their freedom, each lucky victim also happened to be cured of a mortal ailment. Eventually, Ari couldn't stand another minute. But now this festival of extortion took on unsuspected new dimensions: ritual dances broke out all over the place, and more and more worshippers joined them, starting to roll around the floor until the smug preacher invited them to accept Christ. One of the most pathetic characters was a dirty cripple whose leg was missing below the thigh. He wore a frayed khaki jacket and pants and a shoe with holes in the sole and used his weathered crutches to lever himself onstage to roll around on the floor with the others and receive the pastor's blessing.

Michelle went pale. "It's him. Oh my God. Oh, Lord God, it can't be!"

Michelle's knees buckled, and Ari caught her before she hit the floor. She looked in the same direction, but all she could see was a sorry excuse for a man allowing himself to be consoled with melancholy passion. Michelle got hold of herself and stared at him, suppressing a gag reflex.

"No, Lord. Please, holy Virgin, it can't be. It can't be him."

Colônia Liberdade, 1976

Helmut Schwindt was wearing a half-open Hawaiian shirt. He looked like a lost tourist. He'd certainly gone out of his way. The greeting between old friends wasn't especially affectionate. Stobert introduced himself as Aspiazi, and they shook hands, headed away from their bodyguards, and went for a walk on the pretense of taking a tour of the compound.

"How did you find me?"

"Things went well for me after the war. I went to Africa to train indigenous troops and was very well paid for it. Then I moved to Switzerland to set up a private security firm. I had a good relationship with the Algerian *pieds noires*, and that gave me an in with France. Odessa took me back to Germany. Following the rise of the Viet Minh, my services as an instructor were required again, and so my investments diversified. My contacts with the OAS and Spanish regiment were crucial. Today I run a network in Europe financed by the CIA." He smiled ironically. "The communists have been very lucrative for me. As you can imagine, it wasn't very difficult to track you down. I was surprised to find you in this remote corner of the world."

"But you're not surprised by my appearance or my temperature. That makes you the first."

"I have spent much time over the past few years studying. Getting into the protection industry helped; I made contact with families with long histories, former aristocrats, Dutch and Swiss bankers . . . the military past from which we shy in public makes us seem more reliable in private. Word of my interest in the esoteric spread."

"I don't remember your being interested in such things. It was me that talked about—"

"That's true. It was you, until the night we killed your uncle. The chief didn't understand—he was a fool, an idiot with all the intelligence of a lead pipe—but I know what I saw that night. Ever since then, I have developed a . . . passion for the subject that eventually became an obsession."

"You mean you joined a cult like my uncle?"

"No, that wasn't possible. But I did learn a lot. There are circles at the highest level that propagate ancient beliefs, rituals dating back to the Neolithic period. Neither of us could ever gain access to such societies. It's strictly controlled by birthright. Listen to me: I have investigated secret circles: Rosicrucians, spiritualists, magicians like Aleister Crowley . . . they're all frauds. They only con the gullible . . . charlatans who offer nothing but empty promises. But as my company became more prestigious, I got a commission from an old contact: certain groups required special, exclusive, discreet services. These were leading families, surnames I'd seen in advertisements and magazines, people with an incredible amount of power. I became a guardian of what they called their 'ancient worship.' They made me a multimillionaire."

"Did you meet anyone like my uncle?"

"No. I never attended one of their rituals; I'm ineligible. I don't know their ways. But even so, I know that your uncle was feared in those circles. In certain corners, his name is still whispered with caution. And just think that none of them saw what we saw. If they knew what happened that night, if they knew about you, they'd hunt you down wherever you are in the world. They wouldn't hesitate to pay more money than you can possibly imagine to possess you. To study you."

"What happened that night?"

Schwindt frowned as though he'd suddenly switched languages. "What do you mean?"

"I can't remember a thing. I remember nothing from that accursed night in Vienna!"

Henrique, looking nondescript and bereft, left the church and limped laboriously down a back alley. Several blocks farther on, he heard a foreign woman's voice.

"Henrique!"

A pair of women he didn't know were trying to get his attention. The shorter one was speaking to him in Spanish.

"Hello, Henrique. Do you remember me?"

He was hit by a wave of disturbing memories but couldn't tell which applied. She came closer and took hold of his wrist. There was no anger in her gaze, only compassion.

"It's Michelle, Henrique. I was seventeen when you last saw me. Don't you remember me?"

"M . . . Michelle . . ."

"You've been sending me money for the girl."

"Yes, yes. I . . . I've been sending it. When I can."

Michelle hadn't come to confront him; all she conveyed was reassurance. She stroked his face. "I know. Thank you."

Henrique, overwhelmed by this reunion, started to cry. He looked down, avoiding their gazes. "I'm so sorry."

Michelle took him by the chin and lifted his face. "I forgave you many years ago. We just want you to tell us something. Will you tell us?"

"Yes . . . what?"

"Do you live close by?"

"Yes, close by. In a room . . ."

"Would you like something to eat? We'd like to take you out for a meal, if that's OK?"

Henrique allowed himself to be led to a nearby restaurant, where he asked for a glass of water. It took Michelle and Ari a long time to persuade him to have something to eat, but when the food came, he devoured it with long-accumulated hunger. His sunken eye sockets conveyed nothing but misery and resignation. Michelle brought up the time they'd spent together to help him to remember, but he stopped her, saying that he remembered very well: she was as beautiful as ever. Then he let out a brief sob, and she moved to reassure him some more, stroking his thin hair.

"Why, Henrique? Can you tell us? We know that you fathered other girls like my daughter; we just want to know why."

Ari was dumbstruck by Michelle's calm poise. There was no anger, only pity. This man had ruined her life but now was just a ghost of the person he'd once been. Ari wondered how she'd have reacted in Michelle's place. She'd probably have killed him.

Henrique began a stuttering tale from which he broke off every now and again to mumble something to himself before tuning back in. He was slowly getting used to talking in Spanish.

"Michelle, I . . . *sinto muito*, we never really knew each other. I lied; I sinned. I did a lot of harm to *você* and a lot of others. Other poor, innocent, young *meninas*. I'm responsible. I'm a criminal." He grabbed his stump. "And I've been punished by God."

Looking at this man, who had once been the love of her life, Michelle was overcome by feelings of nostalgia and futility.

"I was born in a religious village, founded by Germans. Do you know about the German immigrants to Brazil? A lot came in the nineteenth century to found colonies."

"Colônia Liberdade?" Ari interjected.

Henrique recoiled at the mere mention of the place but recovered his composure. "Before, it had a different name, but my grandfather changed it. I don't know when, but I do remember that he was always the leader. The community lost its religion, and he controlled everything. He's still alive and still there. He decided on everything—he decided who the sinners were, and he punished them. He was a messiah, a prophet; everyone obeyed him. My brother and I lived very well because we were his grandchildren, understand? My mother was Uruguayan, and we learned Spanish from her. You had to get permission from my grandfather to get married or have children. He paid for our schooling and made sure we'd learn Spanish because later he was going to send us out to find girls outside Brazil."

"And I was one of those girls?"

"*Você* were the second. They taught us to do it." He covered his face, avoiding their gaze. "We were born into royalty: nine cousins, five boys and four girls fathered by my father and his brother. We were the grandchildren of the Lord. We could do anything we wanted. They said that we were pure, but it wasn't true. The male grandchildren had it all—we had drugs and a lot of money. The women couldn't say no. We lived in sin, and we didn't care. We went to the city in luxury cars, spending our cash like rich kids without a thought for any-one but ourselves. But my girl cousins were locked away. They weren't allowed out. They just prayed, and after they turned eight, we barely saw them again." Henrique stopped and broke into an absurd-sounding sob, more of a whistle, his face still covered. Finally, he continued very quietly. "We never saw our girl cousins. Much later I learned that we were all my grandfather's playthings. He was obsessed with having female descendants; he only cared about *meninas*. He started with my cousins, doing experiments on them, drugging them and speaking to them in their sleep. The first two were killed by cocktails of drugs; the two others made a plan and killed themselves. Their lives had been hell. We didn't know that then, and we didn't care. I had grown up by then and lived outside of Brazil. My brother found out all this much later. My father and uncle knew, and they allowed it. When my brother found out, he told me, and then he committed suicide too. He couldn't stand it. He knew other things he didn't tell me about, but he killed himself."

Henrique gasped for breath. Michelle suppressed the terror building up inside of her. She feigned indifference and offered Henrique more food. He asked if they could go somewhere else.

"You want to go home?"

"No, I just need some air. To catch my breath."

"But you hear the voices, don't you?"

"There are no voices," Stobert answered sharply. "None at all."

"You have the dreams, Walter. I know that. It affected me, too, although in my case it was just an echo. Nothing entered me, and yet I still hear it from the void. It chases me in my dreams. I tremble just to think about it. The presences took refuge in you; there was no other vessel. They can only be transferred to a relative."

Stobert spun around like a wounded animal. "How do you know that? What are you talking about? You're crazy! We both went mad that night! It was an adolescent fantasy we never got over. What about the chief? He was there—did he see anything?"

"He couldn't see a thing. He was an idiot."

"It's just an old wives' tale. You're a victim of your own superstitions."

"Your hypnotic gaze, Walter, your abilities. I've heard all about your strange cult, your unnatural magnetism."

"It's called collective hysteria!"

Schwindt raised his chin as though he were receiving an order. His voice grew slower and more portentous. "Do you know why I haven't handed you over to those who would welcome me into their circles for just such a gift? When it would be my ticket into the oligarchy that runs this planet?"

Stobert didn't want to hear another word about this madness. But suddenly, a monstrous tremor ran through his body. It came from beyond, from the abyss that had settled in his soul. The weird, incomprehensible language was speaking through him, using him as its puppet. He shivered. "Because the voices ordered you to serve me."

Schwindt's arrogance suddenly disappeared. He now looked like a small rodent. "Then you do know. You can't deny the truth, Walter. It's not you they obey. It's the presences. Just like me, damn it. And yet I place at your service the empire I have built for reasons that shall not benefit me in any way whatsoever. We were cursed that night. Both of us."

"I only wanted to serve the party! If we'd taken the book, we'd have become—"

"What? What were we? A pair of schoolboys trying to prove ourselves in the lowliest party cell run by a tavern drunk who snored while we dreamed. Do you know what we'd have become? What we are: a pair of pariahs. It took me a long time to realize that, but I did. There was no book. Where did you get that nonsense? Who told you about it?"

"I can't remember. I was an orphan; I was raised by my aunts. They had no contact with him, but there were always whispers. They were afraid of him. Why do you think the book wasn't there?"

"I spent years looking for your supposed grimoire . . . all the books about the supposedly arcane arts are nothing but fakes, frauds, hoaxes."

"What about those secret circles you were talking about?"

"Your uncle didn't belong to those groups. I don't know what his affiliation was or where he came from. I imagine it's an oral tradition, like the druids. It works by direct lineage, and that's what matters. Did your uncle have any children or grandchildren? I couldn't find any records after the war. Do you remember having a cousin?"

"Maybe . . . maybe, yes. I remember something, but if they did exist, they died of influenza."

Schwindt's face darkened. "Then listen to me, Walter. More than your life depends on it."

The three of them walked at an exasperatingly slow pace to the shore of the river, where Henrique started to relax. Once there, they looked for somewhere to sit down, and he battled against himself to continue the story.

"Grandfather was terrifying; we were happy not to see him. Once we became adults, our duties as grandchildren were explained to us. He had a list of families that we were to seek out. We had to father daughters with women from those families. Like I did with you. We had to seduce the woman and ensure that the baby was a girl. If it was a boy, we had to try for a girl later on. They didn't want boys. If it was a boy, we had to arrange an abortion or anything else, just so long as we produced a girl later on. It was hard, very tough. It was how we lived, but I never gave it a second thought. Sometimes I felt lonely and sad, but we were given everything we could possibly want."

Michelle bristled. "What list? I was on that list?"

"They told me your grandmother's surname and where your family was: the country and city. They knew everything; I just had to look for female descendants. Your mother was too old for me. I was twenty-two or twenty-three. So I chose you. That was how it was with all of them—I never knew more. Only Grandfather knew. That was our world: we didn't ask questions. We never considered refusing to do what we were told. Later, of course, after acting that way for many years, we started to have doubts. We didn't live at the colony anymore and started to think differently. One of the cousins wanted to marry a girl who gave him a son and promised to have a girl in exchange, but they were both killed to teach us a lesson. They took the baby out of her belly right in front of him to make an example of it. My brother was smarter. He found out what they didn't want him to know: he found out about my girl cousins. He sought me out to tell me. He had realized that we were monsters for fathering girls like that. We were just the same as they were. He had learned more but decided not to tell me. But he did make me swear that we would never again make any more daughters. Then he killed himself. I had eight daughters I never met, and everything started to get more difficult. I thought hard, suffered, and didn't know what to do. In the end, after the accident, I was no use to them anymore." He touched his stump. "I went back there, but they rejected me. They didn't care about me. They threw me out. I didn't have a job. I didn't know how to do anything. I didn't have any experience. I ended up begging and sleeping in doorways. Fortunately, my friend found me and helped."

"What friend? From the colony?"

"Yes, I often went back to ask for help from outside. Some days they gave me some, and on others they didn't. One day they said that if I ever came back, there would be trouble. My friend Santiago lives there, and he helped me. They allowed it because I'm a grandchild. He brought me to Joinville and taught me how to claim social security and look for odd jobs, some Spanish classes, customer service . . . and he brought me a little money from them every month so I'd never go back. I know that they allow it so they'll never have to see me again. I tried to kill myself, too, but I was too afraid. Then I started to come to the church, and I remembered my brother and my cousins, who never received help from anyone. And I realized that I had never helped anyone either. I searched for the mothers of my daughters. I found five, but two of them had lost their daughters and never answered me. I sent as much help to the other three as I could. And my life changed. I work when I can, and the money I have goes to the church and my daughters. I keep some to pay for my room and for food. And so I try to make up for all the evil and sins I have committed. Now I have my faith in God."

"The two of them who lost their daughters: Did they tell you how it happened?"

"No. I never heard. I heard from people I knew, like when I came looking for you. They said that they didn't have the girls anymore. I wrote but never heard from them."

Michelle was trying to stay calm.

"Henrique. There's something that I don't know if your brother knew about. I think that your grandfather always did the same thing. They kidnapped my daughter and brought her to him, maybe the other two girls too. I think maybe all of them. I think they spied on them, took them, and brought them here. We have a list. I want you to look at it so you can tell me if your other two daughters are on it. I need you to tell me everything you know, Henrique, anything that might help us. Do you understand?"

"No . . . that can't be. It can't be true. It can't . . ." Henrique began to shake like he was in front of a giant insect. An insect that fed on his guilt. "Não pode . . . Não pode."

The sky turned dark at an ominous wink from Schwindt. The clouds roiled as he continued his story.

"As the years went by, I began to hear myths and legends. At first I didn't believe them, but later I found that they're taken seriously by those at the top level. Not that I've ever found any corroborating evidence. People whispered about necromancers, secret gatherings at which incomprehensible beings were summoned, dark secrets that predate writing, passed down by blood until the fall of the last European empires. Bloodlines that were wiped out by the two world wars. I heard all manner of superstition. Until an antiques collector led me to an old Polish peasant who described a pagan ritual a noble had performed on his sister in Greater Russia when he was just a boy. It was his most vivid memory. The ritual, Walter, was the same as the one I saw your uncle perform in Vienna. That half-mad peasant had been affected, just like me."

Stobert began to feel dizzy. "Who was my uncle? A kind of witch?"

"I don't know. I don't know if they really existed. And if he was, why allow himself to be killed? Think of your power, Walter, the way you control people. He could have made us eat our own insides before we became a threat. That bothered me for decades. I wondered if it was because of your family ties, a weakness he had for his nephew. Or maybe you had disappointed him, and this was his punishment."

"I barely knew that creepy old man."

"I don't have any answers, just theories. Listen, nothing is written down, nothing about these people, just rumors and folktales. On my travels, I crossed the Iron Curtain, and the most fruitful source of stories came from remote farms in Ukraine, fragments of memories from before the revolution. They refused to talk about the strangers, not even in tales by the campfire. They feared them even more than the nobles, with whom they had some relationship I couldn't determine. They had mastered some kind of . . . dark art that was transmitted directly to their children and grandchildren of both genders. The important thing was that the lineage never be broken. The lore was based around the transmission of . . . the presence of a master onto their disciple before they died. Think of a slave master controlling the most wretched creature you can imagine, passing on their unique knowledge and power but only so the creature can escape and swallow up the unfortunate victim."

Stobert felt a lump in his throat and grew even colder.

"Transmission of the presence to one's own blood and the ability to control it through dark knowledge. The greatest risk, the only thing they were afraid of, was dying without ejecting it from within them first. Otherwise . . ." Schwindt shivered. "They had to transmit it and the apprentice had to receive it so they would become the new master. That opened my eyes. If your uncle had lost his children, might he have transmitted it to you, Walter? Could we have provoked him? And if you die without passing it on to someone else—"

"Quiet! Don't you think I worry about that every day?"

"But not all my questions were answered. You're not a direct descendant, so you couldn't be the recipient. This raised another question: What happened in cases like your uncle's, when they lost their offspring? It wasn't uncommon. That's where their servants, the vassals, come in. One of them gave me an old manuscript he'd treasured for many years. It was no more than a list, a set of names they called 'vessels.'"

"You said that there was nothing written down."

"And this might not be real, but I'd like you to take a look." Schwindt reverently handed over a yellowing, moldy parchment.

"These names are all connected. They look like family trees."

"Exactly. To them, other humans are simply livestock, and that includes nephews or even children that haven't been initiated. That is why they raised a parallel lineage with their servant girls, peasants, or orphans; it didn't matter. They had plenty of bastards: empty vessels to whom the presence could be transferred until another master recovered it. These were the recipients. And if the recipient died without passing it on, they were still cursed, but who cared?"

"You're telling me that I was my uncle's vessel?"

Stobert could feel the voices close by. Voices from a frozen hell beyond his understanding.

Schwindt shook the page. "You haven't read the list properly. Doesn't it remind you of something?"

"My uncle . . . my uncle had a list?"

"That's what I believe. It was the only document we were able to obtain that night."

"Where is it? Did you keep it? No, it must have disappeared decades ago." His brain lit up with a solution. "Forget it—I have two sons and a grandson on the way. They can be my vessels."

"We need to get the list. Your uncle must have been a great master to be able to use you, but I doubt we'll be able to. Your children are a long way from the original source; we can't take the risk. You need to return to the main branch—you need to mix the two bloodlines again and join them both together. Your offspring will produce offspring with the people on that list. The list was never lost. You know very well who kept it: the man who posed as our leader."

"Our section chief. Is he alive? Have you found him?"

"He was much easier to find than you were. He never saw combat, never left his hometown, and as Austria wasn't de-Nazified, he was never pursued. He didn't even have to hide. He got fatter and fatter like a pig, and now he's a venerable town councillor. You must come with me to Europe, Stobert."

"I don't know if it's a good idea to go back to Austria."

"We'll meet him in Switzerland. He'll come to us."

Michelle and Ari went back to the apartment without saying a word. They each went to their own room. Time seemed to slow down. Each minute shattered into shards, and sleep never came. Michelle was wide awake with a lump in her throat so painful she couldn't even cry. Henrique had been overwhelmed by what she'd told him. He hadn't been able to go on. They'd left him their number, just in case, but weren't very hopeful. Then they'd made contact with Caimão, the mercenary, and arranged to meet the next day. But this prospect didn't help Michelle out of the pit in which she found herself. The image of the girls locked up and forced to produce children made her heart race until she began to hyperventilate. She stood up, gasping, and wished she were dead. She destroyed everything she touched. Even worse, her entire life had been a lie; everything she'd done had been to help someone else. She'd tainted the only pure thing she'd ever known.

She destroyed everything she touched, corrupted and ruined it. Nothing about her was useful or healthy. All she could think about was the punishment she deserved. She didn't care what it was so long as those around her were unharmed. Michelle wrapped herself up in the sheets, thinking about saving Michi and about disappearing, being consumed by darkness. Fading away.

Halfway through the night, she was frightened by a shadow at her door. A sleepy Ari was leaning on the frame.

"I know you're awake. I could hear you tossing and turning."

Michelle didn't know what to say, while Ari didn't know what to do.

"I don't know what you're feeling, but I can imagine what you're thinking. This is a completely irrational situation. I'm struggling to process it myself. But it's obvious that they didn't take Michi to . . . they waited until you were . . . old enough to . . . you know. They didn't come looking for you at twelve years old. Whatever happens, you don't have to worry about Michi. They went to a lot of trouble; she must be very valuable to them."

Then Ari left just as abruptly as she'd arrived. However, her curt words were a balm. Michelle was still upset, but now her anguish had been reduced to manageable levels. She was able to cry under the pillow for the rest of the night.

The Grande Dixence, 1977

At six in the morning, the impressive view of the Grande Dixence dam was at its absolute best. Swathed in the early-morning mist and completely devoid of visitors, it looked like a futuristic complex abandoned by a civilization that had melted into the mountains. It was a ghostly wall, a thousand-foot drop into an unseen valley. The rainstorms of the previous weeks had accelerated the ice melt, and the safety sluices had been opened, letting out a thunderous roar of gushing water. The sluice gates, which were functioning at maximum capacity, produced a furious waterfall that fell as a funnel into a hazy white chasm, a raging maelstrom that sent foam rising back over their heads hundreds of feet above.

To one side of the cascade was a parked Citroën DS, the famous Shark, while a yellow BMW E21 emerged from the cloud of water and parked a few feet away. Out of it stepped a rotund, bald Teutonic man with a small moustache and a nervous demeanor. He wrapped himself up in his coat and hat, which he had to hold on to, to prevent from flying into the gorge. Leaning on the railings overlooking the abyss were two individuals. One of them had gone hatless while the other was wearing an *ushanka*. They both wore long Barbour jackets.

Their greetings, said from a distance, were drowned out by the roar of the water. The mayor walked closer, but even when he was a foot away, he had to shout to be heard. Schwindt and Stobert stretched out their hands. He was sweating nervously, in spite of the cold.

"Please, I've done no harm to anyone! My life, my family, everything will be ruined if my past comes to light! I'm a respectable man!"

"Do you have the list?"

"Yes, I have it right here, just like you asked."

"Why did you keep it?"

"To be honest, I don't know! I didn't take it to the party; all that shit about mystical cults was just nonsense! Your uncle was a Mason and deserved to die! But I never felt like throwing away these stupid parchments! My wife has asked me about them several times when she was tidying up, but just the mention of them makes me angry!"

Schwindt and Stobert looked through them. Their former chief patted them on the back out of camaraderie. As one, they grabbed him by the lapels and dragged him over to the railings.

"No, no! What are you doing? I did what you asked! No, no!"

The body fell into the foam at the bottom, the scream swallowed up by the noise from the sluice gates. Every trace of him had disappeared by the time he hit the bottom. The two comrades got into the Shark to look through the pages. They found their answer in some notes in the margins.

"This is what your uncle wasn't counting on. Look: peasants, day laborers, nobodies. But after the breakup of the Austro-Hungarian Empire, there was a major migratory movement across Europe—entire villages set out for America. He wrote something down here when he went to look for vessels: nobody was left."

Like so many things in life in which one places great expectations, the moth-eaten page was a disappointment to Stobert. It contained just five names; he'd been expecting dozens. "Do you know how we'll find them?"

"I know little more than you. I barely know the terms of the ritual. You need to mix the bloodlines and then test each girl in her dreams until you find one that is sufficiently receptive for the transition to occur naturally."

"Why a girl? What about the boys?"

Schwindt was surprised by the question. "The boys? Do you really not remember anything about Vienna?"

"No, I don't know what you're talking about."

"The mansion burned down to its foundations. I can't remember how the fire began; it was all too chaotic. Your uncle brandished a weapon and called us ruffians, fools, and bandits. Our section chief fired at him, and you tried to help him, but he grabbed on to you like a leech and said something I couldn't hear, making gestures I didn't understand. Both of you fell into a trance, as though you were asleep, but just for a few minutes. When you woke up, he was dead. Also . . . ," he stammered, "we weren't alone. I saw someone else, a translucent figure. Oh God, there was a girl there with us, something like the ghost of a girl. I can't explain why, but I know it will only work with a girl."

The meeting with Caimão was set for midafternoon in the town park, a green area with a row of trees that provided shady privacy for their meeting. It was to take place in a paved circle similar to a map of the world with a ring of stone benches around it. The gray sky suggested that a storm was coming; dark clouds prowled around like packs of fantastical animals. A tall, imposing-looking young man was sitting on one of the benches looking at his iPhone. His hair was shaved into graffiti-like symbols. He wore a tight-fitting sleeveless vest that showed off his swollen pecs, designer pants, and sneakers. He clearly took care of himself, adopting an aesthetic made famous by soccer players. When he saw them come into the park, he narrowed his eyes like a hunter and met them with a smile and impeccable English.

"Welcome. I'm Caimão. No one told me that my clients would be so pretty. I was expecting a pair of pale gringos."

Ari spat into the sand in disdain before speaking. "I guess it's only to be expected. You just assume that your clients are going to be white men. You weren't expecting a Latina and a black woman. Are you racist, man? Because my father was a Latino, so I'm no good to you there either. If it bothers you, we can go."

Ari's skin gleamed dark and tough in the sunlight while her curly hair cascaded down over her shoulders, bouncy and chaotic. Her nicely featured face, with its spread eyes and fleshy lips, was similar enough to Michelle's to suggest that Ethan had a type. She wasn't tall, but her legs were athletic, long, and strong, making her look bigger. Her body was tough and toned, her breasts small, and her abdominals were naturally well defined. Everything about her screamed warrior.

Caimão laughed with forced joviality. "Don't be like that, honey. I was just glad to see how pretty you are. White women are soft and brittle—their flesh is spongy, and they move like puppets. It's a pleasure for me to deal with such pretty clients. Once the job is done, I'd love to show you the beaches of this lovely state."

"We came to do business, but obviously that's not going to happen," Ari said to Michelle, turning around.

Caimão blocked their path, amused. "Where are you going? Don't be so sensitive. Let's sit down. Or would you rather go for a drink someplace nice? Everyone around here knows me. I have friends in all the right places. I get free drinks wherever I go. It's because of the music. I'm friends with a lot of musicians, you know. Famous ones. Or we can talk in the park. It's dangerous here—people get mugged. But you won't have anything to worry about with me. It's all under control."

Ari began to feel the aggression building up inside of her. "I'm shaking in my boots, you bastard."

He towered over her. "You should be. This isn't a safe place for a pair of pussycats."

Michelle tried to come between them, and just the feel of her thumb on his bicep magically seemed to calm him down. He was a textbook ladies' man. She bet that this alpha male's aura was navy blue fading to black. The darkness put her off.

"Excuse me; I don't think we've been introduced. My name is Michelle, and this is Ari. What an ox!" Her laugh was an octave higher than usual. "Forgive me—it's Caimão, isn't it? I don't know if I'm pronouncing it properly."

"You pronounce it like a forest nymph."

"Oh, don't be silly, you. Honey, you haven't even given us a chance to introduce ourselves. You're too aggressive." She wrinkled her nose in a childish way.

Caimão laughed with pride. "I'm warm blooded."

"We've come a long way, and this is very important to us." She stifled another patently false sigh.

Caimão blushed. "OK, you're right. So much beauty all at once drives me crazy. But you have to promise me that you'll let me show you all the most beautiful places in Santa Catarina."

Michelle went to sit down next to him while Ari stayed standing.

"I hear you want to steal something from some Mennonites."

"Mennonites? No, they stole something from us."

"They're not Mennonites. They worked with the dictatorship. They're very dangerous," Ari interjected.

Caimão winked and frowned. "That changes things. What is it you want to get back?"

"I'll take care of that. I need you to get me inside and then provide the usual backup. I'd like to get hold of some long-range weapons—is that possible?"

Caimão slapped his knee, as though she'd told a good joke, and said, "You're coming in with us?"

"Us?"

"I don't know you, and if we're going into a compound that had something to do with the dictatorship, I'm not going alone. I already have the guy in mind: 4:20." He winked at Michelle. "He's nuts, but you'll love him. He collects weapons. You won't find more firepower outside the gangs. He's got an AK-47 with a GP-25, a grenade launcher. Just in case we have to knock down any walls. I'll give him a call, and the four of us will meet up tonight. I'm going to take you to some very pretty places."

Ari and Michelle debated at length over how much they should put up with in exchange for help. Michelle shared Ari's frustration and had no problem with the way she'd treated Caimão, but she was still willing to accept his help. Really, she said, it wasn't so different from what she'd experienced her whole life. She even offered to go to the "meeting" alone. She'd been caught in worse traps. Ari was exasperated by her sanguine reaction and ended up accompanying her to a tropical bar on what seemed to all intents and purposes to be a double date. Caimão was constantly showing off, saying hello to every girl in the bar who passed by, especially the more provocatively dressed ones.

"See, my dear? I'm not interested in white women. They're nothing to me."

4:20 was much shorter than his friend but just as muscled and spoke the same tourist-oriented English. In spite of his moniker, the drug he offered "to make the night memorable" was cocaine, and although Ari managed to get them to guarantee that they'd be a part of the raid on the colony and that they'd be supplied an assault rifle each, as well as the grenade launcher (he showed them photographs and videos as though it were a baby), he seemed just as uninterested in the mission as Caimão, whose only goal appeared to be to get Michelle to dance with him.

"What you need is to dance. You've never danced like this before. We're the best dancers in the world. You can't imagine how good 4:20 is at dancing; he can dance with your stuck-up friend all night. He'll wear her out."

Michelle continued playing the bimbo role but turned down every offer. The evening soon split into two separate conversations as each would-be lothario focused on his assigned target. The music and lights had their numbing effect. Caimão and 4:20 tried as hard as they could to buy the drinks, but Michelle insisted on going to the bar herself, where she bought sodas for the women. Ari made it clear that she wanted to leave, but the two comrades-in-arms worked hard to keep the evening going for as long they could. 4:20 was more friendly and relaxed than Caimão, and his conversation wasn't so self-centered. In fact, it was almost pleasant, but he started to go to the bathroom, and every time he came back, he grew more rude and arrogant. Ari knew very well why that was, and when he came back from his third trip, she made sure to keep a healthy distance between them. She looked to Michelle for support, but she was busy putting up with Caimão's self-aggrandizing bluster. Then 4:20 appeared with a nonalcoholic drink for her. He seemed to have noticed her efforts to stay away and was trying to make up ground. The music continued to bore into her skull. Caimão put his hand on Michelle's thigh, telling her how sexy she was. The bass was shaking the table to the beat. 4:20 smiled, surrounded by pools of magenta and yellow in the darkness. He held the glass out to Ari, who took it, grateful for the change in his demeanor. He modestly called for a toast. The drums banged in her ears. Michelle was looking at them. Ari lifted the glass, but a woman's hand knocked it away, spilling some of it. Michelle's expression had turned wild.

"Ari! Did you get that drink?"

"It's not alcoholic!" 4:20 quickly interjected.

Ari saw what Michelle was saying and pushed 4:20. "What did you put in it, you son of a bitch?"

4:20 gaped and giggled a little. Caimão observed them from a distance while the tables around them went silent.

Ari pointed to the glass. "Drink it!"

4:20 blushed. "What do you mean?"

Ari held it out under his nose, and he took it as though he were accepting a challenge.

"I will!" But instead of doing so, he put it down. "I don't know what's going on, but maybe we should get out of here."

Ari couldn't tell whether he was guilty, but her blood was pumping. Before 4:20 realized what was happening, she'd hit him with the reverse of her elbow, knocking the table to the floor with a huge crash. 4:20 brought his hands to his bleeding nose but was then knocked off balance by a knee. He stumbled back into another drinker, who pushed him away angrily. Caimão then stepped over to punch the new guy, sending him all the way back to the wall. Ari and 4:20 were lifted up by a trio of bouncers, who unceremoniously ejected them from the bar. Caimão apologized to another while Michelle ran after Ari. The other group also came outside, their blood boiling, but Michelle, thinking very quickly, stood in front of a taxi, opened it, and pushed the disoriented Ari inside. 4:20 furiously started to shout insults while Caimão came out to prevent him from following them.

The Jackal stepped out of the plane. He didn't like the airport, he didn't like the country, and he didn't like the climate. He was awaited by Thiago, one of the Bloodhound's former assistants.

"We don't have any news as yet. Their administration guy is beating around the bush. I think they're going through some upheaval."

"The old man must still be in control. I remember how afraid my father and grandfather were of him. Let's get a team of top mercenaries together. Four SUVs full, just in case."

Thiago smiled. "So there's going to be some fireworks, boss?"

"No, but it's a cult, and you need to be careful with cults. Double or triple the bribes: the bosses, the guards, everyone that can be bought—however much it takes. There aren't many left. And keep them under surveillance. I don't want so much as a bicycle getting out without knowing who's riding it and where they're going. I want them to hand over the granddad, not a bloodbath."

The next morning, Michelle told Ari that Henrique had sent her a message and she was going to meet him. Ari didn't worry about her safety; Henrique didn't pose a threat. In fact, Ari didn't say a word—she just drank her coffee, upset that she'd ruined their only option. Michelle looked her in the eye and said, "You did the right thing. They're pigs."

Ari didn't answer. Depressed, she wandered around the small apartment, trying to think where they could go from there. She thought about going out for a walk. Then she started flicking through the television channels and ended up writing to Ethan to find out how he was doing. Ethan asked her about their progress and when they'd make the raid. His recovery was going well, and he still wanted to be a part of it. She told him about their unsuccessful encounter with the mercenaries. Like Michelle he told her that she was right, praising her actions. But he didn't offer up any new ideas, and his support wasn't a comfort to Ari. After they'd said goodbye, she just felt emptier and more of a failure. Finally, she found an answer. It wasn't about being right: it was about owning up to one's flaws. The only thing she'd ever known how to do.

Michelle came to a motel consisting of three floors in a U shape around a parking lot. The shabby rooms led off a main outdoor corridor. You had to climb up a fire escape to reach the upper floors. The facade was cracked, damp, and stained with urine and vomit. The halls were lit by a bare light bulb, and the general atmosphere was one of unhealthy neglect. Henrique lived among rooms belonging to prostitutes and drug addicts on the ground floor. His door had been left ajar. Michelle rapped on it with her knuckles and pushed it open. "Hello?"

A short corridor led to a bathroom and then a kitchenette with a table, two chairs, and an old television. Behind them was an opening onto a single cot in the shadows. Sitting on the table, Henrique was waiting with a man of a similar age but who looked in much better shape, both physically and economically. Henrique smiled at Michelle sweetly. Nothing about him reminded her of the playboy who had lit up her world when she was a teenager.

"Let me introduce you to my friend Santiago. He has helped me a lot over the past few years."

Ari returned to the same park, where the same large figure awaited her, although this time he wasn't playing with his phone. He gave her a welcoming smile. Without getting up, he got straight to the point.

"You called me. Here I am. You didn't bring your friend."

"And you didn't bring your 4:20."

"You said you wanted to talk. It'll be easier this way."

"I still need your guns and your help. I don't know if you have another reliable contact, but I don't have anyone else to go to."

Caimão sneered. This time, he was the one to spit. "You've got balls, no doubt about that. I saw your moves. Muay Thai?"

"And Kajukenbo, among others."

"And you know how to shoot, of course. You're some kind of Amazon?"

"If I were a man, I wouldn't have had to prove it to you. You would take my word for it."

Caimão shrugged. "I'm not passing you on to anyone else. I'm willing to continue working with you. The price stays the same. 4:20 comes with us and charges the same as me. They're his weapons."

"How can I trust him after what happened last night?"

"After the way you turned on him, I think you're the one who can't be trusted. Is that clear?"

"I don't know if we're going to make a good team."

"4:20 and I do, and that's good enough for me. Take it or leave it. I can start to check out the place right away. What you said about the dictatorship gave me an idea. A lot of those people have connections to martial arts; I can get information."

"And you can also sell me out for double what I'm paying you."

Caimão gave her an ambiguous smile. "I hadn't thought of that. It would be a good deal."

Ari didn't smile. Caimão reached behind his back and took out a small Walther P99. He held it out by the barrel so she could take the handle. Ari took it with her finger on the trigger.

Caimão continued to smile. "It's loaded. It's yours. You decide whether I can be trusted or not."

He let it go, and Ari pointed it at him.

He spoke to her as though she'd overlooked something important. "But why do you think I'd sell you out? They're just white pieces of shit."

His gleaming smile only increased her doubts.

When Ari got back, Michelle was waiting for her. When Michelle saw her, she jumped, trying to show joy and happiness, but it didn't work. Her happiness was forced and her expression empty.

"She's alive, Ari! She's alive and well. She's alive."

Santiago, Henrique's friend, had told Michelle that they had Michi and another girl in an old hospital that no one was allowed into. There was general consternation about the future of their leader, so much so that several families had fled. He also told her the best day to make their raid. Ari allowed herself to be hugged and told her about her meeting with Caimão. It seemed as though they had plenty to celebrate, and Michelle went downstairs to get a cake. Still, they were both more comfortable while she was in the store, when they were each alone and didn't have to pretend. Ari felt worse for Michelle than herself. Why couldn't she enjoy it? Had she been through too much to accept that something good had happened? And what counted as good after all they'd been through? Michelle came back and set out some candles as though it were some-one's birthday. A lonely birthday in a neutral space. Ari was encouraged by her willingness to make an effort to continue with the act: loneliness was even worse when you were with someone.

The false celebration lasted until Michelle went to bed, and Ari called Ethan to let him know about the latest developments. His admiring praise was a comfort. It was her progress he was praising, not the news. And Ari was encouraged by this return to reality, the fact that they could now plan the next step. They didn't have time for hope; it was a luxury they couldn't afford. The only thing that mattered was the next few days. Once they'd confirmed the date, Ethan bought his ticket without thinking twice about whether it was a good idea for him to come back. Ari didn't raise any objections.

Santiago, Henrique's friend, stopped on his return journey to help a Toyota that appeared to have broken down. He was promptly knocked out and abducted. Several hours later, the Jackal met Thiago in his suite.

"So? Who did he meet? What did he want?"

"He met one of the grandsons, one of the ones they used as an inseminator. He's a cripple now."

"I don't want his life story. Why did he go to see him?"

"It seems that they see each other quite regularly—they're old friends."

"I imagine you required him to be a bit more creative."

"Don't you know it. He didn't look that tough when we took him."

"How long did he hold out?"

"Almost three hours. He was still breathing when I left, but he wasn't going to last much longer."

"Well then, a true believer. See how well they're trained?"

"Oh, it wasn't that bad. It's just that sometimes the truth can be rather surprising."

"I'm all ears."

"Well, in the end it seems that it had nothing to do with the old man. One of the cripple's old girlfriends has apparently come looking for her daughter. She's one of the girls they're still holding on to. The cripple wants to help the mother get her daughter back."

"Don't tell me that you believed that."

"My initial reaction was the same as yours. The problem for him was that it was the first thing he said, before we'd even started. Who's going to believe something like that? But that's how stupid it was."

The Jackal laughed. "You're kidding."

"No. And he was telling the truth. In the end, once he'd lost his eyes, we had to believe him. It seems that the lady wants to break into the colony to rescue her. He told her about the security measures and told them to go during the anniversary celebrations."

"Hahaha! That's priceless." The Jackal cackled. "It's the funniest thing I've heard in a long time. She's really going for the daughter?" He paused to think. "She might be doing us a favor. It seems as good a day as any. They're trying my patience with their internal negotiations. We need to draw a line somewhere. The celebration is a good time—resistance will be at a minimum, and we'll be able to take him discreetly while they're distracted by their banquet and the guards are busy with the intruders. Tell the colonists about the raid. They'll thank us. Also, put the cripple under surveillance. I want to know when he shits, everything. Don't let them complain that we haven't made it easy for them."

The next day, Michelle went back to see Henrique and thank him again. She realized that their conversations were the highlight of his day. In his lonely eyes, eyes that had once been her whole life, she saw that he had made peace with his past. She started going back every day. They spent more and more time together, and her affection for him seemed to soothe an inner void that had been tormenting her. With physical attraction and personal interests out of the equation, she found that a purer relationship had bloomed. For the first time she felt free with a man without having to thank him or reject him, without fear of abuse or being chased. In contrast to the self-help books she'd read hungrily over the years, Henrique didn't offer up any answers or solutions; his only motivations were what she saw right in front of her. Nothing was conspiring for or against her. Nothing promised to give her what she needed. In Henrique she found a soul even more lost than she was, and his company kept her in a continuous present. His affection made sense to her for the time being. Nothing else existed. She even planned to introduce Michi to him without telling her who he was. The girl had a right to meet her father and maybe in the future to know the whole truth so she could decide for herself.

The final days before the raid were tense and dull; they seemed both to drag on and go by in a flash. Ethan arrived the morning before the agreed-upon date. They rented a car to go pick him up, but after her experience at the hospital, Michelle decided not to go, and Ari made no effort to persuade her. His flight was delayed, and she wandered through arrivals for an hour before a crowd of passengers surged out through the automatic doors. Then she saw Ethan; he was still walking with a pronounced limp, and his face was still covered in scars. When Ari went over to take his bag, he was so distracted by the worry in her eyes that he forgot to greet her.

"I've made a surprisingly fast recovery. With a medical girdle I can run and jump without any trouble—it keeps everything compressed. It's just a pinprick." Then he looked around. "Where's Michelle?"

"She decided not to come."

They stood awkwardly facing each other without touching. Then, after a few absurd moments, he stammered something and hugged her while she inhaled. She just wanted to smell him. It was Ethan. Ari was in denial about how much it reassured her to know that he was coming with her on the raid. They went straight to the last meeting before the operation, and on the way she shared her fears about whether Caimão and 4:20 could be trusted.

Caimão met them in his warehouse, giving Ethan a friendly smile and a pleasant welcome. He was the alpha male, but he didn't regard the intruder as a threat. 4:20 kept to a safe distance. Ethan tried to examine them and detect whatever might be hiding behind their beaming smiles, but all he could see was the Latin spark, a front they had long perfected. The two friends were an enigma. Caimão laid out several aerial images of the area and laughed.

"It's all a lot easier with Google Maps. The property is about a mile wide and four long, but we're only interested in a small part of it. The rest is crops and barns. The road leads to a wall with surveillance cameras, but the rest of the perimeter, which is pure jungle, is fenced off with triple barbed wire and cement posts every four feet. It's not even electrified. It's more a deterrent for livestock and casual passersby. I don't think it'll give us any trouble." He winked at 4:20. "We've broken into far more heavily fortified places."

"What about guards and staff?" Ethan said.

"That's the good part. You need to be careful of these people, my friends. I spoke to an old army captain, and he told me that they were once very mean. Even the army didn't mess with them. He said that even if a soldier disappeared, nothing would happen. That was how close they were to the high command. But that was before any of us were born. Now it seems more like a front they put on, scaring people with their tales of long ago. They say that today there are just over fifty colonists living there, compared to a thousand at its peak, and about fifteen have fled in the past month. Half of the cabins are uninhabited. I don't know what security staff they have, but they can't monitor the entire perimeter."

He highlighted several points on the satellite images. "This is the main entrance from the road. It heads right to the center, where the social buildings are, and that esplanade on the right is where they'll hold their anniversary celebration. I don't know what these houses are, but the old hospital is the building at the back, about half a mile to the left. That's very good for us. We can enter here, in this forested area. These sheds come before the hospital."

"For storage maybe?"

"I don't know, but they're a good hiding place. We can check out the area before going in. I don't think we'll see anyone, but it would be good to have a secure hideout. I imagine there'll be a couple of guards—nothing we can't handle. The most difficult part will be getting back with the package."

"What if it's not in the hospital?"

"That's the information you gave us, man," Caimão said with a laugh. "You tell us. 4:20 and I have no problem improvising." They bumped fists. "The most important part is getting around so we can come in from behind, from the jungle. If we pass through the town or go by the road, they'll be ready for us before we've even got close. Their neighbors have been living with them for half a century; they see everything. Which is funny because that's where we got our information too. It's easier to buy someone's conscience than their silence."

These words echoed around Ethan's head on their way back. He shared his doubts with Ari. He had no idea who they were working with. Ari stopped the car in front of the building and gave him the keys to the apartment.

"It's number three. I don't know if Michelle's still there or not. I'm going with them to check on the weaponry, but I need you to rest."

"You're going? Now? You can't go!"

Ari was frustrated by yet another example of his lack of sensitivity; it was almost endearing.

Ethan was still confused and upset. "I don't know. I was thinking . . . over the past few days, I've been thinking, and I'd like to talk . . . to you . . ."

"We'll have plenty of time to talk. I'll still be living in the same city."

"What about working together? Have you thought about it?"

"Yes. And no. That's not going to happen, and you know it. I've thought hard about it, and it's over. That world is over for me, Ethan. It's in the past. I want to go on studying and get my degree."

"I'm sorry. I fucked it all up."

"After everything I've seen, I can't blame you. It all seemed so ridiculous, but in the end you were right. I don't know what to think. I haven't had time to consider it. I think I just don't understand. I don't know, Ethan; I don't know what we're doing, but we need to see it through, and I don't think we can talk about anything else before we do. In fact, now I think it's been a good thing. It was good for us—it helped us to get our lives in order."

"But I . . . so we're done?"

Ari shrugged. "What do I know? You never know what tomorrow might bring."

As Ethan walked up the stairs, his nerves grew tense at the prospect of having to confront Michelle again. Suddenly, he realized that Ari had left him alone on purpose. He was as stupid as she said he was.

On the other side of the door, Michelle was waiting for him, and for the first time ever, she was more nervous than he was. But Ethan opened the door with his sheepish little boy's look, and before she could say a word, he was looking down in shame.

"I . . . behaved badly, Michelle. I know I hurt you, but it wasn't because of what happened. It wasn't because of . . . when Ari told me, I . . . was very weak and wanted to tell you, but she said that I wasn't strong enough, that I wouldn't be able to, and . . . I couldn't even look you in the eye."

Michelle let him talk and waited for him to finish. She felt a weight in the pit of her stomach melt away with this strange apology. It was like a gift. She went over and stroked his scars maternally. "It doesn't matter. I never thanked you for everything, Ethan. In all these years."

"I know it was terrible not to say anything. I know—"

Michelle quieted him. She didn't care. "It's all OK. You always treated me better than I deserved. I know that. Everything I said was garbage. If I regret anything, it's taking Michi away from you. She didn't deserve to lose you. You were the only father she ever had."

Ethan moved toward her, choking up. He didn't know what to say. He never knew when he was with Michelle. He leaned on her shoulder and took her hand. A loud motorcycle rumbled down the street. She squeezed and stroked his hand. He felt as though he were miles away. Michelle gave herself up to the nostalgia of regret, the ancient wound caused by everything she'd left behind. An old memory came to her. She didn't know if it was real or not or an echo of the intimacy that might have been. A truth a million miles away from her present situation. A need for affection and trust. A refuge. Just like back then. Then she looked at herself: nothing from that time was left.

When Ari came back, they had a long discussion over the sleeping arrangements. Michelle was determined to sleep on the sofa to give Ethan her bed. He and Ari needed their sleep. Ethan didn't argue. He went into the bedroom, changed, and fell onto the bed, sure that sleep would come, but he was distracted by Michelle's smell, which was on everything. He saw her sitting next to him hours before and wondered if he should have made a move. If she had been expecting him to. He was bombarded by thousands of jumbled-up memories. He saw her cinnamon skin, the small, curvy body that was so familiar to him. He knew that nothing was over, much as he might want it to be. Everything was still undecided among the three of them.

In the morning, when Ari and Ethan came into the kitchen, Michelle was making a breakfast no one would eat. Out of a superstition they refused to recognize, they avoided saying goodbye, and she thanked them with all her soul.

"I'll see you in a few hours. Good luck—everything's going to be fine."

"What are you going to do until we get back?" Ari asked.

"I'll be with Henrique. I find his company comforting."

For the first time, Ari hugged her. "I'm going to get that girl out of there if I have to go to hell and back."

Michelle watched the exhaust belched out by the old Suzuki Santana that drove off with the four raiders inside. She had been embarrassed to admit that her activities with Henrique would consist of praying, staying close to him in the conviction that their combined faith would help them from afar. It was what she'd been taught as a child.

Michelle got to the door of his apartment, which was always open even though the neighborhood was so unsafe. As usual, she called out a greeting before opening it farther, waiting for Henrique to reply. The TV was on, but when she went in, she didn't find him sitting on the table.

"Henrique?"

Michelle immediately sensed that something was wrong. She peered through the doorway and saw a shape lying on the cot. Knowing how poor his health was, it scared her to see him lying so still. She went to him, praying that fate hadn't played such a cruel trick, just when she needed him. She kept on saying his name, but he didn't react. As she entered the tiny bedroom, she grew more and more worried. Once her eyes had adapted to the light, she clearly saw a dark stain on the sheets underneath Henrique's unmoving form. She went over, pleading with him to answer, and put her hand on his shoulder. She knew what had happened already, but she still had to turn him over to get a better look. She pulled on his body, which flipped like a rag doll. It was still warm but stiffening fast. His throat had been slit from ear to ear.

Heartbroken, Michelle began to cry, stroking his cheek. "Oh, I hope you've found peace. Please, Jesus, forgive him."

A chair scraped on the floor behind her. She turned around to see a Germanic-looking man smiling scornfully. He spoke in broken Spanish. "The mother?"

Michelle knew that her fate was sealed, but she wasn't going to give in just like that. She jumped and ran, taking advantage of the fact that the man was sitting down. Then she pushed the table in his way and set out into the hall before he could reach her. She headed outside but came up against another body that had been lying in wait. The Jackal, still sitting down, checked his watch while Thiago covered her mouth with a hand. Michelle tried to turn around and felt the blade at her back.

Thiago pushed hard. "Too late."

The knife went into her flesh, and blood began to spurt between his fingers. The knife pierced her stomach, and Michelle couldn't make a sound. The man withdrew it and then stabbed again at her lungs. He let her go, and she collapsed to the floor. He nodded to the Jackal. "They've left already," he said in a callous tone.

"It's time—we should go."

But Michelle hadn't died. To the murderers' surprise she got up on her knees and dragged herself to the door, mumbling a warning only she could hear. "Ethan, be careful, Ethan . . ."

They watched her in amazement and curiosity, wondering where she got the strength to keep moving. It was almost superhuman. Thiago made to finish her off, but the Jackal stopped him. Michelle grabbed the door handle, pushed against the wall with her shoulder, and, leaning hard, got to her feet. She rummaged through her handbag, covering it in blood, and took out her phone, but her fingers left a red smear on the touch screen. She collapsed again as she was trying to unlock it and stared at the door handle as though it was a million miles away. She didn't notice that the phone had fallen from her hands, carried along in the flow of her own blood, or hear how she wheezed in a high-pitched tone with each breath, the bubbles rising and popping in her shredded lungs. Michelle thought she'd managed to dial the number and mumbled so quietly only she could hear, repeating: "Ethan . . . Ethan . . . Ari . . ."

Her face sank into the stain on her chest.

The Jackal stood up, still marveling at her willpower; he let Thiago go out the back window first before following, taking care not to step in the puddle of blood spreading across the floor.

12

The Open Mouth of Hell

Vienna, 1935

At the end of the nineteenth century and the beginning of the twentieth, a unique period when the future was coming into being, Vienna was the grand capital of the Austro-Hungarian Empire. Our contemporary society, the way we see the world today, was defined at that time. A vibrant Europe resounding with new discoveries could be seen in Paris and London while in Vienna, amid the secessionism and ornate palaces, the thrusting modernity of Loss, Klimt, and Freud clashed with a history that refused to go away, taking refuge in a morbid, decadent beauty. It was a worthy metaphor for Europe as a whole. Thirty-five years later, the empire was just a memory and Austria a small nation begging to be swallowed up by the thousand-year Reich. Like a psychological disorder, nostalgia for greatness had won over rationality.

When she opened her eyes in the smoky room, Michi was immediately aware of all this. She knew that she was present at a moment when democracy had committed suicide. It didn't matter that she had never heard about that city before and knew nothing of the period. The fire had already raged through the rear of the mansion, burning up the servants' quarters and leaping from one tapestry to the next. Soon it would be unstoppable. The books on the shelves warped in the heat from the flames until their spines were gone. They took off like large flaming butterflies, tracing an arc through the air until they disintegrated into ash. The fire was focused in a dining area, separated from them by a lead-and-glass screen that was about to explode, while the smoke hung thick and black like an inverted oily sea. In front of her she saw four figures arranged like actors waiting for the play to start. Suddenly they came to life, as though their puppet strings had grown taut. The oldest of the four characters was lying on the floor; it wasn't clear if he was still breathing. He wore a pearl-gray three-piece suit and patent leather shoes, but his most striking feature was a patch over one eye. Behind the black fabric, it was just an empty socket. Michi knew that she'd seen him before. She'd dreamed of him, and yet he was different somehow. Of the other three, the chief, who was short and squat like a brewer, with a waxed fringe and small moustache, was only thirty but looked older. He was retreating toward the exit and calling to the kids under his command, but they ignored him. They were just children and had all the arrogance, insolence, naivety, bravery, and camaraderie of late adolescence. It had led them straight into the arms of a banned terrorist National Socialist sect. One of them was hugging the dying old man and seemed unable to come out of his trance, while the other, who believed more in friendship than the party, refused to leave the other one alone in the death trap. This was a decision that would change his life and those of many others. It all seemed inevitable, as though it had all already been preordained. Michelle knew that this was a dream but also real, a year long ago that was also somehow her immediate present. It was happening right now.

The Suzuki's fluorescent-yellow chassis stood out against the vegetation, bouncing along the dry riverbed before coming to a stop. They strapped on heavy, old-fashioned bulletproof vests whose efficacy Ethan seriously doubted and shoved small first aid kits in their pants pockets, thinking more of the girl than themselves. Two old FN FAL rifles were handed to Caimão and Ari; Ethan got a Beretta, his only weapon; while 4:20 packed a Kalashnikov. They hoped that they wouldn't have to use them. They drove on for half a mile until they got to the perimeter fence. Birds sang from the thick line of trees that blocked their view of the compound. Just as they'd hoped, they were the only ones there. 4:20 cut the wires, and they stealthily crept onto the grounds. Ferns came up to their waist while their skin was dappled with the light that shone through the foliage. Five minutes on, the area began to clear, the trees were more widely spaced, and the mud was covered in dead leaves, indicating that more traffic went through here. In front of them they saw the first sheds indicated on the map, and 170 feet farther on was the imposing nineteenth-century silhouette of the hospital, an industrial structure of five floors with large windows, most of which had lost their glass panes. In front of the first sheds were gravel paths and tools that had been left out. They kept watch for several minutes but saw no signs of life. 4:20 ran out into the open on his own, crouching low, until he got to the first shed. He hid behind a barrel and looked inside. It was empty. He signaled for the others to come over. They found that the door was locked up with a chain. From there, the approach to the hospital was more risky, a dirt track that ran around each storage shed to a service entrance. There weren't any trees to provide cover, but the prevailing quiet was encouraging.

The Jackal was traveling comfortably in the second Range Rover in a convoy of five. Like his younger brother, he enjoyed flaunting his status, but his manners were more brusque and aggressive. Tactless, the Bloodhound might have said. And yet on this mission the gesture of arriving in force wasn't just gratuitous; even his younger brother would have had to concede that. They were heading right into the center of a cult to snatch its aged founder, a dangerous psychopath who'd enjoyed being a messiah for too long not to put up a fight. Even though they'd already made arrangements with local political leaders, they couldn't leave anything to chance, especially given the value of the target and the potential risk involved. In addition to Thiago, they were traveling with sixteen commandos. The old man would be taken with or without the help of his followers.

The row of cars stopped at the gate, and it opened automatically. The drive went on for seventy-five feet to a small plaza, where an attendant showed them where to park. Behind it was a guardhouse with a barrier, the original entrance, which was still used. The Jackal ordered the entire team to get out, just for the shock value. It had the desired effect. Another attendant in the guardhouse picked up a phone. The Jackal didn't like that at all.

About three hundred feet ahead, palm trees provided shade for the community's main houses and buildings, which today were festooned with bunting and other decorations. Children carrying trays, dressed up as the original colonists, were being led to the right by their teachers. One of them turned to stare at these scary-looking adults with their guns and armor but was immediately chided by a teacher. The big party was being prepared a prudent distance away, protected only by a flimsy barrier from these emissaries of an ominous present.

"Don't make us kill your people," Thiago murmured to the attendant.

Michi stood stock still, a secret spectator to a mysterious act she knew she shouldn't be a party to. But she couldn't move, and she couldn't just wake up because she knew that the distinction between dreams and reality no longer existed. They were one and the same. Then the young man on the ground started to have a fit, and her terror increased. She'd seen this image before: it had been waiting for her since 1935. Then the indescribable began to take shape. The boy, whose name she knew was Stobert, opened his eyes to look at her. His body remained still, but somehow he also floated up like a ghost. Michi shivered when she saw him there, translucent, blind to everything. His friend couldn't see him: he was still trying to wake him up. She knew that she was trapped like a fly in a web of time and dreams. The flickering phantom approached her with opaque white eyes, even though one of the sockets was also empty, and he was in a three-piece suit and patent leather shoes. It was as though the image of the young man was superimposed over that of the dead old one. She realized that the entity inside didn't know who its host was—it had been disoriented and confused for eighty years. But there was no question of feeling pity for it; it represented a pit of pure evil. It was dangerous and wanted to consume her. The being that now occupied the bodies of two men, sucking up their energy and lives without ever really being a part of them, was floating around the room searching for her, stumbling around in no direction in particular. As if the knowledge had always been within her, she suddenly knew that the dead old man had been its master. He had possessed the arcane knowledge that could invoke and control it, but the ability could be inherited only by blood and controlled through generations of committed study, studies that the unfortunate boy did not possess. It had come to him like a curse with the old man's final breath, but both bloodlines combined in her. Michi learned all this about herself in her dream. It was a part of her genetic memory. She thought she heard the words *You were born to be a great master*, but she didn't know where they had come from. And then she realized in horror that the incomprehensible creature standing in front of her like a living memory heard it too. The entity, like the demons of which her grandmother was so afraid, was currently stretched thin and empty between different existences. Then it raised its head like a dog that had detected a scent while its knowledge passed into her: it would need the entire life of this Stobert, her great-grandfather, to prepare for her possession. It would take decades of torture, abuse, murdered girls, and failed experiments, but this was nothing but a rehearsal before they returned to this moment so she could be inoculated in the present, when Stobert himself was about to die. Unable to move, Michi knew exactly what was going to happen. The shadow came toward her, dragging its feet past furniture it couldn't see, its nostrils opening and closing as they picked up her scent. It was establishing a bond with her skin that could never be broken. From that moment in 1935, she would become the next host, and it would grow inside of her, its power increasing. She was a future mistress, but she didn't have the knowledge she needed to defend herself. This beast was from another reality, the stuff of hell itself. It licked its lips as it tasted her on the air. Michi shivered; the cold it emanated burned her skin. Alarmed by the steam coming off of her, she tried to wake up, telling herself that it was just a dream, even though she knew it wasn't. This was real—the two different times had merged into one, on the same date, the same moment eighty years apart. She saw an awful claw emerging from the combined images of the hands. It reached for her, blurry, damp, and freezing, the embodiment of horror. Michi screamed.

4:20 went around the first shed and carefully crossed the dirt track. The second row of buildings was more solid. They were the original medical storage sheds, with brick walls and wooden windows surrounded by a two-foot-wide pavement. He sheltered behind one of the sheds and then signaled to the others. A narrow passage between two of the sheds seemed the perfect way into the empty lot behind the hospital. He checked that it was clear. Then he stepped out, keeping watch for any hint of activity. There was still no one to be seen. Caimão loped casually along after him, followed by Ethan, who remained cautious. Ari brought up the rear. The three of them were halfway between the sheds, exposed without cover, when 4:20 saw a gleam. Something was glinting in the window. He turned around and hissed. "Back, back!"

It all happened in the blink of an eye. A flash and a roar exploded inside the building, followed by a hail of bullets. At the end of the passage a shadow started to fire at 4:20, who shuddered half a dozen times and was sent flying backward, as though he'd been smacked by a car. He landed six feet back from where he'd been standing. Ethan immediately hit the deck as bullets whistled over him. His instincts kicked in, and he withdrew, looking to see where the fire was coming from, but he was blinded by the dust that had been kicked up. The lines of fire crisscrossed. Ari was running for cover at one corner when a burning piece of metal went right through her left wrist. She screamed involuntarily. Caimão was the only one who hadn't moved, and he was laughing like a maniac. Then two bullets bounced off his Kevlar vest, knocking him down, but he didn't seem to care. He raised his rifle and fired blindly at the shed. His straightforward strategy managed to quiet one of the shooters, but fire still came from the passage. Ethan crawled over to him and grabbed him.

"Let's go! Are you crazy?"

Caimão let out an insane cackle. "Fire, gringo, fire!"

A third shooter joined them from the other flank, trapping them in a sweeping cross fire. 4:20 tried to get up, raised the AK-47, and fired back as best he could, but the bullets kept coming, and the new shooter finished him off with a bullet through his hand and two more in the groin, smashing his hip and burning his insides. He writhed around, still shooting in a reflex action. His bent knees fell into the line of fire and were soon cut off at the joint. And yet he continued to pull the trigger. Ethan aimed a little more rationally, looking for puffs of gunpowder. Caimão reloaded calmly, seemingly unhurried. Additional shooters appeared to join the existing ones. Ari, trapped in a corner, ignored the whistling bullets and inspected her wrist, which had a hole right through it. The good news, she told herself, was that it had an exit wound. She wrapped a bandage tight around it. Her left arm had gone numb, so she dropped the now-useless rifle and took out her P99. She was amazed that she didn't feel more pain: it was the adrenaline surging through her. She stepped out to fire back, with no clear idea of her target. From her corner she saw 4:20, who'd gone into shock and was shaking in violent spasms in an expanding puddle of blood. Ethan and Caimão fired back at the shed as the circle closed around them. Ethan tried to pull the bodyguard back, but he was enjoying the senseless exchange of fire too much. His luck would surely run out soon. A bullet knocked Ethan down. Caimão stood up and walked forward as though he were out for a stroll, still firing. He was the only one of the four still standing.

Lucas, the head of administration, hurried over. He was in fancy dress as a traditional peasant, much to the amusement of the commandos. He was flanked by four armed guards, but they hardly presented a threat to the much larger commando team. The Jackal barked at him: "You weren't expecting us?"

"Of course I was, but . . . there wasn't time. I thought you'd get here later, during the celebration so, you know . . . it would be more discreet. And we haven't seen any hint of the attack you warned us about."

"Oh, they're out there. We thought we'd drop by in case they put up resistance."

"We'll find them. We can't cover every inch of ground, but our men have been on patrol since this morning. As soon . . ."

Suddenly they heard gunfire to their left. It sounded far away, as though it were echoing out from the forest. Their walkie-talkies started to chatter.

"West facade . . . located-zzz-west facade of the hospital-zzz-backup."

Thiago and the Jackal smiled.

"It seems that your guests have arrived."

A little farther on, in the garden under bunting and paper lanterns, the teenagers and the children who were left, all in period costume, started to lay long tables for the banquet. They were shaken by the noise, but the guardians supervising their activities told them there was nothing to worry about and urged them to get back to work, strictly enforcing community discipline. From the vantage point of Fausto Aspiazi's greenhouse, one could appreciate the simple geometry of the preparations. At the entrance, the head of administration stood submissively in front of the Jackal.

"We appreciate the warning. You've saved us from a grave threat."

"Good. Now lead us to the old man. We want to get this over with quickly."

"There's . . . um," he stammered, "some disagreement on that point."

The Jackal stared at him impatiently.

"Don't get me wrong: as agreed, Herr Aspiazi shall be delivered to you as soon as the intruders are neutralized."

"That's your problem, not ours. I want him now."

"We . . . we've come to an agreement with the security team," Lucas said. "Herr Aspiazi has requested a few minutes to finish an experiment . . . about half an hour. You have my word—"

"What manner of idiocy is this? This isn't a negotiation. Where's Armando, your head of security?"

"He's not . . . he's . . . with Herr Aspiazi."

At a sign from Thiago, ten guns pointed straight at Lucas and his guards.

"You guaranteed the handover, and the head of security isn't with you? He's the only one of you morons worth a damn!"

Surrounded by smoke, Michi shivered and shouted pleas that no God would ever answer. The air swirled around the presence while the claw felt for her. The nose savored the scent of her flesh like a wild beast. It would soon possess her for all eternity. The girl cried out, and her soul writhed in fear. Searching desperately for help, she called for the only person with whom she'd ever felt safe. Then she heard a voice behind her: "Michi, Michi, where are you?" She saw Ethan. He was far away, walking along a hallway in an abandoned hospital, right at that moment, which was a few minutes in the future, or maybe the past, but also in an unnerving dream from months before about a lavish mansion in flames in a country she'd never been to. "Michi, where are you?" Tears ran down her cheeks. She longed to hug him, knowing that it was the wrong thing to do. She knew she shouldn't call out to him, but she couldn't help stammering, "I'm still alive."

Ari watched the tragedy unfold from a position of helplessness. Ethan was lying still on the ground, 4:20 was having a fit, and Caimão was ahead, darting back and forth to avoid the gunfire with a success that owed more to dumb luck than skill. He finally got to the shed in front and leaned on the wall, but his move only protected him from the first two shooters. He crouched to return fire at the new threat from the side, but his position was precarious. The shoot-out had transformed the area into one big cloud of gunpowder, giving them perhaps their only advantage. Ari ran toward 4:20 with no clear plan in mind. Something moved to her right. Ethan appeared to come to and sat up. The two original shooters turned to them, and Ethan crawled under the low mist.

Ari went on shakily, her arm bouncing off her side like an annoying flap. Every step hurt. She dove to the ground next to 4:20 and reached for the Kalashnikov, but the clip was empty. Foam was bubbling from his lips, and he appeared to be talking to someone, his eyes bulging. His hand wouldn't let go of the grip. The man who had ambushed him in the passage took aim, and she sheltered as best she could against his body. The smoke and dust prevented the shooter from getting a good shot. She raised the assault rifle at the only target that occurred to her and pulled the trigger, praying that the grenade launcher was loaded. An empty click was her answer. Shots from behind her pushed her attacker back. Ethan had recovered and came over to give her covering fire. Ari pulled a grenade from 4:20's belt, loaded the GP-25, and fired at a window. They heard a metallic ping and were then shaken by the blast. The windows exploded, and they felt the force of the shock wave. Everyone was deafened, and the guns fell silent. Thick smoke came from inside.

Ethan pulled her forward. "Through the window!"

Lucas was trying to talk things over with the Jackal when they were shaken by the sound of an explosion. They could see smoke rising in the distance. Flocks of birds rose into the air. Lucas turned to the source of the noise in shock, then back to the Jackal, blinking. The situation had spiraled out of his control. The attendant reached for something, and the Jackal didn't think twice: his unit gunned down those present in an instant, their shots ringing out through the forest. The guards had no time to react; they were cut to pieces by machine gun fire while another attendant sought shelter in the guard post, which was quickly riddled with bullet holes, some as large as a fist. It soon collapsed. Lucas stayed standing for a couple of seconds, kept upright by the shots, then fell back with the others. The shooting lasted for only a few seconds, but blood flowed down the gutters until it formed a puddle around the drain, which was blocked up with leaves. The plaza had been stained with a crimson flower, opening wider and wider at the killers' feet. They regarded it with indifference. Several hundred feet away, children screamed in terror. Their teachers hurried them away, confused at what was happening. As a precaution, they led them into the church, next to the greenhouse. Some of the community came out to see what was going on while others hid in their homes. The entire compound descended into chaos.

The Jackal picked up Lucas's walkie-talkie. "This is Andreas Schwindt. The compound is now under my control. What was that explosion?"

A voice gulped before answering. "We don't know—reinforcements are still coming."

"We're going to continue with the removal. Issue precise orders. I want a clear path."

In Vienna, the fire was spreading, and the neighbors had called the fire department. Twice, Michi tearfully said, "I'm still alive," and something about her effort interfered with what was happening. She found herself back in the present, looking to the future. Now she saw the cell where she'd been sedated at one end of a dark corridor. Ethan was walking down a corridor in a basement several floors below ground, while on another level the creature, which was both one and several, was still surrounded by smoke and stuck between timelines. The refraction reduced its power on her plane. It was because of Ethan. Michi sensed that she shouldn't involve him, but she was too scared to react. Her childish selfishness overcame her resistance. Ethan turned to a window onto nothing and answered a voice only he could hear.

"No, it isn't. She's alive, right now, trapped in that prison."

His face was bleeding. Michi cried when she heard him because she knew she shouldn't answer; she didn't want to doom him, too, but she was afraid. She called to him like a little girl calling her father in a dream. He walked down the corridor, unaware of the approaching danger. Michi tried to warn him, confusing reality with her imagination: "Don't go any farther, or they'll catch you."

Ethan looked toward her, but he couldn't see her. The creature reacted to his presence.

"Your voice, Michi. They'll hear you."

"They can't right now. For now they're blind, worried about the fire."

The conversation went on, although she didn't understand it herself. She was confused by the different experiences bombarding her all at once.

"Are these the men that kidnapped you? Are they the men you're afraid of?"

"I'm afraid of the other one. Very scared."

Michi knew this was wrong, but she couldn't help it. She was just a girl. Her reality flickered. Ethan turned back to the window, to the place that didn't exist, to answer a question no one had asked.

"I'm there right now. With them."

Black smoke billowed out of the shed, and the guns went silent. Ethan's ears buzzed. Just like those of his enemies, he imagined. He went to the window and jumped inside. Several shards of glass stuck into his arm, but he didn't feel it. Ari was right behind him. He took her by the armpits and helped her in. She grunted in pain and doubled over her left arm. Ethan saw the blood seeping through the bandage. The warehouse was full of dark smoke and the disturbingly sweet smell of burning flesh. The remains of a young man were plastered against the wall, framed by a charred outline. Next to him was an M16 submachine gun that Ethan picked up. He went to a window, but no one was in sight. Outside, the gunfire started up again around Caimão, but it sounded far away. Ethan inspected Ari's wrist.

"Are you all right? Can you use my pistol? We need to get out of here quick—this is a death trap."

"Yeah, don't worry. It's nothing. How about you? I saw you fall and get back up like a zombie."

"It felt as though I'd been hit in the head with a metal bar. I think a cartridge must have hit me in the temple."

Ari snorted and grabbed the gun with her right hand. "This time, my dear, we're truly fucked."

The colony's loudspeaker system broadcast a couple of warning notes followed by warbled instructions: "Go back to your homes. I repeat: go back to your homes, or take shelter in the church. This is an emergency. We are being helped by some visitors. You must cooperate with them."

The announcement spread through the air, followed by a siren that sounded like an air raid warning from wars past. Thiago sent out four of the 4x4s, which drove slowly, providing cover for the commandos. The path was mostly clear, but when they got to the main buildings, figures appeared. A silent group circled them slowly, looking like sleepwalkers. The loudspeakers repeated the warning: instructions from on high.

"Move away! Listen to the pastor! Go to the church!" Thiago shouted in Portuguese.

One of the onlookers finally stepped forward.

"Kill him! Kill the monster!"

Shots came from one of the windows.

"There! On three!"

Twelve barrels aimed at a window from which a small plume of smoke emerged. In a few seconds it was reduced to smithereens. The commotion was accompanied by the screams of the civilians, who were fleeing in all directions. Covered by the rest, two mercenaries ran along the side of the building and entered. A minute later, the radio crackled: "Pacified."

"Smoke," Thiago ordered.

The team put on infrared goggles and fired dozens of smoke grenades that covered the plaza in a slate-colored cloud.

Michi was blinded by the flash. She repeated a few weak phrases that she knew would help Ethan. He stared up at her from a dark, indeterminate space, and a lifelong love welled up from her past. His being near was a comfort, but she knew that he wouldn't be able to control it either. He'd be willing to sacrifice himself, and this knowledge was too much for her.

The figure raised something like a claw, an image that existed only in her mind. Michi saw a nail coming closer to him. Ethan was entirely oblivious to it.

"Don't worry, Michi—no one is going to take you anywhere. I'm going to come find you."

She wanted to stay quiet, to put up with the pressure, to be strong and ignore him. She held her breath for a moment, but her need for succor was too strong. "Are you coming to find me?"

"Of course, but I need your help. I need to know where you are. Something."

Michi scratched herself, knowing that she was acting badly. Vibrations from another time disrupted the frequencies and disoriented the creature, which stretched out a claw through the bubble and into the hospital.

"He's coming now. You have to go."

"Michi, listen: nothing's going to happen. You're dreaming."

She wanted to warn him, but she knew that it was too late. The evil was trying to get to her, but it was lost; it didn't know where she was. It was torn between her and Ethan. The room faded, as did the memory, and the shape drifted away, toward the hospital.

"Get out!" she screamed.

The entity, disturbed by this new presence, opened its eyes, scorching its pupils in the raw light of these different realities, trying to locate whatever it was that was getting in the way of the connection.

Stobert woke up.

Ethan told Ari to cover him and ran to the door that opened onto the passage. Ari aimed the P99, looking for movement. Ethan took a deep breath, raised his arm, and opened the door. There was no one outside. He pointed his weapon and ran. There were no shots either. He could hear a loudspeaker in the distance and tried to hear what it was saying, but he didn't understand the words. It sounded like chanting or a call to prayer. He got to the next shed. The only noise came from the echoing sound system. Then he clearly heard shots coming from the same area, the center of the compound about half a mile away. Meanwhile, the movement around them appeared to have ceased. The situation was getting stranger and stranger. He leaned on the doorframe, gripped the handle, and opened it. The layout was a mirror image of the other shed, with the same door on the other side. Inside there were tools and machinery. It appeared to have been abandoned. He heard a whisper from behind. Ari had come out of her shed and gave him a questioning look. A few seconds later she crossed the space and joined him.

"I prefer my hideouts not to have dead bodies in them."

"They've gone. Something's happening. Whatever it is, right now that's good for us."

But she put her hand over his mouth, pointing to the door. They saw a shadow pass by in the crack between the wood and the floor. Ethan moved to the next window, and Ari covered the entrance. The intruder had to pass him by to get to the door. Ethan stood behind the glass, ready to pounce.

The most prominent roofs of the community were hidden by the clouds of smoke, imbuing the air with a ghostly gray tint as the smoke swirled around objects like a living creature, distorting their outlines like fluctuations of a miniature hurricane. Children watched from the church windows as the commandos ran quickly through the fog, helped by their infrared goggles. Thiago climbed the stairs to the greenhouse. They dragged out the last two guards, who threw themselves to the ground, whimpering without putting up any resistance. They were taken to the Jackal, who was waiting by the vehicles, and forced to kneel at his feet with guns at their backs.

He looked down at them disdainfully. "So? Where's Armando?"

"In the greenhouse. It was our duty to protect him."

"In the greenhouse? He locked himself in with Aspiazi?"

Meanwhile, Thiago burst into the minijungle. With the space superheated by the immense tanks of propane, it was impossible to distinguish body heat. He took off the goggles and let his eyes adapt to the light. He made out a shadow waiting for him at the back of the room.

Outside, the guards who had surrendered were being interrogated.

"No, Herr Aspiazi isn't in the greenhouse. He was taken to the hospital with the girls."

They pointed to the imposing building in the distance.

The Jackal was stunned. "That was his brilliant plan? To hide a little farther away?"

In the greenhouse, the soldiers surrounded the person waiting calmly with his hands placed submissively behind his head. Thiago came closer and saw that it was Armando. He looked at his cheeks: he was crying. He was about to ask why.

"Detonator!" one of the commandos shouted. "He has a—"

The explosives connected to the heating system and gas tanks under their feet exploded, setting off a chain reaction.

Ethan was crouching by the window waiting for the intruder when he was blinded by a flash. The sky turned white, and a second and a half later he was deafened by a huge explosion while a powerful shock wave shook the ground like an earthquake and smashed the windows, blowing the glass into his face. He fell back, bleeding profusely.

Ari jumped on top of him. "Ethan!" She took him in her arms and turned him over, but when she saw his face, her mouth went dry, and her bottom lip started to tremble.

Ethan opened his eyes. When he saw that she was about to lose it, he forgot his pain. "What . . . what happened? Did they blow up the whole jungle? Why are you looking at me like that?"

Ari, a lump in her throat, ignored his question as she stroked Ethan's cuts with her finger. It was as though she were tracing out a shape. "Ethan . . . my God. Ethan, those cuts you made in your sleep. What were you dreaming?"

Ethan seemed distracted; he had difficulty answering. "I don't know, Ari. Fuck, I already told you—you want me to remember it all right now?"

Ari didn't know how to describe it, so she took out her phone and held up the screen so he could use it as a mirror. The shards of glass had cut up his face, following the scars he'd made with the razor exactly, as though it had been an act of prescience. Ethan didn't know what to say either.

Ari took his wrist and looked at him in a way she hadn't looked at him in years. "I'm sorry—I never believed you, not in all this time. I'm sorry. I . . . don't know what's going on. Forgive me, please. I'm so scared." She kissed his hand, gripping tight.

Ethan stood up and kissed her back. Ari moaned in shame and let him hug her, but he felt something different inside of him. Images were all jumbled up in his head. He felt himself go into a strange trance that took him a long way away from her.

Before the sound arrived, a white light spread over everything. It was as though the sun had suddenly intruded on a moonless night or the earth's atmosphere had burned away. An unimaginably loud roar spread out in a wave, flattening the earth, knocking down walls and smashing all the glass within a radius of a couple of miles. A whirlwind swept along, lifting, tipping over, and annihilating everything in its path. The greenhouse was utterly destroyed, the mercenaries flung dozens of feet away, breaking necks and backs, crushing internal organs, and squeezing blood out of every orifice. Flames razed everything they touched before rising into a mushroom cloud several hundred feet high while a rain of burning shrapnel fell all around, drilling holes through roofs and flesh alike. The main building was reduced to a melted volcano crater from which flames spurted intermittently. It sank into the ground as the foundations melted, becoming a shapeless hole spouting black smoke and sulfuric steam. It looked like nothing so much as an open mouth into hell itself.

Forty feet away, an ashen body shook spasmodically until it got its limbs back under control and tried to stand up amid the shower of ash. It fell back down three times in the aftereffects of the shock wave before it was finally able to get upright. There was a painful ringing in the man's ears. He tried to shout but couldn't hear himself. The Jackal felt his ears, which were wet with blood. Several minutes later, when a modicum of hearing had returned, he realized that his right ear, which had borne the brunt of the blast, would never be the same again. A few feet on, the remains of the soldiers and surrendered guards, who had shielded him from the worst of it, saving his life, lay on the ground. He sat down and looked for the SUVs, which had been piled up on top of each other. Only one was left intact. The drivers of the vehicle that had been in the rear came to him immediately. Covered in ash and splinters, they started to help him.

"Sir! Thank God you're alive!"

He made them say it again; he couldn't hear a thing. They were signaling wildly, but he still didn't understand.

"Shout, damn it!"

"Sir! We haven't found any other survivors!"

He nodded more calmly.

"We're bringing up the other vehicle. We have two still working!"

He tried to compose himself. They handed him a bottle of water, and he used it to rinse his hair and wash his face before he drank. His scorched trachea throbbed. "What a disaster . . . this is the worst . . . how many do we have left?"

"There are six of us, sir. The two guarding the entrance and us!"

"Get the engines running! We're going to the hospital—the old man is there! We fell into his trap like a bunch of fools . . . we're going to get that son of a bitch!"

A coal-black cloud blocked out the sun like an eclipse. The ominous orange light that was left had an apocalyptic feel while the landscape had turned nightmarish. It was filled with abandoned buildings covered in thick, leaden particles. Fires burned everywhere, and the air had become hard to breathe.

The reflective glass shuddered, and some of the putty came away, but it remained intact. Stobert took a deep breath, returning to reality—or rather switching to a new one. He was back in the old hospital, in the present, although he was finding it hard to tell the difference. His agitated breathing slowed his reaction time. He pressed the call button several times, but no one came. He'd been left alone. The bastards had run off, probably scared by the explosion. "Your sacrifice has not been in vain, my children," was his only thought for the victims who had served him for half a century. His mind was headed elsewhere. "The girl has torn you away," declared a voice from the void. He knew it was right. One of the creatures inside of him had grown extremely anxious. "How could she be powerful enough to attract an outsider, to eject us?" The parasites were squirming. For the first time, Stobert was conscious of them. He was suddenly in communication with them. He could feel them inside of him, and all the horrors of his previous life were nothing compared to the terror of this new discovery. The failed transfer had filled him with knowledge; everything he'd learned throughout his life now made sense: that night in Vienna had been wiped from his memory because it had in fact occurred this very morning, and one cannot remember their future. He realized that death was a release, that the transfer would only occur when his end was nigh, and it was approaching. His whole life had been no more than a rehearsal, an apprenticeship, a parenthetical aside before the return to this very moment. The girl wasn't the host; he was. He had played host to his uncle until he'd brought him to her. But what did it matter? He'd been so close! And yet he smiled; she was still sedated just a couple of floors above. He knew exactly where she was, and nothing could now come between them. He had to release the ghosts so they could hunt her down. He checked the IV bag with the solution and, with great effort, was able to apply a lethal dose. It would take him hours to pass away but only ten minutes to possess her. Then he would fade away and finally rest, free of nightmares for the first time ever. He needed to get to sleep. Sleep . . .

Ari dressed Ethan's wounds with tenderness and dedication as she mumbled declarations of understanding and loyalty. She had become fragile and open, at the mercy of forces she couldn't begin to understand. He still seemed to get lost for brief periods, as though he were daydreaming. Their shock had made them forget the threats all around them. The door burst open, and someone stepped into the shed. Ari tried to react, but the intruder was pointing his gun at them.

"Bang. *Você está morta.* Hahahaha!"

"Caimão! You crazy son of a bitch! You'll lead them all right in here. Did you see what happened? Where were you?"

Caimão, who was completely disoriented, gestured vaguely around him. "Where the shooters were. We exchanged fire for a while; then the loudspeakers came on, and they left. I chased them a little, but then I came back, and the explosion caught me by surprise. Did you see it? They must have heard it across the state."

"Why did you chase them, you fool? Did you hit anyone? Are you all right?"

"I don't know. Maybe. They ran into the trees. Cowards!"

Ari went over and patted his vest. "You're bleeding. You've been hit!"

Caimão looked down in annoyance. "Shit! I knew it!"

"You didn't realize? What are you on, you bastard?"

Caimão didn't answer. He just giggled like a naughty boy. Ethan laughed along with him as though he'd just arrived and had no idea of the gravity of the situation. Ari had to bark at them a couple of times to get them to shut up. Eventually she persuaded Caimão to take off his shirt.

"Did you see the explosion? Do you have any idea what's going on?"

"No, except that it was fucking huge. There was a mushroom cloud. It's like they blew up the whole town. It's a good thing I was coming back."

"Did you see 4:20?"

"Yes." Even in his stimulated state he betrayed a hint of sorrow. "He bled out. We need to go."

"We haven't completed the mission."

"But we're still alive! Why do you think I came back to get you? Look at 4:20! They were waiting for us! We've been fucking lucky."

"You most of all. You were hit under the collarbone; I think it's still inside. How the hell are you able to lift your arms?"

Caimão just laughed stubbornly.

Ethan talked over him. "I don't know what's happened, but this is a gift. Do you think anyone's going to pay any attention to us now? Now's the time—let's take advantage of the chaos to get Michi." Images flashed before his eyes; he had no idea if they were real or not. He didn't say anything. "I'm staying here, Caimão, but it's up to you."

"Fine, we'll go right to the end, but I'm taking 4:20's share too. This is much worse than what we agreed."

"You've got some balls," Ari spat back. "What we agreed? You were the one saying it'd be a walk in the park. Not that it matters—we're not going to argue about money now. Besides, it was already yours."

Ethan blinked hard. The color faded from his vision as though he'd turned down the lights and then came back in waves. He found it hard to concentrate. He felt like he was falling asleep while the cuts in his face started to throb, trying to communicate in a language of their own. He pulled himself together and spoke to his comrades, both of whom were wounded worse than he was. "Can you two go on? I have a plan."

The room began to cloud in Stobert's vision as the drug took effect, but it didn't disappear; it only transformed. Now the walls gave off their own glow. He detected a pair of frequencies above him: the girls in their cells. Now he knew which one he had to sacrifice. And he saw himself walking, turning around, looking back at his prone body, and going out again. He knew that it wasn't him. It was the creatures that had taken his shape, still linked to his uncle in Vienna. They were on the trail of a child's fear and moved freely down the halls like ghosts, looking for someone new to infest.

"Are you crazy? You must be more screwed up than we are. Splitting up will just get us killed one by one," Ari hissed.

"After what's happened, I agree with the gringo," Caimão said. "I think they're all gone. The most important thing now is to get out of here before the police arrive, and the search will go faster if we each take half the territory."

Ethan had suggested they split up. Ari and Caimão would take the upper floors while he took the ones below ground. The reasoning was simple: between the two of them they barely made one able-bodied fighter while although his face was a fright, it was the only damage done to him. He'd been lucky. He took Ari to one side for a little privacy. She didn't want to argue even though his plan defied logic, and he had always been the logical one. He begged her to trust him, concealing his real reasons. He had a vague feeling that this was how it was supposed to be. To Ari, this was the Ethan she remembered from way back: it was his voice and honesty. She agreed to go along with him, as senseless as it was. He hugged her, and she stroked his wounds gently.

"The scars will heal quickly. They won't look bad—they might even make you look a little cuter."

Ethan stammered an apology, but she quickly cut him off.

"This isn't the time."

"It never is. To hell with that." He brought his hand to her cheek. "I've never loved anybody the way I love you, Ari. Never. Why do we only ever learn when it's too late?"

The Jackal climbed laboriously into the passenger seat. He knew that he was bleeding internally and had a few broken ribs. The survivors of the operation were removing the melted windscreens. They had to roll them up like carpets, peeling them off the chassis. What was left of the convoy got moving. He rubbed his temples; a pain he'd never known before was throbbing in his ears. Neither vehicle had any glass left. At the entrance to the forest they passed a pair of guards coming back. When they saw them, the guards raised their arms, pleading for help. They were mown down without pity. Then the vehicles continued down the road until the old hospital loomed ominously before them. The men got out and, before doing anything else, released more smoke to provide cover. Now that their numbers had been reduced so savagely, they took every precaution.

The three of them entered through a side door into the storage area on the south side and split up. Ethan combed the ground floor while Ari and Caimão went up the stairs. Ari and Caimão heard trees swaying in the wind, the call of birds, and dripping water: a tuneless, erratic beat. Some of the windows flapped in the breeze. They went through wood-paneled offices and reception areas that hadn't been occupied for years, past gutted bathrooms and laboratories, until they came to a room that was decorated with childish motifs. It was split into a series of cells with bunks and up-to-date equipment. They checked each cell until they came to the only one with a locked door. Inside, they saw a body sleeping on the cot. As Ari grew excited with anticipation, Caimão forced the door open, and they went inside. A girl hooked up to equipment was lying unconscious. She looked dead, but Caimão checked her vital signs and disconnected her.

"She's breathing slowly, but she's breathing."

Ari compared her to the photographs on her phone, holding her breath so as not to jump for joy. But then she got her biggest letdown since they'd begun the case. "It's not her."

Caimão turned to her sharply. "What? What do you mean, woman?"

"Look for yourself. She looks nothing like her—this is a different girl."

"No. No, no, no. That's it. You have your girl. We're leaving."

"You can't leave me now—we haven't found the girl."

Caimão was furious.

Their argument was cut short by the sound of engines. Keeping to the shadows, they saw a pair of Range Rovers park at the north entrance. Six heavily armed men got out, wearing infrared goggles. Before deploying, they released a huge cloud of smoke that snaked around up to the floor where they were hiding. A few seconds later, they heard footsteps approaching.

"Come on!" Caimão whispered nervously. "Let's go back the way we came before they get here. It's our only chance."

But Ari answered with Ethan's stubbornness. "She's here. We can't abandon her now."

"Have you seen her? We have no choice! I've done much more than we agreed. My friend is dead, but I stuck with you. No. I'm going. This has become a suicide mission. You don't have to die."

She barely took in his words; a deep-rooted determination shone from her red eyes. "At least save this girl."

Caimão looked down at the little girl, abashed. Without saying a word, he lifted her onto his healthy shoulder and limped to the stairs. Ari checked the hallway lined with cells, which was filling up with smoke, and headed into the ominous silence of the floor above. The sound of boots echoed around her, growing louder all the time.

Ethan searched each space as though he was on autopilot, certain that he'd know the right room even though he'd never seen it before. He wasn't overly worried about stealth. An obscure hunch told him that he was alone with his objective. It was burning close by, like an icy flame. He sensed it beyond his own body, lucid but vague, guided by a thought that had led him since the beginning, a thought that told him where Michi was as well as the source of the danger she was in. It was like a revelation, hidden knowledge that his wounds had unblocked. Echoes of his dreams resounded inside of him: flashes of Michi and an abstract shape with one eye that . . . suddenly a shiver ran through him. It felt like something had touched him. But there was no one else on the floor. He instinctively headed for the stairs, knowing that his time was running out. He no longer saw the premonition of the false shaman as a warning but rather a plea. He had covered half the floor when a memory of Michi hit him like a slap to the face: "Don't go any farther, or they'll catch you." He heard the sound of cars braking in front of the building, followed by coils of smoke snaking through the columns. Ethan went down the stairs to keep out of sight. On the first step he suddenly grew cold and dizzy: he had been there before, heading into the darkness, away from the lights and noise, haunted by a pair of women's voices warning him about the danger. Ethan continued down carefully, knowing that his destiny was approaching. It was as though everything had already been preordained, but he still needed to fulfill it. He ducked farther into the shadows.

The Jackal ordered his men to head in different directions: a couple would search the basement while the other four would come with him to search the old clinic. He gave very clear orders: if they encountered anyone, shoot on sight. They continued to keep a screen of white smoke ahead of them to cover their approach. The place felt as though it were under a spell and, fortunately, empty; there was no trace of body heat. After the main lobby, the door behind the reception desk led to a side passage, one of whose walls consisted of reflective glass. The Jackal knew they'd made a significant discovery and looked for the light switch to the observation room. When the lights came on, they were presented with the sight of a hospital bed with its back raised so it looked like a kind of sickly throne. On it rested the withered, decrepit, naked body of an old man. His collarbones stood out sickeningly against his skin, and his ribs were so sunken they looked as though they'd inverted themselves due to a lack of support. His wrinkled abdomen wasn't dissimilar to an empty bag, and his bony, spindly limbs were bulging with veins and arteries like a morbid map. The sight of so much spotted green skin was thoroughly repulsive.

The second-in-command took off his goggles. "Sir, he doesn't give off any heat. He's the same temperature as the furniture. He must have been dead for several days. Was this our target?"

The Jackal wasn't listening. He'd heard stories about the old man and had a vague memory of him from his childhood. A terrifying memory that fit well with what he saw before him. "Go in, and check his vital signs."

For the first time, the professionals hesitated to follow his orders. They looked at each other in amazement, and in the end the most senior man among them decided to obey. No one followed. He crept forward, pointing his gun, until he was standing next to the body. He pressed the gun against his chest, but the old man didn't move. Grimacing in disgust, he took off a glove so he could feel for a pulse. The flesh was spongy like a jellyfish, and an unexpected shudder only increased his revulsion. To the shock of his colleagues, he jumped back. They raised their weapons, but he motioned to them to lower their guns as he caught his breath.

"He's . . . he's . . . got a pulse. He's freezing. It looks as though he's in a coma, maybe an induced one."

The Jackal smiled. "Come on! What are you waiting for? Get a blanket or something. Pick him up."

The abductors went in and carried him out with notably superstitious reluctance.

"Fucking hell, he's a living corpse."

Ari kept on going, not bothering to consider how she was going to get out of a building surrounded by enemies. She was worried about Ethan, but he had a better chance of getting away from the ground floor. She stopped to listen but couldn't hear anything. Nobody had come up yet, and she'd heard no sign of a fight. She followed the same path as the one that had taken her to the little girl on the floor below. Her hunch turned out to be right: she found another ward. It was better furnished than the previous one, with children's beds and a

Disney princess castle that had been used recently. Toys were scattered all over the floor. The ward led to more empty cells, and once again, one was locked. She kicked it open and ran inside to disconnect the monitor from the form lying in the bed. She turned the girl over and for the very first time came face-to-face with Michi. The girl was asleep but agitated. Michi was sweating and shaking, mumbling incoherent phrases that Ari was somehow able to understand. This in itself scared her.

"See? You stopped. But if you move, they'll find you. And then you'll never come back."

Ari acted as she never would have imagined. "Michi. I'm Ethan's friend. I've come to rescue you. Is that who you're talking to? Michi, are you talking to Ethan?"

The girl seemed to relax when she sensed Ari's presence, and her breathing grew steadier. Ari told herself that it was just a dream; she'd been confused by all the strange things that had happened over the past few days. She was trying to work out how she was going to carry the girl when Michi spoke again, this time in a bland, steady voice that made her hair stand on end.

"Yes, I'm speaking to Ethan." Then she addressed the other person. "There are two of them. They're coming down the passage, but I can see them for you. Don't be afraid—they don't know that I'm talking to you."

Ethan peered into the murky darkness of the basement. Behind him the sounds from the real world above faded and distorted, as though he were walking away from a party. Before him was only darkness and destiny. He knew that he was the only one who could do what he had to do. The memory throbbed in his head: "Don't go any farther, or they'll catch you." The passage opened onto a waste-disposal room. "I can't stop; I can't help it."

"Yes, you can. This is part of your dream. If you don't stop, they'll find you."

Ethan stared numbly at the end of the corridor as though he were hallucinating. He saw a flickering light. Sunlight from far away. Moving instinctively, he found an old black rubber trash can, opened it, and, ignoring the stink of rot, hid inside.

"There are two of them. They're coming down the passage, but I can see them for you. Don't be afraid; they don't know that I'm talking to you."

Ethan knew that there were two women's voices, so who did the other one belong to? A few moments later, he heard footsteps. He kept the can closed and waited, following the path of the two armed men in his mind.

The pair of men whom the Jackal had sent down into the cellar found the waste-disposal room. They could see the heat marks left by footprints in the corridor ahead of them, although they were fading rapidly. They seemed to lead around the corner, to where the trash was kept. At the end they saw a staircase leading up.

"What do you think? Someone running away?"

"Let's follow the footprints."

They walked off into the darkness, retracing Ethan's steps. He waited until he thought it was safe and came out of the trash can, retching.

"I'm afraid of the other one. He says he's a man, but I know he isn't. He's one of them, and if he finds me, he'll take me away."

This was his last chance. He started to run.

Ari was paralyzed by a sense of incredulity. She heard Michi saying things that made no sense, and yet she was sure they were addressed to Ethan, maybe now or some time ago. She even remembered some of them herself.

"Tell him that I'm with you, that I'm protecting you," Ari said. "Tell him to come back up before they find him."

But Michi's breathing grew shallow, and her voice sounded strangled. "I'm scared of the other one. Very scared."

Ari stroked her forehead and kissed her to calm her down, but the girl grew more upset.

"He's one of them—if he finds me, he'll take me away," she said in a hoarse squeal.

Ari spoke reassuring words that weren't getting through to the terrified girl. For a moment, though, she seemed to relax. "Are you coming to find me?"

"I'm with you, honey. I'm right here with you."

Ari cried at her inability to soothe the pain in the little body before her. She yearned to comfort and protect her. But then she sensed something behind her. When she turned around, there was nothing there. Michi moved her head toward the door. She opened her eyes, but only the whites showed. She was crying.

"He's coming now," she said in a pleading, childish voice.

Ari knew from the way the hair prickled on her arm that they weren't alone. Something had come in that she couldn't see. She couldn't protect the girl from it. Ari suddenly felt cold while Michi, staring blankly, began to breathe out gusts of condensation.

Then she directed her empty eyes at Ari. "You have to go."

Ari was chilled to the bone, terrified by something that didn't exist and yet was all around them.

"Go away! Leave her alone!" she screamed in terror, struggling to keep back the void. A part of that void took shape over Michi, who kept crying in her icy skin.

Ethan ran to the entrance, praying that he'd get there in time. When he kicked open the door from the basement, he found himself in front of a group of paramilitaries pushing a corpse into a car. Time stopped. He knew that corpse.

Ari hugged Michi in a useless attempt to spirit her away, but the girl was getting colder and colder. She rubbed her hands, crying into her arms.

"No, honey, please. Please don't leave me."

"You have to go. He'll take you away along with me," she said in a very weak voice.

Ari leaned her head on the girl's chest. "I'll go with you—then you won't be alone."

The girl's chest swelled, and her voice transformed into an inhuman howl. "Get out!"

Ari jumped back, terrified. But she stayed there. "No. I'm staying with you."

Ethan looked at the team, and his well-honed survival instincts took over. He identified his only way out: to shoot the man closest to him and head back down the corridor before they could react. The old man was placed in the seat, knowing that the survivors wouldn't follow him because they had what they were looking for and weren't interested in him. The vehicle started up—the door closed. There was no choice. Ethan accepted this cruel reality, and suddenly Stobert became aware of him. Caught in the never-ending dream, he knew that something was wrong. Ethan sensed the empty shell of the incomplete transit, the anguish of the trapped victim. He fired at the vehicle, filling the chassis full of holes. He hit the driver in the liver and lungs, killing him instantly. The same burst of fire cut through the old man's jugular and jaw, obliterating the arteries. The blood flow to the brain was cut off, and his respiratory system was destroyed, causing its immediate collapse.

Stobert leaped like an electrocuted dummy and fell apart over the upholstery. As he faded away, he heard the voices. They were laughing and, for the first time, calling him by name: "Walter." They were now free of his uncle's form. The laughing voices were allowing him to hear them. He suddenly knew. Now he knew everything. It had always been this precise instant. The instant that had sealed his fate for the past eighty years. His pursuer was always going to track him down and kill him, and the thin thread of time had turned against him thanks to the final decision of someone he'd never been aware of. The voices knew that they had lost, both here and in Vienna; the world between worlds would happen and had happened because that was how they wanted it, and now they were laughing the way they would laugh as they devoured him for all eternity. In the clarity of his death, he tried to make himself understand: he'd never had a chance. None of them had. They were just playthings on which to take revenge. He had always been doomed because he didn't learn in time. This tenth of a second was the time he needed to achieve the transmutation; they had judged him there and eighty years before. The path of his life was just one big joke, a horrible, humiliating joke. He learned everything in that moment, in a flash, because that was also the way they wanted it. And from the abyss beyond his soul rose a horror so great he couldn't face it. It was taking a little time to gloat before it swallowed him whole.

The commandos returned fire. Stobert's body bounced against the backrest, and a terrifying, unnatural scream emerged from a throat that had been stripped of its vocal cords, competing with the sound of the guns until one of the mercenaries forgot his training and aimed his submachine gun right at his skull. It burst like a pumpkin, splattering the interior of the 4x4. The rest of them fired at Ethan, who allowed himself to be hit. The stream of bullets riddled him full of holes as he and Stobert fell, the latter emitting a squeak that they mistook for a scream. Ethan could now see the full horror of the transdimensional nightmare as his energy ebbed away with the impact of each bullet. He was happy with everything that had happened in his life, everything that had led him to this moment, to the streaking bullets that decided his fate, a fate that bound him to Michi and her great-grandfather in the blink of an eye. Everything was happening just as it was supposed to. As it would always happen for all of eternity because it was the only thing that existed. It was beyond time.

Ethan fell to the ground. He was dead.

The soldiers ceased fire and pulled out the decapitated wraith. The pair in the basement rejoined them, and they surrounded the Jackal, dumbfounded by their catastrophic failure. "It all happened in a second," he said to himself, before allowing his bodyguards to whisk him away.

Ari held Michi, trying to keep her warm. Suddenly the girl's normal temperature returned. She sat up screaming.

"Mommy! Ethan!" The scream caught in her throat. "No! They, they . . ."

Ari hugged her, but she had no idea how to console her. "I know; I know. I'm here with you."

She let her cry for a few minutes and lifted her up to take her away. Suddenly, she heard a click and jumped back, shielding the girl with her body. A shadow was standing outside.

"It's me! Don't shoot."

Caimão's voice echoed around the room. Ari cautiously lowered her gun, and he stepped forward, carrying Yarlín, who was still unconscious.

"They've gone. I saw the cars go and came back to see what had happened. I found your friend's body. I'm sorry. We need to get out of here right away, and we need to take him and 4:20 with us. The police will be here soon—maybe the army and who knows what else."

In Vienna, Stobert opened his eyes in the dark. He was covered in ash, and his uncle's body lay next to him.

Helmut was staring blankly at a curtain. "My God. There was a girl."

"What? What happened? The house is on fire!"

Helmut came out of his trance and helped him up. Their thuggish chief was searching through boxes, emptying bookshelves and keeping anything of value he could find. He shouted at them angrily.

"What luck—I thought you were dead. So? Can we go now? Are these the wonderful secrets that will shake up the party?"

"My uncle had them."

"That old man didn't have anything. He's dead, but before he went, he took the trouble to curse you. You don't appear to have been a very close family."

"His gun wasn't loaded! I told you he wasn't dangerous—I could have handled him."

"He was a freethinker, a Mason, and he was threatening us with it. What did you expect us to do?"

"He wasn't a Mason."

"A theosophist, a spiritualist, who cares? Decadent cults, just like the Jews. Trash we need to sweep out of Europe. We need to go before the police get here."

Helmut Schwindt picked up the gun. It was a beautifully engraved Luger P-08. He put it in his pocket.

Walter anxiously searched the shelves. "What about the list? It might help us—it might lead us to other leaders of his group."

"Didn't you hear me? They've fled or died or recanted. They're finished! This stuff is nothing but family hysteria. This is what I deserve for trusting a Hungarian." He reached into his vest. "Here's the list. Where are the leaders? They're just the names of farmers. This corrupt aristocracy shall fall like a house of cards under the weight of the new society. And this trash"—he pointed to the exquisite calligraphy on the page—"shall be taken to party headquarters. But I doubt it's worth anything."

Epilogue

In Santa Catarina the amazement of the authorities was matched only by the eagerness of the press, which went crazy. International agencies rushed to file reports across the world, and the news soon went viral. It was too juicy a story: anonymous hero saves girl from mass cult suicide. Caimão, a friendly event organizer and nature enthusiast (many of his friends were rather surprised to hear this), had been on one of his regular drives through the jungle (cue more surprise) when he'd been caught in a huge explosion that had shaken the province, leading many to believe that there'd been an earthquake. The explosion that had destroyed the compound had been set off by fanatics who apparently believed that the world was about to end. Instead of running away, Caimão, true to his generous, determined spirit, had gone to help the survivors, confronted one of the murderers, and had come back, wounded, with a girl who would turn out to have been kidnapped in Colombia. Colônia Liberdade joined other harrowing cases such as the Peoples Temple of Jim Jones and the Order of the Solar Temple in the annals of tragic cults. A morbid fascination with the cult and its kidnappings kept the media busy for weeks, creating yet another forum for paranoid conspiracy theorists who weren't satisfied with the official explanation. Meanwhile, social networks focused on the human side, eating up images of the relieved mother hugging her daughter.

The next day, the police found the bodies of Ethan and 4:20 in a car in Joinville and, given 4:20's background, the case was filed as a settling of scores by cartels. The mortal remains of Ethan and Michelle were sent back to their home countries.

Caimão, meanwhile, enjoyed the fruits of his sudden fame: he had returned a girl to her despairing family with the whole planet watching. He went from talk show to talk show telling his story, which grew more detailed each time. In a few weeks, he'd signed a contract to appear on a reality show about the dangerous world of concert security. He was strong, handsome, and charismatic and could talk the talk. Producers were rubbing their hands with glee.

Back in Central America, Ari learned of Andrés's murder. Calvo studied the papers and told her that she had every right to adopt Michi, who had no other legal guardians left. It was a long, labyrinthine, uncertain procedure, but, as ever, if he got involved, arrangements could be made far more quickly. Even so, Ari noticed that he'd stopped making jokes. Something about the experience appeared to have doused his spark. When they said goodbye, he hugged her, and she realized that the old cynic had a heart after all.

Calvo's voice was choked with emotion. "I'll always wonder: Was it worth it? All that death and pain to save one girl?"

"It's not about whether it was worth it. It was just something that we had to do. That's all."

Ari tried to be with Michi as much as possible, but sometimes she had to get away. She had to find some space for herself so the girl wouldn't see her break down. She went to the hotel gym to lock herself in the shower and cry in the stream of water. She cried until she was exhausted, until she puked. After that she felt able to speak to this abnormally mature girl again. They both sat on the bed. She didn't know if she was capable of making a connection with her.

"What can I say? I don't know what to tell you. Do you want to come with me? I . . . have a little sister. She lives with my older brother. Years ago . . . I didn't dare to adopt her when I should have. I didn't feel mature enough or ready. It was stupid because we'd always lived together, and I'd always taken care of her. But suddenly, making it legal, when the papers came . . . it seemed too much for me. I haven't thought about it again. Maybe . . . you could be friends. I know that you're . . . alone, but maybe I'm not very good at this kind of thing . . ."

Michi curled up in her lap. "Ari, are we both alone?"

Ari hugged her, trying to copy the way Ethan used to hug. He had been like an arch that protected you from the pain of your life, but even though she'd practiced, she came up short, and the gesture only reminded her that he was gone. She got a lump in her throat that she couldn't control and started to cry.

Then Michi joined her. Ari felt Michi's tears soaking her chest and knew that she'd never be able to let her go.

Later, they had dinner at a burger place. Ari reminded Michi about Candy and Bear and how excited they were to see her. For the first time, they both smiled. Michi finished her fries, trying to forget her sadness.

"In the movies, everyone's happy in the end. Is this the end? Is this a happy ending?"

"I don't know, Michi. I've never known. All I know is that we've lost the people we loved most in the world, but the horrible thing that stalked your family is gone too. It's all over, and nothing will change that now."

Their time was running out too. They went back to the room. Michi closed her eyes and felt a phrase unwittingly emerge from her lips. It was like a math problem she'd been puzzling over for months, and now the solution had come to her subconsciously.

"Nothing is ever truly over."

Through the windows, the palm trees swayed in the evening light, filled with birds chattering away in strange, melancholy languages whose origins were lost in the mists of time.

About the Author

Photo © 2018 Laura Pacheco Castro

Guillermo Valcárcel was born in Madrid. He worked in the construction industry by day and studied filmmaking at night until 2008, when he moved to Costa Rica, where he currently lives and works as a filmmaker. He also dedicates his time to writing and illustrating. He is the author of another thriller, *Counterfeit*, as well as *The Wave That Hit Spain*, an influential essay that launched his writing career.

ABOUT THE TRANSLATOR

Photo © 2018 Ar De Bonis Orquera

Kit Maude is a Spanish-to-English translator and editor based in Buenos Aires. His translations of stories by Latin American authors have been featured in *Granta*, the *Literary Review*, and *The Short Story Project*, among other publications. He has translated several great Argentinian and Uruguayan writers, including Jorge Luis Borges, Armonía Somers, Julio Cortázar, Antonio Di Benedetto, and Adolfo Bioy Casares. He was born in Hong Kong and received a bachelor's degree in comparative American studies from the University of Warwick in the United Kingdom.